Blame Hitler

Julian Rathbone is the author of twenty-four novels, two of which (*King Fisher Lives* and *Joseph*) were shortlisted for the Booker Prize; his other work includes a TVM screenplay (*Dangerous Games*). He has been awarded short-story, crime fiction and poetry prizes and has been translated into fourteen languages. *Intimacy*, his critically acclaimed novel set in Southern Spain, is also available in Indigo. Julian Rathbone lives in Hampshire.

D1343823

JULIAN RATHBONE

Blame Hitler

INDIGO

First published in Great Britain 1997
by Victor Gollancz

This Indigo edition published 1998
Indigo is an imprint of the Cassell Group
Wellington House, 125 Strand, London WC2R OBB

© Julian Rathbone 1997

The right of Julian Rathbone to be identified as author
of this work has been asserted by him in accordance with
the Copyright, Designs and Patents Act, 1988.

A catalogue record for this book is
available from the British Library.

ISBN 0 575 40094 3

Printed and bound in Great Britain by
Guernsey Press Co. Ltd, Guernsey, Channel Isles

98 99   10 9 8 7 6 5 4 3 2 1

C.F.R.
1900–1960

In *Blame Hitler* the central character spends some time reading and recalling *Wellington's War* (Michael Joseph, 1984 and 1994), which is a compilation of Wellington's Peninsular Dispatches, edited, with a commentary, by Julian Rathbone. I am grateful to me for permission to use the quotations that appear here.

J. R.

1

Lulled by the warmth of the boat, the subterranean (or should that be sub-marine) beat of its engines, and the nearer though no more audible breathing of his wife and two children, Thomas Somers floated into that state where one can dwell for a time between memory and dream.

'You go and meet him.'

'Me?'

'Yes.'

'On my own?'

'Yes.'

'Why?'

'I'm ... too excited. I'll make a fool of myself. Thomas. Please. Go on. Quick. The bus will be there in five minutes. If he's not there just wait until it comes. Go on now, be a dear.'

Tears in her eyes, not often seen those before, genuine pleading in her voice, vulnerable, not blackmailing nor bullying, not even commanding or asking but ... pleading. Something new here, unsettling. The first inkling that what was about to happen might not be the unadulterated joy he had been told to expect. Things were going to be different from now on.

Thomas, eight years old, bleached sandy hair, very skinny, bags under his eyes, grey shirt, baggy long shorts almost covering his knees, trudged in sandalled feet with grey socks through the thin granite gravel of the ruler-straight path to the little gate. Eyes focused on the flecks of silicates and fool's gold which winked back at him. At the gate he fiddled the looped cast-iron latch keeping his eyes firmly to the left. On the right between the gate-post and the white pebble-dashed wall there was a dark hole fenced with a web where a large striped spider lived. Sometimes he and a girl from one of the bigger houses up the hill pinged the web and with shivering spines watched the spider run out. Not something he'd do on his own.

Safely through, he set off down the hill leaving the semi, also white and pebble-dashed, behind him. Gable End – because it was the last in a row of four buildings, eight dwellings.

To his left two fields, divided by a hedge which ran across the slope. In the middle of the hedge a palm willow with three trunks, one broken off in a gale that had roared out of the Irish Sea two years earlier. It made a cockpit. He and his friend from next door sat in it and the twigs and branches became controls – a joystick, pedals and firing buttons in what had once been a Spitfire, but was now the very latest thing, a Mosquito. The real thing was also made out of wood as far as possible so it wouldn't show on Jerry's radar. *Eeeeeeowwww, ratatatatatat.*

To his right the emerald wheat was already, at the end of May, a foot high and larks sang above it confident their broods would be fledged before the horses with harvesters in tow plodded in. With fuel scarce tractors were almost a thing of the past. The land then fell away to a valley with trees just greening, a church and a tiny hamlet. Beyond the hamlet a purple mountain rose to at least three hundred feet, maybe more, covered in heather and whimberries. On the shoulder facing the sea there was a rocky platform, circled with Scots pines. The 'Plateau' was what he and Mummy called it. From it you could see across the bay to Llandudno and the Great Orme. But not Conway. That was hidden by the even bigger mountain further inland.

And in front? The sea, the sea. Indigo in the distance, greener just below him, Puffin Island a clear hump on the horizon and the bit of Anglesey that sticks out a violet smudge to its left. Puff-ball clouds in a clear blue sky and the first house martins whizzing through it all. *Eeeeeoooow, ratatatatat.*

Thomas pulled a grass with barley-like whiskers from its clinging sheath and sucked sap which tasted like milk. Then he chewed the fibres into a cud which he spat out. The road, metalled with granite stone but not macadamed, became a touch steeper so he had to lean back into the slope before it levelled into a crescent of bungalows. Both horns of the crescent ended on the main road that linked Penmaenmawr with Conway. The bus stop was at the end of the left-hand horn beyond where the bungalows finished. Here both roads ran between high grassy banks crowned with tumbledown stone walls, brambles and briars in bud. Early butterflies, yellow ones mostly, flickered in the air above them. And there was the bus, dark green, trundling up from the small town – he saw it just before the bungalows hid it. He almost ran round the bend that brought the bus stop in view. Only one passenger had got off. At two hundred yards Thomas felt relief. A tall man, in RAF uniform, yes, but brown, almost black, like an Indian, like the Hindus in the *Children's Encyclopaedia*.

Relief, and guilt at feeling relief that it was not his dad. Then the man stooped slightly to put down the battered leather suitcase he was carrying in his right hand. He gave a hitch to the small kit-bag slung from his left shoulder, and raised his right hand in a half wave that became a salute, and suddenly the man's entire stance was a memory forgotten for three years but now surged back on a breaking billow of joy.

'Daddy,' Thomas cried, and he ran, sprinted that hundred yards, into the tall, lean, dark man's arms, was folded against the rough serge of his uniform, felt the hardness of a buckle against his cheek and breathed in odours as strange as the places of war his father had returned from.

Fifty-two years later Thomas stirred in the narrow bunk and wondered at the accuracy of his recall. Was the topography right? Was it really a crescent of bungalows? Was it right that you could not see Conway from the Plateau? Surely the farmers got petrol allowances for their tractors! But the emotions seemed right, and the figure of the man in a peaked cap, slightly squashy the way RAF ones were, and his darkness, certainly that was right. An almost permanent tan from the Desert, the capital D still says which desert, and then the mountains of north Ceylon. But the gesture – the wave that became a salute . . . ? Was that true? Was that not a touch novelistic?

These days Thomas read many novels, classics for the most part and modern Americans – Heller, Roth, Malamud, and Updike too, though he thought the latter a bit flash. So he was suspicious of that wave that became a mimicked salute. Yet there had been something, something which told the young boy that the oriental gentleman at the end of the road really was his father, home, like Odysseus, from the wars.

Novels were still a relatively new luxury. As an Eng. Lit. student, later as a teacher, an Eng. Lit. pro in other words, he had cut them out of his life whenever he could. They took up too much time. Always when he looked at a syllabus he went for the shortest options. *Macbeth* rather than *Hamlet*. Keats rather than Shelley or Byron. Wilde rather than Shaw. And so on. And no novels. Occasionally he came unstuck. An A-level course had landed him with the job of teaching *Mansfield Park*, like it or not. And he did like it. Week by week he kept a chapter ahead of the class but was sadly caught out by a seventeen-year-old blonde who affected spectacles to hide her stunning beauty – a heroine Jane Austen would have been proud to create.

Rashly he had predicted that Fanny would end up marrying the oldest son and so become mistress of Mansfield Park. After all, it's a romantic novel, isn't it? 'Oh no she doesn't,' Valerie Burton had insisted. 'She marries Edmund . . . '

He got out of teaching, bummed around for a bit trying to make a living writing thrillers, failed, went back into education as an LEA Adviser for English and Drama instead. The holidays were shorter but oddly enough he now found he had time to read novels. And marry for the second time. All that was twenty years ago. An ex-student called Katherine Madden, eighteen years younger than he, she now stirred on the bunk above him and allowed herself in sleep what never happened when she was awake – an audible if short-lived and squeaky fart.

If only she would realize that he loved her imperfections even more than her perfectness . . . anyway, he loved her.

Actually right now, he was not reading a novel at all but a book called *Wellington's War*, a compilation of Wellington's dispatches from the Peninsula. Thomas was a Wellington freak. Twenty years ago, when they lived in the south-west of France, he had tramped the battlefields of the Nive, the Nivelle and Orthez. Nobody could understand why he wanted to do this. And indeed it had been some years, decades even, before he himself had realized why. Now, although they were going back to the same area to stay with friends they had made during that time, he hoped to get over the border and visit Vitoria, Pamplona and other battlefields in the Pyrenees.

On the other side of the tiny cabin, Richard, their gorgeous fourteen-year-old son, breathed heavily, while on the lower bunk, barely eighteen inches away, their equally gorgeous ten-year-old daughter Hannah-Rosa seemed not to breathe at all.

'Ricky, you SNOORRED all night,' she would assert later.

'No, I didn't.'

'How do you know you didn't?'

'When I snore I wake myself up.'

A yellow setting moon, just past full, filtered by a salt-pocked porthole, filled the spaces with soft cool light. Thomas estimated four o'clock, French time. They had been in bed two hours, would have to be up in less than two. He guessed that on the other side of the cross-channel ferry the eastern horizon was already dusting the pre-dawn pearl with the rose of day.

Too much Keats. He pushed his way back into dream-like memory.

Dad's hand was lean and dry. Thomas sensed a shyness in the way in which it had welcomed his as they broke the embrace and began the climb back up the hill. A shyness, a reticence.

'Your mother then. Is she all right?'

Mother? Who was Mother? Did he mean Mummy? He looked up at the brown, dark face, beneath the peak of the hat and then at the badge above it. Its eagle spread its wings made out of glittery material, but not brass like the soldiers' badges, *per ardua ad astra*, through hardships to the stars. Under it the large beaky nose jutted above a moustache that filled the space above full lips, the lower one a touch pendulant. The Adam's apple was already slightly scrawny, outlined against a blue sky through which white puff-balls continued to trundle. Everything looked doubting, worried.

'When I rang from the railway station,' the voice not loud or abrasive, not even very deep – later he would tell Thomas with irony that he had a pleasing light baritone when he sang – but very definitely unfamiliar, sounded uncertain too. Thomas again sensed the shifting sands of the whole situation. Three years was a long time. A long time to be away. Things would be different. Not only different from yesterday, but different from three years ago. And not just for him, Thomas, but for this strange dad and his hitherto familiar, very familiar, Mummy, who was already different, who cried and pleaded when normally she was firm, controlled, careful.

'When I rang from the station and said I should be on the bus, I expected her to meet me. Well, both of you, of course. Is she all right . . . ?'

Thomas now wondered if, in this version, his father had suspected some rank infidelity that had to be concealed, covered up. Hamlet senior returning from bashing the sledded Polack on the ice finds a curl of his brother's red (Danish) pubic hair in the matrimonial bed. Odysseus wonders just how far she went with all or even one of those suitors . . .

'I think . . . I think,' young Thomas improvised, 'she wanted to sort of . . . be in the house, welcome you home, sort of thing.'

'Is it a nice house?'

'Very nice. We have maps on the wall. And Mummy pins them with flags. The ones with flags on, you know, the union thing . . . '

'The Union Jack?'

'Yes, that one, to show how we're pushing Jerry back all the time, and the Japs too, and she has another flag, just the one, a blue one, which is to show where she thinks you are . . . Yesterday it was in the Altantic Ocean and she was afraid of U-boats—' Suddenly his tongue was running away, glad to have found something to say, something to get on with. The whole house his father had never seen unrolled in his brain and he longed to rush on, tell this strange man all about it. But Dad interrupted.

'Atlantic.'

'What?'

'"I beg your pardon."'

'What?'

'You should say – "I beg your pardon" or "I'm sorry". Not "what". When you haven't heard what someone says. I said "Atlantic". The Atlantic Ocean. Not Altantic.'

Thomas released his hand from his father's, sensed a relief on his father's part that he had done so, and reached over the gate to release the catch.

'We're here. This is it. Where we live.' With a heart that sank a little he realized that 'we' was now three.

He watched them embrace. His dad put down his case and took off the RAF hat to do so. Many times in the next ten years or so he would say why. 'A gentleman always takes his hat off when he kisses a lady.'

Mummy had used the time Thomas had won for her to replace slacks with a frock. It had short puffy sleeves. And she had pushed her fair, permed hair into a sort of halo, and . . . lipstick? She hardly ever . . .

His father held her away from him for a moment, looked down at her lean, suddenly fragile body, at her smiles and tears, and said, 'I think I have forgotten how to kiss.'

Thomas unsheathed another grass and prodded the spider's web. The web shuddered and so did he and out it came.

He really did say that: 'I think I have forgotten how to kiss.' It struck me as funny at the time and I snickered behind them. That bit about the spider is crap, nonsense. Oh yes, there was a spider in the gate-post, but not an actor at all during that particular scene. I stood behind them, snickered and felt excluded. And now I wonder at that strange remark. It has a false ring I did not then detect. Rehearsed? Probably. Why? Because he had been kissing ladies from Benghazi to Trincomalee? Maybe. But more probably because he genuinely already expected to be at sea, lost and dreading failure.

Many years later Thomas began to suspect Dad had not been much cop at sex. Not at all surprising really. Upper-upper-class males learned how from professionals – nymphos from their own set, or tarts. And so too did the proles. But not the middles, the upper middle, middle middle or lower middle. The middles muddled, and then gave up.

And 'nice'. It was not a word his father ever used, or if he did, then it was with class-ridden sarcasm and pronounced 'naice'. So he did not ask if it was a 'nice house'. What adjective would he have used? 'Good'. 'Fine'. 'Pleasant'. 'Jolly'.

'Jolly'? I think not. Probably 'good'.

Thomas slept. And then woke with the pain in his side, under his left floating rib. Under and behind. Quite sharp. Enough to wake him up. Serve him right.

2

Taaa, taaa, te te taaa te taaa taaaa. So bloody loud, unbelievably loud.

'I don't believe it,' Katherine shouted. 'Turn the bloody thing off . . . '

The Trumpet Voluntary played on a synthesizer in thirds with a thudding base. Thomas swung hairy varicose legs off the bunk, bent over a laminated console set behind the tiny table under the porthole.

'Jesus, what's going on?' Richard lifted a blotched fair face out of the wafer-thin pillow.

'Daddy, Daddeee, turn it off, please turn it off,' Hannah-Rosa screamed, her head inches from his nightshirted thigh.

Thomas twisted knobs and killed the obscene racket. The corridor outside stirred with doors opened and closed, voices. The ship hummed on, the way ships do. He straightened. Outside the porthole a lambent, nacreous, glaucous sea stretched to a horizon marked by a purple line of land. France.

'What's the time?'

He looked at his watch.

'Five.'

'English or French?'

'French.'

'So it's bloody four really.'

'We dock in an hour.'

But Katherine had pulled her pillow over her ears.

If I'm going to drive I need a proper breakfast, Thomas thought. He pulled on enough clothes, went to the cafeteria and had an English breakfast – sort of defiance here since it was a French boat.

Katherine yawned, covered her mouth, finished her hot chocolate.

'Three hours sleep was it? Four? Not enough.'

Nine o'clock now. A break after driving round Caen and getting lost, then through deep woody valleys filled with mist near their rivers.

'You were crying in the night. Sort of whimpering.'

'I was? Dreaming, I suppose.'

'Bad dreams. Anxiety. Stress. A holiday will do you good.'

'Do us both good.'

Briefly he covered her hand with his on the table between them, and then withdrew it, smiled at her. He looked a touch wan but then they had not left the Rock Bar until one o'clock French time. A very slick, over-rehearsed combo played rock standards with note-by-note accuracy. The drummer had been good though, a driving beat.

The lead guitarist had asked the audience of mainly forty-somethings (he was half their age) to suggest rock titles. Thomas had caused Katherine some embarrassment by constantly calling out, '"Wild Thing", play "Wild Thing". We want "Wild Thing".' He tried to get the others to join in.

He knew that as a teeny in the sixties she had jogged away to the Troggs in Worthing Assembly Rooms, and through the first few years of their relationship often, if he was high on booze and sex, he would dance naked around whatever room they were in chanting, 'Wild thing . . . ' until she had had to scream at him to stop.

Now he took his hand away and saw how she smiled, a little sadly. He was aware of the spaces opening up between them caused by their different preoccupations – his growing distress over conflicting issues at work, and she over-occupied with the translation agency she had started a year before. And then there was all this father business he had run into. He'd have to explain that sometime. Somehow. He looked up at her, eyes refocusing, returning from some distant hinterland.

'Where are the children?'

'In the loos. You know Hannah-Rosa – always has to check out the loos in a strange place, whether she needs to or not.'

He looked round. Cane furniture stained dark to contrast with spotless pale grey and pink walls, tropical palms in ceramic tubs. Outside, tall stuccoed buildings, plane trees throwing leafy shadow, a shopkeeper hosing down his pavement, already a warmth that was different from the warmth they had left, a warmth that the cobbles and stones held through the night although this was still the north of France. Laval.

And everywhere, across the street and in the shop windows, flags of many nations – but not Germany – marked the fiftieth anniversary of D-Day, two months before. It had been the same in every town and village from Caen onwards.

'Here they come.'

Richard in front.

'Oughtn't we to be off again? It's a long way, you said.'

'We'll get as far as we can. No need to push it.' Katherine firm, but sort of reassuring too. Exercising control.

'Mummy, there was free scent squirts in the loo. Smell.'

Hannah-Rosa thrust her upturned wrist under her mother's nose.

'I'll pay a visit too.'

'I'll get the bill.'

'Dad, please don't do that scribbling on a pad mime,' Richard whispered. 'It's so embarrassing. Try L'*addition, s'il vous plaît*.'

When Katherine came back, Thomas was standing with a puzzled frown on his face.

'What's the matter?'

'Three hot chocolates, a café au lait, two chocolatines and two croissants. How much?'

'I daren't guess.'

'Seventy-five fifty. That's damn near ten quid.'

The freshness had gone from the morning, the mists burnt off and France was once again what most of it is and most people forget. A great, long, undulating lump of fields and hedges and villages without bypasses strung out along inadequate main roads. Each village with its white cross detailing the church services: *Messe à huit heures, messe à dix heures* . . .

'Messes at any time of day, if you ask me.'

'What did he say? What did Daddy mean?'

Laboriously they explained, but still Hannah-Rosa didn't or wouldn't understand.

'Shall we have some music?' Richard asked.

'Yes. What?'

Katherine delved for the yellow shoe-box beneath her seat.

'The Troggs? Daddy seemed to be into them last night.'

'"Wild Thing"?' The boy's tone held the hint of a laugh. Last night Daddy had been, well, nothing anywhere near pissed, but certainly a touch high. Katherine slotted in the tape.

'Shit! Bastard!'

Horn blaring, a BMW estate, German number plates, with roof-rack piled high and a load of bicycles stacked across the tailgate, swung past in the face of an oncoming ERF truck to fill the safe distance he'd left between them and the Brit camper in front.

The finger. Automatic reaction.

'Don't do that!'

'Oh, he didn't see.'

'Not much point if he didn't,' Richard remarked.

'You're quite right, though. Slap my wrist.' He proffered his left wrist and she did.

'We'll stop at Angers for lunch,' Katherine said, the map spread across her knees.

'Bit early. We'll be there by eleven.'

'We'll stop at Angers.'

Wild thing.

Renault 21, only two years old, electric windows, smooth quiet ride, good family car. Angers, twenty-five k. I need a wee. And that pain in my side again.

An Austin 8 had been his parents' first car after the war and that not until 1954 – I'll never appreciate how poor they were . . . Not my fault. I didn't ask to go to boarding-school, to fee-paying prep school and public school. Indeed I did not.

But.

'He's got a Welsh accent, and he said Altantic instead of

18

Atlantic. Of course it's not your fault. Blame Hitler. Anyway, I think it's time he went to a proper school . . . '

Oh shit, I really do need a wee, rather badly.

'Daddy, I need to do a stream. Badly.'

'Thomas, do it well, or not at all.'

Do a stream? His mother's euphemism. So embarrassing.

Angers fifteen.

Angers seven. *Centre ville.* Long, long interminable road with grey stucco buildings above drab shops, the sky laced with wires, and ancient hoardings on every wall big enough to take them. The hot summer air heavy with lead and God knows what other toxics, and traffic lights every twenty-five yards. Delivery van coming out of a side street, nearly brushed the right-hand fender. Where the fuck does he think he's coming from?

'*Priorité à droit.* In towns. Remember?'

Fucking France. Looks a nice town though, on a steep hill with a castle and a cathedral at the top. Christ, I need a wee. And if it be not to come soon then it'll be badly.

Big bridge across the river, the Mayenne, sign for a car-park to the right.

'If we're going to the cathedral and the castle we should park at the top. I don't want to climb that hill in this heat.'

It's only ten past eleven and we're barely out of Normandy, and it's no hotter than bloody England.

'There's a car-park here. Now. And I need a wee.'

'There may not be a toilet.'

'There is, there must be. There's a bus station, *station de l'autobus.* Can't have a bus station without a toilet.'

A narrow strip under plane trees divided up with box hedges. At the end nearest the bridge a modern, grey and black low building, with bays for buses beside it. Once it had been a small park where ladies in crinolines, beneath parasols, cruised above the river, splashed with sunlight like in a painting by Monet but now *un parking.* Vandalism? No . . . not if there's a loo.

He found a slot, they all piled out. *Payez ici.* Pay and display. Five francs for two hours, seven for three. Cathedral, castle

19

perhaps, lunch, play safe it's horrible to have to hurry. He slotted in a five franc piece, then a two.

'Shan't be a jiffy.'

'No need for the bus station. There's one of those automatic cubicle things, down the end there.'

'So there is.'

He headed off towards the matt stainless steel ovoid-cuboid chamber from outer space with tolerable confidence that he was not going to disgrace himself. Sixty next February. Surely this sort of embarrassment was setting in a bit early? *Occupé*. Shit. But all was not lost. Back to the bus station, two hundred yards. Don't run. Doesn't help. Brisk walk, bent forward, a little stiff. Try to keep hands out of tracksuit-bottom pockets.

The bus station was an agreeable structure, octagonal, tent-like, not large. Inside there was a circular counter, with offices and surely a loo set into the sides of the building facing inwards towards it. Thomas paced round the circle like a caged wolf. Posters – *Visitez les châteaux de la Loire. Visitez le moyen-âge à Tours*. Tried a likely door. Locked. Turned to the gentleman behind the counter. Tapped the car keys to get his attention.

'*Monsieur, y-a-t-il un vay say?*'

'*Oui, mais l'homme qui a la clef n'est pas ici. Il reviendra à midi.*'

Oh dear, this is getting serious. Getting close to a pain in the penis. Definitely a trot now back to the *automatique*. Family, clustered in the shade round the car, look over the waist-high box hedges with concern. At least they're not laughing – yet. Crunch, crunch, crunch through the pea gravel. *Libre*. Hooray. *Pièce de 2 francs*. Right-hand pocket of tracksuit bottoms. Handful of small change but the only two franc piece went in the parking machine. Back to the car.

'Have you got a two franc piece? It's all it will take.'

'I haven't got any francs at all.' He knows that. Why does he ask? 'What about the bus station?'

'The loo there's locked. It must be the staff loo. Man with the key won't be back till midday.'

She knows there must be a snag, else I wouldn't be here, so why does she ask?

I bet he got that wrong, she thinks. His French is awful, especially comprehension.

'I'll see if I can get someone to change my francs.'

Back to the bus station – more likely to get change there, but no, no time for that, head back to *cabinet*. Holding on now with bruising grip, yet feel a leak seep through. Lucky the tracksuit bottoms are a dark purply-blue. I'm not going to make it, am I? And there's no one around to ask for the right coin.

Five yards from the *cabinet*, under a myrtle, into the inadequately high box hedge, no zip to pull, do it over the front of the tracksuit bottoms, over the top of underpants, and what had been a totally deserted area is suddenly crowded. First two young women with french loaf sandwiches wrapped in paper looking for a seat overlooking the river. Then a woman with two small girls in tow and a third in a pushchair . . .

'*Je m'excuse, priez me pardonner . . .*'

They hurry by with looks of deep disdain.

It goes on for ever.

Deep, deep winter. '44–'45. In a marshalling yard outside Leicester on the way to Dad's new RAF station at Melton Mowbray. The three of them alone in a compartment of a corridorless carriage. Ten minutes, twenty, half an hour without moving. Leaden sky, flurry of dry snowflakes no bigger than gnats. An endless freight train loaded with Bren-gun carriers and tanks, part-shrouded with tarpaulins, one to each truck, clanks by beneath a cloud of sulphurous smoke. On their way to the Ardennes, the Battle of the Bulge, Jerry's last push. Dad can wait no longer, hoists up the leather strap to release the window, puts a hand out to open the door. Sudden terrible blast of freezing air laden with that railway smell, and some of his pee blows back, instantly crystallized into blobs of yellow snow . . .

'My father (Thomas's grandfather) always used to say, "The wise man goes when he can, the fool when he must."'

3

'Right. We'll drive up the hill. Like you said, it's too hot to walk.'

Gentlemen do not use 'like' as a conjunction. Fifty years on it was still an act of Oedipal rebellion to do so.

'But you bought a ticket for three hours.'

Thomas remembered – a five franc piece and the fateful two- er.

'Right then. Shanks's pony. Excelsior. There was a youth through snow and ice, bore a banner with the strange device . . . '

'What's Daddy on about?'

'Never mind. But first could you open the car so I can get my bag out.'

A slim shiny leather pouch on a shoulder strap. In the passenger door side thingy.

'I want to know. It sounds funny. I want to know.'

'Not now, dear, it's too complicated and not really funny at all.'

'Sounds like a poem.'

'Richard, you're right.' Thomas was always pleased at his son's perspicuity. '"Excelsior" means higher. But not just in the sense of altitude, though in the poem altitude is the central metaphor for the perfection the youth is striving for—'

'Thomas. Will you please unlock the car.'

Pause. A hint of breeze and the shower of sun splashes shifted across the gravel and the box hedges.

'I locked the car?'

'You got us out. Then you locked the car. Then you left us.'

'Why did I do that? I mean leave you outside a locked car.'

'Don't ask me.'

'Pressure of the moment?' Richard suggested with a slight sly smile.

22

Thomas felt in the right-hand pocket of his tracksuit bottoms, then, with growing dismay, the hip pocket.

'And I didn't leave the keys with you?'

'No.'

'Shit. I'll just have to go back over all the places I've been.'

'Are you sure they're not in one of your pockets?'

'Richard, I am quite sure.'

'Spares?'

'In my handbag. In the car.'

He set off, first towards the *automatique* thinking he might have dropped them on the ground while looking for change. As he went he heard Hannah-Rosa, using the voice which says 'I am pretending to hope what I say will not be overheard.'

'He's only actually *been* in one place, so it shouldn't take long.'

The scene of the crime. Patch still very damp but no keys. Back to the bus station.

'Monsieur, quand j'étais ici il y a quinze minutes, je crois que j'ai laissé mes clefs, les clefs de mon auto, ici.' Should there not be a subjunctive after that *'crois que'*? But your average French peasant wouldn't know a subjunctive if he banged his funny bone on one. And anyway I remembered to use *'laisser'* rather than *'quitter'*. And pronounce *'clefs'* as if it were clay.

The guy behind the counter lifted his shoulders like a gull about to spread its wings and fly and his lips came together in an explosive pout. Finally his palms came up above the counter spread like a mendicant's in front of a passing prince of the Church. It all added up to a pretty definite *'non'*, the sort of *'non'* de Gaulle gave successive British governments when they begged to join the Common Market. Silly buggers.

He went back to the car. Beneath the trees his family stood around it in attitudes of grim resignation. He shrugged.

'Are you sure I didn't give them to you?'

'Sure. Why would you, anyway?'

'Are *you* sure they're not in one of your pockets?'

'Yes, Richard.'

Then reluctantly the right pocket, the hip pocket.

'The left pocket?'

'I don't think there is a left pocket. Anyway I never put . . . Oh shit. Here they are. Would you believe it?'

With some weariness they agreed that they would.

As they climbed the hill he told them about the Plantagenets, and how Henry I of England whose father was Geoffrey the Handsome of Anjou (Angers) ruled a huge empire including . . . Hang on. William I, 1066 to 1087. William II, 1087 to 1100. Henry I, 1100 to 1135, all Normans. It was Henry II not I who came to the throne in 1154. Henry II, 1154 to 1189. He who saw off Thomas à Becket and thereby inspired some pretty dire liderachure, not to mention cinema . . .

'Henry the Second,' he said. 'Not the First.'

'I don't know how you remember all that stuff.'

The large room with tall pseudo-Gothic windows looked out on to gardens deep in snow, so the room was filled with a cool pale light. Beyond the gardens and the lake close by, which you couldn't see from here, there were mountains, rounded out with the snow, rising to a lead-grey sky. It was cold. Almost too cold to make the steel-nibbed wooden pen do what he wanted it to. It splattered blue ink in tiny drops across the pale-blue paper. Printed address: The Links, Preparatory School for Boys, Patterdale, Westmorland.

Round him, sitting not at desks but at the small tables of what had been a hotel dining room, sixty similar pens scraped away. Except for Bransgore's. He had a gold-nibbed fountain pen. A hotel dining room? The Links had been evacuated to the Lake District and was still there when Thomas arrived in January 1944, just before his ninth birthday.

'Sir, please, sir, it's too cold to write. Can't we have some heating on?'

'Do I really have to remind you? There's . . .'

Five or six of the boys joined in the chorus.

'There's a war on.'

Sunday afternoon. Letter-writing time. Get it done quickly, and then you can read what you like. Percy F. Westerman. G. A. Henty. The older boys read Leslie Charteris.

Dear Mummy,

      I am not very happy just at the moment. There is a boy called Bransgore. He's the marquess of Bransgore but we have to call him just Bransgore. He teases me a lot and sometimes hits me. Could you please write to Mr Fetherstonehaugh and tell him so Bransgore will stop it. It's been snowing for days and I'm very cold all the time.

      Yesterday we had collyflower with burnt cheese on top and I was sick again.

Love from

Thomas

'Sir, please, sir, I've finished.'

'Bring it up then, Somers.'

Mr Barber taught French, was generally thought to be a case. He had a wooden leg which was why he was not in the Forces.

'Somers, I have to say that I think this letter will make your mother rather unhappy. And we don't want that, do we?'

Um . . . we-e-ell. He could not verbalize, could only express in tears the bitterness he felt towards the woman who had colluded with the father who had sent him here.

'No, sir, of course not, sir.'

'So, why don't you go back to your table, try again, and try to be a little braver, and a little more cheerful.'

'Yes, sir. Can I have that one back?'

Pause. Sudden collusion between them.

'No, Somers. I'll look after it for you.'

Barber, thin, dark, ill-fitting clothes, peg-leg, was an outsider too, knew all about inventing strategies to cope with the intolerable. Somers knew he would pass on his accusatory letter to the head, and thus Somers would have sneaked on Bransgore without ever having seemed to.

Feeling a little better he went back to his table to begin his second attempt.

But first he looked round the sad, grey room, the dismal whiteness outside. How long had he been here? Three weeks.

In a fortnight's time his birthday. He had never had a birthday away from home before, he had never had a birthday without Mummy. He did think it was a bit thick – Daddy had missed three of his birthdays, and now he was back this one should have been an extra special birthday, all three of them together at last. Why not? Why didn't they want to be with him on his birthday?

Mummy had worn new clothes to see him off at Lime Street Station. A bottle-green suit, padded shoulders, slightly waisted, hem just on the knees, hat to match, a high circle of green felt above her fluffed-up hair. He liked her the way she dressed now. The perfumes, the lipstick ... He had tried not to cry because Daddy had told him that big boys do not cry. He did not think of himself as a big boy. He cried. And she cried a little too, turning away with a slip of a hankie to her eyes as the steam billowed round her. Well, it might have done.

'Get on with it, Somers. Cut out the daydreaming.'

'Sir, please, sir, he's not daydreaming, he's blubbing. Again.'

> Dear Mummy
>   We are learning the names and dates of
> the Kings and Queens of England. So far we have done
> the Normans and the Plantagenets. It's quite good
> fun ...

'I said,' Katherine repeated, 'I don't know how you remember all that stuff.'

'There are some things you never forget. I'll tell you another one.'

'Yes?'

'Wellington, when he was a lad, went to a military academy, here in Angers.'

26

4

By now they had climbed a steep car-free path of cobbles and steps, following the curtain walls of the castle, to the plateau. Morning Glory and ferns splashed cerulean and emerald from the damper patches, but the top was a bore: eighteenth-century barracks, now municipal offices.

'It's hot.'

'The cathedral should be cool.'

Big shadowy spaces. Not too much Arsee mystery, just the usual banks of guttering candles and the not unpleasant odour of six centuries of incense.

Cool, but a bore. Been here, done this. Yet somehow, something in their upbringing prompted both of them, Katherine and Thomas, to feel you should look at the cathedral when you pass through a European country city like this. The leaflet drew attention to the rose window in the north transept. Scenes from the life of the BVM done predominantly in that deep but brilliant lapis lazuli blue. Secret of it now lost, he'd read somewhere. Surely modern chemists should be able to get their heads round that one. Richard sat down in a pew opposite it and looked at it for ten minutes. Ten minutes!

Thomas was impressed. He could look at a Velázquez or a Goya for ten minutes. Even a Hockney. But a circle of blue light, what, fifty metres away?

'Don't go religious on us, old son.'

'No way.' The Boy God laughed. 'It's just I've never seen colour like that before. I'd like an ice-cream.'

'So'd I.'

'Wouldn't we all.'

Their trainers and sneakers, slap, slap, slapped down the almost deserted nave. Visitors from outer space. No, the inner space was the space that was now alien. A giant stone capsule dropped from the past into a world of smart boutiques, conspicuous consumption, local specialities, leather goods and ceramics. And a superior ice-cream outlet. Class sorbets in brandysnap-type cones, retailing at a cool one pound thirty each.

'I'd like a loo now,' Richard remarked, as cool as the sorbet and its price, cool enough to suggest that he might be masking some urgency.

'There's one of those *automatiques* at the end of the street.'

'And following purchase of sorbets we have a two-er.'

'Right.'

He took the coin. Blond, step haircut, Fido T-shirt, cut-down-jean shorts. Robert Redford of the twenty-first century. Would they ever see him again? The *automatique*, even more obviously than the cathedral, was a Visitor. With such a wonder boy in its maw might it not return whence it came?

'Daddy's just going in this shop to see if he can buy a watercolour pad. You'll find us here.'

But the art shop was already closed for lunch.

'I'd forgotten how the whole country shuts down between twelve and two.'

Richard came out only seconds after he had gone in.

'Hi. Did you manage all right?'

'Not really.'

'What was the matter?'

Richard whispered, 'I want a poo, and I was afraid I'd make it smelly for the next person. They're so small inside.'

'But they have air-fresheners, disinfectants . . . '

'I'll wait. There'll be one where we have lunch. We are going to have lunch, aren't we?'

Richard took consideration for others to saintly extremes. Sometimes.

With increasing irritation bordering on bad temper they mooched from one restaurant to another. Too crowded. Too expensive. People smoking. I don't want Chinese for my first meal in France. I want a proper meal not croque-monsieur at a bar.

'This will do.'

'It's just a working-mens' joint. Equivalent of a greasy spoon.'

'And about as genuinely French as you can get.'

Marble-top tables. Bentwood chairs. Calendars on the wall, and a small bar where your typical French alcoholic, grey face with black crevices, beret, and Gauloises ash all down his jacket nursed his fifth cassis of the day. But the madame was plump, rose-cheeked and jolly as she wiped the marble clean and chatted away about what was especially good today. Tripes à la mode de Caen. Andouillettes.

'What are they?'

'Small sausages filled with pigs' innards. When you stick a fork in they split and lots of little worms burst out.'

'That's horrible.'

'That's France.'

They settled for steak frites, with a very crisp fresh green salad, and ice-cream in pewter cups. And for Thomas a Kanterbräu. And another Kanterbräu.

And Richard had no problem with the toilet.

'It was pretty smelly when I went in. I don't think I made it any worse.'

Two hundred and ninety francs. *Servis non inclus.* Thirty-six quid. Maybe more.

'Did you actually get into the *automatique*?'

'Yes.'

'So you used the two-er.'

'Yes.'

Thomas took the two franc piece back from the saucer where he had left a not substantial tip.

'That was very nice. I enjoyed that.'

'That's France.'

Nice? Naice.

'Passed the time too.' It would have passed anyway. 'That art shop should be open by now.'

It wasn't.

'Give me the keys and we'll go back to the car and wait for you.'

'Keys? You've got the keys. All right. Only joking.'

He watched them go down the hill, hand in hand, Richard on the outside, then Katherine and Hannah-Rosa on the inside. Just the way Dad said it should be. A gentleman should always walk on the outside. Fourteen hundred hours . . . Come on! Shit! When did they arrive? Eleven? It's now two. Three hours on the ticket. Wheel-clamp. Towed away. Come on . . . !

'M'sieur?'

Unlocking the doors. Octavo pad, twelve sheets, good quality, and a tube of Winsor Violet. Seven fucking quid!

They hadn't let themselves into the car, but were leaning against the balustrade above the river. They didn't see him coming and for a moment he watched them, through the trees. Katherine tall, only half an inch less than him, long deep-brown hair pushed up and loosely clipped, keeping her figure but not easily – serious keep-fit twice a week, aerobics and iron-pumping – all too aware her life was far more sedentary now she was running an office from the spare bedroom. Hence the loose canvas top with a draw-string worn over cropped leggings – damn fine legs, though. Richard – Adonis, what else can one say? Hair growing longer again and the unflattering step drifting into the past. Hannah-Rosa, long blond hair in a clip like her mother's, elfin face, a bit like Degas' *Little Dancer* but prettier and even thinner. Again imitating Mum she was in cropped leggings, but she didn't fill them. They were laughing, happy. How he loved them! How far away they seemed!

In thoroughly good tempers now, blood sugars are so important, they drove south and west towards Cholet. Thomas thought they were on a road they had been down before. Katherine thought not. Thomas remembered he had driven this way once without her, actually on his way to find her, when he was thirty-eight and she was twenty and surfing with her boyfriend and his mates at Seignosse, just north of Hossegor, exactly where they were now heading. Actually, she didn't surf a lot.

'You never really surfed a lot, did you?'

She laughed: 'About as much as you ever did.'

'*Touché.*'

'What's it like, the surf?' Richard from the back.

'It's fabulous. Elemental. Picture this. Waves a hundred yards long—'

'Metres?' Hannah-Rosa suggested.

'Metres. And twelve feet . . . three metres high—'

'Four.'

'Four?'

'Three into twelve goes four.'

'And they roll in with spray whipped off their backs and they begin to curl—'

'And where the water's thinner at the top it goes pale, glassy green—'

'I was going to say that. And then slowly they turn over and the foam begins to break, and they come crashing in. Fabulous.'

'And all the time there's a low, unbroken roar—'

'The roar comes from wave after wave crashing up the fine white sand which stretches a hundred miles—'

'Really? As much as that.'

'Can't be much less.'

'What's that in kilometres?'

'You should know.'

'And above it all there's always a haze that runs the whole length of the coast, a white haze of sand and spray.'

'And behind it there's the dune. A bit like the film.'

'Only it's kept stable by the squeaky grass.'

That's right. She had told him. 'You'll find me in a hollow in the top of the dune. I shall be sunbathing topless in the squeaky grass . . . '

'Hannah-Rosa's crying.'

'Oh, my poor dear, why?'

'Perhaps because Daddy told her she should know how many kilometres in a hundred miles.'

'I know that, silly.' Sob. 'One hundred and sixty.'

'So what is the matter?'

'You said it was The Dune. Like the film. Will there be a giant worm?'

'No, darling. Of course not. That was just a film.'

'Promise?'

Her mother promised.

Problem was, Thomas reflected, as he drove on through a landscape scorched and dull, with industrial estates and industrialized forest and farming, they were such a close-knit family it wasn't always possible to chase the youngest to bed while they watched a frightening film. And always he let her go to bed with Katherine afterwards, while he slept in hers, surrounded by teddies, beneath a frilly lampshade, faced with the posters of the pantomimes she had been in with Matthew Kelly and Roy Hudd. Juveniles from the Stage Door School of Dancing. But she was the star. Even so, the films left a mark. And he knew. Boy, did he know.

Walt fucking Disney. *Snow White and the Seven Dwarfs*. The transformation scene; he saw it when he was three, in a cinema in Liverpool. Perhaps the first time in a cinema. Queen into mother (albeit step) into witch into nice old lady. Apple into poisoned apple, and on the way it was a skull for a bit. This is how he remembers it now. His memory might not be right because although Hannah-Rosa has the video (and it doesn't bother her, not the way *Dune* did), he's never, NEVER seen it a second time. Not that bit. Even five years later the Welsh children from the council houses could chase him round the lanes and hedges with the witch card from the *Snow White* pack of playing cards. And *Fantasia*! The volcanoes! There were three volumes of the *Children's Encyclopaedia* he would not open because they had pictures of volcanoes in them, and the crust of the earth tortured and wrenched and finally blown apart. And as for skeletons, the 'Night on the Bare Mountain'? Or was it the 'Danse Macabre'? No. The former. Saint-Saëns was a joker, but Mussorgsky . . . That whirling spiral of ghosts and skeletons, some on horseback. He was fourteen before he could look at a skull or skeleton, and then only because he couldn't avoid them.

There was a mock skeleton in the biology lab, and the chaplain had a real skull in his sitting room . . .

In Wales he had nightmares.

'Mummy, Mummy, the mountain (all three hundred feet of it) is a volcano, it's going to blow up . . . '

And spiders. But that was something else again. Not really Walt Disney's fault. Not Walt Disney's fault at all.

Blame Hitler.

5

With tiredness, heat, heavy traffic, and driving for too long, madness and chaos became invisible companions sitting with them in the car, bumming a ride like psycho hitchhikers in one of those American films. They became evident at the Continentale *hypermarché* outside Cholet where they stopped for petrol. First the site itself – a vast plateau of grit, gravel and rubble laced with curbed concrete access roads accessing nothing but the giant shop and its huge car-park.

Odd system of paying, was he getting it right? If you wanted to pay by Visa you had to swipe your card at the pump and take the chit to the drive-through kiosk. Would he get it right? Yes, of course he would with Katherine, who was sitting on the wrong side, that's France, and able to translate the instructions and shout them to him.

'Got that right!' as they cleared the kiosk.

'Yes. Well done. Full up then, are we?'

'To the top.'

Lurched round a roundabout smaller than he had expected and this huge, *Duel*-type truck roared round the other side, so they were like steeds or carriages on opposite sides of a mad carousel. Triple klaxons blared like the horns in Verdi's 'Dies Irae' rather than those on a fairground organ.

'What's got into him?'

'Got the *priorité* wrong again, have I?'

'I don't think so. He was waving, sort of pointing down at us. Across the roundabout.'

'Oh shit!'

'What is it?'

'I left the petrol-tank cap on the roof.'

'You didn't!'

He could see it all in the wing mirror. The petrol slopping out, in ... in cupsful, cupfuls, as he took another corner to get off the main exit. He pulled in.

'Is it all right? Are we in danger?'

'Will we blow up and die?'

Ever the optimist, our Hannah-Rosa.

Of course the cap was no longer on the roof.

They went back to the filling station, driving very carefully, very slowly, and none of the froggies hooted at them or urged them to get a move on, probably conscious that they were following a petrol bomb about to blevvy. Katherine made with the French. No petrol cap. Slowly they followed the convoluted route through the maze of access lanes and ... *YES!!!* all fists in the air, there it is, the black round plastic cap in the gutter. Wow! Or, as the French say, *Pouf!*

They drove on and on. He began to reflect, occasionally aloud if he thought anyone was listening, what if? What if the truck driver had not been the saintly type or had turned up ten seconds later? What if a pedestrian had tossed a fag-end at them as they drove by. Boom! Or what if they had been wheel-clamped in the Angers car-park? What if he had been arrested for committing a public nuisance ... ? That brought to mind a story one of his best friends used to tell at school with very French gestures. Thomas told it again.

'Notice on a wall in France. *Défense de pissoir*. Tramp in front of it, head down, hands in front of him. Up comes the gendarme. Blows his whistle, signals for reinforcements to help make the arrest. Tramp looks over his shoulder. "*Je ne pisse pas. Je m'amuse.*" No, Hannah-Rosa, that is one I'm not going to explain.'

'It's dirty, then.'

If a butterfly flaps its wings at the right moment in China there's a tornado in Kansas. Ray Bradbury put it all down in a short story forty years ago or more, long before anyone called it Chaos Theory. Time travellers, time tourists really, kill a beautiful butterfly in the Jurassic. Result: they return to a much nastier, uglier world. What if, what if? Did Bradbury ever get acknowledged for spawning all that stuff?

'Time we looked for a *chambre d'hôte.*'

'A what?'

'A B and B.'

He looked at the car-clock.

'Only six, we could get a bit further yet.'

'Seven, you haven't altered the clock.'

'Seven. *You* haven't altered the clock.'

She was right, though. The traffic was heavier than ever, they were getting a touch irritated with each other, the children too.

'Richee, Richee, don't. Tell him, Daddy.'

'Richard, whatever you're doing, stop it.'

'I'm trying to massage my foot. Got pins and needles.'

'He was *only* going to take his shoes off. He was! Pongeee. We'd all be suffocated.'

'There's one.'

Too late. They passed three more signs. Two indicating the house was a kilometre or more off the main road, one they didn't like the look of.

Feyole.

Yet another long ribbon of a village, where the road narrowed and the trucks and coaches roared between grey houses.

'Two hundred metres on the left, it says so.'

'Where?'

'Just coming up. Look, an entrance in that wall.'

High, high enough for a hay cart, courtyard beyond, old farmhouse. He stood on the brakes. Six drivers behind stood on theirs. Trucks, coaches, campers, a couple with caravans. Horns spread across four octaves. 'Dies Irae' with a vengeance.

'I'm not budging. They'll just have to overtake.'

'They can't overtake.'

Madness and chaos.

But is it chaos, I mean theoretical chaos, if you will it yourself? If you are the conscious cause of chaos? Hannah-Rosa began to cry again.

'Look. You can't reverse. If you don't want to kill us all and cause the deaths of others too, just drive on till we find a turning point and then come back down the other side.'

God, you're so intelligent.

It was all right. Weird, but all right. New conversion, varnished pine in the rooms, two adjoining, family suite, even your own spanking new bathroom, all on the side furthest from the road. Spotless. Madame, charming. Four hundred francs with breakfast, French breakfast, of course, but all the same.

'Are you sure? For all of us? That's bloody reasonable!'

But weird. The only other guests were three young Chinese, two men, one girl, and one of them played jazz trumpet.

'West End Blues', sweet and sour, spiralled up to greet the rising moon.

The parental bed was big and for a time they all sat or lay in it, wanting to be close at the end of this first day of a new adventure. Thomas tried to read – *Wellington's War*.

Two horsemen appeared, flying over the stubbled down, pumping up the red dust beneath their hooves. They reined in. Wellington touched Pakenham's shoulder with his crop.

'Edward, move on with the Third Division – take the heights in your front – and drive everything before you.'

'I will My Lord, if you will give me your hand . . . '

The others played Who am I?

Thomas joined in.

'I'm dead. I used to work in a shed at the end of my garden, and I worked with very sharp pencils.'

'Did you draw with the pencils?'

'No.'

'Easy-peasy. You're Roald Dahl.'

Eventually they kicked the kids out.

'Are you all right?'

'I think so.' Bloody pain in my side again. Maybe because I ate

37

all those peanuts on the boat last night. Wild Thing. 'Why do you ask?'

'You've been a touch bad-tempered at times. Understandable of course, but . . . And suicidal at times too.'

'Suicidal?'

'Not putting the petrol cap back on. Stopping like that outside here.'

'I'll be more careful tomorrow. It's all been a bit much really.'

'I know.'

But you don't. Should he tell her? Why not.

'There is one thing.'

'Yes?'

He gulped, grimaced. This was the nub, the crux, the root he felt of all that was churning through his mind the way an inadequately chewed salad goes through your gut. Gut feeling: inescapable and sometimes painful.

'I don't think I can tell you.'

'I think you should.'

'Well, all right then. I worked this out the day before we left, looking at the dates and so on. On August the thirty-first if I make it to a quarter past two in the afternoon, I shall have lived longer than my father did.'

Pause.

'And that matters?'

'No. I suppose not.'

Yes, it does. It bloody matters. For a start I don't really think I deserve to. But he said no more. And she didn't press him.

6

A Brief Life of Christopher Richard Tate Somers
by
Thomas Richard Somers

As told by Thomas Somers to himself, as a better way of getting to sleep than counting sheep.

Christopher Richard Tate Somers was born on 12 September, 1900, the third child and eldest son of Osbert Henry Somers and Hannah Tate. Osbert Somers was an underwriter in maritime insurance with his own firm in Liverpool. He died in 1916 having amassed a considerable fortune which he tied up as securely as a Christmas parcel with thick brown paper, heavy duty string and red sealing wax. Hannah Tate came from the sugar family (also Liverpudlian) and with a handsome marriage settlement – the capital of this too was tied up at least until her death. And she lived a long time, dying in her eightieth year in 1957. Come to think of it, she must have been a lot younger than Osbert.

> 'If we're going to call her Hannah after your grand-
> mother, then she's going to be not Hannah but Hannah-
> Rosa.'
> 'Rosa?'
> 'Rosa. After Rosa Luxemburg.'

The Somers were an old Liverpool family of some distinction – ship-owners, traders, politicians, philanthropists and patrons of the arts, they were descended from a seventeenth-century carpenter who built his own boat to trade with the Americas. In spite of what some people say they never traded in slaves and indeed campaigned through two centuries against the slave trade.

'You're doing it again.'

'What?'

'Grinding your teeth.'

'Sorry.'

Christopher Somers went to a co-ed boarding-school, St George's of Harpenden, surely the only school of its kind at the time, and then to Wadham College, Oxford. He read Greats for a year and was then called up, although the war was almost over, to serve in the new Royal Flying Corps for a year. He spoke very little about this period of his life, though when the next war came along and he joined the RAF it was a matter of great pride to him that he was one of the handful of officers who served in both the RFC and the RAF. In neither did he learn to fly.

Returning to Oxford in September 1920 he found he had forgotten a lot of the Latin and Greek he had been taught so read Jurisprudence instead. He obtained a fourth class honours degree, which is really a fail. However, he won a quarter blue at chess, rowed for his college and in 1921 won the silver cup for Junior Challenge Sculls. He was arrested for riding a motorbike too noisily up the High after dark and spent the rest of that night in jail. He was quite proud of that. Years later, elbow on the polished teak of the bar at the Tithe Barn Club, where he was the secretary, he'd say, 'I have been in jail, you know,' trying to impress the membership – spivs, con-artists and other assorted businessmen with their brassy wives and mistresses.

At Oxford he married a woman called April. An achievement he was less proud of. She was the daughter of a college servant and was, in all respects, a most unsuitable match. However, Richard was a romantic with a strong sense of honour and an exaggerated respect for the female sex. He had kissed her – he should marry her.

I have never heard a good word about April, not even from her daughter Fay, my half-sister. She was a terrible snob, hated men and sex, and when my father left her in, I think, 1932, she refused to divorce him, thus inflicting on me the curse of bastardy. And I mean curse, because the way Osbert had tied up that Christmas parcel excluded illegitimate children or grandchildren from any inheritance rights at all . . .

'Go to sleep, please.'
　'Give us a cuddle then.'
　'The children will hear us.'
　'Just a cuddle.'

What in the world can a man with a private income of about a hundred and fifty pounds a year (worth about fifteen thousand in the 1990s?), a wretched marriage and a fourth class degree in a useless subject do? The answer is probably the same now as it was then – teach in a boys' preparatory school. He taught Latin at a school called Homefields in the leafy Surrey suburb of Carshalton. I think he bought a house, a new pebble-dashed semi or even detached, amongst the laburnums and laurels, with money borrowed from his mother and two older sisters. And because he was in effect on two salaries, he lived it up a bit; he and April. They joined the country club, tennis in summer and bridge in winter. Long flannels with his Wadham College tie for a belt – subtle that. To wear the silk square would have been too obvious, clearly showing off. To keep his trousers up with the tie let people know he'd been to Oxford, but sort of signified it didn't really matter. He played cricket too, in the same flannels, slow off-spin with an occasional googlie.

Was he a snob then? Some alter ego in his head posed the question.

One hell of a snob. Which was odd. Because most of the Somers I've known were not. His younger brother and younger sister, my uncle Wilf and aunt Brenda, were not snobs.

How was he a snob? the voice went on. *What was he snobbish about?*

Family and education. He used to say to me, often, Thomas, you are the scion of a noble race, and he said it with such pride I believed it and became rather proud of it all too.

The Somers family has been on the whole a good thing.

Yes. A class actor, a class potter and coppersmith, one of the first women MPs, a strong libertarian tradition and so on. Musicians, writers. Founder member of the British Communist Party. Something, yes, to be proud of and live up to. But not to feel exclusive about, different, pharisaical.

And he did?

Well, yes and no. Intellectually he hated anything pharisaical, anything that said I'm better than you, mate, and I've got blue blood to prove it. But all the same . . . he did think we Somers were a bit special, a bit different.

And you feel that yourself?

Yes. But not because of our genes.

And he thought it was genetic?

I think so. Though of course in his lifetime people were not as *au fait* (that was one of his phrases '*au fait*' – but always used ironically, while my mother would use it without irony) people were not as *au fait* with genetic theory as they are now. Educated people, I mean.

There you go. You are your father's son. He sounds rather insecure.

Very insecure. I think his father's death, when he was only sixteen, came as a terrible shock and one for which he was not prepared. And though he had two older sisters, who were very capable people, in fact tough cookies, he felt that as the eldest son some sort of extra responsibility or burden had fallen on him. For instance Aunt Brenda, who was six years younger, has told me how when she played with her mashed potato, making sculptures out of it, he made her take her plate to the sideboard, which he called the 'Pigs' Table'. Thirty years later he did the same to me. And, of course, his insecurity was not helped by the fact that from then on he contrived to make pretty much of a mess of most of his life.

Really? Perhaps you should go back to telling me the story of it. We were, if you remember, in the leafy suburb of Carshalton. 1932, or thereabouts.

Yes. He and April got involved with at least two other families in the sort of suburban shenanigans that were quite a feature of the time. Tennis and dinner dances. Liaisons conducted by Mr and Mrs Smith in those ghastly roadhouses which were also very much of that period – those big red-brick barns, with 'function rooms' and so on, that went up all over the Home Counties at the junctions of main roads. Servicing the new middle-class, car-owning democracy. My mother, who was called Decima because she was her parents' tenth child, Dess for short, was married to a businessman, an entrepreneur in a way, who imported vending machines, leased them, and took a royalty from each threepence or sixpence that went into them for cigarettes or thin bars of Nestlé chocolate. She had two daughters. But he was carrying on with another woman, and my dad fell for Mum. She was a very pretty woman at the time. Blond hair bobbed, big blue eyes, thin, the fashions suited her.

After all the usual rows, which must have been horrendous, April packed her bags and returned to Oxford with her daughter. As I said, she vowed she'd never divorce Dad, and she never did, and for the rest of her life, and she didn't die until 1973, she got half the income from Grandad's Trust. Meanwhile Dad and Mum went off to Monte Carlo. Yes, they really did. But first they came to an arrangement with her husband whereby, in exchange for letting him divorce her, undefended, they would share custody of her two daughters. And that was the next cock-up – Dad expected her husband to behave like a gentleman and honour a gentleman's agreement, but when they got back he'd got total custody and control.

Bastard. But what about Monte Carlo? That sounds really romantic.

Yes, I suppose it must have been. There's a photograph of them, taken outside the casino. They worked a system my father had devised which was simply to bet each day on the even money chances until they had won enough to support themselves for the next twenty hours or so.

Hang on, I'm not sure I get that.

Well, suppose you need ten pounds a day to live on. Lot of money then. You go in, put ten pounds on black, it loses. Now you need twenty pounds. Black again, it wins, you need ten. Ten on again, let's this time say, impair, odd numbers. Thirteen. You're ten ahead of the game, what you need; you pack it in

43

until tomorrow, go on the beach instead. You have a reserve – say a hundred pounds – and once you're fifty down on a day you stop. It's gone, you don't try to recoup it . . .

I don't believe that would work. Not for long.

Three months.

Really?

Really. Partly because when they were down to their last fifty, Dad said, 'Put it all on one number.' And Mum did, picking her birthday, seventeenth of November. Fifteen hundred quid. A hell of a lot of money in those days. They brought back five hundred and bought a tobacconist's shop in Angmering. Didn't work. Or they didn't enjoy the life, I really don't know. Then Mother got pregnant, with me, something they had not been expecting.

Why not?

After the birth of my second half-sister, Mum's ovaries became diseased – I'm not quite sure how, she told me cancer – and, according to her, she had an operation which left her with half an ovary instead of two and a doctor's promise that it was virtually impossible for her ever to conceive again. Yes, I know that all sounds unlikely, but it's what she told me. Dad's family now intervened – they realized they were stuck with her even though she'd never be able to marry him. Stuck with her and with me. There was a preparatory school in Liverpool renting a large house which had once been a Somers townhouse. The head was shortly due to retire. The family got him to take Dad on as deputy head with the understanding he'd take over the business in due course. So. They moved to another thirties pebble-dashed, bow-windowed, suburban home and I duly appeared. But not in Liverpool. My eldest aunt ran a maternity home in Blackheath, south-east London, close to where they start the London Marathon, so Mum was taken down there when I was due. And that was where I was born.

'Sorry, but I had to wake you up.'

'Why?'

'You were talking in your sleep. Listen. What you said about

44

being older than your dad ever was on the thirty-first of August, what is this all about?'

'Difficult to explain. But I've always had a compulsion to be better, do better than he did, and I'm not sure I ought to. I'm not sure, in this case, that I ought to do better than him, live longer than he did.'

'You'd bloody better.'

And she turned on her side, pulled the pillow under her ear. He lay awake, aware that the sky was lightening. Sparrows chirped in the eaves and the first of the morning's huge container trucks thundered down the road beyond the courtyard, making the window panes vibrate.

It really was a bummer, him and Dad. By and large he *had* done better. He'd made more money, had books published, which was something his dad had longed to do. By and large, after the defeat of being sent to a boarding-school, he'd won the battle for his mum's love. He'd even held him to a drawn game at chess. And because after all his dad had suffered far more than he had, had made more sacrifices, had probably been truer to himself, Thomas felt guilty that he had done all these things, felt guilty that it mattered to him that he had. So, now he was going to feel guilty if he lived longer, felt that in a just world, he didn't deserve to. And, and this really was the bummer, at times he wasn't sure he wanted to.

7

Richard and Hannah-Rosa came through turn by turn to use the en-suite, sleepy-eyed but grinning. Katherine grumbled that she liked a cup of tea before getting up, but finally followed Hannah-Rosa through the bathroom. 'St James Infirmary Blues' played on a silver trumpet by a Chinese offered a mournful comment on the traffic already thundering down the street. While Katherine was in the bathroom Richard sat in the dormer window and sketched the courtyard with its square high entrance, making a damn good job of white stucco, blue shadows, red tiles and a plant potted in a ceramic tub. He even put in a telegraph pole Thomas would have left out. 'He's very good, but he's got to sketch more from life and he has to have a portfolio,' the art teacher had said at the last parents' evening. A strange woman, X-ray thin, very emotional in a way you'd say was affected if she wasn't so patently sincere. Black cropped leggings beneath a leather mini, at forty she was clearly stuck in a time-warp. Aren't we all, more or less? It just depends which of the decades marks us for its own.

Early fifties to early sixties for me, Thomas thought. The Beats. *On the Road*, *The Naked Lunch*, 'Howl'. Trad jazz – Ken Colyer, boyish Barber, suave Humph, sinister Mick Mulligan. Should have been West Coast but he didn't come to that until much later. Rock and Roll, Bill Haley, Elvis and Chuck Berry. Buddy Holly. And Frankie Vaughan – 'Green Door', 'What's That Secret You're Keeping?', 'When you walk in the Garden, the Garden of Eden'. Black jeans and Jesus sandals. The first folk movement – the surviving Blues singers, Blind Lemon and Josh White. Frank Sinatra and *Songs For Swinging Lovers*. Tommy Steele and Cliff. *The Duke Wore Jeans*. First the Cha-cha-cha, then the Twist. Osborne, Braine and Storey. Angry Young Men, and Women. Edna O'Brien, Lynne Reid Banks and Shelagh Delaney

46

as good as any of the men or better. Joan Littlewood. *Fings.* Is Auden any good now he's gone Christian? Beckett, and again Beckett. It helped to pass the time. It would have passed anyway. *The Birthday Party* and *The Fire-Raisers.*

Thomas put it all behind him and read. The Battle of Salamanca unfolded through Wellington's own words.

> The cavalry under Lieut.-General Sir Stapleton Cotton made a gallant and successful charge against a body of the enemy's infantry which they overthrew and cut to pieces . . .

The commentary went on to describe how 'cut to pieces' were the *mots justes* – the Heavy Dragoons used a broadsword which smashed collar-bones and rib-cages, severed limbs, and left its victims horribly mutilated and dying slowly.

> 'By God, Cotton, I never saw anything so beautiful in my life; the day is yours.'

Katherine came out of the bathroom. By God, I never saw anything so beautiful in my life. Plumpish now, yes, but not Rubensesque. Yet it would have been fine with him if she had been. Shoulders pink and smooth. But her hair was wet, that meant the drier . . .

'What's the matter? We're not in a hurry, are we?'

He showered, let the thin warm spray play over his tummy, the warmth soothing the nagging soreness below his left ribs. Then his balls and up his backside. His penis thickened. Should he or shouldn't he? He'd not locked the door, better not. Anyway, another delightful but almost certainly exhausting day ahead, better not start with feeling . . . weary? Brushed his teeth instead. Used the loo. Not easy, try again after breakfast. Pain in the left side better, hardly discernible.

With the drier still playing over her head Katherine was sitting on the bed, skimming through the battle. She turned the drier off as he came back in.

'This is pretty horrible stuff.'

He shrugged.

'Don't know why you read it,' she went on.

Welly. A fascination since he was fourteen when Uncle Apples gave him *The Age of Victory* by Arthur Bryant. Mr Appleby, housemaster, and in love with him. Not the only one, in his first years at public school it had been not so much a case of who's a pretty boy as whose pretty boy. They wooed him with books and holidays and he never surrendered his virtue. Rather wished he had, at times.

'He was a total reactionary, wasn't he? Peterloo, and all that.'

'I don't think he had much to do with Peterloo. He always did what he thought was right. He was brave, very hard-working, and much more of a military genius than most historians recognize.'

'Please yourself.'

She turned the drier back on, raised her voice.

'Won't be long now.'

Of course, the real answer was that Welly was a fantasy father figure, the dad who didn't let you down.

'I don't think I'm going to like any of this.'

In Hannah-Rosa's ideal universe breakfast was Sainsbury's Coco-Snaps (Kellogg's Coco-Pops too chocolatey) with the top of the milk, lunch was lamb cutlets, tea, chocolate Swiss roll, and supper, Sainsbury's small cheese and tomato pizza with Sainsbury's pitted black olives on top. Nothing else would do. Certainly not Charentais brioche, shiny and brown as newly opened sweet chestnuts on the outside, crumb flavoured with honey and vanilla on the inside, three different sorts of freshly baked rolls, and a choice of café au lait or hot chocolate. Madame found some Frosties for Hannah-Rosa who conceded she might try the hot chocolate.

'Why is the coffee and chocolate in those bowl things?' Richard asked.

'So you can dip your brioche in them.'

'Coo-ool.'

'Just that. The liquid cools more quickly in them.'

Richard grimaced, refused to comment on his dad's silliness.

Why did you do that? You're a teacher, an educationist, you ought to know better. You didn't like it when your dad put you down over some triviality, did you?

Richard cleared the air by asking, 'Where are we going today?'

'All the way to Hossegor. Where the surf is. We stay there for four days with Pierre and Elvira. Do you remember them?'

'Just. I think. They came and stayed for a day or two, didn't they?'

'When you were five. Mummy and I shared a flat with Pierre in Pau about twenty years ago.'

'And after that? I know you've told me but I didn't really take it in when we were at home.'

'We stay with Monique in her parents' flat in Biarritz, and then in her flat in Pau. And maybe from Pau we'll go into Spain for a day or two. You know Monique.'

Katherine's best friend from the year they had spent when Katherine was an *assistante* in a Pau secondary school, Monique had been coming over to brush up her English pretty regularly once every two years ever since.

'I'll be able to buy bangers in Spain.'

'Maybe in Pau.'

'Or saltpetre to make gunpowder. You said so.'

I say some pretty silly things sometimes, showing off to him about the things I used to get up to at his age, Thomas reflected.

Back to the rooms; I'll just use the loo. Much better after two bowls of coffee.

'Pooee, Daddy's done a stinko.'

She of course never does. Thomas yes, Richard usually, Katherine not often, Hannah-Rosa never. Eats like a sparrow, shits like a sparrow.

Pack up, back to the yard, *Merci, Madame, merci beaucoup*, it really is only four hundred francs, she'll see you out into the road, it's not easy, she says.

Not quite ten o'clock, warm, bright, sunny, but still fresh.

A huge field of sunflowers. Look at them! Later their heads will droop, their petals curl but now they welcome their master, sun-worshipping acolytes, hierophants of the sun, thousands of them following their father . . .

Gently downhill most of the way now, and the light is changing from the heavy blues and greys of the French plateau, the dusty greens, dark with a summer already over-ripe. Now it is brighter, paler, more pure, of course: although it is still some miles to the west, we are near the sea, dropping into the coastal plain.

Katherine unfolded the double-sided Michelin map, refolded it the other side up. The South at last.

'Let's have lunch at La Rochelle?'

'Let's.'

Hannah-Rosa had *haché*.

'What's "*haché*"?'

'Proper beefburger, just freshly ground mince, salt and pepper, nothing else. Like Daddy makes.'

'Not like a Whopper, then.'

'You got it.'

'I don't want it all bloody inside.'

Katherine and Thomas had moules frites, mussels with chips, seemed reasonable at forty francs until you realized that was only a bob or so short of a fiver. Richard went for it. Seafood platter. When it arrived they oohed and aahed and wondered could he possibly get through it. Code, on the part of Katherine and Thomas anyway, for 'go on, give us a bit!'. There was a whole crab, a large helping of mussels, some fried small-fry, shell-on prawns and langoustines like baby lobsters, soft-shelled Dublin Bay prawns and four oysters, all with a garlicky mayonnaise dip and frites. Thomas had the oysters.

'Ugh, it's like phlegm.'

'They're alive you know. And they can twist round the thing that hangs down at the back of your mouth and strangle you.'

Essence of sea. Not salty, not fishy. Just . . . sea. Sea in a bed of nacre, shaped like a tiny petrified wave. Chablis a bully – Maine et Sèvres, just right.

'Jolly lucky to find this place.' Thomas looked round. They

were in a wide, car-free alley between two fish restaurants sitting out in hot sunshine but cooled by the breeze from the sea. Just a hundred or so metres from them a high square tower marked the entrance to the inner harbour. Its huge tricolour shifted in the light airs, its dark blue a bruise against the perfection of the cerulean sky.

He breathed a sigh of satisfaction, snaked out a thieving hand and began to peel a Dublin Bay prawn. Katherine, her father's daughter, sniffed the dead man's fingers on the crab, checking for freshness, and showed Richard how to crack the claws. Her father knew all about shore fish, fished the Bognor beaches with rod and line at dawn and bought live crabs from the fishermen almost as soon as the prows of their boats crunched in the shingle by the pier. All gone now. Most of the pier in a storm three decades ago, and the fishermen crippled by bureaucratic regulations on how they could dispose of their catch.

Lucky – and there had been more luck on the way in, deciphering the unfamiliar signs, coping with dreadful traffic, including a girl on a scooter whose hair had got in her eyes. Avoiding her as she swerved he had nearly put them under an outrageously big container lorry which had no business at all to be juggernauting down a leafy avenue near the centre of the town.

'Watch it!' Katherine had shouted.

'I bloody am!'

The tiny gust of wind that had blown the girl's hair unexpectedly forward had no doubt been the latest in a series of tiny climactic occurrences set off by a butterfly that stamped on a hill outside, say, Aix-en-Provence the day before yesterday. If the butterfly had stamped a second later, the truck would have been that much closer . . .

Thomas looked up and around, breathed in the sea and fishy smells, the coffee smells and the Gauloises on the next table which Katherine found offensive but which he secretly rather liked, even envied. Above all it was the seaside lightness of it all, the glassy ripples on the ultramarine water, the streaks of pure white foam echoing the flag, the mewing of the gulls. Poor Dad.

'This is the life.'

'Can I have an ice-cream?'

'Why not. And I'll have another glass of vino.'

He'd already drunk most of a half-litre.

'Should you?'

'Holidays, you know?'

'But I can have an ice-cream, can't I?'

'Of course. Richard?'

The lad put down the latest of the crab legs he'd been chewing at, wiped his mouth on his fifth paper serviette, looked over the battlefield of broken shells, and grinned.

'I think I could manage one.'

Rolling hills, just steep enough to be interesting, robed in the brilliant viridian of vineyards with medieval abbeys, châteaux nestling between them. *Dégustation gratuite*. Twenty-four barrels of Bordeaux, ho-ho. Thomas sang it, remembering a song the school choir he and Katherine had sung in when he was head of English and she was just a good friend – still in the upper sixth. Signposts for Bourg to the right, St Emilion to the left.

'When Wellington was a young man he did what all young officers did – he drank six bottles of claret a day.'

'Calling it claret is poncey. Pretentious.'

'It's what he called it.'

How do I know that? Fact is I don't. It's what his biographers called it: Philip Guedalla. Richard Aldington. Or was it Elizabeth Longford? He couldn't remember which he'd read it in. Possibly all three.

'Anyway. He realized it was over the top so he cut it down to two. Stuck with that for the rest of his life. Eighty-four when he died.'

'Remember scrumping for grapes?'

'And sweetcorn.'

Richard was fascinated.

'You *stole* grapes?'

'Point is, I might make it to eighty-four if I drink two bottles of clar . . . red wine every day.'

'You might . . . if you cut out the beer and the gin.'

Do I want to be eighty-four? *Ought* I to be eighty-four? All the fossil fuels I will consume. The animals that will be killed for me. The Colombian peasants who will break their backs producing the only coffee I'll buy. The tons of paper, cardboard, plastics . . . the turds that will settle on the bottom of the English Channel or be washed up on Highcliffe Beach.

'Can we stop and scrump some grapes?'
'They won't be ready yet. Hard, green and sour. Give you the runs. That's what happened to the British army in Spain.'

The commander of the forces requests that officers will take measures to prevent the soldiers from plundering and eating the unripe grapes . . .

'Look at that!' A moment of contemporary, man-made beauty – the twentieth century at its best. Because they had kept off the autoroute they were crossing the Gironde on the old bridge and upstream to their left they could see the new autoroute bridge above the wide gorge, suspended from two piers soaring above the panaches of the poplars. A tracery, a web of metal and concrete spun thin like white sugar. Far below in the cappuccino water the barges and coasters chugged to and from the new port. There was an airiness in the light, a cool haze, an unexpected loveliness, a sense of purpose, of commerce and exchange, but all in this open broad setting of woods, water and man's skills working in harmony . . .

They came off the bridge, their road merged with the autoroute, they closed up into the tailback of a solid three carriageway traffic jam.

Later Thomas decided that this was where the nightmare started . . . nightmare? Not all bad. Dream, fantasy. Much of it chosen. But pretty nightmarish at times, for all that.

8

The first nightmare was the road accident that was holding up the traffic: a jack-knifed caravan which a container truck had hit broadside-on, traffic police, ambulances that weren't proper ambulances at all but converted hatchbacks, people standing or sitting on the kerbside looking shattered, shell-shocked. You don't pass accidents like that without a touch of 'there but for the grace of God' in your mind.

'Why was the fire engine yellow?'

'The French are funny like that.'

'The French are funny in lots of ways.'

'What's a *stade nautique*?' Hannah-Rosa again. 'It says two minutes to the *stade nautique*.'

'Sports pool, I should guess,' Thomas answered. 'High diving-board, Olympic standard, that sort of thing?'

'Actually no,' said Katherine. 'More a fun place. Like Splash-down at Tower Park, or Romsey Rapids.'

'Can we go? Can we go?'

Three o'clock. Not expected before eight. Over a hundred miles though.

'Yes,' said Katherine firmly, just as the slip-road arrived on his right.

Richard spent most of the time on the slides going down forwards, backwards, sideways on his stomach and on his back head-first making Thomas's scrotum creep with terror and provoking the attendants to blow whistles at him. Hannah-Rosa almost immediately made friends with a French girl her own age and they walked about with ice-creams in their hands and spoke to each other endlessly, she in English and she in French, and clearly understood each other perfectly, though neither understood a word of the other's language. Katherine chatted gently with the girl's mother, who was on her own – in French, of course, which rather left Thomas out of it all. He wandered about, keeping half an eye on the kids and three-quarters of an eye on adolescent topless wonders. When he remembered to he hauled in his tummy. He wondered if he could get a beer. And, by golly, he could! The kiosk sold not only ice-cream but Kanterbräu in cans. They order, said he to himself, this matter better in France.

There were other delights – under a big cantilevered roof but open to the fresh air, waterfalls, two jacuzzis . . .

He'd never been in a jacuzzi before. Sitting with one thigh against Katherine's he mused not only at the mildly erotic pummelling he was getting from the water, but the sheer, jolly, uncomplicated, democratic hedonism of it all. Moments like this were rare in his mum's and dad's lives, and when they did happen they tended to be stolen or shredded with other guilts.

There were hot rooms too.

With sweat pouring off him in the dry heat room, a dark wood-lined cave, and briefly on his own, Thomas recalled what they called the 'Covered Passage' in the house his aunt let them use after they went broke in 1947. It was really a narrow conservatory running alongside the garage linking the back door to the little room they had given him to keep his books and paints in. It was known as his 'Muck Room'. Anyway, there was a dry old grey bench, whose legs could be folded but never were, against the glass and the knee-high brickwork below it. Through one summer holiday, maybe two, his mother used to put a towel on this bench and sit on it with her back to the glass, and no clothes on at all. And she made him sit next to her. He was a frail youth, very pale, very thin, and probably already fighting the pulmonary TB that would be diagnosed two years later. Meanwhile, and quite erroneously, she believed long doses in the sun would help put things right. She said.

And there they'd sit, baking, facing the odoriferous tomato plants against the wall (still an aroma, when hot and under glass, that thrilled him), sweat streaming off them, sometimes reading, sometimes chatting, and slowly, rising up from a score of new pubic hairs, he would get an erection, and she would pretend not to notice . . .

Thomas came out of the heat.

'What did you think of that then?' Katherine asked.

'Super. I could get really hung up on that sort of thing.'

'Unblocks your pores. Makes you feel much better.'

By then his fifty-year-old mother's breasts had been flat and a bit droopy, the nipples brown and quite large, the areoles pimply. But, for someone who had never seen breasts of flesh rather than stone or bronze, and who had no hang-ups about how breasts should be, they were beautiful. Lovely.

But what had she been up to? Did she know herself? By then she only kissed him when he went back to school or came home – but, he recalled, those kisses could be very close, she clinging to him, especially when he was leaving. But sweating naked in the Covered Passage there had been no longing, no passion – just sweet, sweet eroticism.

Pierre and Elvira lived in Rue Anatole France, a rue which proved elusive. They found they were in the centre of Hossegor and knew they had gone too far.

'This can't be right.'

'We could stop and ring them up.'

'Wouldn't even be able to tell them where we are.'

They turned back again and Thomas spotted an Intermarché with a car-park and a map set in a vandal-proof frame. Anatole France. He'd read *Le Crime de Sylvestre Bonnard* for A-level. About a bibliophile who made platonic friends with a pre-teen girl and got into trouble as a result. One line he always remembered. Monsieur Bonnard employing a house-keeper/cook showed her his library. *'Que de livres!'* she exclaimed. Ever since, he tried to impress French friends with the same idiom. *'Que de poissons!'* he'd say. *'Que de montagnes, que de l'argent, que de neige . . . '* whatever. What a lot of . . . ! It was his boast that he had three French O-levels (though the first was the old School Certificate), one genuine the other two consolation prizes for failing A-level.

'There it is. An-at-ol-ee France.'

Hannah-Rosa was right. The tiny plaque, white lettering on blue, high up on the wall of what actually turned out to be the house they were looking for.

'So you gave up writing? Altogether?'

'No money in it, not enough.'

'You were making a living when we first stayed with you in England.'

Nineteen seventy-eight? Summer? If so just before Thomas went back into education, first as a part-time lecturer at the Isaac Watts College of Education, Southampton, later as deputy adviser then full adviser in English and Drama to the LEA.

'Not really. What I made had to be topped up with Katherine's post-graduate grant and that was peanuts.'

He took a good slurp of Pernod, relaxed back into the cane chair and looked around. A big marble-floored dining room/kitchen, assorted chairs and benches; patio doors open on to a flagged terrace and a big wooden table that was half outside half inside. At the far end of the kitchen Elvira, lean, brown, huge dark eyes, petite with a halo of frizzy long hair that sometimes looked bleached but could have been white with age though she was not yet out of her forties. She was briskly chopping salad vegetables.

At the end of the table, out in the open, Pierre leant across to him. Behind him on a small sandy plateau planted with pines, mimosa, hibiscus and a palm, the dusky air rang with the screams of the children – Richard and Hannah-Rosa water-fighting with Jean-Luc who was the same age as Hannah-Rosa. They had buckets, a hose and plastic water-guns. Pierre said they could do what they liked so long as no water got indoors – it saved him from having to hose the threadbare grass, and it meant there was no need to shower the salt out of the kids' hair.

'How many books was it then?'

'Six. All thrillers.'

Two already published while he was still head of English in a huge comprehensive, the others during the first five years he'd spent with Katherine after giving up the day job . . .

prematurely. It was during the second of those two years when she had been doing her year abroad as part of her French and Spanish degree that they had first met Pierre, but not Elvira – she came into his life later.

'Do you not miss writing? Don't you do any in your spare time?'

'Not really. I mean, I don't miss it. And I do actually keep my hand in. I review thrillers for a couple of papers and magazines. I go on meeting writers. I go to conferences and so on. The last publisher I had is still a very good friend. And I knock off the odd short story every now and then.'

Indeed just a few weeks earlier he had been to a party in the publisher's home celebrating the launch of an anthology of short stories which included one of his. Dick Cass, who wrote as Ray Butcher had been there, looking like Death at the Feast. Poor Cassie. He'd said to Katherine when he got back, 'Cassie's on his last legs. He won't be around for much longer.'

'Anyway,' he went on now, 'there are better things to do with spare time.'

Like sitting in the dusk, sort of half in and half out of doors, breathing sun-warmed air, eating garlicky olives and drinking Pernod.

'But it must have been satisfying, you know? The creative urge fulfilled . . . '

Pierre was persistent. Perhaps he was finding these first few hours of reunion a bit of a strain, and having latched on to a subject to talk about, was reluctant to give it up.

' . . . a sense of achievement, yes?'

'I suppose so. But I got that just as much, for example, from setting up a three-day residential course for drama teachers and knowing it had all worked out well.'

There were lies swimming like sharks below the surface of this. His job during the last three years he had been an adviser had been more concerned with directing teachers towards career opportunities outside education, that is giving them the boot, than enabling them to maximize their potential, that is help them to be better at their jobs. The thing was that a teacher straight from college cost the authority and central government less than one with thirty years' experience. Better for everybody – except the kids, sorry, I mean customers.

It all added up to frustration, despair, chronic depression. He had given up teaching in the first place because it had become less and less to do with helping personalities to fill out and realize some of their potential through language, literature and drama, and more and more to do with the acquisition of the language skills other disciplines required you to have. And literature had been reduced to acquiring entirely artificial analytical skills (Examine the role of the Nurse in *Romeo and Juliet* and assess her contribution to the success of the drama) rather than any ability to respond to what it was really all about.

Driven by financial imperatives, Richard a hoped-for twinkle in their eyes, he'd been dead lucky to get back in – he thought. But now he realized he'd have done better borrowing money from the bank and opening a shop so it could be boarded up ten years later. Hence his move to a private firm of educational consultants, which already he was learning to hate, and hence this holiday. He needed a break. Privately what he thought he needed most was a nervous breakdown.

9

'Hello, here I am.'

'Katherine! Was the shower good?'

'Fine.' Then to Elvira. 'Is there anything I can do to help?'

'No, no.' Hair silvered by kitchen spotlights she waved a large kitchen knife so it flashed above the work-surface. 'It's nearly ready. Pierre will get you a drink.'

'Do you have dry white . . . ?'

Pierre smacked his forehead.

'Only red or rosé. The rosé is very good. Local, you know, very dry . . . '

'I'll try the rosé. I get migraine if I drink red. Could I have some mineral water in it? Half and half.'

Thomas watched and listened as Pierre poured Katherine a rosé spritzer. Pierre over six feet, with a slightly oriental cast to his features, long very straight black hair, well-built, masculine in shorts and T-shirt; Katherine glowing from the shower she'd had, in fancily patterned cropped leggings this time and a fawn-coloured floppy, crinkly cotton shirt, all smiles and ready for a good laugh.

'I like Pierre,' she'd said several times in the run-up to the trip and on the way down. 'You can have a good laugh with Pierre.'

And Elvira. Elvira had married, very young, into a dour Catholic family; the boy, a fellow-student, a serious, introverted character, whose melancholy had appealed to her. But his bourgeois upbringing led him to believe he had acquired a property he could treat as he liked – which included brutality, neglect, marital rape and denial of her right to continue being a student. She had had a nervous breakdown.

Pierre rescued her, looked after her. He was generous, extrovert, boundlessly optimistic by nature, was sure he could turn her round. It had not been easy. How could it be? But one thing was sure. If she was to get over it they had to be out of France. So they taught English in French schools, *outre-mer*. Now this was the part Thomas could not understand, and not for the first time brought it up. This was not Algeria or French Equatorial Africa, he said. This was Mauritius, Tahiti, Martinique. They got free flights back at least once a year, and salaries fifty per cent higher than they would have earned in France ... And yet, they had always seemed to think of it as an exile, a second best.

'Oh, it was not so wonderful, you know?' Pierre was insisting, his voice deep, even gruff at times, but always the twinkle in his eyes behind his spectacles. 'There were always sharks. For example, one day, we were out fishing in a boat, and Elvira said she wanted to swim ... '

'It was not like that.' Heavy emphasis on 'like', her voice hitting a high note. 'I just got so boo-o-ored with them sitting there not catching anything ... '

'And this big shark ... '

'Really big?' Richard had joined them, was fascinated.

'Oh-h-h-h, yes. Really big.'

'How big?'

'Oh, poof, three metres?'

'Mu-u-uch bigger than that.' Elvira put a huge bowl of salad on the table. 'At least four metres.'

'And it swam round and round her, not attacking her, you understand, but not letting her get back to the boat ... '

It was almost completely dark now. Hannah-Rosa came in and Katherine towelled her hair, then sent her upstairs to get into her one-piece Mickey Mouse pyjama suit, Pierre set a huge round barbecue going with pine-cones beneath the charcoal.

'That shark,' Thomas managed to murmur to Katherine as more and more plates of food were added to those on the table, and Pierre popped corks out of bottles, 'was almost like an allegory, an image from her past, threatening to separate her ... '

Katherine was annoyed, almost angry.

'What bollocks. It was a shark, that's all. If I were you I'd lay off the Ricard.'

'It's Pernod, not Ricard.'

She looked at him with that almost blank but slightly pitying expression in her eyes.

'Same difference,' she said.

Sliced chorizo, pork loin from Pamplona over the border, impregnated with paprika and with a honeyed after-taste, Bayonne ham, best Charentais melon, Tursan wine, red and rosé, salads green, Niçoise and Caesar, *tabbouleh* – cold couscous with loads of oil, olives, mint and parsley, loads of bread. It was a meal and a half even before Pierre had done barbecuing. Blue smoke drifted around him, coals hissed and sparked in the darkness. He looked like a wizard or shaman casting spells.

His sister Thérèse, older than him, plump, a touch butch, joined them from next door. Next door? It was one house, a large Basque-style building on a small hill with deep eaves and lots of exposed woodwork, traditionally green, white and red. It had been their parents' home. Their mum lived on the other side, well over eighty and still elegant. Thomas had seen her briefly, earlier in the evening, a grey thin figure in cloud-coloured silks. She had a seventy-year-old boyfriend who looked after her, for though she was still physically able her mind had begun to go. Thérèse was on a brief holiday . . .

'From what?' Thomas asked.

'From my shop, I have a boutique.'

'Here, or nearby?'

He was thinking of Biarritz, Bayonne or St Jean-de-Luz – all places stacked with boutiques.

'No, a long way off. In Germany, just. Aachen, on the border with Belgium.'

'Aachen?' he asked. 'Is that the same as Aix, Aix-la-Chapelle?'

She agreed that it was.

'Then it must be the Aix in the poem . . .'

'*Poème* . . . ?'

"I sprang to the stirrup, and Joris, and he
    I galloped, Dirck galloped, we galloped all three . . .'

Suddenly aware of the conversational pitfalls not just ahead but all round him (for Katherine, sitting beside him now, was eyeing him with a mixture of concern and reproof), he stammered into silence.

'It's a famous poem in English . . . '

'Fairly famous,' Katherine interjected.

'About some guys on horses bringing some good news from Aix to Ghent—'

'Ghent to Aix.'

'Really? It's not important. Don't know why I thought about it—'

'Ghent?' Thérèse was puzzled.

'Gent,' Katherine supplied, giving it the full French pronunciation.

Fortunately Pierre now intervened with huge leg-steaks of lamb, baked potatoes and merguez for the children if they didn't want the lamb. The baked potatoes were topped with soured cream, garlic and onion. Thomas reached for the Tursan.

'Do you think you should? You've only just finished one.'

But from the back of the mind again Thomas produced, '"As I poured down his throat our last measure of wine, Which the burgesses voted by common consent, Was no more than his due who brought good news from Ghent." To rhyme with con-sent. But you're right. From Ghent to Aix. Not the other way about.'

Browning. Dad liked Browning. His mind drifted back to his earlier conversation with Pierre. Getting a book published was one up on Dad, who'd written a couple but had had them turned down. Dad would have been so proud of his son, had he lived to see it. Nevertheless, it was one up on the old man. I did it, and you didn't. He shuddered inwardly, pushed it all back into the cupboard – old broken toys you can't quite throw away.

He leant across to Thérèse, determined to play the polite guest.

'Living, and working, running a business in Germany. How do you get on with them?' he asked.

'The Germans?' She shrugged. 'It's my business. I have to get on with them.'

'But not easy, eh?'

Pierre, overhearing as he leant round his guests' shoulders

piling their plates with yet more meat, pulled himself up to attention, loaded his voice with mockery. 'Discipline and order,' he cried.

'They pay their bills on time,' his sister remarked drily.

'Not all of them,' Thomas murmured. 'They fucked up both of Richard's grandads' lives, and to some extent those of their wives and children. They still owe.'

'Last October we were in Munich,' Thérèse said. 'My boyfriend and I, at the end of the bier-fest, and we were sitting in the Augustiner—'

'Where it all started,' Thomas put in.

'Exactly. I was sitting next to this man, about your age, Thomas . . . '

Fuck off. How does she know how old I am?

' . . . early fifties . . . '

That's better.

' . . . and for some reason he thought I was English. He went on about Margaret Thatcher and what a great person she was, had been, and then he touched his nose and this is what he said, "I am not a fascist . . . but my father was." I tell you, my blood ran cold.'

They all had similar stories to tell or invent. Katherine recalled a German lector at Southampton University she had known quite well during her brief spell as part-time Spanish lecturer.

'She was my age, born in the early fifties, and she really believed that we started the bombing of big cities. In Southampton, for heaven's sake, where they wiped out the docks and the entire city centre at least two years before Dresden, Cologne and Hamburg. She also made a big deal of how her eldest sister was born in a bunker below Dresden during the fire-storm. Well, I had the answer to that . . . '

She paused.

'What was that?' someone asked.

'My father, Richard's grandad, was a prisoner of war there—'

'Like Kurt Vonnegut and Joseph Heller, I believe,' Thomas chipped in. If Katherine resented this wholly irrelevant interjection, she concealed it well.

'— and he was actually in the town. As a private soldier, not an officer, he could be asked to work, and he was living with a family who owned a bakery . . . '

So it went on. Thomas sank into a little reverie, recalling the first time he had met Bill, Katherine's dad. In a pub in Bognor called the Orlando. It could have been a deeply difficult confrontation – Bill had a reputation for being deeply difficult – and here was a married man, not far off forty, who had been living with his now twenty-one-year-old daughter for six months. Amazingly it had gone off all right. Blame Hitler. Very early in the conversation Bill had said he was in the Desert in the war. They worked it out together. For six months from late nineteen-forty they had been within miles of each other, his dad and Katherine's dad. Then Bill, trained in the Signals and attached to an infantry platoon, had been sent to Crete by Churchill on a military blunder not far off as stupid as Gallipoli had been in the war before, where of course he was taken prisoner. Not though until he had undergone the sort of horrors that leave you a bit mad for the rest of your life . . . on a par with those Thomas's dad had undergone on the retreat from Benghazi at much the same time.

'What's yours, Bill? Nina?' Because Katherine's mum had been there too.

'Generally we have a Bell's before we go.'

'Two Bell's please and another Double Diamond.'

'Large ones, Thomas.'

'Large ones.'

He went for a wee, downstairs loo, came back.

What were they laughing at? Katherine was telling them all about his exploits in Angers, his failure to find a loo and the 'lost' keys. Oh well. It would be Cholet next and the petrol-cap saga. He leant back in the cushioned chair, raised his glass and let the red Tursan trickle round his tonsils. Drunk and suddenly emotional as he was, the insect repellent torches Pierre had put out on the terrace defocused into flickering orange suns blazing in a black, blank universe. O for a beaker full of the warm south, full of the true, the blushful Hippocrene . . . What the fuck is a

Hippocrene, oh yes, I remember, the fountain that inspires the Muses on Parnassus, struck out of the rock by the hoof of Pegasus, hence 'hippo'. But 'blushful'? You can see why the refeened types north of the Border called him the Cockney Poet. And it was warm, a warm midnight. Worth travelling for, a warm midnight. Cease upon the midnight with no pain.

Que de vins!

'Apple omelette? Gosh, yes. Why not? With cream. *Mit rahm.* Wow.'

Katherine sighed and he knew why. Talking like someone in a Wodehouse novel and throwing in, God knows why, that bit of German, meant he'd soon be sounding like something from *Finnegans Wake*.

'What's that row?' he stood up, a touch unsteadily, hand on the back of his chair. Bright lights shone through the pines, there was amplified music, then an unintelligible voice on a PA system. Next a recorded trumpet call, not unlike the fanfare that announces the start of a bullfight.

'*Cours de chasse*. Greyhound racing. In the sports arena on the other side of the road.'

'Pierre told you about it earlier. He even asked if you'd like to go.'

'So he did, so he did.' Though Thomas had no recollection of it. 'For a moment I thought it was a dashed corrida. Hey, I'd love to go to the old *torear* again. We could nip over the border for a nipple of kites. Couple of nights.'

What he was really angling for was a trip to Wellington's battlefields.

'Bayonne is *en fête*, next week,' Pierre said. 'There are bullfights there. You don't have to go to Spain.'

Greyhuns. Huns of Gawd in grey hablitzs, bad hablitz, black hoodz. Hunned Dad down Paddy's Dayo, after meeting in the gloaming at Bricht-helms-ton.

Gawn to the Dawgs.

Hlame Blitzler.

10

Square of grey light. Daylight. Already? Need a pee. Whoops. Floor nearer the bed than I expected. Where am I? Not on the boat. Not at the B and B. What came next? Oh yes. Gottit. Pierre and Elvira's. Good meal. Lots to drink. *Que de vins!*

Door surely opens inwards? No, the other way. Small landing, two doors. One has to be a loo. No. Small dark boy in a bed, larger boy on a blow-up mattress, smaller girl ditto. Wotsisname, Richard and Hannah-Rosa. Not a loo. Must be the other door. Low bed, big one, room filled with daylight. Pierre, big male body like a lion flung across it, barely decent, black hair streaked by sweat across his cheek. Out cold. Not surprising considering the quantity he put away last night.

Bloody racket those birds are making. Elvira not with him. Humm. Ho-Hummm.

No loo. Swore there was a loo up here somewhere. Definitely one downstairs.

Steady now. Wide but steep and shiny wood. A tumble could be nasty. Very. Right to the kitchen/dining room, and the great outdoors beyond. Water the plants if I don't find it soon. Left – big, very big L-shaped room, sitting room, big low comfortable sofas and armchairs, two desks, books on shelves and all over the floor. PCs. Apple-Macs, lucky bastards. Nice pictures and, if I remember right, the loo is up the end of the L by the front door. Yes. Got it. Magellan would have been proud. Captain Cook ecstatic. Weeeeeee, Whoof. That's better. No, really, it was nothing really. You see I knew the world was round and so I was sure to get to the other side if I went on long enough. Now I have to get back.

Oh my god.

Elvira.

Sitting at the desk by the window. Reading a book. And me in the Emperor's New Clothes. But she doesn't look up. Even though the flush crashed like an Atlantic roller. Even though before that I pissed like a horse with the door open. Why not? Good book, is it, Elvira? No. She was there all along, saw me come through and is now being terribly civilized, hoping I'll get back without noticing her. Good on you, Elve.

He touched his forelock at her back and tiptoed up the stairs.

'Where have you been?'

'The loo.'

'There's one next door.'

He thought of saying, I didn't want to wake you up, but left it too late.

'You should never have had that plum brandy.'

'What plum brandy?'

'The schnapps Thérèse brought. Present for Pierre and Elvira. From Germany.'

'Oh *that* plum brandy.'

Part II of
A Brief Life of Christopher Richard Tate Somers
by
Thomas Richard Somers

Again? Do we have to?

Only way I can get back to sleep. And get back to sleep I must: it's only half-past six. I'll be a wreck if I don't sleep.

You'll be a wreck anyway.

More of a wreck.

What's your first memory?

This is meant to be a history of Dad, not me.

Never mind.

All right. But this is not really a memory, it was what I was told later in life. My parents were surprised and totally delighted at my arrival, a blessing they had not really expected. Not only had their illegitimate union been blessed, but with a boy too, after they had had three girls between them.

And then – disaster! Pyloric stenosis at the age of three

months. My stomach refused to pass food through the pylorus, the gateway to the duodenum. Lying on my back in my cot my projectile vomiting hit the ceiling, thus setting a high in athletic achievement I have never surpassed. I was at death's door. The doctors said fifty-fifty. Chance of surviving an operation, fifty-fifty; chance of recovering without one also fifty-fifty. My father called in his brother-in-law, my uncle by marriage, who was a specialist in piles and varicose veins. He said, unequivocally, not the knife.

My aunt, not the pile man's wife but the one who ran the maternity home where I was born, also had a hand in my recovery. The problem was, she said, psychological. I had responded badly to my mother's refusal to continue with breast-feeding. It was of course by then too late to return to nature, and wet-nurses had long gone out of fashion, but, she insisted, I would recover if I was properly mothered, cuddled, pampered, held to the breast and generally made much of, especially at feeding times. The fact was my parents were ready to spoil me rotten, and even more so than before, if my life depended upon it, but they simply did not know how. People didn't in those days, especially the middle classes.

Story of my childhood, much of it anyway. Parents desperately fond of me, suppressing all or most natural desires to kiss, fondle, stroke, hug, protect in the name of bringing me up properly, not just as a man – my half-sisters suffered the same deprivation – but as a civilized, rational person, with a soul and a mind, both infinitely more important than the body. They were inconsistent, but more so with themselves than with us. They admitted their own failings, their occasional lusts, their reliance on alcohol and nicotine, were determined that we should do better.

Hence too, in amongst all the suppressed desires, the occasional forays into less conventional displays my mother gave way to – the nude sunbathing, the passionate kisses, there were others . . .

After that? I mean the memories?

The next four or five are of things that happened after my

father became headmaster of Hollylea School. I am not sure what order they came in but they all took place when I was three or four. I remember a red pedal car with me pedalling like mad down a drive between high laurel or holly hedges. Why should it stick? I suspect because what followed was traumatic and suppressed. Possibly I was shouted at, even smacked for going too near the main road, something like that. No, I've got it. There was a bend in this drive and a car coming in a touch too fast could have squashed me into the tarmac like a toad.

That sort of thing can be very painful for a small child, especially when it follows a moment of extreme gratification – parents' love proved by the present of the pedal car and then catastrophically withdrawn. What else?

Two memories merge, both probably pre-dating the pedal car. A huge thunderstorm, a lightning bolt striking the house, the school, Irish maids crossing themselves in fear and me hunkered in my cot defecating a perfect coil of shit. Source of great pleasure, a present I wanted to offer to those I loved best, again probably followed by devastating rejection.

Next tonsilitis and tonsilectomy. A nursing home, with starched nurses, great triangular head-dresses. A swab taken from my throat by an evil-smelling doctor using a long bent sort of scissored probe thing, stainless steel. My throat painted with a foul tarry unguent on a long brush also bent and somehow quill-like. Firelight flickering from a small cast-iron fireplace. Promises, promises.

Promises?

That when I woke up it wouldn't hurt.

And it did?

Like hell, what's more there was blood pouring from my mouth . . . Terrifying. Then a treat to make up for it all, first visit ever to a cinema to see . . . *Snow White*!

Don't you have any pleasant memories of that time?

Yes. At the kindergarten I attended I won a prize, a framed picture of rabbits in a bluebell wood.

What for? What was the prize for?

Dancing the polka. One, two, three, hop, one, two, three, hop. I can still do it.

*

Thomas eased sleeping Katherine's nightdress above her buttocks, above her waist, pulled himself in as close as he could and got his hand on her breast. But still he couldn't sleep.

That brief period when he was headmaster of his own school was the happiest period in my father's life. My mother's too. They weren't broke, he was his own boss, Mother had a couple of Irish maids, a cook and a gardener, they were accepted by professional, even bourgeois Liverpool. I recall grown-up dinner parties, the full soup and fish, Dad in his black tie, where I was made much of before being packed off to bed. I remember prize-giving – a table covered in brilliantly white starched linen laden with silver that gleamed so brightly it hurt your eyes and of Father handing the trophies to a grand lady with a fur stole, who then handed them to the boys who'd won things. He used to take assembly, wearing his gown and his red silk hood. Bow our heads in prayer. Sing hymn number 76. He who would valiant be, follow the Master . . .

The school was inspected by HMIs and got a glowing report. Father wrote a long article about it all which was printed in the *New Statesman*. He was proud of that till his dying day. That he'd been published in the *New Statesman*. He won a couple of competitions too, and believe me the standard was a lot higher in those days.

You too. You won a comp. You even set a comp. And they published an article . . .

Ah, but only a book review.

Lots of letters, though.

Oh, Dad was always getting letters in.

Well, there you go. What went wrong? With the school?

Blame Hitler. I actually remember the day war broke out. Driving through the Mersey Tunnel and on into North Wales. Excitement, awe, in the air. Not much fear, not then. Not even though they'd lost older relatives in the first lot. From then on they always called the Great War the First Lot. What did you do in the First Lot? they'd ask each other, those who were old enough . . . I think there was relief too. They'd known for a long time it was on the way. They'd agonized over Libya, Albania, Abyssinia and Spain. They'd built up some sort of understanding of what fascism was, and they knew it needed a war to stop it.

So why were you going to North Wales – on the day war broke out?

Father believed that Liverpool would be bombed and that therefore his school should be evacuated to somewhere safer. He found a school in North Wales, in Penmaenmawr, not far you see, by road or rail, which had spare accommodation, and we were going down so he could talk it over with the head there. I don't remember anything else that happened that day but they must have come to an agreement, because, by the time term started, only a fortnight or so later, we'd all moved out of Hollylea and into this other school. Ferndown, it was called. Things went all right for a time. I remember the winter, huge falls of snow tumbling beyond high sash windows so heavily you couldn't see beyond the flakes, and the big room, with all the boys assembled, seemed to be levitating.

Wading through the snow past a big vegetable garden, where the cabbages and sprouts looked like small snowmen, Munchkins or whatever, up a footpath towards a big white mountain, like a flat-topped whale.

Then spring and Father in his khaki uniform – Home Guard or rather Local Volunteer Defence. He was very proud because they'd done target practice with five live rounds each, all that could be spared, taking it in turns with the one ·303 Lee Enfield that worked, and he'd done best of all of them.

And then everything went wrong. The forty or so pupils he'd brought leaked away, went back to Liverpool. And he'd already sold Hollylea, the building that is, to a convent of nuns.

Why? Why did the pupils leave?

Blame Hitler. He didn't bomb Liverpool, or anywhere else, not for nearly a year. And most of the boys had been day-boys, not boarders, and their parents couldn't see why they should pay boarding fees to avoid bombs that never came. Of course they were wrong. Hollylea was hit when the blitz did come. In the end Mr Rhodes, that was his name – I knew it would come back if I just waited – bought what was left of the business off Dad and offered him a job as a teacher. He was a nasty little fat man with a red face and a red bald pate above a haze of white hair. Pointed mean nose. Dad would have nothing more to do with him. Joined the Raf. That's what they always called it – the Raf. Dad didn't have to, he was forty on 12 September 1940, he could have got through the whole war without joining up. Mind you, at that age there was no question of him flying or getting into combat. We supposed.

I imagine he wanted to do his bit. Was that it? You've said he was politically aware enough to be strongly anti-fascist.

Yes. Those damned birds. There may have been . . . I mean he probably had other motives too . . .

Such as?

Well, the alternative was going back to what they called ushering, being an usher, a prep-school teacher with no stake in the business, a hireling. And after being the headmaster . . . But it was either that or . . .

Or join up?

Yes.

You feel a bit mean about saying that, don't you?

The lavatory flushed. Next door. Woke him up. Katherine climbed back over him, buttocks briefly glimpsed. I could eat you. She always slept on the side of the bed furthest from the door.

'It's five past ten. The children are all up.'

'It never is!'

'Be a sweetie and get me a cup of tea.'

'It'll be Liptons.'

'No it won't. We sent them a pound of Twinings English Breakfast for Christmas.'

'Now that was clever.' He kissed her, got out of bed, pulled on T-shirt and jeans. 'Oh my God.'

'What's the matter?'

'Never mind.'

He'd remembered Elvira, sitting at her desk, pretending not

to see him. Well, what I'll do, he said to himself, is pretend that I didn't see her. Then neither of us need feel embarrassed.

Later, in the bathroom, he looked himself over in the full-length mirror as if he were a doctor with a new patient. Or a car mechanic. *It doesn't seem to have the pulling power it used to. Definite loss of energy, especially going uphill. There's a nasty vibration too if I go over sixty* . . . You're not over sixty yet, he told the big mirror, and indeed his body didn't look it. Overweight, but not over sixty. And even the weight was really only below his rib-cage and above his pubes. If he pulled it right in . . . really more a matter of muscle-tone than flab. His thighs were solid and well shaped, his knees had held up well since the lady who cut their hair had advised him to wear a copper bracelet, and that's as far as the mirror went. (He had been brought up in a family that never referred to ladies as women – not, at any rate, any lady, any lady at all, you might talk to. Thus even the woman in the greengrocer's shop was the lady in the green-grocer's shop. Even as late as 1994 he'd argue that he was right – by derivation a woman is a man with a womb. A lady is someone who is loved.)

He looked down – the varicose veins had been there since he was fourteen, but he didn't like the look of his ankles and feet. The ankles swelled up if he stood for too long, his left foot had a bunion just like his mother's, the big toe sort of crawled over the one next to it and there was a lot of permanent bruise-like discoloration. By nightfall there would be deep ridges where the elasticated tops of his socks had been. The nails were ridged and uncuttable unless he soaked them in a hot bath for ten minutes. And of course he was stone deaf in one ear, had been since he was twelve. Jack it all in, get a new model . . . but you can't, can you?

He set the shower going, determined to get himself back into a good mood, a holiday mood, slurped gel on to his short greying hair, into his armpits, round his genitals and anus. Such a small little button of a circumcised prick unless he managed to stir some life into it. He remembered the Yugoslav nudist holiday, pushing Richard, then a year and a half, round the peninsula's perimeter after lunch, trying to get him to go to sleep. Hell . . . for five days. Then at last he saw an adult bloke with a prick as small as his.

Dad's wasn't any bigger, really, about the size of his thumb.

He sluiced off the surplus water, tied the towel round his waist and watched it slip off. One of Elvira's and too small. Or his tummy was too fat. Oh well. Better shave. He hadn't shaved yet in France and he looked a wreck once it had got to designer stubble length. Baggy eyes, but he'd had those at birth – just like the King a Welshman had said when his mother took him to church in North Wales, but such lovely blond hair, like an angel. Those bags go back at least as far as great-grandad Philip Henry Somers, though Thomas had been spared the eyelids that drooped at the corners. Good nose, a bit big, strong, almost aquiline, not in the Duke's class, certainly not, not even in Dad's. Dad's was a real conk. And a much better chin than Dad's, who hadn't been far off a chinless wonder. Thomas reckoned he'd done well in the genetic lottery, the best features of both parents.

Could have done with a man-size prick, though.

11

By the third afternoon Thomas knew that Richard was having a ball. Plucking the body-board Pierre had lent him out of the swirling water he strode into the surf for what must have been the thirtieth time. It had all turned out even better than they had said it would. The noise was still a surprise, the steady, rolling, unvarying monotone of thunder. And the stark colours. Sand yellow where the sea had reached it, white where it hadn't. The sea violet on the horizon, then blue-black, ultramarine and finally transparent green on the bow of a wave as it curled over and crashed spilling the foam like milk or snow, rushing up out of the ocean to lap your feet like a puppy. After the first day on the beach Richard had gone on and on about it. How you first felt the force when it was below your knees without a wave but up to your chest when one came by. Then there was the rush back out sucking the sand from under your feet if you stood still, all swirling in foamy patterns on the surface.

He really was getting the hang of it now, Richard was, the way he dived through the breaker like a dolphin, getting through to the break-line. Thomas put down his paintbrush, stood, shaded his eyes, searching for him amongst the bobbing heads, sensed Katherine beside him, the long hair blowing in the wind almost touching his shoulder. She was in a black one-piece that gave her the look of a sea mammal, something between a mermaid and a sea-lioness.

'Your son,' she said, smiling across at him, even teeth, the top front slightly gap-toothed, sign of lechery, he had told her when he was teaching her *The Wife of Bath's Tale* twenty-four years ago, probably the first flirty thing he ever said to her, 'is in serious danger of becoming a surf-head.'

Your son, when he was doing something she felt was naughty or made her uneasy. But she was smiling.

'Hey, he's on a really big one this time,' she added.

'Great.'

Katherine too shaded her eyes.

Here he comes, he's holding himself on top of the wave, he seems to be able to steer a bit now, hair plastered, thank God he's given up on that step haircut, letting it grow long again, oh dear me, he is going fast, what a lad, what a hero . . . !

But Richard was in trouble. Later he said it was like being on the roof of a train, and even though it was a body-board he would try to get up on one knee, straighten, then the wobble, then over he went, the board, attached to his wrist by a velcro painter, smashing him from behind, water in his lungs, the back-tow sucking him round, a proper drilling . . .

Katherine grabbed Thomas's hand, but it was all right; Richard was on his feet, had the board secure again, shaking his head, coughing and spitting. All the same she wanted to run into the surf, make sure he really was all right, but she knew that would not do at all, not now, not now he was a young man of fourteen.

She called out to him, high above the thunder of the surf. 'Wipe-out!'

Richard could see they were laughing now, so he wasn't going to come out and tell them about it. He turned, pushed his way back into the waves. As he did so a huge blond youth, he looked like eight feet of *Baywatch*, skimmed past him on a proper surfboard, narrowly missing him.

'He shouldn't be there,' Katherine said.

'Who?' Thomas looked up at her. He was already back on his knees painting, trying to get the slanting perspective on a parasol just right. God, I'm bad at this, he thought. Why do I do it?

'That lout on the surfboard. This area's for body-boards. He could cause an accident.'

But Thomas was back in his private world. The sky violet, turquoise, cobalt blue . . . the dune behind climbing halfway up the sky with the blue grass that can cut you, and between it and the water's edge a thousand parasols and windbreaks, all in primary colours, casting purple shadows over rugs and mats and cooling boxes. Only problem was the wind. A touch chill from the north, so when you came out of the sea it dried you too quickly, and the evaporation brought your skin temperature down, before the burning sun could heat it up again. Thomas felt he was getting a chill. No, he bloody knew he was. And his insides were not right either, and this just after he felt they had been getting better. Trouble was he hadn't 'been', not properly, since they'd arrived at Pierre's. Just rabbit droppings . . . well, goat droppings; hard, dark pellets.

'Enjoying yourself?' Pierre, just out of the sea.

'Oh yes.' He set aside the brush he'd been painting with, hoped Pierre would not look at what he had been doing. It was awful. Bloody awful. The sand kept blowing across his paint tray, clogging up the Winsor Violet, the ultramarine and the watered-down Hooker's. 'Children all right?'

'Oh yes. Of course. They are enjoying themselves.' Pierre stooped to pick up a towel. He looked like that Greek guy with a discus or a snap by Mapplethorpe. Katherine, who had gone back to reading Highsmith's *Ripley Under Water*, lying on her stomach, rolled over and looked up at Pierre, arm thrown over her face to shade her eyes again. She would, wouldn't she?

'Are you sure? Shouldn't one of us keep an eye on them?'

'It is not too necessary, I think.' Pierre towelled broad brown shoulders. A touch chubby for perfect fitness, Thomas thought, but then a hell of a lot less chubby than me. Why aren't they fat, Pierre and Elvira? They bloody ought to be, the amount they eat. Pierre went on, 'Rick swims well, and as long as he does not go out too far he will be all right. The tide is coming in. And the little ones keep near the edge.'

They had had this conversation every day. More than once every day. It always ended in the same way.

'I think you ought to keep an eye on Hannah-Rosa and Jean-Luc.'

I'm painting, you do it. I can't swim in this sort of sea. Well, neither can I – nobody bloody swims in it, do they? But that was the bit that always got left unsaid.

Thomas hauled himself up. Suddenly dizzy he made a grab for the parasol – silly bugger, as if that would keep him up.

'Are you all right?'

'Yes . . . fine. Cramp, pins and needles, that sort of thing.'

He set off towards the water's edge and Pierre lay down with his wife. And Pierre lies down WITH my wife? What's going on here? Surely that should be 'by', or 'next to', for Christ's sake, not biblically 'with'? He glanced back. She was on her side now, one knee pulled up so the swoop and rise of her torso and full hip and then the long slope of silky legs put him in mind of the rise and fall of certain downs in Dorset. Pierre must feel . . . attracted? More than that, surely.

So. Where were they, the little ones? He pushed into the water until he could feel the elemental force behind the rushing small force, and then stopped, where a lot of people stopped, not wanting to go further. Parents like himself trying to spot their kids, girls watching out for their surf-head boyfriends, not many girls actually seemed to surf, but a lot of them were topless . . .

Get a grip, Thomas. You're not meant to stare.

But that girl over there, to the right. They're fucking perfect, pert and firm, a nice gap between them you could run your tongue through, taste the salt of sea and sweat . . . And have that hunk she's with hang one on you? No. He wouldn't bother. He'd just kick sand in my face.

'Daddeee, Daddeee, look at me, look at me.'

'I am looking at you, honey.'

Terrible to think that in the last ten minutes, no even less than that, I've probably seen more tits for real than Dad did in his whole life. Poor Dad.

Hannah-Rosa riding the tail-end of a big one, thin fingers clutching the curve of the bow of Jean-Luc's body-board, swinging her lithe body this way and that to steer round his varicose legs before beaching in the sand beyond him. She dances so well, she can dance lying down on a board in the water, lithe body making the board carve snake-like ellipses in the foam.

'You're getting quite good at that.'

She pouted solemnly, her usual reaction to praise.

'Isn't it time Jean-Luc had a go?'

'He's all right, he's building a sandcastle. Watch me go again.'

She strode off into the surf, pushing the waves aside until they got too big, then turning as the wall of foam hit her, throwing herself on to the board, paddling furiously to keep on the crest and then, securely mounted on her white horse, she rushed past . . . but this time she wanted to show off for him, steered too far across the flow and tipped. Distressed for a moment she got up, hauled on the painter, pushed her long hair out of her eyes and mouth. Her bottom lip trembled, but then she smiled, grinned at him.

'Wipe-out,' she shouted above the din with pride, proud she'd survived it, proud she knew the jargon.

A presence by his side. Thomas half turned and caught a very different sort of grin from an unknown woman at least as old as he was. She had a copper tan, hennaed hair tied back under a puce and purple scarf. Gold glimmered on her breastbone, small bare breasts sagged above her X-ray ribs, much like his mother's, and a small swathe of stretched skin sagged above her minimal briefs. That he rather admired – for here was someone you felt sure could have paid to have had a tuck taken in here and there. What lay behind the grin was unmistakable.

He turned, gave a tiny nod to the presences behind him, she smiled with wry understanding and moved on . . .

Meanwhile, all hell was breaking out.

Pierre first, moving through the surf like a galloping horse, then Katherine. Richard on his knees, face twisted in pain as another wave smashed and toppled him forward. Pierre got to him, hauled him to his feet, supported him as he arched his head back and his hands as the pain came sharper than before.

'Christ, what happened?'

'Didn't you see? What the fuck were you looking at?'

'Hannah-Rosa,' he lied.

'That great oaf with fair hair, the one you told me was such a fucking good surfer . . . Oh, forget it.'

Because now, already, the lifeguards' red beach-buggy, outsize tyres carving valleys out of the wet sand was behind them, and two men in red T-shirts over trunks were helping Pierre get Richard out of the water. Katherine went with them. Hannah-Rosa grabbed Thomas's hand and began to sob . . .

'He's dying, I know it,' she wailed.

Thomas hauled her out of the water and held her with her chin in his neck and her bottom on the step of his waist, legs scissoring round him. He felt her weight, and the way his heart protested.

They all gathered round, chattering like starlings. All? At least five hundred. Thomas had to push his way through. *'Je suis le père,'* he insisted and they gave way.

Probably, they later told him, because the crowd thought he was a priest, come to administer extreme unction.

But Richard was alive, indeed much, much better already, embarrassed by the fuss. The lifeguards palpated his back, got him to do sit-ups, and finally walk.

'Oh, he's all right,' Pierre asserted. 'They are all paramedically qualified. It looks bad but it happens quite often. They know what they do.'

In relief Thomas could not help but reflect that after twenty years or more of overusing the English present continuous Pierre was now getting it wrong by cutting it out entirely. He also recalled Pierre's classic mistake twenty years ago which they had giggled over ever since. On being told it was Jane Austen's one hundred and fifty-ninth birthday (he was studying *Emma* and hated it), he had said 'You are pulling my mickey . . .'

'Why are you giggling? Why?'

He put Hannah-Rosa down and gave his wife a rare hug.

'Because he's not hurt, I suppose. Not hurt.'

Something had happened. Nevertheless: something happened.

81

12

Mornings they spent in the village. Next morning was market-day. Sauntering through the narrow alleys between the stalls Thomas had a headache and an unaccountable desire to pee every half-hour or so, but only when they were at least five minutes away from the nearest loo. He thought the headache was accountable. At his age and with his drinking record behind him he only very rarely copped serious hangovers. However, the evening meal, after several Pernods, had started with Assiette Landaise. This consisted of foie gras, actually pressed and canned by Pierre himself, duck or goose giblets, and dry red fatty bits from some other part of the bird, served with salad. Then the inevitable barbecue – huge, seriously huge, pork chops. Much the same as the night before, only the barbecue had been big, yellow, Landaise chicken legs. On both nights vast amounts to drink and riotous games of Trivial Pursuit, the English version, so Thomas teamed with Elvira and Pierre with Katherine to make it fair. They flirted outrageously, of course, but no more than flirted.

One boon of this pair of boozy nights had been that he had gone to bed drunk enough not to have to send himself to sleep by telling himself the story of his father's life. In fact for a day or two he'd hardly thought at all about his dad and his possibly impending doom on or before the day he reached his dad's age.

But now they were in the market. Richard bought a yin-yang enamel on a leather cord which secretly he knew would cure his bruised back. Katherine and Hannah-Rosa scoured the place for espadrilles for Hannah-Rosa that would match her mum's. Thomas looked for loos and then wandered round the fish stalls and the ones selling *specialités Landaises*.

Later they had a little wander up and down the seaside streets; a seaside town even though you couldn't see the sea:

palms and acacias, gift shops spilling out over the pavement, busy-ness building up as the morning wore on. They looked at the posters for restaurants and discos, jazz at the town hall, *courses de vaches* in the sports stadium.

'I want a go at that,' Richard demanded.

'What, in the ring with a mad heifer? No way.'

'Especially not with a bruised back.'

'Pierre says you have to be fifteen minimum.'

He and Katherine still achieved a sort of unison in front of the children, a practised act they'd got together, so it didn't matter which of them said what, they got it right.

Richard loved the surf shops. Thomas did too, especially the really sharp ones. He even liked looking at the price-tags confident no one was going to ask him to put his hand in his pocket.

Oakley shades he especially liked, the styles and the slogan: *protection contre réaction thermo-nucléaire*. Laboriously he explained to Richard that while you were meant to be put in mind of hydrogen bombs, it was in fact an accurate description – the sun is a thermonuclear chain-reaction. An angry star. Shades protect you from it.

They bought postcards. Hannah-Rosa said she was going to send one to herself, so it would be there when they got home.

'Why?'

'I'll remember the day I bought my espadrilles. All the nice things. Help me forget bad Richard not getting drowned.'

She'd been more frightened than any of them, and blamed Richard still for the fright she'd had. But this was too much for Thomas.

'Tempting fate, a bit.'

'Why?' Katherine asked. She knew why but wanted to get it out, these waves of angst he had that sometimes deepened into depression, make him talk about it.

But the possibility that something might happen to Hannah-Rosa before they got back, so the postcard would be there but she would not, was not something he was prepared to talk about. Nor why he was plagued with such thoughts.

'Hey, look at this.'

A huge glossy poster with a surfer riding a crest above a forming pipe. *HOSSEGOR – RIP CURL PRO CHAMPIONNAT DU MONDE DE SURF, 22–28 AOUT.*

'We'll still be here for that. Can we go?'

'Maybe. But we should be in Pau by then.'

Richard was downcast but Thomas hardly noticed – there was another poster: *FETES A BAYONNE – LES CORRIDES, 21–28 AOUT.* It was all happening. He loved bullfighting and they had actually been to the Bayonne corrida twenty years ago.

'Why does it say RIP,' Thomas asked. 'Rest in Peace, *Requiescat in Pace*?'

'It's the name of a make of surfboard.' Richard tried very hard not to make it sound like a snub.

They bought a plant for nearly forty quid in the sort of posh flower shop you never see in England, not even in the West End. Like their *confiseries*. How do they do it? Money and taste. Bastards. This plant was four feet high, a mass of large blue flowers in a plain ceramic pot, a present for Elvira.

'Really, you know,' said Katherine, 'for what it is, it's a snip at three hundred francs.'

If, Thomas thought, I don't drop it on the way back to the car.

Thomas found a small supermarket, left them on the pavement guarding the plant. He bought a bottle of Pernod to replace all he'd drunk.

After lunch, cold pork chops, of course, they went back to the beach. But it had clouded over now – on what was planned as their last full day at Hossegor, the weather was having a hiccup. The grey sky drained the colour out of a sea that was less surfable, the offshore wind flattening the swell into choppy, irregular waves. The tide was wrong now, at half-past two as far out as it went. Thomas kept on T-shirt, tracksuit bottoms and deck shoes, but got them wet when Richard and Hannah-Rosa both insisted he took photos of them on the boards. Problem was the lens on his old Pentax SLR zoomed up to no more than 70mm, so no way could he get close enough.

He began to shiver, the headache got worse, he snapped at

Katherine and at Hannah-Rosa too, when she whinged that Jean-Luc was not giving her enough of a go on his body-board. At four o'clock they called it a day and walked back to the car-park, Richard kicking at the plastic bottles on the high-tide line.

'Cheer up, Rich,' Katherine said. 'You can surf on the beach at Biarritz. And if you really want to we can come back here for the last few days.'

'What, and miss out on going to Pau, the mountains, the drive over to Jaca?' Thomas was suddenly angry. She tried to calm him down.

'We can do both. Three or four days in Pau is probably enough. And certainly three days rather than a week in Biarritz is quite enough. There'll be time to come back here.'

'I should think Pierre and Elvira will be fed up with us. They won't want us back again.'

'Not at all.' Pierre behind them stuck his oar in. 'We are dreading your departure. We shall not know what to do with Jean-Luc without Hannah-Rosa and Rick.'

Don't call my son Rick, you greasy frog bastard. Thomas stopped, pulled in breath. Why did I think that? Get a grip. Pierre's a mate.

He hauled himself and the parasol, and his unused painting things, and the towels and the bathers and the sun lotion up the steep slope of the dune, pausing on the bend of the zigzagging path. His wet tracksuit bottoms clung to his shins. His claggy deck shoes were caked with wet sand. A gleam of distant sun ran a streak of white gold along the horizon, but kept well away from the land. A squad, no other word would do, except possibly *einsatzgruppe*, of Germans, not bronzed but, he was pleased to see, quite savagely burnt across their backs, pink skin peeling through their yellow body hair, stormed past him. A surfboard carried on the last one's shoulder swung with the bend and he had to duck. Fucking krauts.

'Are you all right?' Katherine called from the crest of the dune.

'I'm fine. Just a bit puffed.'

*

Back in their room, little more than a boxroom, the low double bed, a cheap bookcase filled with a child's books, in French of course, a small basin, he lay on the bed and watched while Katherine got together what she needed for a shower.

'What's this then, about coming back here?'

'Richard and Hannah-Rosa love it here. If Elvira doesn't mind, why not?'

'Because it's not what we planned to do.'

'So? There was nothing rigid about what we planned.'

'Moni will be upset if we come back here.'

'I doubt it. She wants us to go to her parents' village for their fête. So long as we do that she won't mind if we come back here for the last few days. Or maybe come back here between Biarritz and Pau.'

Thomas felt confused, bothered.

'Anyway, nothing's been decided,' she added.

'But that's just it. Everything's been decided. And now you're changing it all.'

'No, I'm not.'

'It seems to me you are.'

She gave him the long slow look. As devastating in its promise as a nuclear deterrent.

'I'm not going to have a quarrel about it. I'm going to have a shower.'

You're always having a bloody shower.

He pulled *Wellington's War* up from the floor, tried to make himself comfortable, but couldn't. He ploughed through the first-aid kit, found a Boots tub of aspirin and codeine, washed a couple down with water from the tap. Was that wise? Cholera? Or just plain good old dysentery? He could do with a dose of diarrhoea. When was the last? Properly? Back in the mists of time.

He got back on the bed, opened the book, wrenched it a little to make it lie flat on his knees.

Wellington was also having a bad time. Salamanca, the liberation of Madrid, the glory of 1812 had sunk into the tragic cockup of Burgos, which he failed to take. The only notable failure in his career. Now, in appalling weather, his army was in retreat, back towards Ciudad Rodrigo and the safety of the Portuguese border. Worst of all, he too was suffering from people who liked to change arrangements without consultation, and as a consequence got lost.

Wellington went to look for them and came across the officer in charge of the baggage.

'What are you doing, sir?'
'I've lost the baggage.'
'Well, I can't be surprised . . . for I cannot find my army.'

They marched by a road leading they did not know where, and when I found them in the morning they were in the utmost confusion, not knowing where to go or what to do. This with the enemy close to them, and with the knowledge that, owing to the state of the roads and the weather . . .

Some accounts of the actual confrontation say that a white-faced Wellington said nothing to the generals when he found them, simply got on with sorting out the mess; others that he remarked in a voice like cold steel, 'You see, Gentlemen, I know my own business best.'

The book slipped off his knees and back to the floor. For no particular reason a dream-memory swung across his inner eye in the seconds before he slept. A happy time. All on bicycles. New bicycles. Nothing swish, upright, no gears, but new. Dad in civvies, a short-sleeved Fair Isle pullover, grey trousers, bicycle clips, Mum in a pale blue cotton dress with large pale yellow flowers. It billowed up over her knees so she had to ride one-handed to keep the tops of her suspendered stockings invisible. Thomas on his new Hercules. They had been blackberrying in the countryside near Melton Mowbray, and his parents' bicycle baskets held jars of the fruit. (Odd, you think? But there were no plastic bags or plastic punnets in those days, and mostly you took jam jars when you went blackberrying.) Anyway, they were all hurtling down a steep hill, hallooing and shouting, his dad leaning forward over the handlebars, and making as if he were on a racehorse, whipping it up to get ahead of Mum at the winning post. Such storms of air, such delightful fear, such shouts and ecstasy beneath a blue sky tumbled with clouds and full of Dakotas dragging gliders, black gliders, south and east towards Arnhem . . .

I want to ride my bicycle, I want to ride my bike . . .

13

This was the big one, but it all went a bit wrong. The big one because Moni came over from Pau on her way to her parents' flat in Biarritz. Thérèse's boyfriend, Norbert, was also coming to spend a week in Hossegor. Thomas took his usual place at the end of the table under the sky so his good ear faced everybody else and his bad ear the thunder that prowled beyond the pines and the sports stadium.

Thoughtfully, but perhaps not wisely, Pierre left the jug of iced water and the Pernod bottle in front of him, before driving to Bayonne station to pick up Norbert. Which was where it started to go wrong. Nobert got off the train at Dax. How it was sorted out Thomas never quite discovered, but the result was that the meal did not properly start until gone nine o'clock with the Pernod bottle (45% by volume) a third gone.

They all talked French, at least thirty-six to the dozen. Thomas knew he was lost as soon as he heard Katherine start in on the lingo to the manner born. He filled up his glass, stood. Pain shot through his knees and up his thighs, lodged in his left hip joint. Shit, he thought. So much for the copper bracelet. Arthritis strikes again.

Before getting the bracelet he had taken his knees to the doctor. The doctor, using patronizing doctor-speak, said it was down to Anno Domini and there was nothing to be done but to give him a painkiller. He prescribed an ibuprofen derivative and, as a result, Thomas had appalling wind for three days. If he sat down for a meal, took a mouthful or two, his stomach swelled up so he had to loosen his belt. He had belched and farted like something out of Rabelais. All of which was why he had been so grateful for the relief the copper bracelet had brought him. But now it was all back.

He took a good pull at the Pernod, topped it up again, took

his drink for a walk down the terrace towards Pierre's mother's half of the big house.

He peered through the french windows into an ill-lit room where the two old people were watching television. Then the thin grey old lady, in her pigeon-coloured silks covering her pigeon chest got up, opened the doors, saw him (or had she got up because she had already seen him?) and spoke quickly and sharply, spitting as she did.

Telling me to piss off, I've no doubt.

He muttered apologetically, backed away. Her voice rose, ended on a question. Oh shit, what do I do now? Is she asking me to do something, pass a message to Pierre or Thérèse or something? Or is it just a question of the what the fuck do you think you're doing order? He grinned weakly, turned, staggered, and the thunder, playing Grandmother's Footsteps, came closer.

The two children, Richard as well, were watching a video: *The Jungle Book*. Baloo singing and dancing through the 'Bare Necessities'. Thomas loved it, stayed and watched, watched the pawpaw drop and the prickly pair, no make that pear, how Baloo made a kebab of it all. How the banana bunch arched down and Mowgli squeezed one out of its skin. Then the two of them getting exquisite relief rubbing their backs against a palm tree and a rock, while nannyish jaguar Bagheera sighed and grumbled. Then how Baloo and Mowgli floated down the river past exotic flowers and through rapids and over waterfalls . . . until the monkeys appeared. The bare necessities.

He went back to the dining area, stood in the shadows and watched them. Moni, Monique, especially. Their closest friend, she had been the teacher Katherine had been attached to in the school where she had been an *assistante*. Of all of them she was the only one who had not married, and who had not done well, financially at any rate. She had never managed to get the final qualifying exam and was now teaching English in an agricultural college, but at least it was back in Pau, the town she thought of as home.

Thomas liked Moni a lot. She had thick, dark, chestnut hair, whose cut had not changed in twenty years, though the colour shifted – always it was a heavy bob that spread behind a face that was still heart-shaped. She had large, warm, brown eyes, good bones, but her figure ... Her face and top half took after her father, a thin, even elegant man, her bottom half after her mother who was decidedly broad in the beam all over. For Moni the result was a handsome face, thin-boned shoulders and arms, long fingers, small breasts and a thin waist all mounted on hips and a bum that belonged in the fields.

She was a lot of fun, though Katherine sometimes found her too French by half, bossy at times, and indeed she had done her best to organize this trip for them – a few days at Hossegor conceded a touch grumpily, then a week in Biarritz and a week in Pau with her. She was also obsessed with health as the French almost always are, and far too ready to scoff at British culture and cuisine. British *what*? Thomas asked himself. Though never married she always had a boyfriend, usually not living in, if she could avoid it. Like a company director with the company car, she traded up every two years.

Quietly, but never doing anything about it bar prolonging the old *baiser* a second over the odds, a mutual squeeze of the hand, they fancied each other ... in the past, quite a lot really.

In the past. On his fiftieth birthday, almost ten years ago, *almost ten years ago*, she had sent him a card, A Marcel Leméné photograph, *Pomme encadrée*, a red apple placed in white paper which reflected the redness, on a white foreground and a vivid blue background. This is what she wrote on the back, in English: Happy Birthday, Thomas, my best wishes for your 21st birthday. I hope you will enjoy this book on Truffaut. Love XXX Monique.

He was glad to have the book, though enjoy was not quite the right word. It was the *Cahiers du Cinéma* special memorial number. She knew Thomas adored Truffaut, perhaps had not known that he had been very upset indeed when the bastard upped and died. His French was good enough to read most of it with a dictionary, though he had not read much. It was mostly testaments from people even more shattered than he. *Il me manque. Il nous manque* ... Jean-Pierre Léaud said it all. He looked through the photographs and stills though, often, until his eyes blurred.

A year or so later, when she came over for one of her brief stays to refresh her English he asked her ... Why the apple?

'I think because once you were over fifty, you became forbidden fruit,' was the answer that was almost a declaration.

But married to one of her very best friends, forbidden fruit was what he had always been. And now at nearly sixty what was he: fruit withered on the bough? He kept the card, along with a hundred or so others, blu-tacked to the wall of his study and over the ten years the colours had faded, especially the red. I'll go when all the colour has gone, he thought.

Meanwhile he remembered Sterne. It has always been the singular blessing of my life to be miserably in love with someone. Trouble is, I'm in love with all of them, he thought, as they stumbled over each other, pushed round each other, got in each other's way, gesticulated, waved flashing knives at each other under the kitchen spotlights, argued, called for the salt, the garlic, the pepper, the blender, whatever, dipped fingers in each other's concoctions, pursed lips and asked for more oil, more vinegar, what do you think Elvira? More oil, assuredly.

He loved them all: mysterious Elvira, already anxious because her husband should have turned up by now with her sister-in-law's boyfriend; Moni showing Hannah-Rosa, who had seen *The Jungle Book* too often and anyway was hungry, how to make vinaigrette; even Thérèse, whom he hardly knew and who was making a Gorgonzola sauce that would not thicken; and Katherine letting loose again and again the very jolly laugh which company always produced, and he himself hardly ever. Thinking of the old lady next door, he sighed with the fleeting loveliness of it all. Ah well. Anno Domini. *Un Pernod encore. Oui. Encore un Pernod.*

Pierre eventually arrived with Norbert. In his late forties, Norbert had dark hair (dyed, perhaps?), glasses. Thomas never discovered if he was German or French. Sort of Alsacien, he decided, a bit of both. Alsatian. Bow-wow. He was thin, a scientist it seemed and serious. Presently, having been rather perfunctorily welcomed by Thérèse who blamed him for the cock-up, he brought his drink to the table and sat beside Thomas. His English was not good.

'One is disquietened by the news from Bosnia, is one not?'

Inwardly Thomas sighed, but pasted in place the thin, serious smile he felt this warranted.

'One certainly is.'

'One wonders where it will all lead.'

To tears before bedtime, was the reply Thomas choked back.

'Ah,' he said.

'Nationalism has been the curse of the twentieth century.'

'I wonder,' Thomas managed, 'what will be the curse of the twenty-first?'

Across the table, behind his specs, Norbert's eyes narrowed and his lips tightened. Shit, he thinks I'm taking the piss. But no, the scientist was giving the matter serious thought.

'Industrialization of the third world,' he suggested. 'Leading to trade wars, and of course pollution, the environment. What is your idea of it?'

'The gap between the rich and the poor, the employed and the unemployed, everywhere. It will get intolerably wide and then we shall all fall into the chasm.' History a sequence from a *Road-Runner* cartoon. Uh-uh-uh-uhuh. Not that I'll see it. 'I say, don't you think it's got a bit chilly? I think I'll go and get a pullover.'

Norbert looked surprised, and indeed not cold at all. Thomas, however, was genuinely shivering. He stood up and it felt as if he was banging his head against a low ceiling.

'Won't be a tick,' he murmured, clutching on to the back of his chair, as the room and pine trees beyond keeled and swung like a boat rising on a swell. I can't be that drunk.

On top of everything else he suddenly felt sick as he battled his aching legs and creaking knees with red-hot daggers in them up the stairs to their room, a sort of hollow, empty sickness, that could well have been as much to do with hunger for the delayed meal as anything else. But then as he slumped on to the low bed he realized at last what the matter really was. He had flu. He hardly ever had flu. In spite of all the other things that had been marking Anno Domini these last few years he had not had proper flu for more than a decade. He'd forgotten what it was like.

He delved in their first-aid kit again, found a thermometer, stuck it in his mouth. Not, he thought, up his bum. He remembered Moni's story from when she was living in digs in England as part of her degree course. She caught flu, went to bed. Her landlady had come in and said she should take her temperature. 'I am,' Moni had replied.

He snorted through his nose, lay back on the pillow with his eyes shut. The light above his head scorched through his lids.

He saw it. His prophecy, premonition. He didn't have to verbalize it at all. He saw it. The village where they lived surrounded by surveillance cameras, heat sensors, electrified fences. Outside the forest burnt. The poor – dirty, unshaved, hungry and cold, clutching shotguns, sickles, knives – tried to filter through the blazing trees. Suddenly they were caught in the lights of ten or a dozen four by fours, Range Rovers and the like, and a volley of small-arms fire tore through the poor, shredding flesh, shattering bone.

He woke with a start, pulled out the thermometer. It's metric, goddamn metric. Over thirty-eight, nearly thirty-eight point five. Multiply by nine ... you're joking. What was normal? Thirty-seven. So. One point five times nine divided by five. Do it the other way round, dumbo. One point five divided by five equals three. Times nine. Twenty-seven. That can't be right. He felt his blood pressure rise as he grappled with the problem, a weight in his chest, his arms and hands going tense. Must be a point somewhere, call it two point seven. Plus thirty-seven. No, plus ninety-eight point four. One hundred and one point one. What's that in pounds, shillings and pence?

'Are you all right?' Katherine was standing over him, looking down, not sure whether to be angry or concerned.

'Touch of flu, I think.'

'Richard too. He's on his way to bed. Perhaps you should stay here.'

'I'll stick it out a big longer.'

He could hear how downstairs the dining area was exploding with life and jollity.

'All right. But try not to drink much more. Pierre and Norbert have got the barbecue going. Tonight it's steak. Huge lumps of it.'

They passed Richard on the stairs, Thomas and Richard pausing to kiss goodnight.

'You'll be better in the morning. Take some aspirin.'

'Mummy's going to give me some.'

'Back all right?'

'Back's fine.'

Already, although at fourteen and nearly sixty perhaps they were doing better than most, it was becoming increasingly difficult to talk. But at least they still kissed, mouth to mouth. He picked his way carefully down the remaining stairs and remembered how at the age of thirteen, on Bognor station, his father, seeing him off to school, had said: 'When men . . . and boys reach . . . a certain age . . . they stop kissing each other.'

What do they do instead? Thomas had wondered. Shake hands? No, not even that, apparently. And he had got in the train. Not even a proper steam engine – the green-liveried Southern Railway, about to be nationalized, had been electric since well before the war.

14

Of course he went on drinking. And with a sweater on now, and the aspirin and codeine beginning to take effect, the more unpleasant symptoms of flu receded, leaving the pleasant ones – a pleasurable weakness in the limbs; a heightened sense of reality, heightened partly because both the eyes' and the mind's foci were narrowed; a feverish delight in food, women, talk; and the instant sympathy he won as a victim of seasonal *chaud-froid*.

Not that the food was as good as usual. Too many cooks. The prawn and rice salad lacked Elvira's sharpening finesse, the rice a touch claggy; the Gorgonzola sauce had remained obstinately runny and anyway represented the sort of colour supplement cuisine he normally despised. But no, he was not to be put out of sorts. How could he be? The Tursan rouges et rosés flowed like water, and Pierre's superior sound system offered Mozart 22 with that swinging dancing rondo finale – de dum de dum de de de daaa dedaaa. Aural champagne.

'Who's playing,' he asked, as Pierre went by with a plate heaped with charred meat.

'Alicia de la Rocha.'

'Oh, I love her.' He turned to Moni. 'She's heaven. Have you ever seen her? She's small, dumpy, short stubby fingers the way many of the best pianists have, looks a typical Andalusian peasant woman in her black dress and corsets – but listen, just listen . . . '

Silver noise cascading answered by the pompous gold of the horns.

Moni frowned, concerned arrow-heading lines between her plucked but full brows.

'Are you sure you shouldn't be in bed?'

With you, yes, with you all! But he managed, just, not to say it allowed, that is, aloud.

'Thérèse,' he called across the kitchen. She waved back at him. 'This sauce is divine,' he lied, and sawed through black into crimson. The meat bled into the sticky rice.

Bored with her boyfriend she came and sat at the head of the table on his other, deaf side, bringing the plate Pierre had just given her. To hear her meant that he had to turn his back on Moni, but she knew all about his disability, and anyway was relieved not to have to sustain a conversation about concert pianists.

'You have spent your time on the beach since we saw you, yes?'

She was not the sort of woman Thomas was usually attracted to, a touch butch for him perhaps, but this evening she had dressed up for the occasion in ways that would not have occurred to the others – dark silks, browns with highlights of electric blue, and sun-kissed greens. Gold chains and bangles. The scent she wore enveloped her like the mist that surrounded Greek goddesses when they appeared to mortals. Coty? Maybe.

'Almost all of it. Yes, apart from le shoppeeng in the mornings, yes, every afternoon.'

'It's strange I think 'ow most youmans are 'appy on the beach.'

Thomas took a deep slurp of the blushful and waited as the tastes and fumes expanded like a benevolent explosion filmed in slow motion through a body and mind deliciously at one with each other. There are few pleasures so exquisite as when the person you are talking to has handed you the reins of one of your three favourite hobby-horses. The other two were, for Thomas, Wellington as the greatest Englishman after Darwin and Turner (Waggle-dagger came fourth), and the homoerotic relationship that fired and fuelled Beethoven (the greatest youman ever) through his mature life (NB: Homoerotic – sex didn't come into it). The object of his passion? The Archduke Rudolf.

But his favourite hobby-horse was the semi-aquatic moment in the evolution of youmanity.

'Not strange, Thérèse, not strange at all.'

'Why not strange?'

Blessings upon this woman. Clearly she retained some of the elements of a sound feminine bourgeois upbringing. That is, she knew it was part of her social duty to listen with apparent interest, nay delight, to the drunken piffle of an older man.

'Thérèse, we were born to sit at the edge of water and do nothing, or only as much as we need to do to prevent us from dying of boredom. Which when we are sitting in front of, or swimming or wading in water, or lying near water, is very little indeed.'

''Ow do you mean . . . born.'

'Involved. Evolved. It was sitting by the water and spending a lot of time actually in it, that youmans became youpersons.'

She glanced up fleetingly as Pierre passed. I must, thought Thomas, get on with this before she gets bored. Thunder growled again too, the storm that had been padding around them for some hours, sniffing out its prey, was moving back in, and she, and he, at the end of the table were actually out under the stars. He looked up. Clouds. Black as . . . well, very black, except when the heat lightning flickered.

'No, seriously.' He began to gabble. 'There was a bloody great big lake in the middle of Africa. Game swarmed all around. Animals. Predators. None of them too good in the water. But a few, very few to begin with, of the *Homines* found if they stayed by the water's edge and ran into it whenever a giant pussy came along or a hungry Neanderthal or whatever, they were safe. Under circumstances of this sort Natural Selection, combined with a quickly growing cultural element and probably very intensive inbreeding, favoured the survivors, that is those who got on in the water better than those who didn't.'

Pierre sat down opposite him, scattered salt over the last three steaks, filled their glasses.

'What would be . . . ' Thérèse struggled for the English, 'the 'er favouring things?'

'The flavouring characteristics were many. First those who had the slightest tendency to adipose tissue below the skin were better insulated in water than those who weren't. Those who most readily stood perfectly upright, not stooped at all, got deeper into the water and were safer.'

Pierre looked up, over his meat.

'No sharks in this lake?' he asked. 'Not even freshwater sharks?'

Thomas felt a very rare twinge of doubt, as if his hobby-horse had stumbled or shied from a rabbit in the hedge, whatever.

'No sharks.' He was firm about it.

'Nor,' he added, pre-emptively, 'crocs.'

'Go on. What else?'

'Oh lots. We have hair on our heads and thin skin because we keep them out of the water; what body hair we do have follows the flow patterns of water round us when we swim; female youmans give birth most satisfactorily in water... But the thing I find most convincing is the aesthetic sense and the pleasure principle. Where we came in. The basic aesthetic we like is of contrast between light and shade; we love sparkling jewels, water and land contrasted, the horizontal cut across a picture, and so on. We just love spending our time in family groups as part of loose seal-like colonies, on the edge of water or in it. It is our favourite recreation, in the fullest sense. It recreates us, we come back from the seaside refreshed and we retain a year-long nostalgia for it, as for a lost Eden.'

'So those who prefer mountain-walking in the summer are ... deranged?' Pierre again.

'Probably. But no, not necessarily. The whole youman race began on this lake-side, but over millennia the lake shrank, grew again, the population pressures fluctuated. When there were severe pressures, clans, maybe just family groups, upped and walked. All the way in some cases from the centre of Africa to Tierra del Fuego.'

Pierre looked doubtful, refilled their glasses.

'I thought we were meant to be descended from hunter-gatherers in a savannah habitat.'

'Maybe. But that was before the aquatic development. Here's another factor. The physiological differences between men and women. These are often explained as the necessary source of sexual and familial bonding. *Vive la différence* and all that. But you see the actual differences need to be explained. Why men are hairier, have less adipose tissue, and so on. Because the successful aquatic youperson clans were ones where the women were more aquatic than the men, could take more readily to the water when predators approached, carrying their infants with them, while the men remained on land fighting off the attackers ... And of course when men get older they get fatter and lose their hair, so it wasn't only the infants ...'

'This is not a view that will recommend itself to feminists.'

'Pouf!' said Thérèse, pouting the whole tribe into outer darkness.

Thomas felt a sudden wave of weakness, breathlessness, flood over him, and he slumped back in his cane chair, eyes sparkling, glistening sweat beading his forehead.

'Has he been boring you?' Katherine at his elbow.

'No, of course not.' Pierre was emphatic, but Thérèse quite readily surrendered her chair to Thomas's wife.

'Wellington, was it?'

'Wellington? The Duke of Wellington?' Pierre laughed.

'No. The semi-aquatic origins of mankind.' Thomas put his hand on her thigh. 'Katherine, I think I ought to be in bed.'

'I think so too. Come on then.'

She made him say goodnight to everybody as if he were Richard or Hannah-Rosa. And once she had seen him into his nightshirt and given him two more aspirin and codeine with water, she went back down again.

That quite surprised him, even saddened him a little. She muttered something about there being an awful lot of washing up to do, but he knew very well that there was a dishwasher ... He slept, dreamt feverishly, but the sort of dream you choose, compose.

A huge sheet of still water. The colour of pewter, its millions of ripples caught by the risen sun sparkled with diamond intensity. An uneven transparent mist hung above it: in places thick enough to make a wall, in others just enough to soften the outline and blur the detail on the mountains twenty miles away on the other side. With the sunrise the air filled with sound. Troops of monkeys chattered in the trees across the bay, a dawn chorus in the trees above him built into a symphony of song punctuated by the calls and cackles of the bigger birds – parrots and macaws, birds of paradise impractically ornate, gloriously feathered in colours that became extinct when they did. Far out on the lake a huge host of long-legged birds thrashed the water with their wings and swung up into the sky for no particular reason but the hell of it, before swooping in a great white dense arc back on to the water again.

Thomas rubbed his eyes, sat up, then stood. The air now felt a touch chill after the warmth of his nest. He rubbed his arms with his hands and ran on the spot for a moment, his hard-soled feet cracking the friable shells and twigs on the little shingly beach. Then he turned his back on the lake and moved inland across mangrove roots and through the curtain of vegetation that filled the shore.

The forest proper was still dim. The warm and damp composted litter on the floor was filled with grubs and larvae some of which were good to eat, but he was thirsty too. Soon he came on what he was looking for – a bromeliad with a pineapple-like fruit in the centre of its bright spiky leaves. He topped that up with a paw-paw and a prickly pear which he managed to open without spiking his fingers on the spines, peeling back the skin to reveal the dark, seeded, scented flesh within. First pangs satisfied he wandered on, taking in the big home he was part of and shared with such an abundance of other life: there were big black butterflies that shone like gold when the sun caught them, hundreds of flowers, almost never two of the same species together, some huge blossoms in strange shapes from dreams, others clouds of purple or bright blue stars hanging from the canopy in frangipane-scented swags. Jacaranda? Bougainvillaea? There were more sinister plants as well – spikes crusted with red berries, and others with bright vermilion phallic protuberances. Plants that caught and ate insects, even small amphibia.

He paused to rub his back against the abrasive bark of a tree, revelling sensuously in the relief it brought.

Presently he came to the part of the forest he was looking for, and the chatter of the white-faced monkeys was leading him to – the giant trees that sheltered their colony, because there, below the monkey-pot trees, he knew he would find some of the big nuts the monkeys occasionally dropped.

He was lucky. Not just single nuts but a whole pot – a large shell as big as a coconut which he reckoned probably held five or six of the large meaty kernels.

He was about to prise open the round lid there and then and eat a couple, when a movement on the forest floor over to his right caught his eye. A black-phase jaguar, belly to the ground, tail swishing, was edging inch by inch towards a group of creatures somewhere between a small pig and a large rat browsing near their burrows off saplings and creepers.

Thomas backed off. He knew the jaguar would make his move on the coypu first – if he got one, he'd be satisfied. But if he didn't then Thomas might be on the menu.

Still clutching the big nut-pot he reached the forest curtain again, pushed through it and, stumbling and stubbing his toes on mangrove roots, got back into the water, scaring a flock of small, bright kingfishers in the process. He pushed through the warm water until it lapped his genitals; then he waded along the forest edge until he came back to the tiny cove of shingle on whose edge he had spent the night. He felt safe there. The only large predators that could penetrate the curtain were the stooped shaggy men who lived on the savannah in the uplands beyond the forest and they only ever came down here for Mother Nature's remedies – herbs, seeds, leaves and flowers that could cure diseases and help wounds to heal. If game was short, or they were feeling lazy about hunting it, or they just felt like it, they were quite capable of seizing and eating one of the lake people.

The dazzle of the water was even more intense now though already the mists were forming into a lowish cloudbase which would dim the sun as it rose, and protect the lake people's hairless skin from its ultraviolet. He put the soles of his feet together in front of him, spread his knees and put the nuts in the space between his feet and his genitals. And he waited. This was the third day, the first day on which she might come to see how he had survived, fending for himself. He reckoned he had done well. She should be pleased. He wouldn't eat the kernels, not yet. He'd keep them for her. As a gift. In case she came.

Meanwhile he rested. At ease.

The heat built. Time passed. Presently thunder rumbled round the mountainous periphery of the basin, heat lightning flickered. A few heavy drops of warm rain clattered on the big leaves above him . . .

And then he saw her. At first just her head, a tiny black spot right out in the middle of the lake. Clouds parted and the sun, now almost directly overhead, shed a pool of light that drifted with her, accompanied her in. Presently he could see the tan whiteness of her face, then her features beneath the streaming hair: her high broad forehead, the dark eyes above high cheek-bones, a small but straight nose and full lips, that parted and closed as her strong arms lifted her forward and up in a slow easy breaststroke.

Fifty yards out she could stand, with the water lapping just below her loose breasts, then her waist, her tummy. It rippled and broke in a bow wave as her thighs pushed through it, and the droplets glittered in the hair between her legs. She scooped it with her palms and as she did the rain came on more heavily, pocking the surface about her. A rainbow formed an arch of promise behind her.

Mitochondrial Eve. The Mother of us all.

The fragrance, the odour of tomato plants hot beneath glass . . .

These, he said to himself, are the bare necessities. And the thunder crashed again.

15

Flash, bang, wallop. Christ, that was close. He came out of the dawn of youmanity and heard the rumbling rain, waited for the next bolt. 'Sorry, God,' he murmured. 'Just joking.'

Katherine was climbing over him, trying to get into bed on the far side. What dreams! Had he dreamt all that from the moment she had entered the room and begun to undress in the darkness, while the thunder rolled nearer?

'What did you say? You said something.'

He was aware of her knees swinging up from under her as she got herself on to her back and slid beneath the sheet beside him.

'I was just telling God the Daddy that I don't want to be struck by lightning just because I don't believe in Him.'

'I wonder if the children are all right.'

Code for: why don't you go and check?

'Of course they're all right.'

Code for: I've got flu and I'm not getting out of bed.

'If Hannah-Rosa's bothered she'll come and tell us.'

Code for: I'm on the wrong side of the bed to get out, and I've only just got in. Then she went on, 'You're soaking. And terribly hot. Are you all right?' Code for: sorry, I forgot you were ill. 'Do you think you should have some more aspirin?'

'Don't know. What time is it?'

'About two o'clock.'

Two o'clock? He had come up at about half-past ten, nearly four hours ago. What had they all been doing downstairs? What had he been missing?

'Nearly four hours. Should be all right.'

She climbed back over him after all, turned on the light, shook out two pills, handed him water. Then she went to check that Hannah-Rosa was sleeping through it. Outside the lightning flashed and the thunder rolled. She came back, turned out the light, climbed back over him, pulled the duvet up from the bottom of the bed and wrapped it round them.

Thunder and rain assaulted the house, the mildly erotic delights, enhanced by fever, of all those lovely women at dinner, the red meat and red wine, the dream of Mitochondrial Eve, the warmth of Katherine's backside against his front... The thunder crashed again.

A night of strange noises – a distant steady rumble from high, high above. The wailing siren a mile and a half away in Penmaenmawr. Then the crump, crump of falling bombs. The Luftwaffe was on its way home, from Liverpool, and shedding here what it had not been able to drop there. The light came on, stark and bright and his mother got into bed with him. She lay on top of him, careful not to smother him or confuse him with her weight (not that she was heavy, indeed she was always thin until in old age the doctor put on her steroids), but nevertheless her warm body covered all of his. His nostrils prickled with the talc she used, L'Aimant by Coty, and since she left the light on he could see her breasts hanging in the loop of her long nightdress, and feel the murmur of her lips in his ear. Why? Why this sudden unexplained access to the ravishing mystery of her body?

'Why?'

'There are spiders on the ceiling, and I was afraid they might drop on you.'

It was true. In his memory they became the biggest of big black widows. Perhaps they were. From that moment, to his phobias for volcanoes and the witch in Snow White was added an arachnophobia worse than the others put together. He got over volcanoes. He just about got over the witch. But at nearly sixty he still ran from large spiders and it was Richard who had to trap them in a two-litre ice-cream box and take them outside.

And it was only three years ago that he had actually worked out just what was going on. His mother lay on top of him that night because she was afraid they might be hit by a bomb and she wanted to protect him. Greater love hath no man than this –

that his mother will risk her life for her son by lying on top of him during an air-raid . . .

Blame Hitler.

Katherine brought him tea, made him take off his wringing-wet cotton nightshirt (she'd made it for him, for a birthday present) and got him into a T-shirt instead. She sat on the edge of the bed, covered his hand (hot) with hers (cool).

'Do you think you'll be able to drive?'

In England when they were together she always drove, but she hated having to acclimatize herself to the wrong side of the road.

Unable to answer because of the thermometer in his mouth, he shook his head. She took the thermometer out.

'Not yet,' he said. 'In the afternoon, perhaps.'

'Thirty-nine; that's quite high, isn't it? Richard's is only thirty-eight.'

'How is he?'

'He says he's almost better. I think you both ought to stay in bed until this afternoon. If you're not better, I'll drive. After all, it's not far.'

Twenty miles to Biarritz and the flat Monique was borrowing from her parents who kept it for seaside holidays, though the sea was two kilometres away.

'I can't remember the way.'

'She drew a map. With directions.' She shook out two more tablets. 'Take these. Drink your tea. Sweat it out.'

She pulled the duvet round him.

'What will you do?'

'Mooch about. Take Hannah-Rosa down to the village maybe. It's not a morning for the beach – windy and much cooler after the storm.'

He finished the tea then curled himself up in a tight ball inside the duvet.

The 'Bungalow'. That's what they called it, perhaps that was what it was called. That was where his mother lay on top of him to save him from the bombs. It was in a road grandly called Merthyn Howell Drive – that's a phonetic approximation, the Welsh was probably different. It was a lane, not a drive at all, beneath the purple mountain. At one end there was a farm where they bought milk. If they were lucky they could be there while the milkmaids, landgirls probably, were milking, and chatting to each other and the big russet cows in Welsh, briskly, like the brook on the other side of the lane. Brown hands in the dark stable, pulling the long pink- and cream-coloured teats in that firm but loving caress that made the milk rhythmically hiss. There was a dog, a Welsh collie, that scampered anxiously around, begging for a squirt and occasionally he'd get one, catching it and lapping it into his mouth, long red tongue scooping the last drops from his grey muzzle. Then the milkmaid would fill a chipped Silver Jubilee mug from the year of Thomas's birth, and fill it to the brim.

'Drink it up, *bach*, it'll put some fat on your bones.'

Actually it gave him tubercular glands.

The Bungalow stood in the middle of a wilderness, a strip of land between the lane and the cemetery. Apart from the scrap of lawn round the building itself there was nothing but trees and undergrowth with a small ditch or second stream between it and the graves. A dark place and very damp. It was blamed for the TB. But it was there Thomas, alone for much of the time with his mother, discovered himself.

What else? The jungle. There were strange plants in it – spikes crusted with red berries, and others with bright vermilion phallic protuberances left over from a time when there had been more cultivation than there was now. Plants that caught and ate flies. The sweet smells of rotting vegetation and the water that drained down from the graves. There were thickets he could hide in, and once he hid there with a girl of his age from up the road. She showed him what she didn't have in her knickers and he showed her what little he did have. Fascinating. Then they went indoors, into the lavatory, to show each other how they worked and his mother caught them there. She was neither angry nor distressed, but he had no recollection of ever meeting that girl again.

There were other ways of being naughty. There were big stoneware jars in the pantry. One, he knew, held the powder from which drinks of cocoa were made. Catering size, because, like many other things at this stage of his life, they were left over from the time his mother had been in charge of the domestic side of running a small school. One day when he knew she was busy with her mother, he put his finger into the deep jar and licked the brown powder . . . but what he scored was curry, not cocoa.

His mother's mother?

Granny Murray was there for a time. Wheelchair-bound with, yes, arthritis, she had been found in her sitting room in Welsh Newport with the chimney wall still standing and facing her, and the roof and two floors above in rubble around her. For a few months she was an intrusion in their lives: a gaunt helpless figure with deep-set eyes and a halo of white hair. She couldn't do a stream or a busy without a bed-pan. His mother had to clean her up and his mother was a very fastidious person. Granny was also too heavy to lift. One day he ran at her, pummelling her with his fists, 'I hate you, I hate you, you make everything horrible.'

Later in the day, the same day? it felt like it, he crept into the sitting room to say sorry and, just as he had already discovered eros, he now found himself face to face with thanatos. She was slumped in her wheelchair, chin on her breastbone, face glistening lead-white, and her yellowed top denture half out of her mouth, askew, concealing her bottom lip.

'Mummy, Mummy, Mummy, Granny's dead,' he screamed.

Mother came running from the garden or wherever and as she burst into the room Granny sat up, and her denture clicked back into place.

'Oh no, I'm not,' she said. 'Just sleeping.'

For once his mother was really angry, and slapped his thigh. Why? She should have been pleased he'd got it wrong, that Granny was after all still alive. Perhaps she had run from wherever she was with hope in her heart and it was disappointment rather than anger that lay behind the slap.

But no.

'God, you gave me such a fright, you stupid boy.'

After a year in the Bungalow he fell mysteriously ill, lost weight, had stomach cramps. A grumbling appendix was diagnosed. He was put into hospital in Llandudno. He wasn't at all frightened because he was told he was going to have an operation. He knew all about operations. They stuck a needle in your arm or your bottom, and it pricked for a moment, even hurt, but then it was all over.

But on this occasion, after his mother had left him, promising to be back in the evening, they came and painted his stomach brown, took off his pyjamas, which he thought was disgusting of them, put him in a gown and on a trolley. The rest was nightmare.

They rolled him off the trolley and on to a table. At that moment he panicked and began to fight. If he could have he would have slithered through these white-gowned monsters, pelted along the corridors and out into the street. But some of them held him down, while others fastened leather straps over his chest and thighs just like when Moriarty strapped Sherlock Holmes to the table and started to bleed him to death, drop by drop. A bright circular light came on over his head, masked figures told him to count slowly to ten, a cotton-wool mask was planted over his mouth and nose and they began to drip ether on to it. He fought to get it off, his arms were still free, but they held them down too.

The light spun, turned red. There was a terrible roaring. The light came closer, spinning faster and faster, threatened to engulf him. He knew if it did he would die, he knew that this was what it was like to die . . .

His mother was sorry. She had not realized he had confused the two words – injection and operation. She read aloud to him from *Swallows and Amazons*, and later in the week he finished it himself, the first real book he ever read unassisted.

The operation and the ten days in hospital cost seventy guineas and were all unnecessary. His appendix was fine, though since they were in they thought they might as well have it out anyway. The problem was glands infected with TB, tuberculosis. He had to rest, rest for a year. No school for a whole year. And they had to leave the Bungalow, and move to an airy, drier house, Gable End, on the side of Jubilee Mountain. It was the happiest year of his life. Because it was the only bedroom with a fireplace he slept in the large front room, in the large bed, all through the first winter, sharing it with his mother; and even in the summer, when she put him in the back room, during the daytime when he was meant to be resting or when he caught a summer cold, he still used her bedroom with its alluring fragrances, the powder puff, the valanced dressing table with its three mirrors . . .

She read to him, Grimm in an old Arthur Rackham illustrated edition, more Arthur Ransome, and together they listened to Masefield's *Box of Delights* on the wireless. She tried to keep up with some of the schoolwork he should have been doing, but there again – he was not to be made tired. Once or twice they did really outrageous things together. For instance they made floating ships out of blue cardboard Tate & Lyle sugar cartons, floated them in the bath and set fire to them. Because of the still encrusted sugar they burnt too well and the conflagration gave them a fright.

They had spats: one day he ran away from home with some biscuits and a favourite toy – a Dinky toy Buick – done up in a handkerchief and tied to the end of the walking-stick Granny had left behind. He hid in a hedge until he heard her calling for him and caught sight of the really worried frown on her face. Another time, picking whimberries on the side of Jubilee Mountain, he refused to come when told.

'You're a spoilt brat,' she called across the low windswept shrubs.

'Look who spoilt me,' he shouted back.

'Wait till your father comes home . . .'

Father came home.

So that first morning, in the early grey light, fearful that the mountains would erupt, that skeletons would drop out of the cupboard, or the spiders that lived behind the wainscotting might come scuttling up the counterpane and over the earth-heavy eiderdown, he came out of the small back bedroom and got into bed with them. On Dad's side of the bed.

And presently, wanting to be close and friendly, even loving, to this strange new presence that smelt of tobacco, he sought under the bedclothes with his hand to find his father's hand. And got hold of his father's thumb. He thought.

Dad was suddenly still, and very quiet.

And presently poor Thomas realized that it was not his father's thumb he was holding but something about the same size, softer than a thumb.

He let go as if it had been an electric eel. He went bright red, not just his face but maybe all over his body, certainly he broke out in a sweat. Sweat it out. Presently he went back to his own bed where he tried very hard not to cry with the embarrassment of it all, and where for a time he felt more lonely than he had ever felt in his life. More lonely even than when he was in hospital.

Sweat it out.

Thomas woke at about twelve-thirty, felt something stirring in his lower bowel. At last, he thought. He swung his legs out of the bed, straightened his still aching knees. It seemed a long way up, and his head began to bang again before he got there. He looked down. Beneath the hem of the T-shirt his tiny prick bobbed above loosely sacked but adequately sized balls. I'd better put something on, he thought. He cast about for under-pants, suffered a sudden swing of dizziness, found them, thought about sitting on the low bed, thought better of it, leant against the wall and pulled them on, first one leg then the other. All to negotiate a couple of metres with no risk of being caught . . . with his pants down.

Once in the loo he pulled them down again. But the effort of getting there had put a brake on things and, though he sat for ten minutes and pushed a lot, he brought forth not a mountain nor a mouse but again a small handful of hard black pellets. He had a chuckle though, remembering how Richard, at the age of three, had burst in on Katherine's mother in a similar position and had called out, 'Big one – push, Nana, big one push!'

Back in bed he picked up *Wellington's War*. Nosey too had had a big push, up from the Portuguese border in a series of forced marches manoeuvring the French from every defensible position they had a mind to stand on, and finally thrashing them at Vitoria. The army picked up the biggest booty ever captured on a field of battle – the French, led by Joseph, Napoleon's older brother, were trying to get out of Spain with just about every valuable object they could lay hands on, and the Brits copped the lot. Including the splendid Velázquez and Goya canvases that to this day adorn the walls of Apsley House, Number One, London.

Still under the influence of the stars (for it is the Italian for that phrase which gives us the word *influenza*) Thomas had a sudden sense that as he (and his family) moved south towards the Pyrenees, Wellington moved north . . . to meet him?

'It would be a good thing,' he said to himself, laying the book back on the floor, 'if we could meet.'

And he slept for an hour or so, a healthier, less troubled sleep than before.

112

16

No one to say goodbye to: Elvira and Pierre with Jean-Luc had gone to a friend's baby's christening. Moni had left earlier to open up her parents' flat. They loaded the car – the body-board Pierre was lending Richard so he could continue to surf in Biarritz went in last. Then they piled in. Thomas now had to reverse down a narrow, steep drive with a bend in it, and squeeze between narrow gate-posts out on to the road. He reversed badly at the best of times.

'Shall I get out and guide you?'

'No. I'll manage.'

'Guiding' him in this sort of situation often ended in a domestic. He blamed this on the fact that she would never position herself where he could see her in the mirrors and so follow the signals she was making. Whereas she blamed it on his deafness and his inability to remember which was his left and which his right.

Something he forgot exactly then, because reversing out on to the road he ended up on the left instead of the right. It was the first time he had got it wrong during the whole holiday.

Pierre's house was on the corner of a junction with the main road out of Hossegor – a junction with traffic lights. These were green and a bus was hurtling towards him across the intersection, horn blaring. The only way to avoid it was to turn sharp left into the track of another car. Fortunately, since this was approaching a red light, it was decelerating and had time to pull up before hitting him. At last he got over on to the 'right' right-hand side of the road.

'Are you trying to kill us all, or what?'

Hannah-Rosa began to whimper.

'I think you should let Mummy drive,' said Richard.

'A chance would be a fine thing,' Thomas replied.

Beside him Katherine's mouth set in a grim line.

'Which way?' he asked.

She looked at Monique's bold but not overly legible handwriting.

'Take the signs for the autoroute. Junction seven. And please drive on the right.'

Chaos again? Hardly. You can't blame chaos when you've behaved like an idiot.

'What's this place we're going to?' Richard asked, once they were safely cruising along the short stretch of autoroute – pine-forest on both sides with here and there Basque-type chalet houses of some substance.

'Moni's parents' flat,' Katherine answered. 'They don't live there but just keep it for when they need a break. They let Moni and her friends use it whenever they don't want to be there themselves.'

'Is it grand?' Hannah-Rosa asked with lip-licking anticipation.

'Not particularly. Why do you ask?'

''Cos where we've just been was pretty posh.'

'Moni's parents' *pied à terre* in Biarritz is a model of under-stated petit-bourgeois pretension. If you ask me.' Thomas added his two-pennyworth.

'Nobody did. Keep your eye on the road.' Katherine turned to the children. 'I suppose what your father means is that the furniture and so on is rather old-fashioned and a bit big and heavy for the size of the rooms. It may have all changed since we were last here.'

'When was that?'

'Thirteen years ago. You were one and a half and you had a cold as bad as Daddy's is now. We had to get the doctor in.'

It was exactly as it had been: functional kitchen at the back, and two bedrooms. In the front a living room with double glass doors framed in dark wood separating it from the hall, heavy settee and armchairs in dark brown embossed moquette, a glazed cabinet and sideboard with, Thomas was sure, the half-

114

empty bottle of Carpano that had always been there. Then a tiny loo and finally her parents' bedroom. Between this and the bedroom at the back was a small bathroom. Moni gave them her parents' bedroom. There was just room for a pink dressing table with white mouldings and a glass top beneath the mock-rococo mirror. She gave the children a bedroom each and she herself slept on the settee.

'Don't worry, I'm used to it. I sleep there more often than not.'

At the front there was a veranda with patio doors to the living room, shielded by a cypress hedge from the small concrete driveway.

At about half-past ten the next morning the doctor came. Moni insisted. Tom had gone to bed early after eating a boiled egg and drinking three glasses of white wine with water. In the morning his temperature was thirty-nine point five and he felt awful. Nevertheless it was not a situation he would have called the doctor in for, not for himself anyway, and certainly not when their medical insurance required them to pay the first twenty-five pounds. And in any case Monique was, he knew, as much a hypochondriac about other people as she was about herself.

The doctor was a young man who pretended to speak English – worse still he pretended to understand it.

He listened to Thomas's chest. Made him breathe and hold it and breathe out. All the usual stuff. He palpated Thomas's stomach. Thomas winced, especially when the doctor got his stubby fingers into his left-hand side, just under his ribs.

'You have been going to the vay say much?'

'Yes. But whenever I go I do very little, just very small hard turds. I haven't been properly for days.'

No use. The doctor decided he had *gastero-enterite* as well as *chaud-froid*. Probably he'd decided this before he came, for he added, in French which Katherine translated for Thomas later: 'Everyone who has this *chaud-froid* has mild diarrhoea with it.'

He prescribed paracetamol and an anti-diarrhoea mixture.

Moni stood over Thomas and made sure he took them, then they all went off to the beach and left him there.

He tried to read *Wellington's War* but could not keep his mind on it, but neither did it send him to sleep. He station-surfed on Richard's Walkman, found *France Musique* at 92.7 but there was too much chat and the music was all early baroque from some festival or other played by authentic nuts. He took off the ear buttons and savoured the near quiet – but not for long. The flat was on the ground floor. The woman upstairs began to wash her balcony. She sluiced water across it and a lot of it came tumbling down into the cypress hedge. The noise was exactly that of someone vomiting heavily. The woman then began to shift things about, things that screeched like animals in pain. Thomas guessed that she was moving heavy ceramic plant holders across polished terrazzo flooring. Then the vomit crash came again, curtaining sheets of dirty sudsy water into the hedge, and the screeches once more. He pulled the duvet over his head, turned from the window and faced the wall.

Was it ever a good time after Dad came back? Yes. Thomas had scarlet fever at the beginning of his first summer term at The Links. 1944. He got over it quickly and was then quarantined for a fortnight. Dad took leave and both parents came up to stay in a hotel that had not been requisitioned. They spent a lot of time rowing on the lake. It was like *Swallows and Amazons*. The boat nudged through the sparkling ripples. Purple shadows chased emerald patches of sun across the big round mountains. Often they went to a small cove on the further shore. The prow of the boat crunched in the shingle beneath scented pine trees. He and Dad had a pine-cone battle while Mum watched. Then they paddled and watched the dark brown minnows scattering away from their feet over the lighter brown of the stones. The steamer from Penrith chugged into the little landing stage just below the hotel where The Links was, a mile away or more.

One afternoon Dad and Mum wanted to swim but they had no bathers. Yes, Thomas thought, in bed in Biarritz, that was

116

what they called them – bathers. They told him not to look and took off their clothes, but when they were in the water he did. His dad looked like some sort of strange animal from the veld or something. His face and neck were still dark brown. And so were his arms to just above his elbows, and his legs between his knees and where his long, pulled-up socks would have come. And the rest of him was livid white. His mum was livid white all over.

If, Thomas in Biarritz now thought, I wanted to make a fiction of all this I would have them come out of the water and make passionate love, or even stage a marital rape. But they just sat in the sun until they were dry, and presently smoked Woodbines to keep the midges at bay. It really was a happy time. For them. He, in recollection anyway, felt excluded. After all, it was him they had come to see.

Less happy after they had gone. The Marquess of Bransgore decided Thomas should be punished for having brought scarlet fever to the school, for in spite of quarantine just about every boy who had not yet had it got it. The punishment was simple. The dormitory, a double room in peace time but now with six beds squeezed in, had a big sash window. They lifted the bottom half and stuck his upper torso through the gap and then lowered the frame into the small of his back so he couldn't move. And then, led by Bransgore, the five of them took it in turn to hit his bare buttocks as hard as they could with their slippers.

And that put Thomas in mind of a humiliation almost as bad. No. Worse. Worse for being self-inflicted. Each boy had a chamber-pot under his bed. Waking in the darkest part of the night Thomas had knelt beside his bed, fumbled for the pot and picked up his bedroom slipper instead. He peed in it. And remember, Thomas in Biarritz said to himself, Mum and Dad colluded in putting me in that hell.

Think of the hols, think of the holidays. They weren't so bad, spent in Melton Mowbray, getting ready for D-Day and then all that followed. They had digs off the base down in the town owned by a woman called Mrs Warner. An elderly but jolly soul who let them have the run of quite a lot of her large house. Thomas slept in a big bed with a reading light over the headboard operated by a nut-shaped, dangling, push-button switch. One summer evening, double summertime, it *never* got dark, he unscrewed it and gave himself an electric shock. That was quite an event. He knew he had been naughty, fiddling about with the switch. And he liked being naughty – in a private on your own sort of way. Still did, Thomas in Biarritz thought. And he'd often wondered what an electric shock was like and now he knew. Perhaps he'd try it again. But he never did. Well, not on purpose.

Dad had a huge Smith and Wesson revolver kept in a pale blue webbing holster. He also had lots of bullets for it. He kept the bullets separate from the revolver, though one night he and his mother had a terrible row and Dad tried to shoot himself with it. Thomas heard the row but did not know that the gun had been out and loaded. It was only after his dad died that his mother told him about it. Died? Was killed. Killed himself. In effect he really did will the kill, if not actually kill himself, fifteen years later.

Anyway, Thomas loved that gun. It was heavy and solid and smelt of fine oil and when you pulled the trigger (almost too stiff for a nine-year-old) the chamber went round and the hammer, which had a pin-head on the end of a curved beak, came back and then click! and it slammed forward. Thomas used to put Swan Vesta matches in the groove which the hammer entered on its way to where the base of the chambered round would be, if it were properly loaded, and the match would flare and fill the air with sulphur. Was that happy? Certainly it was fun.

It was fun too on the rare occasions when Dad took him up to the airfield, especially the day they let him sit in the cockpit of a Mosquito. He would have liked it to be a Spitfire, but Dad explained how the Mosquito was just as good an aeroplane in its own way, had cannon like the Spitfire but could carry small bombs too and go almost as fast.

Thomas rolled on to his back. The woman had stopped washing her balcony and a slight haze or rain was curtaining-in the space that separated Moni's shoe-box block from the next one. He thought of them all on the beach. Perhaps they'd be back early because of the rain. He turned away from the window, thought of Melton Mowbray again, and a sky filled with the thunderous roar of Flying Fortresses. Later he learnt how there were American day raids to Dresden, Hamburg, Cologne and the rest, which smashed the streets into splinters. These were followed at night by the RAF who set off the fire storms with incendiaries.

He remembered a summer's day, early summer perhaps, a cricket field, a cricket match. Dad a flannelled fool, slow off-spin, occasionally with a Chinaman or a googly thrown in. Which? What was the difference? Thomas had no idea then, and had no idea now, but he remembered he enjoyed the cama-raderie of the men, the way they treated Dad, well, each other really, with a sort of mutual respect. They called Dad 'Pop'. Which meant 'Dad'. Why did they do that? He was Thomas's dad, not theirs. For the rest of his life the family called Dad 'Pop'. Thomas never did.

When she was washing-up Mrs Warner always insisted on leaving saucepans to the end on the principle that God might call her away to higher things before she got to them. Also she often left them to soak, and for years after all of them, that is Dad, Mum and Thomas would say when faced with a particu-larly recalcitrant saucepan, 'Give it a Warner'. Of course in those days detergents, washing-up liquid, plastic scourers and so on were uninvented, and metal scourers were not available because – 'there's a war on, you know.' Vim was around, or perhaps came back. It was at Melton Mowbray that Thomas had a banana again. He'd forgotten what bananas were like. It was like your first ejaculation – the pleasure was such an enormous surprise. Subsequent bananas were just as good, but never again would there be that shock of delight.

All of which was displacement activity, if lying in bed trawl-ing your memory can be described as activity. Dodging the issue, the one memory of Melton Mowbray that troubled.

His mother took him to the pictures. They walked there, hand in hand. She was wearing white gloves. Women wore gloves a lot in those days. They were not going to the pictures to see what they often jokingly referred to as a 'flim' because that's what his half-sister had called them when she was five. They were going to see the newsreels, because Mummy thought they ought to.

What they saw was the opening of the camps.

A learning experience. Thorough too. It lasted, in memory at any rate, all of an hour. The images, which are now as much part of the baggage our minds carry with us as, say, the dome of St Paul's, were there – unheralded, unmediated. New. The piles of white bodies, skeletons with skin on; the survivors like ghosts with hollow eyes; the guards forced by the British and Americans to load the bodies into the backs of lorries; the huge grave, with the bodies tumbled in anyhow. The plummy commentator, original Mr Voice-Over Man, explaining how many of the survivors had been killed by the liberators who gave them food straight away, food their stomachs could no longer cope with . . . and so on, and so on. Not believing she could have wittingly inflicted this on him, Thomas turned and looked up at his mother's face, flickering in the light reflected from the screen. She sat up very straight, chin up, and tears were tumbling down her face. Aware he was looking at her she took his hand in her white gloves and held it in her lap.

Thomas in Biarritz did not think he had been harmed by the experience. Scarred, yes. He knew from then on what fascism is, and why his dad had had to go off and fight it. He knew because that is what his mum told him when they came out of the cinema. It was knowledge that he built on for the rest of his life. It underpinned many things he would later become and believe – attitudes that, by now, almost sixty years old, had hardened into atheism and hatred of all power structures.

That summer, before they caught the boat to Caen, they had gone to see *Schindler's List*. Well, Katherine and Richard had. It was a multi-screen cinema, so while they saw *Schindler's List*, Thomas and Hannah-Rosa went to *Sister Act 2*. He reckoned seeing the real thing when he was ten was enough, and besides Hannah-Rosa was way under age. Richard too, but only by five months.

There was another difference. Back in 1945, in the newsreel, there was no mention of the word 'holocaust', nor, Thomas was pretty sure, of the word 'Jew'. Just that these were ordinary people the Nazis had taken against for no good reason. This still seemed right to Thomas. To him the point was not who these poor people were, but what had happened to them. Later he found it annoying the way American Jews, in particular, referred to the holocaust as an event that had been suffered solely by Jews – he felt the holocaust had been hijacked.

On the way back to Mrs Warner's digs Thomas and his mum passed a large dead dog lying in the road in a vast pool of blood. Its body had been crushed by a lorry. She pulled him in, into her side, and covered his eyes with her hand in its white cotton glove.

'Don't look,' she said.

'Dad, Dad, Daddy, we went to the aquarium. When it rained we went to the aquarium, the sea museum.'

Hannah-Rosa was first in, and on to the bed, expecting to be hugged and listened to. The others crowded in behind her.

'I could have gone on surfing,' Richard said stoically. 'It doesn't matter if it rains when you're surfing.'

'But it's not a lot of fun sitting in the rain and watching someone surf,' said Katherine.

'No, Richard, it's not.' Hannah-Rosa was firm.

Poor lad. They're ganging up on you.

'But the *musée de la mer* was OK?'

'Oh yes. Glad we went.'

Katherine took up the story. 'All the stuff we saw before was still there, but there were lots more live fish and tanks than before . . . '

'A shark, a big one, Daddy, like in the film . . . '

'A big white shark . . . '

'Cruising round and round and round . . . '

'Poor thing,' said Thomas, arm now round his daughter, the other two at the end of the bed.

'Not really,' said Richard. 'We learnt about goldfish at school.

Less than five seconds conscious memory. Once round the pool and it's, "Oh, I haven't seen that waterlily before, how interesting." I expect sharks are about the same.'

'Maybe worse,' said Thomas. 'They are, I believe, lower down the evolutionary tree.'

Twelve years earlier he and Katherine had looked after his mother in their own home. Two years of hell – well, anyway, a bad time. Towards the end, Mother, aged eighty-five, would ask for her lunch five minutes after he'd cleared the tray away. She also thought Thomas was Christopher, his dad. And that Katherine was the help, and also his mistress. She believed that young Richard, by then nearly four years old, was Thomas, her son.

Sometimes she'd try to climb into the wardrobe they'd got her from MFI. 'Mother,' he'd ask, 'why are you trying to get in the wardrobe?' 'I'm late for work.' Which was all very well but this scene was often enacted at three o'clock in the morning. Goldfish had it made, permanent Alzheimer's. Memory can be an evil thing.

17

Six in the morning. Something moving at last. Big. Big one push. Thomas staggered out into the passage and into the tiny, totally enclosed loo. A dark cupboard of a place with a forty watt lamp. Maybe twenty. The bowl at least clean, which it was not thirteen years ago, nor had it been five years before that. There has been, he thought, as he hoisted his nightshirt, washed, dried and pressed by Katherine in a day, a revolution in France. Until quite recently they did not bother with loo-cleaners. The bowls below the waterline were always walnut brown, stained in permanent walnut juice. Thinking of which was probably a way of displacing what was about to happen. After nearly a week with half the fibre and three times the animal protein of his normal diet, topped up with an anti-diarrhoea medicament prescribed by a mad French doctor, this was not going to be easy.

Big one.

Push.

His mother's word for the business had been 'busy'. He's doing a busy, she'd say. Have you done a busy today?

Big and filled with razor-blades or shards of broken glass, his busy did not drop, it fell, it plunged like a cannon-ball.

He lifted himself up, turned and looked. The water was red, bright red, and he could only just discern the big black brute that lay below the surface. He wiped his bum, looked at the paper. It was sodden with blood. He cleaned himself up with more paper and decided that it was not the small exposed haemorrhoid he'd had for years that was bleeding, but that the blood had come from above the sphincter. In short, with his sphincter closed he was not bleeding. Externally, that is.

He got back into bed and lay on his back, thought about it. He realized he was frightened. But he also knew this was something he must try to keep to himself. Tell Katherine, tell Moni, and it would be the doctor again – internal examinations, a hospital almost certainly, surgery. Inconceivable even in England – but in *France*? Impossible. No way. Two weeks – as much as that? Could he hold out? That is if the bleeding did not stop? Just how much was he bleeding? He recalled how swiftly blood spreads in water and really how little is needed to stain quite a large volume. A bad nick shaving, and only a few drops colour the water in a basin. As the light grew and the oblong of sky above the cypress hedge, seen in the mirror in front of him, took on the colour of a fair-weather dawn, he guesstimated he'd probably lost no more than a tablespoonful.

But where was it coming from? Why? He chewed his knuckles and suppressed a desire to whimper. Then he gave it some more thought. Surely there was nothing really to worry about. Surely that big, hard, rock-like turd had merely scraped the wall of his colon. Once his digestion was operating normally it would heal. Surely? Don't call me Shirley. Pantomime joke – he'd been in the chorus of the village pantomime back in January, knew a lot more like that. The reason I'm so beautiful is I bathe in asses' milk. Pasteurized? No, only up to my knees. He giggled.

Ten past six. Of course, there may be more to it than that. This is the reverse of Montezuma's Revenge. This could be Dad's way of seeing him off before or on the crucial thirty-first of August. Bled to death over nine days. Again he remembered Sherlock Holmes strapped to an operating table, his life blood dripping away.

Which led him back to the Penmaenmawr flea-pit where he'd seen *My Friend Flicka* (or was it *Flicker*?), then walking home – a good mile and a half – blubbing all the way. Until his very recently returned dad told him to be a man; he must learn to face up to things like that, terrible things like that (the shooting of Flicker at the end of the film) really did happen. It was worse than when Bambi's mother died. Worse than when the old stag left his monarch of the glen position – too old to sustain the role any longer. My God, there was stuff in those old Disney films that went pretty deep . . . Remember the nymphet fairies in *Fantasia*? Tiny titless boobs jogging, flashes of pert bums. The centaurs in the Pastoral . . . suggesting that bestiality could be jolly?

Be a man. And on top of everything else to be made to walk all the way home instead of catching the bus. But now of course he knew that maybe Dad had been talking to himself, telling himself to be a man, to face up to what he himself had . . . Even so, he could have given Thomas a bunk up, a ride on his shoulders.

Thomas recalled a time when he had. At Hurst Park . . .

Where?

Hurst Park. The races. In the holidays he often took me racing. Sometimes Mum came too. This must have been one of the first times, spring maybe, early summer of forty-six, though I remember a cold, grey day. Anyway there was a big crowd, so perhaps it was Easter Monday. We were in the Silver Ring, quite a distance from the winning post, and I couldn't see a thing. So Dad put me on his shoulders: although I was eleven years old I was a very weedy eleven. I knew I had to cheer on a horse whose jockey was wearing the pink and primrose colours of Lord Roseberry.

It was a long race, twice round a figure of eight, maybe as much as two and a half miles.

'Charlie Smirke's in front,' a bloke in a brown derby, holding binoculars, told Dad.

'They'll let him stay in front till they get back to the straight,' a small, wizened gypsy added. 'He's the only one who knows the way.'

I forget, indeed I forgot the name of the horse, for I remember shouting for pink and primrose, pink and primrose, come on pink and primrose. It won. Catching Charlie in a pink hat with a black circle on top in the last furlong. Dorothy Paget – wasn't that the owner's name? And it was a damn good thing it did. Cold, heavy, wet clothes, the smell of Woodbines and Weights.

Why?

Probably paid my school fees.

That was not a good time. Probably the worst. Christmas of forty-five we moved to Mottingham, no, not Nottingham, Mottingham – a suburb of south-east London. The border between Kent and London went through our back garden. Mother never forgave Dad for that move. She loved Gable End.

But Dad refused to go back to being a prep-school usher and he and my uncle Wilf, who lived in a house owned by Granny Somers in nearby Blackheath, across the road from my aunt's nursing home where I was born (which had been bombed), put together this crazy scheme. They set up an agency in Lewisham (or was it Lee Green?), for window-cleaners, plumbers, odd-job men. They had to be ex-service, preferably ex-Raf. Dad and Wilf did the advertising for them, looked after the paperwork and so on, and kept ten per cent of the takings. Well, of course, the men only declared half of what they earned and as soon as they had an established clientele of their own they ducked out.

The capital for all this came from the sale of Hollylea to the nuns and then when it went bust, in a matter of months, Dad used what was left to buy a partnership in a bookmaker's. Thomas never did get to know the ins and outs but that went very seriously bust and Dad lost it all. Maybe they refused to pay protection, or were at the wrong end of a fixed race – it was a crooked business in those days, and especially in south London.

I remember, Thomas said to himself, Dad filling a green baize bag with a silver teapot, fluted, hot-water jug, creamer and so on, Georgian heirlooms (he was the eldest son), and going up to town with them and coming back with fifty guineas and being very upset about it all. Fifty guineas was about what my school fees cost for a term, so I didn't feel too good about that either, I can tell you. Especially since I hated the place anyway.

Destitution faced us. For two years they tried to live as professional gamblers. Mother stayed at home mostly and worked with the form books. They concentrated on two-year-olds . . .

Why?

Because the races are short, only over five or six furlongs, and straight, there's no luck of the draw: all that makes the form more consistent. The best time was towards the end of the season when you get handicap races. Mother then tried to do a better job than the handicapper, work out when he'd put in a colt or a filly at a couple of pounds lighter than her own rating. She got good at it, studied Time-Form and filled blue, ex-Hollylea exercise books with lists and calculations. Nevertheless they reckoned it was important that at least Dad should be on the course – to pick up any whispers that were going round, take advantage of sudden changes in the betting. So in the hols he took me with him. Hurst Park, Kempton Park, the south London courses. Once we even got as far as Salisbury.

But it wasn't only racing. They held night-long poker parties which were almost certainly illegal, inviting friends from the Raf, who were encouraged to bring their friends too. Women as well – dark hair stacked in curly flounces, they always wore slacks, scarlet lipstick and smoked incessantly. Most of these parties took place while I was away at school, but I remember one very clearly. A huge amount of noise all night, the whole house filled with tobacco smoke, and dozens, it seemed to me, of glasses and bottles left lying around in the morning. The first time I got tipsy was through finishing off a couple of half-empty glasses at eleven o'clock on a Sunday morning. Luckily I couldn't, then, stand the taste.

Did it work?

For some of the time it must have done, since there was no other income apart from half of his share in Grandad's will, the other half going to wife April, remember? And at times they got lucky.

How so? I mean what effect did it have on you when they did?

Well, my school reports were never that brilliant, and the one thing they always harped on about was my handwriting, so Dad promised me Bertram Mills Circus if I got a Christmas term report which didn't mention bad handwriting. He was betting on it you see, and so was I. And I won. So I got to see Bertram Mills Circus at Olympia in its heyday. I was terrified! The clowns, the trapeze, the lions . . . Oh, Jesus . . . But I loved it too, and not so much for what it was but for it being the three of us on a family outing together. And another time we went Up to Town was to see Olivier's *Henry V* in the Leicester Square Odeon, but first we went to see the Crown Jewels . . .

In the Tower?

No. In an amusement arcade, penny in the slot machines, in Oxford Street . . .

There was this deep narrow arcade and at the back two amazing things. The first was a huge sculpture carved out of yellowish stone, *Jacob Wrestling with the Angel* by Jacob Epstein . . . I must be making this up. No. I think it was there because some pundit had said it was obscene and Epstein couldn't get it shown anywhere else. Something like that. Jacob did have a stylized prick and balls. And then behind the sculpture this wonderful cave of light, brighter than any artificial light I had ever seen before, filled with these marvellous jewels, the Crown Jewels. I was flabbergasted. Moved by the brightness and beauty. Filled with the glory of a to me then untarnished monarchy, an Empire whose rightness had never been questioned.

When we got back outside, into the fog and greasy dirtiness of an Oxford Street by no means recovered from six years of war, Dad could see the brightness in my eyes, the excitement that still tingled like electricity all through me and he felt forced to admit it . . .

What I had seen were replicas. Not the real thing at all. And with the bile of acute disappointment welling up in me I put on a cheap grin, as phoney as the jewels, and said, 'Yes, Dad, of course they are. I knew that.'

What was Mottingham like?

Awful. And after North Wales, hell. It was another pebble-dashed semi called, this time, The Rowans. But it only had one, one rowan, the other having been destroyed by the stick of bombs that had smashed a hundred yards of houses on the other side of the street. When we arrived they were a boarded-up row of ruins that smelt of damp, broken brickwork. Not completely destroyed however: you could see some rooms almost as Jerry had left them – flapping wallpaper, charred furniture. There was even a toilet with a cracked lavatory bowl exposed to the street – I thought that very rude.

Below our house there were drab allotments and then a small shopping parade. I remember queuing for potatoes there and being told by a cockney greengrocer that I had to take seven pounds; you always bought potatoes in multiples of seven because a quarter, a quarter of a hundredweight was twenty-eight pounds. The point was that I could hardly lift the bag once he'd filled it: I really was a very weedy lad.

There was also a toy shop where I bought balsa wood aeroplane kits: Spitfires, Hurricanes, Wellingtons, Heinkels, Messerschmitts and the dive-bombing Junker 87. Or was the dive-bomber the 88? They cost maybe half a crown and came with tiny tubs of enamel paint and tiny tubes of transparent glue which you closed with a pin. I can smell it all now, the paint and the glue, and indeed possibly, without knowing it, got a little high on them.

The balsa wood came part shaped; you had to finish it with a penknife, sandpaper and then paint. I loved it all, put them together very quickly, strung them with cotton and drawing-pinned them to the ceiling. You could do this easily because the ceiling was made out of composition material, Essex board, something of that sort, which was there instead of the plaster the bombs had brought down. And one day Dad said, 'Thomas, I am not going to let you buy any more of those kits until you make them properly.' Scales fell from eyes: I realized in a horribly painful flash of self-knowledge that I had been making them very badly, the knife marks still unsandpapered, the paint blotched so the raw wood showed through where I had not filled in the spaces between the green and brown of the camouflage. What had been magic was tawdry, as tawdry as the Crown Jewels.

Sorry, but I think I've got to go to the loo again.

Hang on. What else do you remember?

It was cold, cold and grey all the time. The Peace. People used to say, 'Don't you know there's a Peace on?' The only sun I remember was the summer of forty-seven, the holidays of which I spent in bed in a darkened room with measles. Seriously bad measles. Then we caught a coach to Bognor. I had never been on a coach before. We went by coach because we couldn't afford the train. And the reason we went to Bognor was so we could see the house my aunt was going to let us live in for virtually no rent. The Rowans had to be sold to pay off debts. My fucking school fees amongst them. The gambling must have come unstuck, or maybe they just weren't making enough. And it was the first day, towards the end of the summer of forty-seven, that it rained. God, how it rained. Oh yes. Round about then father had another crack at shooting himself but my mother persuaded him not to.

But he no longer had the Smith and Wesson.

No. But my cousin Graham, who had been in the Tank Regiment, brought back a tiny .22 German pistol with eight rounds of ammunition. And he gave it to his aunt, my mother. I don't know why, but he did. I've still got two of the bullets – I keep them in the silver cup Dad won at Wadham.

What happened to the pistol?

A few years later Mother shot a blackbird with it. It was eating her raspberries and she just meant to scare it, but from ten yards or more, firing through the open kitchen window, she took its head off. Some time later Dad stuck it in the waistband of his bathers and swam out as far as he could at low tide and dumped it. I really do have to go to the loo now.

Eight o'clock. Thomas again made it to the tiny cupboard of a loo. More blood, a lot of pain and a lot of shit, a bucketful.

'Are you all right?' Katherine asked, as he got back into bed.

'Fine,' he lied.

Before breakfast they took his temperature: Moni and Katherine. Normal.

'I'll come to the beach with you.'

'Good.'

But after he had had a cup of tea and a madeleine he felt awful again and went back to bed. Katherine took the children to the beach. Moni said she had letters to write and stayed behind.

Thomas slept.

18

He woke at twenty to twelve needing a wee. There was more on the way, but just for the moment the wee was enough. He went into the kitchen wondering if he could find a beer or a wine, or even get at the Carpano on the cabinet in the living room. But he could see Moni, first through the glazed double doors, then through the open patio windows beyond. She was sitting at the long table on the veranda reading the paper, half in sunlight, half in shade, with the cypress dark behind her. Framed by the doors she made a picture – quite an ordinary picture, unless you were Monet, but beautiful. He wondered at his lack of desire for her. Not that he would have attempted to exploit the situation even if there had been any. Yet it seemed sad that there was none. Old? Ill? Fat?

Nevertheless he was touched, touched by the ephemerality of the scene, the way its unimportant perfection was of its own kind, unrepeatable, and that he was the only person who saw it, or even knew of it.

His slightly naughty desire to scrump alcohol forgotten he got back into bed, picked up *Wellington's War*. The chapter was called 'Apotheosis of Our Hero'. Thomas wondered why. He couldn't recall any really notable victory between Vitoria and Toulouse – which was a year later. But there was a map on the facing page which quickened his interest. Bayonne and Biarritz itself featured at the top, and Pamplona at the bottom. He began to read . . .

Finding the enemy had already advanced so far upon their march as to render it impossible for me to cut them off at Jaca . . .

Jaca! Lovely town filled with lovely memories for Katherine

and him. It was still their aim, his anyway, that they would get there from Pau on 31 August, the fatal day . . . He read on:

I discontinued the pursuit with the allied British and Portuguese troops; and they are on their return to Pamplona . . .

The story unfolded – a melodrama, tragedy averted but only just. The British generals Cole and Picton withdrew from the Pyrenees in the face of double their numbers, but they went too far, back to a position on a hill just north of Pamplona above a village called Sorauren. Too far, because if they were now defeated the British centre would be exposed, Pamplona relieved, the siege of San Sebastian on the north coast raised and Wellington would have to go right back to the Ebro to regroup. But Wellington himself came literally galloping to the rescue and saved the day.

Letting the fat paperback fall forward from his knees and on to his chest he realized again what a fine thing it would be, what a fine thing indeed, to walk over those passes and down the valleys, taking in the major battlefields, especially Sorauren.

Shortly after twelve thunder rumbled in the distance, somehow reinforcing his daydream. Then much nearer, an ambulance sounded its two-note siren – the third he'd heard during the morning. Cooking smells drifted in and made him feel hungry for the first time since *la grande bouffe*. Some of them came from Moni's kitchen – he could hear her moving about and he wondered if he should get up and offer to help. But really all he could think of was how he wanted to go to Sorauren, and perhaps on to Pamplona.

'Daddy, Daddeee, Richard got whistled by the lifeguard. Bad Richie!'

'Oh, Hannah-Rosa, do shut up.'

'No, tell me all about it.'

'How are you feeling, love, any better?'

'Yes, I am actually. In fact if you all get out I'll get up. But first tell me about Richard and the lifeguard.'

'Well, there was quite a big swell today, and high surf, and they wouldn't let anyone swim out with body-boards unless they had flippers. So we had to get him some.'

'What a con. I bet they're in league with the surf shops.'

'No, Dad. I don't think so. It really was much better and safer with flippers.'

'But we've got at least three pairs at home . . . '

'And a fat lot of use they are there. Look, don't go on about it. We've got them, Richard needed them, end of story.'

Thomas took a deep breath. She'd got close to going over the top. Should he take it further? Better not. Not much point really. He let the breath out.

They ate lunch on the veranda. It was warm, even hot, though only intermittently sunny. Up in the mountains thunder continued to rumble. Lunch was not a success, not for Katherine anyway. All right, the French always undercook meat . . . but pink pork? In hot thundery weather? And cauliflower?

While Moni was in the kitchen all three of them tried to offload the offensive stuff on to Thomas's plate.

'She knows we can't eat cooked green vegetables.'

'I expect that's why she's taken all the leaves off.'

'It's still cauliflower.'

'I know that. But she probably thought it was all right without the leaves.'

'You could have told her.'

'How should I know she was cooking cauliflower?'

'You must have smelt it. I did.'

Later, while Katherine was washing up and he was drying, she asked, 'Are you coming to the beach this afternoon?'

'I'd rather not. I don't think I'm quite up to it yet.'

'I wish you would.'

'Why?'

'It's the walk. It takes nearly half an hour coming back up the hill. And carrying all the gear too.'

'You could take the car.'

'Moni says it's impossible to park.'

'We'll go in our car.'

'No. If you don't feel up to it, you'd better stay here.'

'All right. But I'll buy and cook supper.'

'Daddy, can we have lasagne?'

'Maybe. Spaghetti bolognese anyway.'

'Well,' said Katherine, 'go easy on the garlic.'

Christ, why is she so bloody edgy, niggly?

Almost as soon as they had gone he went back to the toilet and produced a huge, loud, explosive fart. It was as if he had blown out a cork. And floating on the surface of the bloodstained water was a dollop of white mucus, about the size of a half-crown, and a small turd. Again it frightened him, but at the same time he felt a lightening, a normality in his colon. Perhaps, he thought, things are working themselves out. Through and out.

First he checked what Moni had in her cupboards, then crossed the road to the scruffy, run-down grocer/greengrocer, almost opposite the driveway to the flats. He bought a kilo of tired-looking mince, soft onions, tomato purée in a can, Knorr stock cubes and some *fromage rapé*. Then a bottle of Jurançon for the ladies and Tursan rouge for him. Two-twenty francs, twenty-five quid! As he set about making a bolognese sauce he remembered that awful day in early September 1947.

Back in those days, during the summer holidays, thousands of coaches, charabancs, sharrabanks or 'sharras', headed out of London for the South Coast every day of the week loaded with daytrippers. Thomas didn't realize it at the time but it was the cheapest way to get there. They took an ordinary bus to Bromley and caught the sharra on a bomb-site near Bromley bus station. It was already raining.

The sharra itself was a surprise to Thomas, used to London Transport and the slatted wooden benches of the trams. It was new, gleamed with masses of chrome runners and fairings, had even a gesture at tail fins. On the inside the bench seats were soft with new Dunlopillo, and upholstered in deep-pile moquette – indeed, he reflected in Biarritz nearly half a century later, it was probably a sight more comfortable than a modern coach for all their crass attempts to emulate economy class on an aeroplane.

They sat in the back half and were soon surrounded by a warm acrid fug of tobacco smoke. Dad and Mum were sullen, reticent. He didn't know why. The trip had been presented to him as 'a bit of a day out and we'll have a look at this house your aunt Helen's got. If we like it we might move there.' Baffled by a sense of their misgivings and defeat, he rubber-nosed the window for the whole trip. It soon steamed up but he wiped it clear with his handkerchief and watched the raindrops stream horizontally across the glass as they went through bombed south London, then the leafier and less damaged suburbs of Croydon, Carshalton, Sutton, Leatherhead, Dorking, and so into the rolling downland of Surrey and Sussex.

In those days there were woods and hedges, the roads were narrow, dual-carriageways and bypasses for the most part still to come. Orchards, the trees laden with apples and pears, filled spaces later given over to prairie farming and industrial estates. Men on ladders dropped the fruit into blankets or sheets held by the women below. As well as orchards there were countless market gardens filled with vegetables and flowers for cutting. In the fields the cows were chestnut, yellow, all black and all white as well as just black and white. There were hops on canes and strings, eight feet high. The people who worked the fields lived in tied flintstone cottages in tidy villages clustering round pond, pub and church. They still, in 1947, drank cider with Rosie and went with Denis Potter to village schools run by dragonesses. Maybe, thought Thomas in Biarritz, they had straw in their mouths and wore smocks decorated with cross-stitching across their chests. Maybe not. Anyway, since it was chucking it down they were all indoors and not picking apples at all.

At the east end of Bognor prom, where Butlins is now, there was a huge sharra park already half-filled. With a couple of hundred other trippers, they had to walk into the town along the prom. To the left the grey heaving sea, to the right terraces of four- and five-storey hotels and guest houses, one lot set in a magnificent mid-Victorian crescent, then two hundred yards of amusement arcades. These were already caves of light and delight, bright lights, crushed humanity smelling of wet clothes, south London determined to have a good time in spite of the rain. Thomas would have liked to join them; after all, it was meant to be a bit of a day out.

'Not yet. First we have to catch another bus to see this house.'

Almost in front of the pier they turned up a narrow side-street past W. Jones's Garage, with its art-deco forecourt, and Gough Bros the art shop. Thomas wanted to visit the pier. It was splendid with square twin towers, two live theatres, tea-rooms, licensed bars and a diddy railway to take you to the silvery band-stand at the end. Campbell steamers for daytrips to the Island, speedboats to take you on daredevil spins, and men in old-fashioned swimsuits who set light to themselves and dived into the water. But not then, not on that wet, dull day they first came to Bognor Regis.

Picture them as they left the prom where the brass band did not play tiddly-om-pom-pom: Dad, thin, tall, still dark, baggy eyes tired, worried, in a grey trilby with a broad black band, a grey beltless mac that came lower than his knees, his demob suit whose turn-ups were already frayed above black, cracked, down-at-heel shoes; Mother with a scarf over her head, a mac over a bottle-green suit, lisle stockings and sensible shoes; and Thomas, the smartest of the three, that's where what money there was went, in a new dark blue mackintosh, a school cap with a pale blue Maltese cross for badge, and The Links school tie, grey jacket, grey shorts, grey socks, all good quality, and shoes that kept the wet out.

The bus station was art deco too: glazed cream and green tiles, every corner rounded, curved metal-framed windows almost filling each floor fronting a big hangar where the double- and single-deckers rumbled in and out at the rate of at least one a minute, or trundled through to the big yard beyond. They were to live in Bognor until Thomas went away for good twelve years later and were carless for almost the whole time. That bus station became very familiar. Gone now. Of course.

Dad made enquiries at the big semicircular counter and then took Thomas up the curved shallow stairs to the cantilevered gallery on the first floor and a huge Gents. Big porcelain urinals with gleaming brass and copper pipes and outlets polished till they shone like gold. Well, the gold of the Oxford Street Crown Jewels.

'Wise man when he can,' Dad said. 'Fool when he must.'

He always said that when they shared a Gents, just as on the London Underground he always said, 'Thomas – one word of wisdom which will never let you down: "Follow the green light for Victoria, and you can't go wrong".' Little square lights on the ceilings of the passages at Charing Cross, now renamed Embankment while Charing Cross itself has moved up to where Strand used to be . . .

Follow the green lights. But they've gone, along with most other moral certainties.

And, Thomas in Biarritz discovered, there's no nutmeg, and no lemon. Just as well, perhaps. Few people understood why he always put a zest cut from a lemon in spag bol. One day, in the future, perhaps the not too distant future, they'd say to each other: 'And do you remember how you always found a slice of cooked lemon peel in the bolognese? Why did he *do* that?'

19

I suppose, thought Thomas, as he ground in extra black pepper to make up for the lack of nutmeg, that was about the most important day of my life. Katherine's life too. Though she was still nearly six years off being born. And, of course, Richard and Hannah-Rosa owe their existence to it. Supposing Mother's objections to Seventy-One Fairway had carried the day (and there were lots of other 'ifs' as well, but one will do), then we should not have gone to live near Bognor, I should not have taken a job there twenty-six years later to be close to my mother, I should not have met Katherine . . .

What's all this 'should' stuff. Most people would say 'would'.

The best people, writing or speaking in the first person singular or plural, use 'should'.

Not any more they don't.

There are not many best people left.

Moni has dried basil which is virtually useless, like chucking in tiny shreds of green paper. But *faute de mieux* . . .

Do the best people say 'chucked'?

Seventy-One Fairway was, in retrospect, the oddest dwelling in the oddest place. But a twelve-year-old is still young enough to find amost everything new odd, and therefore everything odd normal. First though they had to take the 55 bus to the end of Barrack Lane and then walk the length of Fairway, Aldwick Bay Estate. The creation of a Captain Galway MC, who had dreamt it up as a way of fighting off madness in the trenches, the Bay Estate was to be the perfect environment for the well-to-do and even rich. There were two flint gate-posts and a barrier, only lowered once a year to reassert its legal status as private, residents only. Thomas wondered – we're not residents yet, are we allowed? There were palm trees and other exotics. The first houses the three of them walked past, looking wonderingly about them, were very large and in different styles: Georgian, Tudor, seaside art deco. There were two islands on the way, planted with shrubs and trees which cars had to drive round but which you could walk or bike through.

At the far end of Fairway the houses were smaller but still extraordinary. Seventy-One was the last, with fields in front and to the side. A vacant lot, waist-high in grass, went with it. It had the high gables and low eaves of a fairy-tale cottage and a balcony above a veranda framed by timber beams and supports.

A dark sullen lady welcomed them. Sullen? Well, she faced eviction. Thomas lagged behind as she showed them round. It was bigger than it looked from the outside. Downstairs there was a sitting room and a dining room both with french windows on to the veranda. The furniture was either thirties oak from Heal's or turn-of-the-century from Grandad's house. There was a glazed cabinet filled with Aunt Helen's treasures: Venetian glass, pottery and copperwork from Morocco and Turkey, knick-knacks from all over – a plastercast copy of *Head of a Roman Boy* and an Egyptian cat from the British Museum, Nefertiti from Berlin. And lots of pieces from the Della Robbia pottery in Birkenhead, the work of a distant cousin on the Tate side of the family.

There was a small bedroom downstairs and a vast kitchen with an Aga coal-fired range and a walk-in larder. Upstairs three more bedrooms, the one in front with twin beds. The one at the back was light and airy and had a single, but large and very comfortable bed. The middle one was a bit poky. They all had washbasins, a luxury Thomas had never seen before except on the two or three occasions he had stayed in a hotel.

Some of the furniture was really very odd even to a twelve-year-old: a low chair with low arms was described as a nursing chair, designed for easy breast-feeding. Thomas did not know what breast-feeding was. There were bedside tables on wheels with adjustable tops that could be placed over the beds. There were several basins, kidney-shaped dishes and buckets made out of enamelled iron. And so on. Eventually, but certainly not on that first day, it was explained to him. Aunt Helen, who owned and ran the Blackheath maternity home where he was born, had bought this as a refuge to which she could send unmarried mothers with their new babies until they could be found a secure and friendly place to go to, and also mothers whose husbands beat them.

She was an extraordinary woman this aunt Helen. In 1914 she had become engaged to a man who was killed in the first Battle of the Somme. She remained loyal to his memory for the fifty-five years she still had to live. She had already trained as a nurse and worked as such all through the war. As soon as the war was over she travelled: North Africa, Venice and later Germany – who knew where else? She reached Istanbul where, for a time, she took a post as nanny to a diplomat's family. In the early thirties she set up the maternity home where the clients were billed absolutely according to their means and by no other criteria. Since she was an excellent midwife and a brilliant organizer the whole business flourished to the benefit of all who worked there or used it.

Then it was bombed.

She sold the ruin and reopened in the Lake District, where she also looked after her ageing mum, Granny Somers. However, she still had two houses on her hands, one in Blackheath and this one, four miles from Bognor. She had already virtually given the London one to Uncle Wilf and now she was willing to let the Bognor one to Thomas's father for a nominal rent. That is if Decima, still in law no more than Pop's concubine, agreed.

As they walked back through the rain to the bus stop Thomas realized it was not certain she would.

'It's so dark. It's such a dark house.'

'Anywhere would be dark on a day like this.'

'And all that stuff . . . She said I must look after it all for her. That's right, isn't it?'

'Some of it's very good. There are some very good pieces there.'

Not naice. Good.

'But we've already got all the furniture we need. What will we do with our things?'

'We'll have to sell them. With the house.'

He meant The Rowans in Mottingham.

'But they're *my* things. And if we ever want to move again, we won't have any furniture of our own, so we won't be able to. We'll be stuck there for ever.'

Thomas heard the tears in her voice, though she pretended the actual tears were rain. He felt the great blanket of despair that each of his parents wore over their shoulders, but two separate blankets. She did not want to live in a house charitably made available by a sister-out-of-law who looked down on her; she did not want to be caretaker and custodian for a load of things that she had never even seen before, let alone chosen. She did not want to lose the furniture, pictures and so on that she had chosen and bought with what little money she had ever had of her own.

And Dad. The only way he could get out of debt, escape the writs and summonses that were already fluttering in like confetti was to sell up in London, take his sister's house, and get a job . . . as a preparatory-school usher.

They faced each other at the bus stop. Thomas looked around, tried to move himself psychically away from the blackness. It was where the 55 terminated: a gravelly space just big enough for a double-decker to turn. On one side a high hedge filled with ivy already bobbled with flowers flanked a track which led first to a shed then to a large but run-down house with a market garden around it. On the other side there was a brook and a strip of uncultivated land, woodland really, between it and the road that led to the sea and, if you took a right turn, the Bay Estate. The whole area was overhung with giant elms, long since gone, through which the rain then wept. In spring there would be primroses and violets, in early summer, bluebells. And in the middle of it all a shack with a counter that sold cheap sweets, cigarettes, soft drinks and vegetables from the market garden. Miss Newport's. Already forty or more she had iron-grey hair, a gypsyish face and a sharp wit. They would get to know her well by sight, though they were never properly acquainted. For a shilling a week she let you park your bike in a shed so you didn't have to walk the length of Fairway and then some to catch the bus.

It occurred to Thomas now, stirring the pot and adding more tomato purée, that Miss Newport must have been some sort of proto-crypto hippie.

'There's no other way?' Mum. But it was hardly a question. She knew she was stuck with it.

'Not on the horizon.' Dad.

'All right. If we have to do it, we'll do it. But if it was going to happen anyway, I don't know why we had to make this trip.'

'Your idea. You wanted to see the place before—'

'Oh, please be quiet.'

The bus arrived. They went upstairs so they could smoke. Thomas sat with Dad over the driver's cab. Mum sat on the other side. She looked out of the window away from them and let the tears flow with the rain that streaked the glass and Dad felt awful and so did Thomas, though he was not too sure why he should feel bad.

Mother turned, looked over her shoulder at them.

'I shan't be able to keep all that clean. Not on my own. Not without a woman.'

No washing-machines then. No dishwashers. A hand-powered Ewbank carpet-sweeper. The only polishes were beeswax, no aerosols, no spray-on/wipe-off. And there were a lot of polished surfaces in that house. The tiled floor of the kitchen would be scrubbed with a big bristled brush, using a block of yellow domestic soap. There were no detergents – only soap-flakes that left a grey scum round the basin. The Aga had to be cleaned out of clinker; fuel, coke for the Aga and anthracite for the sitting room fire, had to be carried in from the bunkers twice a day and the dust of ashes settled over everything. There were a lot of brasses too, and, Thomas reflected, that's about the only area which has not been new-ed and improved. Brasso remains much what it always was. And quite a bit of the brass still cluttered his and Katherine's home.

In Bognor they still had three hours before the sharra would take them back to Bromley. They had pie and boiled potatoes in a tiny café next to Gough Bros and then drifted to the prom. The after-lunch pubs were turning out and the amusement arcades were packed. Dad, no doubt feeling that there was light at the end of the tunnel, got a pound changed into real pennies (two hundred and forty of them) and they had a wonderful time. Shuddering with fear, which mysteriously transferred itself to his groin, Thomas spent five of the pennies one after another watching tiny automata chop the head off Mary Queen of Scots, again and again and again. He did not see What the Butler Saw because Dad told him not to. He won two cigarettes on a crane thing in a glass box that sank silver claws into all sorts of treasure and dropped them into a drawer. He gave them to his mother and she cheered up a bit. He rolled pennies which, if they didn't cross the lines when they fell flat, won up to six back. Everything in those days was twos, threes, fours, sixes or twelves, never fives or tens. The trippers all smelt of beer and fish and chips.

His parents sat next to each other on high stools and rolled balls up boards so they would drop in numbered holes. The balls landed on switches which powered wooden horses to move the number of lengths designated by the numbered holes. There was some skill involved and often they won against the other six players.

On the sharra the Londoners were all happy. The rain had not spoiled their day at all. They sang 'My Old Man', 'Tipperary' and 'Roll Out The Barrel'. They sang 'Lili Marlene'. And they sang 'There'll Be Bluebirds Over The White Cliffs Of Dover'.

Katherine was in a seriously bad mood, almost a temper, when they came back. It had been a really hot day, the beach had been very crowded and Moni had spent most of the time chatting to friends of her parents. Thomas got the message: he was to be ill no longer.

'The walk back was a killer. I'm not doing it again.'

So either he was on sole beach duty the next day or they were to take the car.

He dished up the spaghetti bolognese. Everyone liked it, Hannah-Rosa especially. They stayed up late drinking the wine and watching a performance of *La Flute Enchantée* on the telly. It was a live performance from some festival. Thomas wanted to stay up at least until the Queen of the Night had done her coloratura bit and that meant sitting through a long interval filled with interviews – the conductor, the director, members of the audience. During it Thomas went to the toilet. Toil, sweat, blood and tears. He took a couple of aspirin and codeine.

The Queen of the Night was perfect – much better than anything that had come before: the sets had been modern, not post-modern, but brutal modern and on the cheap, the singing competent but not particularly great. But the Queen of the Night was good – a kid listening to her slagging-off dad as a murderous brute would happily go along with her interpretation of events.

They went to bed. Thomas dreamt. He had to enter a cave. Swags of moss hung from the rocky roof, between the stalagmites and stalactites. But no . . . not moss but the skins of flayed poets. Then there were bones and skeletons instead of skins. They rattled and chimed in a cold breeze that wafted in from the outer air behind him. A voice told him that the rock was, of course, volcanic. He was surprised that there were no spiders, but then perhaps the flayed skins had not been skins and the moss not moss, but spiders' webs. And then a light grew and out of it came Katherine. She was wearing a nightie or shift or some such. She seemed bigger than he was. She took his uplifted face in her hands and began to kiss him. Again and again and lingering more and more. Then she put his head between her breasts and stroked his hair.

He woke. With an erection – and that pleased him. As usual she had her back to him. He pulled in closer, shifted her nightie up her thighs, and caressed her flanks. He wondered if she could feel the erection. If she did, she gave no sign that she had, and presently he slept again, dreamlessly and deeply.

20

He woke at nine and felt fine. Admittedly a loud fart in the loo released a tablespoonful of blood, but it was bright red which meant, he was almost sure, that it was from the very lowest reaches and probably still the result of the wound created by the razor-bladed turd, or the passing of the coin-sized mucus. If it was further back it would have had time to turn darker, even black. What he was really saying to himself was: this is not cancer or disintegration of the lower bowel, what is happening is that the wound is really an external wound – after all, at what point do you think of your body as having an inside and an outside? Is it an outside turned in or an inside turned out? Think of simple organisms like the hydra. Doesn't work for most of the youman body, but, yes, for the very lowest bowel. Surely. Don't call me Shirley.

He took Richard and Hannah-Rosa down to the beach on his own and on foot. He liked Biarritz. A sort of successful Bognor. Bournemouth really, but with warm sea. The main beach was a wide bay with a rocky island or two in the middle. Behind the beach were the casino and the Grand Hotel which had once been Napoleon III's summer palace.

Richard went off with the body-board – the surf was not high and there were few surfers, so Thomas reckoned he needn't keep more than a perfunctory eye on him. Instead he helped Hannah-Rosa build a sand-castle, and then they decorated it with the smooth marble and agate pea-shingle they found along the high-tide mark, together with tiny pearly shells.

When that was finished they stood hand in hand in the sea and let the white foaming water surge round his thighs and her waist and watched Richard waiting for the big one. He rode it in, and for the last ten yards or so got on to one knee, with arms spread out as if he were flying. He even managed to jump off without falling over, just before the board grounded.

'You're a lot better at it than you were.'

The boy grinned and turned, striding back into the waves, happy as Larry.

Back on the rug Thomas pulled out his watercolours and the pad he'd bought in Angers and for once quite pleased himself with what he did – the rock and the lighthouse and a not bad impression of the surf between. Perhaps he'd work it up later in a second version with Richard holding his body-board in the foreground.

By midday it was hot and he realized he'd forgotten the sun lotions. He'd be in dead trouble if after all the care Katherine had taken he now let the children get burnt, so he called them in and they went up on to the terrace by the casino where he bought them ice-creams, while he had a beer. Actually two beers. In spite of the fact there were far fewer topless girls than there had been in Hossegor it was all very jolly and so he felt a touch bothered, even betrayed, when Richard, scraping out the end of his ice-cream, said, 'Mum says, when we go back to Hossegor, I ought to have a go on a proper surfboard. Pierre's got one that's small enough. He got it cheap for Jean-Luc but Jean-Luc's not big enough yet.'

'Then I can have the body-board instead of sharing the little one with Jean-Luc,' Hannah-Rosa added.

'But that's not the plan. Tomorrow we're going to stay in Pau for a few days, and go into Spain. That was the idea.'

'Mummy says it will be too hot away from the sea.'

Thomas's feelings about all this worsened as they made their way up the long though gentle hill back to the flat for lunch. Clearly a lot had been going on that he was not fully aware of. He hated changed plans and, more than that, he hated going back. They'd done Hossegor and the surfing at Seignosse. Been there, done that. And he felt another bout of daily barbecued meat in unacceptable quantities would probably just about do for him.

On the way back (past Rue Pringle, named after one of Wellington's generals – one of the many who settled in the area after the wars were over) he grumbled to himself that this was *his* holiday, to get him out of the bother and pain he had begun to feel at work: why shouldn't he do what *he* wanted?

He was ready to have it out but Katherine and Moni were already laying a lunch of cold meats and salads they had bought in the big Leclerc Hyper. And not only food . . .

'Daddy, look at my new plimsolls. We tried them on the other day, so we knew they'd fit.'

'Good aren't they,' Katherine added, standing behind Hannah-Rosa. 'She insisted on wearing them.'

'I'm not surprised. They're lovely.'

They were decorated with beads and sequins which sparkled when she moved as she did now in small unconsidered dance steps. He bit back the desire to ask how much they cost until, that is, they had had lunch.

Bayonne ham, foie gras, fresh baguettes, cold Landais chicken thighs, a mixed salad with vinaigrette prepared by Hannah-Rosa according to Moni's strict proportions: two of oil to one of vinegar, which Thomas felt was too much vinegar, but both Katherine and the children preferred to his over-oily mixture. Then he asked her.

'Oh, I forget. One forty-nine, something like that.'

Oh shit. Seventeen quid for plimsolls she'd not even be allowed to wear at school!

'Does it matter?' Katherine went on, making the question as militant as a challenge thrown down with a mailed gauntlet at a medieval tournament. He backed off.

'No, I suppose not.'

Moni came back from the kitchen with cheese – including black-rinded Pyrenean sheep's cheese at over one hundred francs a kilo.

'It's only money, after all. They weren't dear, those plimsolls, were they, Moni?'

'No, no. *Très bon marché.*'

The big department store in Liverpool had been called the Bon Marché. Bombed in the war.

'He's always on about how much things cost. I don't know why. I mean, he's not mean.'

'Older people are often like that . . . '

Ouch!

' . . . My parents too. They never throw anything away either. For instance there is right now enough bolognese sauce in my refrigerator to feed one not very hungry person. Why? Why not throw it away? I would, you would, but not Thomas.'

Thomas shrugged, beamed at them all, anxious not to let the good mood they were in drift into a bad one. But the images that flooded through his mind were answer enough. His mother, at Gable End, slicing green beans into earthenware jars and salting them down in layers so they'd still have a green vegetable other than cabbage at Christmas. Filling an enamelled bucket with a solution of brine (or was it isinglass?) and then lowering a wire cage filled with eggs into it. The eggs always came out tasting 'nesty' but could be used for cooking up to three months later. Milk-puddings because there was milk left over and no refrigerator. Bathwater four inches deep and always used twice. Bedrooms where the condensation froze in the night on the inside to match the frost on the outside. He could remember, almost with nostalgia, that very particular sort of light you got through windows triple glazed because of the ice.

And later, during the really bad time just after they had moved to the Bay Estate, both his parents shredding the tobacco from dog-ends to make roll-ups out of them in a gadget which had two rollers and a looped strip of thin rubber. Above all the constant refrain that had rung in his ears throughout the war, and on and on for ever after, amen: 'It's got to be finished up . . . it's too good to throw away.'

It was why every year, just as his mother had done, he made green tomato chutney, once the tomatoes stopped ripening, and brown sauce from the surplus plums. Mother though had bottled them – a tedious and expensive process nowadays involving Kilner jars and excessive use of fuel. He still went round the house turning off lights and verbally abusing the children who had left them on. He fumed at them for not practising the piano, not on the grounds that they might not be as good as they could be but because of the money laid out on a decent instrument (nearly a thousand pounds) and weekly lessons. He worked out minutely the balance between heating the house and water from oil and just heating the house but not the water from the wood-burning stove. He'd turned the heating off and on maybe three or four times a day when he was at home and refuse to light the wood-burner until all four of them were in the house and not likely to go out again.

In short: Blame Hitler.

But on the other side he was not, as Katherine had rightly said, mean. Like his dad he spent money when it was there with what his dad called 'careless abandon'. And not particularly on himself. Theatre tickets, concert tickets. Extravagant presents. Food and drink. Books, videos and CDs.

In short: Blame Dad.

The telephone rang. Moni went back through the french windows to answer it. Katherine and Thomas looked at each other across the table. He took a deep breath.

'We're meant to go to Pau tomorrow.'

'We're not *meant* to go anywhere. It's not a coach tour, you know? With a courier and a fixed timetable? If this is Biarritz it must be Sunday. If it's Monday it must be Pau.'

The children fell silent, a quick glance between them, then they looked at their plates. Richard looked up again, catching Thomas's eyes with a look that combined anticipation of pain with a plea that it might not happen. His parents did not row often any more but when they did it crucified him.

They listened to Moni's voice rattling on, nineteen to the dozen, then breathless pauses: '*Oooway, Oooway, d'accord.*'

The argot pronunciation of '*oui*' indicated she was talking to someone she had been a student with. '*Ooway, ooway, d'accord . . .*' then, in English, 'OK, I ask them. *Moment, moment!*'

She came back on to the veranda, face lit with expectation.

'It is Pierre. They want to come by this evening and then we all go on together to St Jean. There is a fête, not exactly *une fête* but every Sunday in the summer a good band in the *place*, it is very animated and jolly and first we could go to a restaurant. They have a babyseetair for Jean-Luc . . .'

'But we can all go? Richard and Hannah-Rosa too?'

As Thomas often did when faced with someone speaking emotionally in an accent, he felt himself slipping into the accent too – or rather a vaudeville send-up of it. He looked helplessly at Katherine – who nodded agreement.

Moni hesitated. Then shrugged, the way the French do.

'They planned you should share the babyseetair . . .'

'Back in Hossegor? I don't think so.' Katherine standing firm.

'But if you are going back there tomorrow anyway, why not? I'll drive them over if you like.'

A nonplussed moment.

A lot of thoughts can go through your head in a moment.

Thomas thought: this is a plot to ensure we all go back to Hossegor tomorrow.

Katherine, without actually believing it, sensed the possibility of the adults ending up back here at Biarritz in the early hours with no children in the way, drunk, and wondering how to end a wonderful evening . . . Not her scene.

Moni read a united front. It was something that had always puzzled her (and many of their English friends felt it too): how with Thomas and Katherine, Richard and Hannah-Rosa nearly always came along too.

'All right. I tell them.' Back on the phone: 'Pierre? *Ecoute* . . . !'

'Do you mind . . . ?' Katherine leant across the table towards Thomas. 'I didn't want them all that way away with a strange babysitter . . . I wouldn't have been able to enjoy myself.'

'Me neither,' Thomas murmured – though he suspected the babysitter would be Pierre's sister.

'It's settled then,' Moni cried, returning. 'They will come by at seven and we all go on to St Jean.'

Katherine thought. Then –

'Look. Can we go to St Jean now, and meet you there . . . at half-seven? Tell the truth, I've had enough of Biarritz *plage*.'

And so it was arranged. They'd meet in the square at St Jean at half-seven.

While she gathered together what they'd need for the rest of the afternoon, Thomas picked up a copy of the local freebie – *Sud-Ouest Dimanche*. There was a picture of the Pic du Midi d'Ossau on the back, the great tooth of a mountain on the Spanish border, due south from Pau. He'd been hoping they'd go for a walk in the mountains near it. They'd done some splendid, and terrifying, walks in the mountains during their year in Pau. Now it looked as if they might never get there.

He leafed through the rest of the paper and ... shit! The black French beret worn very straight, the tired, ill, gaunt face he had last seen six weeks earlier at a party given by his publisher. Though then the face had been even more cadaverous than it was in this photograph. Cassie. He read: *Ray Butcher est mort* ...

Shit.

He felt the presence of Katherine behind him.

'Ah,' she said. 'You found it.'

'You knew already. And you didn't tell me.'

'I didn't want to spoil things for you. I was going to tell you at the end of the day, or when nothing much else was going on.'

Shit.

'You know you were expecting it,' she went on. 'You told me how ill he was.'

Thomas felt his throat burn, his eyes prick. He swallowed hard.

'Fucking good bloke, though. Fucking good writer. Cassie. Shit.'

21

'We don't want Espagne, do we?'

Yes, we bloody do.

'No, keep to the coast road.'

Silence. Richard looked out of the window.

'He was only sixty-five.'

Mortality.

'And I'm nearly sixty.'

'Does that mean Daddy's going to die in five years' time?'

No worries there. Five years is a long way away when you're only ten.

'He drank continuously and chain-smoked.'

'And Daddy only drinks.'

Continuously.

Did he have high blood pressure? Did his bum bleed?

'There's a sign. Keep left. We'll soon be there.'

There is where we'll soon be, thought Thomas, with a heavy heart. But he cheered up when they caught a brief glimpse of the sea, the wide bay and the headlands.

St Jean-de-Luz. One of his favourite places and not least because of the light itself. Set in the very centre of the arc which turns the coast through ninety degrees from France into Spain, it fills a tongue of land at the mouth of the Nivelle. On the inland side of the tongue there is a small fishing port and marina, on the other side a wide egg-shaped bay a mile across and open to the ocean only through a gap between long moles with forts that double as lighthouses. The bay itself is therefore almost always calm and has a long sandy beach. The old town has narrow alleys which were once the homes of fishermen, boatbuilders, chandlers and the like, but are now boutiques, gift shops and cafés, punctuated by small palaces with a distinctive architecture that is not un-Venetian. Maurice Ravel lived in one of them.

That afternoon and early evening should have been the jolliest, happiest time of the whole trip – the only time, apart from the almost equally jolly spell in La Rochelle, when they were a family together with no one else around. And indeed, perhaps it was. Cassie's death added a bitter sharpness to the day, bitter but not distressed: if anything the knowledge that he had gone enhanced the joy and delight. If his ghost was with them and Thomas sensed he might be, he was saying as loudly and clearly as his grating, wine-and-Gauloises voice would allow, 'Have this one for me, Thomas, have this one for me. I shan't be having any more.'

They meandered through the alleys, had ice-creams and beers at the Madrid Café in the square. There was a big band-stand in the middle, large plane trees hung with lights, and a small selection of stalls, boarded up now, but later they would open into bright shallow caves selling crêpes, *gaufres*, *véritable nougat de Montélimar*, soft toys – the *sine qua nons* of a French fête. It all looked very promising. The beers were big, half-litres, and Thomas helped Katherine finish hers.

Then they strolled down to the quay and looked across the shimmering water towards *chez* Maurice. The light flashed on the ripples in front of it and lent it all a soft transience like the passing of music. Katherine found a public phone from which to call her office and check out that her friend was managing it without problems. She would not use Moni's phone, or Pierre's when they were in Hossegor, because she knew they would not let her pay.

While she was on the phone Thomas drew Richard's attention to La Grande Rhune, the conical hill, well, mountain really, at nearly three thousand feet, that lay eight miles or so to the south – the first pimple of the chain that climbs into the Pyrenees.

'Wellington fought a lot of small battles round here. One of them resulted in the capture of that hill.'

'Oh yes?'

'He used Spanish troops for it. They were our allies against the French.'

'I think Mummy's finished now.'

They spread themselves on the beach and for once all swam together. The water was warm and buoyant, turquoise on the ripply waves, shaded with mauve in between. The sun, dropping towards the left-hand mole a mile away became orange through the violet haze, and what had been a very hot day became pleasantly warm. The beach slowly emptied, leaving large spaces free around them.

'This is an awful lot better than Biarritz,' remarked Katherine, sitting up on the woven nylon rug and towelling the ends of hair she had managed for the most part to keep dry.

'Richard may be missing the surf.'

'I don't think so. Look at him.'

A quite large raft with a scaffolding diving board eight feet high had been anchored about a hundred metres or so out. Richard was jumping in off it, swimming round, hauling himself out, climbing the ladder and jumping in again.

'I think it belongs to one of those areas you have to pay to get into.'

To their right there were enclosures with games and beach toys, table-tennis tables, beach-huts or tents, volley-ball nets and so on.

'Well, if it does, no one seems to be bothered. I'm just going to tell Hannah-Rosa not to try swimming that far.'

She got up, and Thomas watched as she walked down to the edge of the water. If only it was always like this. His backside seemed a bit better too. The blood before lunch had been thicker and darker, which frightened him at first, but then he realized that it was a clot – the movement had shifted a clot from the wound, which meant presumably that it was trying to heal itself, not that it had travelled some way down the lower intestine. This self-diagnosis was borne out later, just before they left, when the blood had been bright red again. Always he removed every trace of what was going on from the bowl and checked that he wasn't leaking in between times: he still reckoned that the worst thing he could do was to put himself in the hands of French doctors. And since he seemed well enough in other respects he remained determined to keep it all to himself until they got home.

If they got home. If *he* got home. Even on the beach of St Jean-de-Luz his father, wearing a grey and stained trilby and a raincoat, pedalled the three miles down Barrack Lane and Aldwick Road through driving rain to get to the crummy prep school where he now taught maths and Latin. The fact of the matter was, Thomas realized, Dad had been a far better person than he ever was, had fought bad luck with real stoicism, constantly made sacrifices beyond, to use a favourite phrase of his, the call of duty. This discovery dawned on him like a huge rock slowly uncovered by a receding tide – it had been there all along and he shivered with awe as it broke the surface. He did not deserve to be older than his dad. There seemed indeed to be something almost obscene, however irrational, about the idea of being older than one's own dad. Suppose they met in a hereafter Thomas did not believe in, but anyway suppose, if he lived to be eighty he'd be twenty years older than his dad when he met him again. Not on.

Meanwhile Katherine and Hannah-Rosa walked along to the end of the quay where there were real rocks and stones alongside a slip-way. He knew they would be scouting through the tiny pools looking for sea anemones and shrimps. She loved all that, did Katherine, because that's what she used to do with her dad amongst the rocks to the west of Bognor, just when she was the same age as Hannah-Rosa was now.

Fathers.

He dragged Welly out of the big beach bag and turned to the very end of the book.

On the right, the troops of the army of reserve of Andalusia attacked the enemy's posts and entrenchments on the mountain of La Rhune in two columns, under the command of Spaniards only . . .

He looked up again and around. Perhaps Katherine was right. What was he reading this stuff for? Why was he doing it?

Le Patio (sic) turned out to be splendid. An old converted Basque house with a stone ground floor and timbered first floor with deep eaves, it was crowded and full of *animation*. They were asked to go upstairs, where tables were pushed together to accommodate them all, and the waitress, a stunningly beautiful young girl with a low-cut tight black top that showed a lot of creamy cleavage, brought huge flagons, two-litre carafes of house white, fruity, dry and so cold that the glass frosted up even as she put them on the table. They were a big party – Thérèse and her boyfriend Norbert had come too, so there were seven adults and two children. They almost all ordered fish in some form or other; most of them having paella, though Richard had fresh grilled sardines – six of them – and, since fishfingers were not on the menu, Hannah-Rosa had *haché* . . . again.

Thomas looked at the menu.

'What's *bar*?' he asked. It was the most expensive item.

The French went into a long discussion about what *un bar* was. The final consensus was sea-bass.

'I'll have that.'

Katherine looked up from her menu.

'In that case,' she said, 'I'll have the lobster.'

The service was slow, the place crowded, they drank too much. Well, Thomas did, starting with a surreptitious libation for Cassie.

As usual in such circumstances he had manoeuvred himself to the end corner of the table so his deaf side was by a small window open to the street below, with Elvira on his right. In front of him, above Moni's head, was a handsome reproduction of Van Gogh's *Irises* nicely framed in plain black wood with a thin gold mount, and near it a crude still life of which a central feature was a woven basket. The basketwork had been done in broad brushstrokes slashed across each other to suggest the interweaving of the straw. Since Elvira was rattling away in French to Katherine, who was opposite her with Hannah-Rosa between her and Moni, and Moni opposite him was quizzing Hannah-Rosa about how they'd spent the afternoon, he allowed himself a reverie about these pictures.

Which was more real? Clearly the irises were, even though Vincent had made no attempt to disguise the fact that what you are looking at is paint. He also used bold dark contour lines which had no basis in what he could see. So why were the irises so much better? The basketwork. If, the painter had said to himself, I push paint over the paint I have already put there, so the bristles of the brush drag it crosswise across, then that will say to the viewer – basketwork! And many, many people will feel rewarded because they have read the code.

Cassie, Ray Butcher, wrote like Van Gogh. Dark contours but never code, always the real thing, the darkest places in the human soul.

The nubile goddess took away an empty vessel and replaced it with a full one. For a moment those creamy mounds, they really were creamy, just a hint of yellow in the skin and a surface somewhere between matt and silk, divided by the beginnings of a dark valley of delight, were within inches, well, a foot or so, of his face. He wondered: were her nipples brownish or pink? He settled for a brownish brick-red, then dragged his finger through the tiny beads of moisture that frosted the curving glass and felt a sunburst of euphoria: the bright lights, the dark corners, the pale topaz of the wine, the perfumes of women and their breasts. He recognized that he was obsessed with breasts, an obsession that had grown over the years, when really it ought to have got less.

Which was the Truffaut film with that immortal line? Two blokes, middle-aged to elderly, and one says to the other, 'If I had breasts I'd fondle them all the time.' One of the Doinel films, perhaps *Baisers Volés*, though it was not one of Jean-Pierre Léaud's lines.

Elvira put her thin small hand over the back of his. Oh dear!

'You are very quiet, Thomas.'

'I was thinking of my favourite moments in cinema. Running through them, one by one.'

'Which one was in your mind just then?'

'A Truffaut film . . . '

'*J'adore Truffaut.*'

The full French 'r', not rolled as Béarnaise Moni rolled them, but coming from the back of a throat that has to be seasoned in Gauloises for a century or so to get it just right.

'And I know which one. *Le moment exact!*'

'You do?' My God, she probably does.

'The old man who says if I had bosoms I would caress them all day.'

Jesus!

'How did you know that?'

'The way you looked at the waitress.'

It was that obvious? He glanced across the table. Had Katherine heard? She was smiling sweetly, not always a good sign, so probably she had. He looked down at the plate which had at last arrived in front of him. Head-on sea-bass, the king of fish, but eyes chalky, so perhaps overdone. Chalky and dead. He rushed on.

'Another great moment is when the severed leg drops through the hole in the submerged boat in *Jaws*. We actually saw that in Pau in seventy-six. The whole audience gasped.'

'And the week after,' Katherine leant across the table, from the far side of Hannah-Rosa, fork upraised, with a pink pizzle of coral from a lobster claw on the end, the candlelight from a wax-encrusted bottle playing on her face, 'we saw that early Dépardieu film where he cuts his willy off with a Moulinex electric carver.'

Ouch! Pause.

'And is that your favourite moment in cinema?' Elvira was sly, probing.

Katherine's smile became broader.

'Perhaps!'

And she popped the fishy morsel in her mouth.

Presently Hannah-Rosa got up from her place between Moni and Katherine, who had returned to talking, literally though perhaps not metaphorically, over her head and came and sat on his knee.

'That burger,' she whispered in his ear so her breath tickled, 'was so bloody I thought it was alive.'

'Did you eat it?'

'No way! Only the black and brown bits on the outside. I ate the chips though.'

Vive la belle France et les pommes frites.

'She ate hardly any of the beefburger,' Katherine breaking off her conversation with Moni.

'She just told me. A touch rare. It doesn't matter.'

'I know it doesn't matter. I was just telling you.'

Women, his dad once told him, go through difficult spells at times. Not their fault. Your ma's a bit like that at the moment. It'll blow over though. It always does.

Now this was really strange. For surely he'd been talking about menstruation. PMT and all that. Yet Thomas's recollection was that this conversation had taken place in 1950 or 1951 by when Mother would have been fifty-two or fifty-three. The thing was Dad probably did not know that she had already gone through 'the change'. The mood swings he was explaining away were almost certainly the result of advanced pulmonary TB.

And now, it occurred to Thomas, here in St Jean-de-Luz and having not a whale but certainly a sea-bass of a time, Katherine might well be in the throes of PMT. When had she last had a period? He had no idea. A pretty pass. Things have come to a pretty pass when a bloke no longer knows, no longer *needs* to know when his wife is due . . . He reached for his glass.

'Da-ad!'

'Yes?'

'Please don't drink continuously. Like the man's who's dead.'

She looked down at the street below, wriggled on his knees. So she does care.

'Where are all those people going?'

'To the fête perhaps. The square, the dance place.'

'Then why aren't we going?'

'We will, we will. I need a wee.'

He shunted her off his knees and found his way to a Gents. He unzipped, peed. You'd need a pretty skilful butcher to get

159

that off with a Moulinex, he thought. A surgeon with a scalpel might manage. I just farted. Have I bled? Not enough to be seriously aware that I have. He zipped, set himself on course.

On the landing above the staircase there was another print. And this one was very familiar, they had it hanging in their downstairs bathroom back home in England – a Degas pastel of a red-headed woman hunkered down in a shallow blue-black enamel bath, sponging the back of her head.

Revelation: the whole point of mimesis *and* the role of the artist. Just like that. *She* was real. There really was a moment in time when a real woman crouched in her bath, just as she does in these magic pastels. This was no pretence, or fantasy. This was not imagination or madness. This happened.

Fair enough, but so what?

Don't you see? The significance of all this is what is not there – the presence of the artist himself. She was there, but so was Degas! And he took endless pains, using not only his own skills but centuries of perception and technique, right back to Giotto and beyond, to get her down on paper, to present to us her reality. And he does it so well we know she was real. It's the interplay of the two realities . . .

I'm not sure I follow you. I think you've maybe had a tad too much to drink.

No, no, no, NO. It's the fact and the image, merging, mixing, shifting, interpenetrating each other that justify him, don't you understand, he has put on record *his* ability to be there and see.

I'm going to say it again. So what?

It's the whole humanist tradition, the right of every human to exist and be in their own space, their own individuality, it gives the lie to all totalitarianism, to all rule, bossiness, intervention, it gives substance and importance to the flesh, it shows us how flesh and spirit are indivisible and holy, it shows us that there is only one morality, only one political agenda . . .

Which is?

Act in such a way that the principle upon which your action is based may be made a principle of universal action.

Kant.

Do unto others as you would have them do unto you.

Jesus!

Kropotkin too.

'Hi, Richard. Having a good time?'

'Yes thanks.'

'The loo's at the end of the corridor.'

'I know. I went earlier. Mum saw you here and told me to tell you we're going quite soon. Coffee in the square.'

'Fine.'

'And she thinks we should pay.'

'For everybody?'

'Because they've all been feeding us all the time and all that.'

Nearly forty quid for that pot plant we gave Elvira. More than a gesture, surely . . .

Don't call me . . . Never mind.

'Yes. I'm sure she's right.'

'So she says why don't you get the bill now, and pay it, then they can't argue.'

'Good call.'

Richard winced, aware that his Dad was teasing him by using *Wayne's World* speak.

In fact Thomas was pleased. The theatricality of the gesture. He went downstairs to where the manageress or owner presided over a computerized till. Reading off the scrawled order sheet the waitress had stuck on a nail on a board behind her, she fed into it the items they had had one by one and it seemed to go on for ever. Well it would, wouldn't it? Nine of them, say three items each? His heart began to sink again. This was surely a touch Quixotic. Timon in his heyday, entertaining the freeloaders of Athens? One thousand two hundred and seventy-three francs. And they'd only had three of those flagons of wine – he had expected there to be twice that number on the bill, he reckoned he'd had most of a whole one to himself. So, about sixteen quid each – for a fish supper in a tolerably posh restaurant, in a tolerably posh resort, in France. Not bad.

'*Servis inclus?*'

'Oui, monsieur.'
'Prenez-vous Visa?'
'Oui, monsieur.'
That's all right then.

A gesture which worked. For at least ten minutes he was the
hero of the hour. They promised they'd pay for the coffees. And
a brandy, he said to himself. Brandy for heroes.

22

Spread out across the street and broken up in shifting groups they made their way beneath fairy-lights down the main drag to the square. It felt, Thomas thought, like the still from *Reservoir Dogs*, the famous one that isn't actually in the film itself. Hannah-Rosa spoilt the Tarantinoesque illusion that they were all on their way to a jewellery heist but made him even happier by taking his hand.

'It's going to be ages before we get to bed. Will it be the latest ever?'

'Maybe.'

They passed a street vendor who carried a big tray filled with tropical colours.

'Oh, Daddy, can I have one? I do want one.'

'Want what? Oh. I see. Parrots.'

They were birds made out of paper-thin plastic and card on a simple wire frame, with wind-up elastic that drove the wings and made them fly. To the innocent they were magic. I should, Thomas thought, buy the trayful, let us all have one, so we can fly them in flocks over the heads of the dancers. But no, just the one.

And here was the square, *La Place*, *La Plaza*. The band was very French, the lead instrument an accordion, but a rock band was due on at ten. The stalls were open, rectangles of bright light against the darkness of shops now shuttered; the odours of vanilla, candy-floss and sizzling crêpes drifted in a haze of blue smoke around them; the floodlights and fairy-lights above the band turned to acid-house green the plane tree leaves, some of which swung below the wrought-iron marquee of the stand.

They pulled white plastic tables together, scouted for spare chairs, ordered coffees (camomile infusion for Katherine – she sensed a migraine in the offing which coffee would exacerbate –

so maybe it was PMT), and yes, for Norbert and Thomas, brandies. Good guy, Norbert, Thomas thought, I'd have felt a bit out on a limb if I'd been the only one. Pierre sat next to him.

'So you're coming back to Hossegor tomorrow. Jean-Luc is pleased. Already he is missing Hannah-Rosa.'

'Are *you* pleased? You must be sick of us all by now.'

'Oh no-o-o-o. Quite the contrary.' Pierre leant back, big grin, lights flashing off his spectacles. 'You know what a long holiday it is for us. We'd go mad on our own.'

'We were going to go to Moni's parents. Their village fête.'

Moni leant across.

'I don't think it's such a good idea now. Papa has not been very well, and Maman has bad legs. They are afraid they will not do the occasion justice.'

How all occasions do inform against me, thought Thomas. Perhaps her parents' indisposition had lain behind the change in plan all along. Nevertheless, he should have been consulted. He would far rather have gone into Spain.

'So just what are we doing?'

'I told you. We're going to Hossegor tomorrow,' Katherine from the other side of Moni. 'For a week. So Richard can see the Pro-Surf World Championships. Then we'll go to Pau on Monday week, tomorrow week for three or four nights in Moni's flat, and that'll give us two or three days to get back to Caen.'

'What about Spain?'

'If you're really stuck on it we can go over the mountains to Jaca for one of the days we're in Pau. All right?'

Coffee and brandy arrived. Super. I'm not going to let anything spoil this evening.

Applause. The local band were packing up their instruments. A new lot, leathered and with long ponytails, were climbing over the railings of the stand to take their place. A tasselled arm beneath a wide-brimmed cowboy hat swung a white electric guitar high above his shoulder. Richard stood up, moved briskly towards them, waited a few moments then came back, almost prancing with glee.

'It's a Fender,' he crowed. 'And the strap is exactly the same as mine.'

Hendrix Experience.

'I didn't know you wanted to watch these surfing championships.'

'Yes you did. When we saw the poster in Hossegor. And you said "maybe".'

'Did I?' But he remembered the ones for the bullfights in Bayonne.

'Well, can I?'

'Looks like you're going to.'

'That's all right then.'

Feedback boomed. The drummer rattled off a couple of riffs, the lead guitar a bluesy lick.

'I hope that cowboy gear doesn't mean C and W.'

'Sea and double you?' Pierre asked.

'Country and Western. Can't stand country.'

'No, no. They play rock standards, some rhythm and blues, some soul.'

This was enough to make Thomas want to dance, and dance he did – with each of the women in turn. It was a politeness his father had taught him. Moonlighting from his ushering job he had become paid secretary to the Tithe Barn Club. The excellent Captain Galway had caused this Sussex flint erection to be built on the Bay Estate as a social focus for the residents. It was a big oak-beamed hangar of a place with a full-size snooker table, a sprung dance floor, a bar and a huge open fireplace where real logs burnt throughout the winter. Passions too. Every second Saturday there was a band that played foxtrots and quicksteps until eleven, when it finished things off with a slow waltz beneath dimmed lights. And while Dad, wearing his single-breasted, high-collared soup and fish, built to last twenty years earlier, did not dance with all the ladies present, he certainly spread himself around. About his suit he would say, 'The thing is, Thomas, fashions repeat themselves, so this dinner jacket is always either five years out of date or five years ahead of its time.'

What Thomas could not now understand was how his father had been able to maintain the same figure for twenty years so the damn thing always fitted him. Probably by cycling eight miles a day in term-time, rain or shine, and looking after a double garden. Though they had a charlady whenever they could afford it, they never had a gardener.

Meanwhile he went through the motions with Katherine who declared she was not in the mood, which disappointed him since they danced rarely but when they did danced well together.

Thomas could only do one sort of dancing – an old-fashioned jive learnt forty years ago in live thrashes dancing to trad jazz. He moved on through Thérèse, who was jolly about it but refused to submit to his jivery, to Elvira who tried but gave up with a laugh because she would not be led by a male partner either in dancing or anywhere else.

'Daddy, why don't you dance with me?'

'Golly, Hannah-Rosa, why don't I?'

So he did. He picked her up and whirled her around until he stumbled on the cobbles and she told him to stop. By now he was more than breathless, his heart rate was up if not actually palpitating and his legs felt like pillars of fire. Heart attack or stroke? Stroke please, there's less pain. Back to the table.

'*Un cognac encore? Pourquoi non. Que de cognacs!*'

'You'd better give me the keys.'

At last. She's going to drive.

And finally Moni. He had danced with Moni before and it always went well with her. She'd been taught to jive by *her* dad who had learnt the art from the GIs who liberated *la belle France*. So they spun and twiddled, and passed each other under each other's arms, and changed hands back to back, and he spun her away, and spun her back so his arm ended up round her waist, and so on and so on. Occasionally the parrot he had bought Hannah-Rosa whirred between the leaves and the lights above their swinging heads. And her dark hair bobbed above her shoulders, and the black vest she was wearing became damp with sweat, and the full skirt which hid her mother's peasant bum swirled this way and that, and . . .

'Mummy says can you come and help.'

'Why Richard? What's happened?'

'That parrot you gave Hannah-Rosa. It's stuck on the roof of the band-stand.'

He climbed on to a table, and on to a chair placed on the table and found the damn thing was still a foot beyond his groping hand.

The band was packing up, the other dancers were drifting away; soon they'd turn the lights out. And the bright plastic still stirred and sussurated in the midnight breeze, and the reds and oranges and blues shimmered so for all the world it was a real bird, injured, but not dead.

Richard's face loomed up alongside his. He was on Pierre's shoulders. He was standing on Pierre's shoulders. *Standing?* Yes. From his back Richard had reached up and caught the outer edge of the band-stand's roof and hauled himself so his feet were on Pierre's shoulders.

He was a strong, agile lad; karate and death-defying feats climbing trees with his friends. But his unprotected head was now something like eleven feet above a cobbled floor.

'I think you ought to get down.'

'I think you ought to get down. You're not going to get it like that.'

Katherine had spoken from below. Moni and Katherine were holding the chair he was standing on. His head swam. Slowly he lowered himself using one of the slender iron pillars that supported the roof.

Richard empty-handed too joined him on terra firma. Pierre went *oooof*. Hannah-Rosa declared, albeit tearfully, that it was only a stupid old toy and she'd rather go home. They drifted back up the main street towards where the cars were parked. The breeze continued to ruffle and rustle the parrot's plastic feathers, but not enough to shift it.

23

For two or three years things seemed a bit better. In the first place I left The Links and went to Minster Hill which was a much jollier place altogether, though virtually hopeless as a place of formal education.

Yet your dad sent you there?

Faute de mieux. You see, I had to have a scholarship. And I was not a clever boy. I passed the common entrance for Winchester – out of the question with no dosh to help pay the fees. Lancing College offered me an exhibition of fifty guineas a year – not enough. Going downmarket I finally got the necessary two hundred quid a year at Minster Hill. In fact I was top scholar with another lad for that year, which shows how academically unambitious the place was. Dad still had to find fifty-five quid a term at a time when he was earning only double that as an usher.

That must have made things very tight then.

Yes. Which is why he was moonlighting at the Tithe Barn Club, where he was responsible for just about everything except cooking, cleaning and serving behind the bar, and he even did that quite often. He kept the accounts, looked after the licensing, did all the ordering, seeing the reps and so on ... on its own it was a full-time job, and he already had one, teaching, often weekends too since it was a boarding-school. He had long school holidays, of course.

The club was owned by a broke baronet called Sir Ronald Gunter. He wasn't really broke but his father had apparently tied up all his capital – he was spending hundreds on lawyers who were trying to break the trust for him – so on a day-to-day basis he was broke and always robbing his own tills, which drove Dad to distraction. And drinking a bottle of Scotch a day out of the stockroom ... and so on. 'It's only pennies, after all,' he'd say. 'Look after the pounds and the pennies will look after themselves.' He bought my bike from me when I grew too big for it. It tickled me to think it was going to a penniless baronet, but it turned out it was to be a present for the son of the captain of his yacht.

Dad also wrote a lot. Upper-middle-brow journalism for now-defunct magazines like *The Hibbert Journal – A Quarterly Review of Religion, Theology, and Philosophy; Blackwood's*; and *Collins Magazine for Boys and Girls*, later renamed *The Young Elizabethan*. For the boys and girls he wrote jolly scientific articles on things like optics and simple electricity, mugging them up from his 1921 edition of the *Britannica*.

Mother did her bit. First of all she kept up with the two-year-olds and through that got propositioned by the local bookmaker who was fed up with her systematic wins. The upshot was that all through the summer months she was put in a garden shed on the local caravan site where she took illegal cash bets for the bookmaker from the holiday-makers. No betting shops in those days, and to keep the working classes in their place all off-course gambling was meant to be done by phone on credit.

Wasn't she in danger from the law?

Not really. The village bobby was one of her regular customers. And the bookmaker, Bob Murfett was his name, was so well in with the local constabulary that when a policeman came into the pub where he was drinking one lunchtime to tell him to move his Jag which was causing an obstruction in Aldwick High Street, he just looked at the copper and said, 'You're new here, aren't you?'

So. Between them, three, four jobs to keep you at a useless school. And this was a good time?

I think so. We were quite jolly for much of it, it seemed to me. But then things began to go wrong again.

How?

Well, first off, I had left The Links with just about enough Latin to get School Certificate. Two years later when I actually took the exam, I failed. And it mattered. You see, in those days you couldn't get into Oxford without Latin. It was then I realized what the ultimate purpose of all this endless self-sacrifice was. It was to get me to Wadham, where Dad had been. That way I'd be a gentleman. That was one of the four definitions of a gentleman current at that time. One, you were armigerous – first son of a first son of a gent who had been granted a coat of arms. My great-grandfather made the mistake of being a second son. And anyway my escutcheon was ir-redeemably besmirched by the bastardy wished on me by the dreadful April. Two, you had the freehold of an estate imme-morially owned by your family. No way I was going to do that. Nor was I going to enter Holy Orders. That left number four: you had an Oxbridge MA. Only Oxbridge, mind you.

And that mattered?

To Dad, yes. He wanted me, the scion of a noble race, to be a gent. I, personally, had never seen him as upset as he was when that result came through. Seven years of penury and hard labour down the toilet. I vowed, I promised, that I'd pass the December resit.

And you did?

I'm not sure.

?

I took the crib for *Aeneid II* into the exam and consulted it when I needed to. The invigilator was an old man who used to compose music while on the job. He'd look at the ceiling, close his eyes for long spells, and sing softly to himself before scrib-bling notes down on manuscript.

I passed, in the sense that I got a certificate, but whether or not I would have passed without the crib remains, until the Day of Judgement, unknowable. But it was Dad I cheated for.

You don't want to go back to Hossegor tomorrow, do you?

'You don't want to go to Hossegor tomorrow, do you?'

'Shit. I was nearly asleep.'

'Well, I'm not. I'm lying here awake, worrying.'

'Worrying? About Hossegor?'

'About Hossegor. And about us.'

'Do we have to have this conversation now?'

'I think we do. We never get time together on our own to talk things through.'

'But at three o'clock in the morning?'

'You don't want to go back to Hossegor.'

'No.'

'Well, I suppose I can understand that. But you've got to understand it's going to be far too hot for me in Pau and probably for the children too.'

'I thought we'd spend most of the time in the mountains. Walking.'

'But what you really want to do is go into Spain and look at those battlefields.'

'I suppose so.'

'Well, for goodness' sake say so.'

'I just did.'

He heard and felt how she turned on her side away from him in the darkness.

'And us. Why are you worried about us?' he asked.

She mumbled.

'I can't hear you.'

'You never seem to have any real time for us.' She turned on to her back and her voice came through clear as a bell, sharp as a knife. 'You don't share things any more. You daydream all the time and won't tell me about what. You're sullen with me but as soon as there are other people around, like tonight, then you drink too much and you get frightfully jolly,' this said sarcastically with a posh accent, 'and everyone has a wonderful time.'

'I'm sorry. I've not been very well.'

'I don't suppose you've noticed, but none of us have been too good. Richard had what you had, and I think I might be going down with it.'

What, bleeding from your bums?

'There's this other thing too . . . ' He was determined to get her to understand.

'About your father and how old he was when he died?'

'Yes.'

'Well, I think that's just too stupid for words. And it's making *us* miserable, seeing you going about so miserable most of the time. I think you should just forget it and try to make what's left of the holiday a good time for all of us.'

'I'll try.'

'Good.'

'But I'll do it better if I have a decent night's sleep.'

Again, flouncing the pillows and banging her shoulder down, she turned away from him. Quite right too. It had been a silly thing to say.

The sister at Minster Hill did not like the way I caught every cold that was going, and had a persistent cough through much of the winter. She said I should have my chest X-rayed. The X-ray showed up a shadow, a small lesion at the top of my right lung. I remember the interview well. It took place in what must once have been the drawing room of a small country house. Not quite a stately home, but not far off. Aldingbourne Chest Hospital. The specialist was Dr Wallace, a tall, kind man with black crinkly hair, a lot like Elliott Gould. His sidekick was Doctor Pillman, a woman of extraordinary elegance, thin, with a sharp face that might have been severe if she had not smiled often and broadly . . .

Why are you telling me about these people?

They were in love. But Wallace's wife was crippled with rheumatoid arthritis and he would not leave her. Eventually she died and after a decent interval, Wallace and Pillman married. They too died not much later, and within months of each other.

?

You see every day for years they had both supervised the taking of X-rays. Worse than that, they carried out live scanning procedures. Every patient they had, and often they had as many as a hundred at a time, maybe more, was scanned once a fortnight, that is they were X-rayed behind a screen, a monitor, so the doctors, who sat in front of the machine, could see what was actually happening in our lungs, live, moving. Those doctors spent hours every day being continuously X-rayed.

So they cured hundreds—

Thousands.

Of TB, and died of lung cancer?

And cancer of the spleen, the liver, the pancreas and any other organ within range.

It's almost like a fifties film. Black and white, very tender, Extended Encounter, selfless sacrifice, a doomed love. They don't make them like that any more.

They don't make people like that any more. They were very much of their time.

Was your dad in that class?

Almost. He aspired. Anyway, there I was in this converted drawing room being told by this kind dark man that it really was not at all serious, it shouldn't take more than a year to cure. A YEAR!

'Put a good face on it,' Dad said. 'We don't want to upset your mother.'

He'd do almost anything to escape a row with Mother. You see the thing was I had this touch of TB but what we didn't know was that she had it really badly, not far off galloping, which made her tired and irritable. She'd probably been fighting it off and on ever since we drank the infected milk in North Wales, and I'd probably copped my lot from her. And for some reason she slipped through the net – that is, once I was diagnosed she should have been X-rayed. Dad was. But the card or whatever never reached her . . .

Or she suppressed it.

Goodness, I never thought of that before. Yes. She might well have done.

But why?

Believed Dad needed her at home. Me too during the hols. Keep the home fires burning, that sort of thing. Dr Pillman once asked her, 'Surely, Mrs Somers, you were in pain?'

'Well, yes,' mother replied. 'But after a certain age one always is, isn't one?'

What I was getting round to was this. During that period, and especially during the spell when I was convalescing at home a year later, and Mother was bedridden waiting for a bed – yes, there were waiting lists in those days too – they did have some colossal rows. I remember one occasion. During the holidays Dad always found an excuse to go to Tithe Barn during the afternoon.

'There's the Watney's rep coming,' he'd say. Or the man who fixes the pinball machine ... And an hour or so later he'd come back saying how Sir Ronald had dropped by, very miserable, and had insisted on taking a bottle of Scotch out of the stock cupboard while they went through the accounts. Mother and he used to row about this in front of me and I always took her side. Adolescent boys do, don't they?

Especially if they have spent hours in the nude with their mothers in a sauna-like situation ...

Yes. That may have had something to do with it. Anyway on one occasion Dad sat on the edge of mother's bed while she was having a go at him and he lit a Weights.

'Careful,' said I. 'If you blow the match out you'll turn yourself into a flame-thrower.'

Meaning?

Oh, come on! That he had so much alcohol on his breath it might catch fire. He was hurt. Very hurt. Didn't speak to me until the evening.

And that hurts you now. Even now. What you did to him.

Yes.

Which is why, Thomas said to himself, if we are heading for a major domestic, it must not be in front of the children.

He slept. At last. In his dream Cassie stood at the end of the bed, lighter poised beneath a Gauloise, looking at him from under the rim of his black beret.

'Dear boy, this is all we have, you know. This is not a rehearsal for the hereafter.'

The lighter flared and he disappeared in a puff of smoke. Just like that.

24

'So. You're going.' Elvira, rolling out pastry at her kitchen table.

'I think so.'

'Either you are or you are not.'

She smiled at him, a soft, gentle smile starting from warm dark eyes. She pushed a strand of sun-bleached hair off her forehead with the back of her hand.

'Sometimes,' she said, 'a couple need a break from each other.'

'I'll go and get what I need.'

He climbed the shallow wooden stairs to the small room they had had before. The house seemed very quiet and airy, peaceful, with no one in it apart from the two of them. When the children came back the telly went on, they played noisy water games outside and then the place would fill up as dusk fell with grown-ups, friends and guests, chatter, noise, music.

What would he need? Not a lot. Passport. Money. How much? Five hundred francs and a Visa card. He'd leave Katherine with the traveller's cheques which were in her name. Toiletries – a towel, a piece of soap, toothbrush. They shared toothpaste so he'd have to buy some. Disposable razor, one would be enough. Three pairs of underpants, which, if they got bloody, he'd chuck. Comb. *Wellington's War*. What could he carry it all in? Centre Leclerc *hypermarché* plastic bag? Why not?

He looked round the room and his eye fell on Katherine's nightdress which she had folded neatly and left on her pillow. He felt a wave of angst, of sadness too. Was this really such a good idea? She'd thought so. At any rate said so, firmly, half an hour ago.

It had started with a pointless row about early youmans.

Joking, not attempting to score points, she had said, 'I can't understand why you don't enjoy all this.'

The beach, the surf, the surfers.

'I mean,' she went on, 'according to your semi-aquatic theory about the origins of mankind, you ought to be in heaven.'

Niggled he had launched into an old fogy's attack on the *Championnat du Surf* – a circus that toured the world, like Formula One racing, visiting every viable surfing place where crowds were guaranteed too. If you wanted a decent view you bought into enclosures, even took a numbered place on temporary stands. If you didn't do either of these then really you needed binoculars. It all meant huge crowds, a travelling trade fair with over-priced peripherals, and the smell everywhere, not of the Atlantic but *gaufres*, crêpes, merguez. For seven whole days . . . ?

'Listen,' she had said. 'You're clearly in a state and fed up with us all, and have been for the last few days.'

'It's not you or the children I'm fed up with.'

'Richard would be devastated if we left now with the championships only halfway through. Hannah-Rosa is having a wonderful time again with Jean-Luc . . . '

'And what about you?'

'I'm all right. Now what I suggest is you take our car back to the house, ask Elvira to come and get us at the usual time, take what you need and go . . . '

'In the car?'

'No. I may need it. You'll have to take buses. Whatever. It's not fair on Pierre and Elvira to make us completely reliant on them. And anyway the documents are in my name and if you get in a mess in Spain you won't have me to do the talking. Now I think it's best if you just walk off quietly, no fuss, no upsetting the children.'

'When shall I . . . when, where shall we meet up again?'

She had looked up at him from under the parasol, dark eyes solemn, even a little puzzled.

'When . . . which day is it that you'll have lived longer than your father?'

'Wednesday. The thirty-first. A week today.'

'No,' she said patiently. 'A week yesterday. Today is Thursday. Actually that works out quite well. We'll go to Pau on Monday, or Sunday evening after the championships are over, and drive over to Jaca on Wednesday. Do you think you'll be able to get to Jaca?'

'There'll be a bus, maybe a train. If the worst comes to the worst I'll hitch.'

'All right. We'll meet you on the steps of the cathedral, the west door, at one . . . no, make it one-thirty, on Wednesday. Don't be late. Now go.'

He had stooped to kiss her, but all she offered was her cheek. He squeezed her shoulder.

'We could have lunch at La Fragua.'

'If it's still there.'

He squeezed her shoulder again.

'Take care. I mean it.'

'You too. Don't do anything stupid. You're not going to come to any harm. You are going to make it through to Wednesday. You'd bloody better. And if you get to Pamplona, keep off the pacharrán. You owe us all that much.'

And now he wanted to go back to the beach, say he was sorry, that he would make everything so much better, he'd even sit with Richard in the stands . . . He sighed. No, I bloody won't, he said to himself. He sat on the edge of the bed and, thinking there might be some serious walking to do in the Pyrenees, changed his deckshoes for Wrangler boots. Then with his Centre Leclerc bag clutched by the neck like a chicken he went back to the kitchen.

Elvira was standing in front of the sink, wiping her hands. On the table in front of her, uncooked in a flan dish, a *tarte à moutarde* – mustard spread on the pastry. For a moment he watched while she layered it with thin slices of scarlet tomato.

'I'll be off then.'

She laughed gently, with amused tolerance.

'What will you do at nights?' she asked. 'Where will you sleep?'

He shrugged.

'*Chambres d'hôtes*? B and B?'

'It's not a thing you get much of in Spain. And this time of year you'll be lucky if you get a room.'

'Out in the open? It's warm enough.'

'You'll need a sleeping-bag. Come on. I'll lend you one.'

He followed her back up the stairs. She was wearing a white cotton smock over jeans. Following her like that it did not hide her butt. Still very slim. She talked as she climbed.

'We have very good ones. Thermal but very light. And they pack away into nothing.'

She took him into her and Pierre's bedroom, stood on a chair to reach the bundles down from the top of the wardrobe. She climbed down, pulled the bags out of their container, shook them out.

'They're zipped together to make a double. But they unzip to make singles.'

With neat competent movements she separated them, rolled one back up and into a small cotton bag. As she did so he had an urge to say : No, don't, leave them as they are, come with me! The mysterious smile that played round her eyes and lips seemed to him to say that that was what she was expecting him to do. Even hoping? Probably not. At least fifteen years older than Pierre, and a degenerate, fat, old, balding wreck; why should she think such a thing? Probably she was remembering how he had gone to the downstairs loo that first dawn, mother-naked, half-drunk, pot-bellied with the smallest prick she'd ever seen. That's why she was grinning.

'Great,' he said. 'That's marvellous. It might even fit into this bag with the rest.'

But she'd also found a small rucksack. She took the plastic bag from him and put it in the rucksack with the sleeping-bag.

'There you are then,' she said.

They went back downstairs.

'So what's your first step?'

'Bus to Bayonne. Then either a bus or a hitch to Roncesvalles.'

'To see where Roland was killed by the Moors?'

'Maybe.'

Actually to see where five hundred Brits held up a French army.

'You know where the bus stop is?'

'Yes.'

'*Au'voir*, then.'

'Yes, indeed.'

Les baisers. Her cheeks soft and lips like the brush of a moth's wings. Come with me? But no. He daresn't. The resultant hassle would be totally cataclysmic if she said yes, and more than a touch humiliating if she didn't. And actually, he admitted to himself, as he set off down the short steep drive, what he really wanted was company and friendship and if he'd had the sense to ask she and Pierre might have agreed to look after Richard and Hannah-Rosa and he might have persuaded Katherine to come with him on this crazy jaunt. And that could have been a good idea. Too late now.

25

By the time the bus reached Bayonne his mood had lifted. School's out, he was determined to enjoy himself, maybe, in the words of the Ian Dury song, 'break a few rules'. The first thing he saw when he got off the bus was the bullfight poster and, forget Roncesvalles, he knew immediately how he would spend the evening. He remembered that the ring, *les arènes*, was out of town in a modern suburb on the bank of the Adour but that the tickets could be bought from a kiosk set up in the small sloping cobbled square outside the cathedral. Since the bus had dropped him by the railway station he had a pleasant walk of some fifteen minutes or so across the Nive not far from its confluence with the Adour. It was a brilliant day, not a cloud to be seen, not yet unbearably hot. The rivers twinkled serenely, the sun blazed from the lead roof of the twin-spired cathedral on the other side.

Bayonne remained one of his favourite towns. The thing about it, he said to himself as he *flâneured* through the winding alleys decked for the week-long fiesta with flags and coloured lights, the thing about it is it is not French. There were more of the green, red and white interlaced crosses of the Basque flag than there were tricolours, and almost as many of the European stars on a blue background.

There were bands out and dancing in the streets. The men wore white shirts, white trousers, red berets and red scarves worn scout-wise with a folded triangle at the back. Their dances were a mixture of jotas and morris dancing, with much banging of batons; the music, fifes and drums. All of which *animation*, or rather *alegría*, made doubly distasteful the fact that the *vente* where the tickets for the corrida were on sale was picketed. By animal libbers. Brits at that.

There were about seven of them standing round a couple of

beat-up campers parked in the cobbled space in front of the cathedral's west door and about twenty metres from the hut where the tickets were sold. They were hippyish with long hair and beads, the men wore leather cowboy hats and the women long skirts that trailed over grubby bare or sandalled feet. They had a banner: *La Corride est le Meurtre*, and a display of photographs of bulls with thick grey tongues hanging out and blood streaming down their flanks, bulls lifeless dragged out of the ring, and gored horses. There were pamphlets too, which one of the women thrust at people as they came away from the kiosk. Two of the men twanged tuneless guitars and two of the women banged tambourines performing a horrible parody of Bob Dylan's *Blowing in the Wind* with a new refrain: ' . . . the cattle are lowing in the wind'. A gendarme stood nearby, smoking, but clearly ready to interfere if they tried any serious hassling.

Thomas joined the queue, bought his ticket, for a seat *soleil et ombre*, near the back of the *barreras*, that is the blocks of seats nearest the ring. It cost two hundred and fifty francs which, such was his mood, did not seem too expensive, though he recalled Katherine and he had paid only nine francs twenty years ago, but that was for the very cheapest seats. And then, as he walked away, one of the women called out, 'You should be bloody ashamed of yourself.'

He was disconcerted for more reasons than one. Clearly he had been singled out as English. But how had the woman known? Sure, he was blond with thinning whitish hair (well, sort of going bald really), podgy, not tall, wearing a pale-pink shirt with sleeves rolled up, chinos with turn-ups and his Wrangler boots. And he was carrying a small rucksack by the straps. So. Not French, Basque or Spanish. But why not Dutch or German?

He paused, then walked on, very careful not to quicken his stride.

'Yes, you, motherfucker. You with the rucksack in your hand.'

And at that moment an eighth turned up, another man, clutching a greasy bag filled with *pains* and frankfurters. Hot dogs. He began to hand them round and the frightful music stopped.

Thomas watched, made sure that he was right about what was happening. Then he walked over to them.

'I appreciate, and to some extent, respect,' he said, keeping his voice low, slow and firm, the way he used to when as a teacher he had had to deal with playground nonsense, 'the views of those who campaign against bullfighting. But only when they are held by strict vegetarians.'

'Piss off, man.' An evil-looking character this. Beneath the brim of his Indiana Jones hat he had a wide beaky sunburnt nose, small blue eyes and a yellow goatee beard. He was older than Thomas had expected. 'There's a world of difference between the humane slaughter of a pig and what goes on in a bullring.'

Thomas thought, this is stupid. He turned away.

'Shithead.'

From the woman again.

He stopped. To accept their insults without argument would, he knew, in their eyes constitute a victory. He knows he's a shithead, they would think to themselves, and the poor fucker can't do anything about it. He turned back. Beak-nose was wiping pink-stained grease from his beard with the paper serviette the hot dog had been wrapped in.

'The pig you're eating lived its entire life in a shedded stall not big enough for it to turn round in,' said Thomas. 'It was force fed, never saw daylight, was stunned not killed before its throat was cut so it could bleed to death. The bulls that will die tonight roamed pastures and forests with almost unlimited freedom living out lives more natural than any other husbanded animal that you can think of. They are mature. If you have ever eaten a chicken under three pounds in weight or "new season" lamb you have eaten a baby.'

'You're full of shit, man.'

'No. You are. And getting fuller the more you stuff your face with pig.'

'If the filth weren't here I'd hang one on you.'

'You and your army.'

Indiana Jones took a threatening step towards him and Thomas experienced a sudden adrenalin rush.

'Leave it out, Matt. There's some truth in what he says.'

This from another woman who had been hanging back a bit. It took Thomas by surprise. Animal libbers were, in his experience, fanatics, as open to the voice of reason as born-again Christians. She was, he thought, about twenty-five years old, had short spiky hair bleached but streaked with rust. She wore a brick-coloured T-shirt which revealed the contours of rounded firm breasts with pert nipples above a long cheesecloth skirt and, like the man, had a rather prominent nose. She could have been his kid sister. She had five or six tiny silver rings in each earlobe. Her eyes were nice and she had a generous mouth painted, and it was a surprise this considering the rest of her appearance, in a crimson Lana Turner bow.

He grinned at her and turned away. As he left the sloping cobbled square he looked back over the parked cars. 'Lowing in the Wind' started up again; it seemed they had forgotten him. But she turned her head, glanced over her shoulder and answered the slow wave he gave her with a grin.

Chuffed at this mildly romantic episode he sauntered down the hill and back on to the main drag. Lunch, he thought. There were café-restaurants down on the quays, he remembered, where you could sit out, but after a moment he rejected the idea. To sit at a table amongst families and couples would, he realized, make him feel lonely, miss his children and their mother. They loved eating out together. So he turned into Nouvelles Galeries knowing there would be food and drink in the *sous-sol*, picked up a wire basket and cruised the aisles looking for goodies.

Being in a Spanish mood he bought sliced chorizo to go with a French stick, a couple of ripe peaches and a bottle of red Navarra. No Spanish cheese, so he picked up a wedge of Chaumes made in Jurançon, just outside Pau. Then with all this packed into a plastic bag he took the escalator up to the third floor where they sold camping and beach stuff and bought a clasp-knife (I'll give it to Richard), a corkscrew which had an attachment for lifting crown tops and a plastic beaker.

Where to eat this feast? He headed for the parks. These were laid out inside the low triangular redoubts of the fortifications designed by Vauban. He found just the spot he was looking for, a grassy patch where he could rest his back against a parapet which on the inside was only a metre high but on the other side dropped three or four metres to a clay tennis court below. It was partly shaded by an acacia, already hung with long black pods, and faced inwards towards the town. He could see the traffic shunting round the inner ring road above the last line of fortifications but was far enough away not to be bothered by fumes or noise. Close by, children played with their families or squabbled over baguettes. In the distance there was always music, the rattle of drums, the squeal of fifes. He wondered if Katherine and the kids were OK. She really was a brick to let him go walkabout like this, though she'd surely claim she was benefiting from his absence just as much as he was.

He broke the bread, slit a chunk with the knife, laid slices of crimson and orange chorizo along its length, folded it in, took a bite. The hot spices exploded sweetly in his mouth. He pulled out the bottle. He had a bit of trouble with the cork, but not enough to be a real bother, though it did break up a bit. Too bad, he thought, I'll have to drink all of it. He let the dusky red wine glug into the plastic beaker. The blushful Hippocrene winked back at him.

He drank, ate, drank, ate and drank again. Reckoning no one would be able to move it without waking him he placed the rucksack in the small of his back, put his shoulders against the warm brick of the parapet and closed his eyes. That I might drink and leave the world unseen, And with thee fade away into the forest dim. F-f-f-fade away. Stones yes, but before that Buddy Holly, 1957 . . .

26

Granny Somers died in 1957 and that enabled the last major changes in Dad's life. By then Thomas and his mother had come through TB – he very satisfactorily, cured by streptomycin, PAS tablets, bed rest and a minor operation that collapsed the top half of his right lung so it could heal. He had to go to hospital every fortnight to have it filled up, that is a thickish needle was thrust between his ribs just below his armpit so some air could be pumped into the cavity between the top of the lung and the wall to keep the lung down. That had lasted for three years, long enough to keep him out of National Service, which his deaf ear would probably have exempted him from anyway, and was all over by 1957.

His mother's case had been very different. She had two long spells in hospitals, and two very major operations. Much of the time she was in St Richard's, Chichester, seven miles away, and Dad cycled over to see her almost every day. Rain or shine.

This also meant that Thomas and Dad had to spend quite long periods, all the school holidays really, on their own together. It worked out better than they had expected, though there were hiccups.

The first crisis came when Thomas failed the Wadham College entrance exam. The second when the prep school that employed Dad moved from Bognor to Millionaire's Row in Godstone, Surrey. For one term he went with them, only coming back at weekends. By then Thomas had left Minster Hill and he stayed at Seventy-One to look after Mum who had a brief spell at home between operations. He used the time to teach himself what he felt he needed to get into Cambridge.

It was also the time he shared the house with his dad that he remembered as being really rather good. They taught each other to cook. They drank and smoked together. When Dad came back from Godstone they went to the Labour Exchange for their dole together, along with all the summer workers – the deck-chair attendants, the men who ran the amusement arcades, the women who cleaned out the hotels, and all the extra staff Bob Murfett took on in the season. Dad must have been on the fiddle.

Why do you say that?

He was still secretary of Tithe Barn.

Look, there's things about your dad I don't understand. He prided himself on being a gentleman, yet he was happy to be a bookmaker, work for a bookmaker and fiddle his dole.

Difficult to explain. He was, as aren't we all, a creature of his period, his decade. About 1925 to 1935, I'd guess. A gentleman was honourable about women, about the people who were his responsibility, in Dad's case his family, *us*, and the men who were in his charge in the war, the boys he taught. He paid off personal debts promptly, business debts if his word to a person he actually knew was involved. But part of the creed was that if you were hard up and the people in your care were threatened, you could not be demeaned by any occupation, or non-personal subterfuge, undertaken on their behalf. So the government was fair game, and so, I'm afraid, were tradespersons.

What's this got to do with his decade?

Oh come on. Think of early Greene. Even the more sym-pathetic characters in Waugh. The whole ethos of distressed gentlefolk finding ways and means of making ends meet. He was seedy. But a flame burnt within. That's how he saw himself. To sum up. A gent does not worry about stealing from a corrupt state, nor does he attach status to occupations. The lower-middle classes do. But a gent is a gent is a gent. A gent is a libertarian anarchist.

Anyway, I know he was still secretary, because in the afternoons, just about every afternoon we were together, we went round to the club and played snooker on the full-size table. I'm still quite good.

*

He remembered his dad teaching him the correct stance, telling him to get right down over the cue so it brushed the middle of his chin, how to put on side for a swerve, top-spin to make the cue ball run on and bottom to make it stop dead or even spin back after hitting its target. Matters of etiquette too – you never *ever* smoked over the table for fear of dropping burning ash on the cloth, so every turn began with you putting your fag on an ashtray on the table where your drink was. And if you were lucky enough to get a longish break going, you'd go back to it every now and then for a slow meditative drag before returning to the table.

Long afternoons – the big leaded windows curtained from the sun, the oblong fringed light above the brilliant table, the procession and elimination of the clicking balls as they thunked through the netted pockets on to plastic-covered runners . . .

'So it's all on the black again.'

'All on the black.'

And Thomas would pot the black.

Of course Dad fixed it so he'd win, partly through a handicap, giving him a twenty-five-point start, but also by throwing the occasional easy shot. And when he fluked an impossible shot, he'd always say, 'Thought I'd missed it,' and when he left the balls in a near snooker, so Thomas could scarcely hit the designated ball let alone pot it, he'd say: 'Blast, I've stuck them up for you again.'

He also taught Thomas poker, with all its variations according to Hoyle, and Liar Die, played with poker die. And chess. They played through games from his ancient edition of Staunton, learnt the Philidor Defence, the Petroff Defence, Ruy López and the Scotch Gambit. Dad had a travelling games set, a box of inlaid wood that opened out into a chequer board with holes in the squares on one side, and on the other a backgammon board and crib board down the spines. The chess men were finely carved ivory abstracts of the conventional Staunton designs, with pegs to fit in the holes. Again Dad offered handicaps – playing without his rooks, then with the rooks but without his bishops; finally they played on equal terms.

The game spanned three days, lasted at least twelve hours, for they took as long as they liked over each move. At the end of it Thomas held Dad to a stalemate.

'Was that a fair result?'

'Of course.'

'I mean you didn't let me off the way you sometimes do at snooker.'

'I don't let you win. Occasionally I don't concentrate as well as I would if I were playing Hibbert or Yallop with a couple of quidlets on the table.'

Hibbert, Dad often asserted, was the other gentleman who used the club – he spoke posh. Yallop being a butcher with a nose like a large fat strawberry was not. Not even Sir Ronnie was a real gent – his dad having made his money in ice-cream.

That marathon game left Thomas mentally exhausted. It was another three days before he could make his tired mind function well enough to read a book. He never played chess again, not even with Richard.

The one game they never played was bridge. Thomas for a lot of his life had been a bridge orphan. Two, three nights a week during the holidays, his parents played bridge at the club. Thomas stayed at home, listened to the wireless, the proms in the summer hols, Al Read, the earliest Goon Shows and plays by Louis MacNeice and Dorothy Sayers during the rest of the year, and read. But the wind rattled the windows, he could hear the sea a hedge and a field away, and occasionally a large black spider would scuttle across the floor. Often he sat on the sofa with a volume of the *Britannica* beside him so when a spider came he'd stand on the sofa and drop the encyclopaedia on it, leaving the volume and the crushed arachnid for Dad to clear up when he came home.

What did you read?

Michael Innes and Edmund Crispin in the Victor Gollancz yellow jackets. A fortnight's pocket money would buy one. I had hundreds. Not only Innes and Crispin, but Allingham, Tey, Household, Ambler and Greene. When they moved to Felpham, on the other side of Bognor, Dad sold them to a second-hand bookshop, them and all the books from my childhood. I was livid. He said there was nowhere to put them in the small bungalow they moved to – but he didn't tell me he was doing it. Or maybe he did but said if I couldn't take them off his hands they'd have to go. Something like that. Ten years later some of them were still in the bookshop, but I couldn't bring myself to pay for them a second time.

They moved to a bungalow in Felpham?

Yes. Well, that's where we came in, isn't it? 1957. Not Fade Away. Granny Somers died leaving him ten thousand pounds of disposable, unentailed capital. Also Aunt Helen decided she didn't need Seventy-One any longer and she gave Dad most of the four and a half grand she sold it for. He bought the bungalow and some furniture of their own, though they kept some of Helen's stuff too. With the income from the ten thousand and no more school fees to pay, he felt he could pack in the day job . . .

He wrote from then on?

Dear me, no. The evening job was running Bob Murfett's office on the evenings when there was dog-racing. He did it four or five times a week. It killed him in the end . . .

Killed him? How can you get killed running a bookmaker's office in the evening?

There were other factors. The move to Felpham was not a success. It was on the opposite side of Bognor from the Bay Estate, far enough for them to lose touch with their bridge and snooker circles. Mother hated it. She didn't like the nasty new estate they were on. She didn't like Father being out in the evenings so often. They had rows. They were not happy. He drank a lot, and that night, 17 March, St Patrick's Day . . .

Hey! What's going on? It was as if he were in bed with Katherine and she had turned over. A bit like that, anyway.

He opened his eyes, found he was on his cheek on the grass. With swift desperation his hand searched behind him for the rucksack. Phew. It was still there. He must have slipped sideways off it. He pulled himself into a sitting position against the brick parapet, and looked around. Five yards away, hunkered with her back against a plane tree, the girl from the animal libbers who had spoken up for him looked over at him. Their eyes met. She smiled.

'Hi,' she said.

27

Thomas looked up, around, beyond her. Where were the others? Behind the nearest tree? Waiting to put the boot in? Make off with his rucksack? His mouth felt dry, he had a headache, he wanted to wee. He realized he had a now subsiding erection and he wondered if it had been visible before he awoke. He spotted the campers at last, parked on the final layer of fortifications in an extended lay-by. Some way off. He could see four or five of the animal libbers sitting on the parapet, easily identifiable even at that distance by their cowboy hats and ponytails.

He focused on the girl again. The sun, which was warming the back of his head, lit her up as if she were on a film set under a reflector board held up off-shot. She shifted her head slightly to one side and the smile, those lips still painted in a forties bow, became a touch quizzical. He stood up, felt a sharp ache in the lumbar region, managed a grin.

'Hi.' His grin slipped apologetically. 'I need a wee.'

'There are loos a couple of hundred yards back there. Through the trees.'

'Oh, great. Thanks.'

She straightened too, rose, brushing down her skirt. Her hands were broad, the fingers long, lots of rings, the nails painted to match her mouth. There were more lines on them than he had expected. Perhaps she was older than he had thought when he first saw her back at the kiosk. But her breasts, cradled in red cotton, still looked like a young woman's.

'I'll come with you.'

'Why?'

She pouted and he realized he had been ungracious.

'I mean thanks. But . . . why?'

'I'd like to talk to you some more. About bullfighting. What you said was interesting ... about them being free, almost wild.'

He gathered up the rucksack and the plastic bag. The bottle, still a quarter full beneath its broken cork, had not tipped.

They followed a gravel track round the edge of the rampart towards a small clump of cypresses. Funny how people plant them round public loos as well as churchyards.

'Really,' he said, looking at the way the dust powdered his Wrangler boots. 'They really are wild. The owners are careful with bloodlines, monitor which bulls run with which cows. They steer them to where there is plenty of natural food, and they watch over them for illnesses, or accidents. But apart from those things they're left very much to themselves.'

'And they pay for this ... luxury by being tortured to death in the ring.'

'Not exactly.'

'No?'

'Hang on.'

He quickened his stride, and she, with a brief giggle trotted to keep up with him, sandals slapping the gravel. Oh God, he thought, suppose it's one of those space capsules like at Angers. Have I got a two franc piece? Has she got one in that woven shoulderbag she's carrying, if I haven't? But it was an ugly flattened box of a building, stuccoed with cement, coloured the grey of death, sitting beneath the low dark boughs and wrapped in a harsh acrid miasma of wine-induced urine – not as sweet as the beery smell of British wee. Inside it was almost dark, lit only by small dirty windows with iron gratings. The floor was wet. He managed to shrug the rucksack on to his back but had to find an almost dry corner to prop the plastic bag in. The urinal itself was a half-pipe set just below knee level. There were several dog-ends in it. He chased them down towards the outlet with a powerful long stream ...

Pleased though he was with his performance, at least his prostate seemed to be holding up, he realized that he was vulnerable. The big man with the beaky nose, the other younger ones could take him apart, steal everything of value he had, leaving him bleeding and naked and waiting for the Good Samaritan. He shuddered, zipped up, emerged blinking into the sunlight, went back for his plastic bag and came out again.

She was no longer there. Gone! He felt disappointment mingled with relief. On the whole relief predominated. Then she came round from the other side of the building. He guessed there was a *dames* on the other side.

She fell in beside him as they strolled out of the copse and back towards the parapet. They found a stone seat, warm from the sun, and sat on it. She spread her knees and her hands fell into a loose grasp in the valley her skirt made between them.

'Is there anything left in that bottle?' she asked.

He delved.

'About a mugful. And I have a mug. Do you want some?'

She nodded. He poured what was left into the beaker. Nearly three-quarters full. He handed it to her. She drank half and handed it back.

'Nice. Sort of blackcurranty. You finish it.'

'Cheers.'

The wine was warmer, smoother than it had been.

'So.' Her hands came out of her lap, stroked her thighs towards her knees. I'd like to do that, he thought as the wine warmed his stomach. 'So. Not exactly tortured to death?'

'No. The bull pays for five years of very good living with twenty minutes, that's the legal maximum, fighting for its life. It's not a bad death. All right, the bull does suffer pain and bewilderment, but it resists, it fights, right to the very end. Its death is more natural and more ennobling both to itself and to those who kill it and those who watch than anything that happens in a stockyard or slaughter-house . . . '

He paused, glanced sideways at her profile. From this angle the nose dominated her face. Her eyes were narrowed into seriousness. Is she taking all this on board, he wondered, or rejecting it for sentimental twaddle? But aware that he had stopped and was looking at her to see how she was reacting, she turned to him and her eyes lit with a bright, open, sympathetic smile which quite transformed her. It went to his heart like an arrow.

'Go on,' she said.

They were very close on that stone seat, but not quite touching. He fought hard against the temptation to take her hand which rested again on her knee.

'Put it another way. Would you rather die in the full glory of your womanhood or as a commodity on a production line? Would you rather go when you have fulfilled everything you can at the height of all your abilities, or of old age, cancer, with Alzheimer's as a side order after twenty years of merciless decline?'

He shuddered again as he said this. That's the way Mother went. That's the way I'm going. Maybe Dad was lucky.

He had a sudden vertiginous sense of what these last ten years or so would be like, slithering faster and faster, and with less and less control down scree and shifting shale towards the lip of the precipice and the bottomless drop beyond. Instead of walking towards it, proud and upright.

He sighed.

'There's no way you can convince people. It's an experience: it can be sublime, it can be awful. But you have to go to know what it's really like. And I don't expect you to do that.'

'Why not?'

'Animal rights. Animal liberation. You're into all that.'

She laughed and the wonderful smile came back.

'Not really.'

'No? Could have fooled me.'

'A couple of them are but the rest of us are just bumming about for the summer. You see we're actually paid to picket bullfights.'

'Paid?'

'By CACTA.'

'Cacta?'

'Campaign Against Cruel Treatment of Animals. They pay us fifty pounds a week to picket bullfights all over the south of France. It's not a lot, but it helps. Pays the petrol and we get to

194

see a lot of nice places. That's why they picked on you. You see CACTA has a guy checking out the people they've paid and we thought you might be him. Every time we see a middle-aged, middle-class Brit we turn up the heat.'

Well, at least she didn't say elderly.

Silence. Just the distant traffic and music. Bands still playing. That's it, he thought, she'll split now, back to her friends, and I'll be on my own again. But her chin came up, her rich lips pouted a little and then, yes, she put her hand on his knee.

'All right,' she said. 'Take me. Take me to the bullfight.'

28

It took a bit of organizing. First, he was now very low in cash and had to stop at a hole in the wall which let him have one thousand four hundred francs on his Visa card. Then they found that the kiosk outside the cathedral had closed – a notice said that tickets would be on sale at the bullring from five o'clock. It was now nearly half-past four. The bullring was some four kilometres away, downriver. For the first time on his walkabout Thomas felt helpless without a car.

A bus? But how often did they run, where did they go from? Walk? Two and three-quarter miles in this heat, get lost, arrive too late to get decent seats together.

The word 'taxi' never sprang readily to his mind. Dad and Mum in their carless days relied on buses and bikes. Only in the most dire emergencies would they use the ultimate extravagance – a taxi.

'Taxi?' the woman suggested.

Not far from the cathedral they piled into the back of an old, but large and leathery Citroën.

'*Plaza de Toros, por fav . . . si'l vous plaît.*'

The woman whispered: 'In French, it's *les arènes.*'

'Of course it is. Silly me!'

'*Les arènes, s'il vous . . .* '

'*Je le sais . . .* ' the driver growled, adding something in Basque which would probably have been a fighting matter if Thomas had known what it meant.

They sat in the corners so they could half face each other.

'I'm Thomas. Thomas Somers.'

'I'm Lucasta. People call me Luke.'

Again that smile.

'Can I call you Tom?'

'Yes. No one else does, so I'd like you to. But you'll have to forgive me if I'm not quick in answering. I'll be looking around to see who Tom is.'

The usual answer was a firm no. But Thomas suddenly felt that if she called him Tom it would put this new relationship, if you could call it that, on a plane set at an angle to the rest of his life.

'Also,' he indicated his left ear, the one furthest from her, 'I'm stone deaf in this ear, so if you get caught on that side of me, don't expect me to answer.'

'How did it get deaf?'

'When I was eleven years old I was at a frightful private school where they made me stand on playing fields for hours on end in howling icy gales. I ended up with an ear abscess – and a course of penicillin, one of the first ever given to a civilian, I believe.'

Christ, I sound like an old fogy.

'Really? When was that?'

'Nineteen forty-six.'

She calculated.

'You don't look your age.'

Whoopee!

Briefly the memories flooded back. The Links had moved back to its peacetime buildings on the Wirral, overlooking the Royal Hoylake golf course and, as the school song said, the golden sands of the Dee. In winter it was an icy, bleak place. He remembered the sanatorium, a cottage separate from the main buildings, a downstairs room with a blazing coal fire, a ferocious fever with nightmares, excruciating pain in his ear, a worried doctor, and then, the sign that things were really bad, the arrival of his dad and mum all the way from south-east London.

They shifted him to a nursing home. In those early days of penicillin it had to be administered as a thick chalky suspension injected into the buttocks once every two hours, night and day, over forty-eight hours. He almost minded exposing his bottom to a strange woman more than the pain. Now, he felt, a chance would be a fine thing.

It cured the infection but left him deaf though he didn't fully recognize the fact until the Latin teacher, a sour, sandy-coloured martinet with a toothbrush moustache, lost his temper with him for not paying attention and slapped him round the head. 'But sir, please sir, I *was* paying attention.' 'Somers is blubbing again.' Next holiday Dad took him to an ear specialist in Woolwich which meant a tram-ride which he enjoyed. The specialist twanged tuning forks and touched them to the side of his head in various places and asked him what he could hear. 'Yes,' he said at the end of the appointment, 'the hearing in his left ear has gone completely. That will be five guineas, please.' Lot of money in those days.

'You're looking sad.'

He pulled his head up, grinned at her.

'Sorry!'

The guy at the ticket office would not take back the ticket Thomas already had and since the seats on either side of it had been sold, he had to buy two new ones – not as good, the third row of the *tendidos* above the *barreras*, and in the sun, but he reckoned since Luke had never been to a bullfight before a little distance might lend enchantment to the view. She offered to pay, but he doubted if she had a hundred and fifty francs on her, or at any rate to spare, so he refused the offer.

With European Summer Time the corrida did not begin until seven so they now had at least one and a half hours to kill. They found a café-bar on the ground floor of an apartment block, but it was a dull, typically French sort of place with leatherette banquettes, electronic fruit machines and low, globe-shaded lights.

'Let's see if there's anywhere better by the river,' Thomas suggested.

There wasn't. But there were seats and it was warm and though the view across to the other side was of factories and commercial wharfs the river was wide and, beneath the clear sky, blue. Thomas loved rivers and ports – always they suggested to him new places, going somewhere, being on the move.

Luke delved into her small woven shoulderbag, pulled out a pack of Marlboro, offered him one.

He hesitated.

'Go on.'

'Jacked it in. Years ago.'

She laughed, 'Be a devil.'

But he refused – partly he had to admit because of the brand. He had always preferred darker tobacco: if it had been a Gauloises, or even a Camel . . . They sat in silence for a moment or two, watching a line of long thin barges loaded with containers being towed downstream, and the three old men fishing fifty yards or so from them under a stand of poplars. He thought about her – this strange, attractive if not beautiful acquaintance he had picked up – or perhaps had been picked up by. What was she really like? Where was all this leading?

'Where are you from, Luke? I mean you don't seem quite like the others.'

'It shows?' She grinned, smoked some more, then, 'Case of running off with the gypsies. Except they're not real gypsies. Just travellers.'

'Why did you run off?'

'Usual reasons, I suppose. Boring old life. Not getting anywhere. Not a lot of fun in it.'

'And this is better.'

'It's different. It can still be a bore, but it's different. I can't stand being bored.'

She leant forward, elbows on her knees, face cupped in her hands, occasionally taking a drag at the cancer stick. That's what his parents called them – decades before the connection was made official people called them coffin nails or cancer sticks.

'How did you get in with them?'

'Road protest. Twyford Down. I belonged to a local group. Tweed skirts, fur-lined boots. NIMBYs really.'

Again he looked at her. Full of surprises. Lucasta, posh name. And definitely a bit older than he had thought. Could be early thirties. And she was, bit by bit, dropping what he now guessed was an assumed cockney twang. She had no accent he could define – educated but classless. There you go again. Educated meant you didn't have an accent. Dad's (and Mum's) snobbery still ran like a poison in his veins. Twyford Down? That probably meant Winchester. She lifted her head, turned to him.

'And you? You're odd. You're a family man, but on your own. You surely have a car, but where is it?'

He explained briefly, sort of: his son's obsession with surfing, the family needed the car, he'd caught the bus into Bayonne just for the bullfight. He didn't say he was to be bumming around on his own for a week.

'How long have you been with these travellers?'

'Nearly a year now.'

'And you just . . . upped and joined them?'

'Juss like that.' She made the Tommy Cooper gesture with her hands in front of her, palms down, a magician's spellcasting motion over a top hat or whatever. 'Juss like that.'

'Any regrets?'

'A few. But it beats PA-ing for a solicitor.'

Thomas's mind bubbled up with prurient curiosity. The communal life, promiscuity even . . . group sex?

'So what's the downside?'

'Not much privacy. Which is why I like to be on my own every now and then. We eat badly, especially when there's not much money – you know, white bread and sweet tea. Police harassment – but there's much less here than in Blighty. Spain's best. We wintered in Spain, in Andalusia. Easy to get good dope in Spain and possession is legal.'

'How do you get money? Apart from being rent-a-crowd for animal libbers?'

'Busking . . . '

'Not a lot of talent that way from what I heard.'

'Stop knocking them.'

Suddenly her face was dark, turned in and away from him. She dropped the butt end of the Marlboro and ground it savagely beneath her heel.

'A couple of us are really quite good. I play classical and

Spanish,' guitar obviously, 'and a guy called Jeremy is good on the flute. We go well together.'

Spasm of jealousy. Already I'm feeling possessive about a woman I've known barely a couple of hours. Well. Barely not at all. Not yet known her bare. Maybe later. But she was still talking.

'And in Andalusia last year we met up with some Dutch people and for a time we toured as a sort of cod circus. Flame-eaters, simple juggling, pretending to do real circus tricks. It was a laugh, and went very well till we quarrelled over the take and split.'

He remembered the circus people in *Hard Times* – images of freedom and co-operation against the utilitarianism of Gradgrind. Presumably this lot were like that and only beguiled gents on the cusp of being elderly before mugging them when they were really hard up. He pushed the idea away and scolded himself for being an old grumpy guts. Must be low sugar levels – or most of a litre of red leaking into hangover. Either way there was an answer.

'Let's go back to that caff and have a sandwich or something. Don't want to see your first bullfight on an empty stomach.'

'Now you're making me feel nervous again.'

But she grinned.

29

And so fortified with croques-messieurs and a couple of large cognacs each, they made it to *les arènes*, a big hollow drum of terracotta bricks. On the shady, *ombra, ombre*, side exactly half of it rose a further three floors beneath a roof to accommodate galleries with wrought-iron rails on the lowest level. The whole structure enclosed at its centre the perfect circle of orange sand, flawlessly raked in concentric circles and walled with heavy timber. Steep terraces of narrow concrete benches climbed from it to the galleries or, on the sunny half, to a lower parapet with its back to the river. Thomas recalled how, twenty years ago, Katherine and he had sat two rows below that parapet in the very cheapest seats, except they weren't seats at all but numbered spaces. As indeed were all the places apart from the very poshest. And then they had not even been able to afford to hire the leatherette cushions the attendants hawked round the terraces.

Feeling obscurely guilty that she was not with him now instead of this strangely exotic but slightly tacky pick-up (very tacky, Katherine would have said: in almost every way you could think of Luke represented the sort of woman Katherine most despised – or feared) he hired cushions and, a true gentleman and his dad's son as ever, indicated the way from behind her rather than leading her.

The atmosphere was good – hot, no breeze, the place full, the sun dropping but not quite in their eyes, an amplified buzz from the full crowd. Next to them a Mediterranean beauty with a face by Murillo, a body by Michelin and a floral dress out of Kew Gardens parked herself with her ten-year-old son last seen as the altar boy in El Greco's *Burial of Count Orgaz*. Spaniards for sure, possibly all the way from Seville or Granada, on holiday in one of the campsites. Meanwhile, another small boy, dark and

Arab-ish, street Arab anyway, Caravaggio type, roamed about trying out seats until someone with a ticket arrived and turfed him off. Clearly he had squeezed through the turnstiles without one. Thomas found his spare ticket, the one for the far more expensive seat down in the *barreras* and gave it to him. The boy checked the print to make sure he wasn't being hoaxed and then grinned at him as if he were St Peter, the guy with the keys to heaven's gate.

Luke approved.

'That was a very nice thing to do,' she said and the heart-stopping smile came again.

Feeling as though he had won the pools, Thomas sat down and she took his hand and squeezed it. Not the pools, the lottery. Although it was France, there were a lot of Spaniards including *peñas*, supporters' clubs, for two of the toreros – Robles and Espartaco. Three rows in front of them five huge fat men with Zapata moustaches and huge sombreros thumped drums in tango rhythms.

Everyone seemed to have seen someone they knew, ten, twenty, thirty yards away. They shouted greetings which extended into long conversations. ('How's your sister, has she had her baby?' 'Why weren't you at the Blah-di-blah last night, we had a great time'), and occasionally they slung leather wine bottles up and down the terraces ... ('This is a good one, my uncle made it, go on try it ... '). The aromas were amazing, a cocktail of expensive perfume, eaux de cologne, cigars (*en fiesta* one smokes cigars), sweat and anticipation.

Then, at last, *al punto, à point*, at seven, a cornet squealed a fanfare and the *alguacils*, in their black velvet and black plumed hats, mounted on prancing ponies, led in the glittering procession.

'Here we go,' said Thomas, and squeezed her hand back.

The three toreros with their heavily embroidered ornamental capes wrapped over the left shoulder and arm, their slightly less resplendent *peones*, and their mounted picadors, laid out a slowly wheeling phalanx which arrived in front of the president's box. They saluted him, he saluted them, then they wheeled away, and immediately the *peones* of the first torero shook out the real capes that had been left folded on the *barrera* some time before, floated them in the air, testing the wind or lack of it, the humidity even.

The cornet squealed again, high and silvery . . . And here he came, the first bull, a big black giant storming through the *toril*. He paused for a second, then, spotting the flap of a cape, went after it like an express train and the *peón* scrambled behind the *burladero*, one of the small but thick and sturdy screens that protects the entrances on to the sand . . .

The first three bulls, taken, as the custom is, by the toreros in descending order of seniority, left everybody with a feeling of frustration, of chances lost. The picadors spent too long with the first two, weakening them, leaving them incapable of proper *faenas*, the last act when the torero faces the bull alone with only a scrap of red cloth, the *muleta*, and a wooden stick before taking the sword and killing him.

'Why does the bull go on charging the horse, even when his shoulder muscles are being shredded?' Luke asked.

This was, as Thomas had expected, the bit she found difficult to take – but at least it was the bull she was worrying about, not the spavined, drugged and heavily padded horse.

'Because he's driven by the satisfaction he gets from feeling the weight of the horse on his horns. That moment tells him there is an enemy he can reach in the ring, and from then on, right up until he dies, he will be looking for the same satisfaction.'

The kills were not as good or quick as they should have been. The president awarded only one ear, to Espartaco, but the crowd thought it was not enough.

Interval time and everybody was restive, anxious, angry with the president, and beginning to sweat in the increasingly clammy heat.

'What do you think of it so far?'

'Brill, wicked, deadly.'

'Something to eat?'

'Whatever's going.'

Thomas got to his feet and went in search of food and drink, arriving back with two beefburgers and two beers just as the fourth bull charged out of the *toril*.

He was magnificent, the best of the evening. At five hundred and twenty-four kilos he was well-muscled and sleek, not a pure black but a *moreno*, a deep, deep brown the colour of plain chocolate, and it was clear immediately, as Robles strung together the first of a magical sequence of passes with the cape that he charged true, was strong and brave.

Back he came into, but never quite touching, the folds of cerise silk so tantalizingly moved just inches in front of him, and never completely lost from sight, so the maestro was able to string together fluid, graceful veronicas, making an art of the uncertain choreography of the ring, three, four, *o-o-o-o-lé*, before spinning the cape round in the graceful swirl that left it held on his left hip and draped around his feet. He turned his back on the bull with his right hand flung in the air saluting the cheers of the crowd, slung the folded cape over his arm and sauntered back to the *barrera* across sand which his black slippers scuffed. Behind him the panting bull pummelled the surface with his hoof, wondered where the elusive enemy had gone.

The *faena* was superb: after string after string of perfect passes, Robles, trusting the bull's and his own honesty, lured him into a final true charge, came over the top with one toe still on the ground, and plunged the sword deep and with perfect accuracy so the blade cut the vena cava and the bull dropped like a rock, dead before his head hit the sand. The crowd erupted, Thomas looked at the woman beside him and found tears were streaming down her face. He seized her hand and squeezed tightly, she responding to his pressure. The Zapatas in front of them whacked their drums as if the Archangel Gabriel had commissioned them to wake the dead.

Two ears. But the crowd chanted, some of them anyway, 'What do you have to do to get the tail as well? Fly?'

From high drama to farce. The fifth bull, Espartaco's second, was a disaster. It emerged from the pens, stood, gave its shoulders a shake. A *peón* flapped a cape, the bull seemed to notice and trotted forward, picked up a little speed, lowered its horns and then passed him, missing him by a clear three feet. The *peón* ran across to Espartaco pointing two fingers of his right hand into his own eyes. The bugger's blind. Well, anyway, ought to be wearing spectacles.

Espartaco shrugged, came out, called, shuffled elegantly nearer and nearer the bull, called again and the bull came, but once more well wide of the mark. The crowd's protest was muted at first, incredulous that this should happen to them, and then even more incredulous that nothing was being done about it.

A storm of protest rose but the president remained unmoved. After three or four more attempts at the *capeo*, the picadors were summoned, and this was the signal for the crowd to go wild. If the animal was pic-ed, then the whole charade would have to be completed. Half an hour in from the interval and there were thousands of empty beer and soft-drink cans in the stands. The woman who threw the first might have felt she was taking a chance, but within seconds it was raining cans. They were not being thrown to hurt or even hit anyone, but simply to make the continuation of the farce an impossibility.

The president took his time but gave in, showed the red handkerchief that ordered a substitute. This bull would be taken out to be killed by a butcher, and a new one brought in. Four steers appeared, not true *toros bravos* but sway-backed, neutered males with brindled markings. The theory is that the defective bull will surrender to its herd instinct and follow them.

But this one could not see a cape properly and could not see its fellows either. It declined to follow them.

The farce continued for forty minutes. The crowd began to amuse themselves with the Mexican Wave. Again and again it circled the ring. Up they all went, Luke and Thomas with the rest, arms in the air, waving, with a great rising and falling cry, leaving them rocking with laughter at the fun of it. On the wave went, curling back round to them, a simple but splendid thing, an act of rebellion and a symbol of unorganized, spontaneous oneness.

Dusk fell and the lights came on. At last the president signalled that the bull should be killed in the ring. The *peones* slung cans back into the crowd, or gathered them into bin-liners and the picadors came back. Espartaco's chief *peón* attempted a quick kill without a *faena*, but this is almost impossible with an ill-prepared and defective bull. It took six attempts before at last he dropped.

The substitute was a *deslucido manso*, a dull coward, and Espartaco was no doubt emotionally drained by the previous three-quarters of an hour. He made what he could of it, but killed badly, low down almost in the flank of the animal. It took a long time to die.

With swifts still high in the glowing sky, now shot with the scarlet streamers of sunset, and the first bats squeaking out from under the beams that supported the roof of the galleries, the third matador, Pedro Castillo, returned, his white and gold suit glittering in the lights.

But nothing now could surpass Robles' great *faena*, nor the raging and conflicting emotions that came after. The crowd too were exhausted, and many were already leaving. However, the bull was good; Castillo took his own *banderillas*, and coaxed the animal into long raging charges, halfway round the ring, so he was moving really very fast when the *banderillas* were launched, and the slightest misjudgement or stumble would have cost him his life.

Castillo began to put together a credible *faena*, but he was trying too hard and he was caught – the bull's right horn sliced into the outside of his upper right thigh. That brought back the crowd's attention all right. Screams, gasps and cheers as Castillo pushed back the human shield his *peones* had made, retrieved his *muleta* and took the sword. The blood, brighter than a bull's, spread swiftly across the white and gold.

Limping and wounded though he was, he took the sword, made a cross of it with the *muleta* furled on its stick, and went in over the top to produce a kill as quick and as good as that of Robles. Medical attendants carried him away, and his *peóns* remained to receive the one ear awarded, and again the crowd went wild, demanding a second.

But it was only one that the *alguacil* in his black-plumed sombrero was allowed to hand to Castillo's *peón*, before the plumed mules were beaten into the ring for the last time. The yoke was hooked to the dead animal, and in a swirl of stained sand he was gone.

Now it was the thin, flat cushions that rained into the ring: the crowd's final demonstration of its execration of the president, and many remained behind to continue booing and whistling.

Thomas and Luke took one last look at the ring, then he turned behind her as she climbed the steps to the exit. For a second he relished the swing of the loose skirt over her buttocks, the way he could see the reversed triangle her briefs made beneath it, the slimness of her waist. The twin gods of love and death, Eros and Thanatos, performed a pavan in his head.

'Wasn't all bad then, was it?'

She half turned so the lights made the tiny rings in her ear glitter, and her nose and mouth were in harsh profile.

'Best I've ever been to,' she said.

'?'

'Whoops!'

30

The euphoria generated by the corrida leaked away like air from a ripped tyre. He followed her out into the dim concrete galleries which circled the terraces and would not have been out of place in an abattoir, and down the zigzagging flights of stairs. Through unglazed lights latticed with ochre brick he could see the chaos of the car-parks, dust swirling in the cars' headlights, youths playing the matador, passing their jackets or T-shirts over the bonnets, the occasional shunt, the heady altercations as two Frenchmen blamed each other for what had happened, the angry gestures, the shrugs, the waved arms suddenly switching to the finger or the fist jerked up at the elbow, the swung fist.

He let her stay in front of him, protecting her from the idiots behind who wanted to lean on and tip everyone in a heap to the bottom. He'd been taken, no doubt of it.

In the car-park she turned on him.

'You're pissed off with me, aren't you?'

'A bit.'

'Would you have bought me the ticket if you had known I was a paid-up member of the *peña taurino del mundo*? Probably not. And I learnt a lot from what you said while it was happening. A lot I didn't know. Look, over there we can get a bus back to the town centre.'

She was right. *Centre ville, les arènes, centre ville* – a shuttle service. But perhaps she knew already – after all, this was the fourth day of the fiesta, *les fêtes de Bayonne*. Who had she conned the afternoons before?

In the bus they stood, strap-hanging, swaying against each other, hips banging together, a longer contact on the bends.

'So, what didn't you know about toreo before you picked me up?'

'God, you're a bastard. Full of male shit. You were priding

yourself on picking a bird up, half your age, and now because you've discovered it might be a bit the other way round your pride is hurt. Which is bollocks when you think about it. You should be pleased I thought of picking you up.'

'A free ticket more like.'

She took three deep breaths. Then, 'The bit about the satisfaction the bull gets from feeling the weight of the horse on its horns.'

That sounded pretty genuine.

Bayonne does not have much of a centre. There are no big squares, only small ones which in daytime hardly figure as squares at all as they are merely roundabouts for the traffic. But at night, *en fête*, the three or four largest were closed to cars and filled with crowds.

The bus dropped them close to one of the largest. They could see the floodlights, the fairy-lights, hear the music. Thomas hesitated on the crowded pavement, wondered what would happen next. He felt empty, ready to be lonely, almost ready to walk back across the river and see if the last bus to Hossegor had gone.

Luke pulled out her Marlboros, stuck one in her mouth, fired it up with her tiny lighter. She took a drag, placed it carefully between his lips, and fired up another.

He remembered, as from another life, the old adage – if you put a fag in someone else's mouth and they don't have to adjust it, then you really are compatible. Well, actually, you're soul partners.

He managed not to shift it, though he wanted to. He puffed at it, took it out of his mouth, grinned and let the smoke out.

She smiled, and again the smile almost physically winded him.

He did not inhale. Him and Wimp Clinton.

'Lover,' she said, 'I need a drink.'

Miraculously two people left a café table just as they pushed past it and Thomas grabbed the seats ahead of others who were moving in on it. A moment's stand-off and they conceded.

It took their waiter twenty minutes to reach them. Thomas

looked at the oddly shaped bottle of water that already stood on the table engraved with a familiar logo.

'Ricard,' he said, when the waiter came. 'Deux verres avec glace et un demi de Ricard.'

'Last of the big spenders?'

'Not really. It's just that he's so busy it might be an hour before we get a second.'

He drank two stiff ones quite quickly while she lingered over a much milkier, weaker shot, and the euphoria built again. It was really very jolly: the fifes and drums, the swirling dancers. He counted six eights, all wearing elaborate costumes of lace, bells, flounced shirts, embroidered shirts and flared trousers. A repeated moment in the dance came when each individual spun on the spot for a bar or two and it put him in mind of the music and dance of the spheres, each one separate in his or her own space, but still part of a constellation.

Luke sat with her elbows spread on the table, her chin in her hands. The posture pushed her breasts together, exaggerated the cleavage and produced a wider gap at the top of her low-slung T-shirt.

Two more large ones for him and another for her, and the half-litre was gone. He toyed with the small bottle for a moment or two, wondering whether or not to order a second. Ricard. Richard, and he felt the pang of loss, and guilt too – were they all right? Were they managing without him? Of course they were. When all was said and done they didn't really need him all that much – they'd even get by financially now Katherine had her own business.

'Come on . . . '

'Eh?'

'You can dance, can't you?'

The folk-dancers had finished, were mingling with the crowd, talking to friends at the other tables, and an ordinary band, much like the first one at St Jean-de-Luz, maybe the same one, had struck up, accordion, fiddles, brushed drums.

He stood up, swayed a little, she steadied him with a hand on his elbow.

'Are you all right?'

'Fine. I'm not leaving that on its own though.'

He meant his rucksack. She helped him to shrug it on to his back.

The square filled as soon as the band got properly going and there was no question of jiving even if the music had been right for it. Which it wasn't. It was very French, chirpy but sentimental. They danced in the way every other couple there danced, close together, her forearms on his shoulders, her hands clasped behind his neck, his in the small of her back, swaying back and forward, jogging slightly up and down. Occasionally the rucksack bumped other dancers.

She was small, smaller than Katherine, yet her body fitted to his so easily, so naturally. He could feel those breasts, warm when they were close, moving across his chest when the tempo was more lively.

'This is nice.'

'Ummmm.'

Images of the day went through his head. The wine in the park, the perfection of Robles' *faena*, the Mexican Wave, the blood spreading on Castillo's thigh. It had been a good day after all, a very good day, and that it should end like this . . . He felt her tongue in his ear, then she whispered:

'You're very nice you know.'

'So are you.'

What an adventure! Supposing it came to it. *It*.

Would he, um, be up to it? Judging by the warmth that was spreading through his groin that shouldn't be a problem. Never had been much of a problem except when he'd drunk too much, or was ill, or seriously overweight. But premming . . . That was another matter. He'd never been unfaithful to Katherine in actual deed, only in imagination and fantasy, but even with her after all these years premming could be a problem – and with someone entirely new, and half his age and . . .

'What's wrong?'

'Sorry, nothing. Nothing at all.'

'You were miles away. Worrying.'

He pulled back, smiled at her. Such understanding. Such empathy. Then that smile. Like a sword.

'Oh . . . Luke.'

He closed in, felt her warmth nestle into him. Presently he began to kiss her and her tongue flickered over his teeth. Definitely no problem about being *up* to it. Her palms and finger ends began to knead the back of his neck. He slipped his hands inside the elasticated band of the top of her skirt and she wriggled against him again, dropping her hands from his neck to the small of his back. Assent.

Don't rush it. He stumbled on an unevenness in the road surface, opened his eyes, put the side of his face against hers and swayed. All around, jostling like an overcrowded bumper-car attraction at a fair, but in very very slow motion, the other couples nudged, and sometimes the men, catching his eye, would wink. Occasionally the rucksack on his back got in the way because he'd forgotten it was there, and they'd mutter at him: *putain, cochon, con*, and then slowly, like giant copulating jellyfish they'd swing away. Indeed it was like being in water, an aquarium, with the fairy-lights above fencing off the sky. He stumbled again but this time on purpose, making of it an excuse to let his hands slip lower.

Brief briefs. His finger ends were inside them, his palms now resting on the upper rise of her buttocks, one thumb nestled in the top of the cleft. He could feel dampness there, sweat. America, my new-found land. Allow my roving hands to go – above, beneath, around, below. Something like that, anyway.

'This isn't quite fair,' she murmured.

'No?'

Her hands came round the front, loosened his belt and undid the top of his chinos. Jesus, he thought, I'll end up with them round my knees. But then her hands went to his back again and slipped under the loosened waistband.

And for the first time since he had left Hossegor he remembered his problems. September! November! These vintage years to be spent bleeding from his bum! It's a long, long time from May to September, but not so long from September to

November. Yes, somewhere in the mishmash the band was playing he could make out the tune of 'Autumn Leaves'. Fucking defector. Brecht went back. Weill stayed and wrote this hideous song . . . She pinched the top of his bum.

'Ouch!'

'You went away again.'

'Sorry.'

Good excuse to get a bit lower. His hands were now cradling warm, silky, soft flesh. But how to get round to the front?

'Where are you going to sleep tonight?'

Is that what she really said? Is this really happening? I thought you'd never ask.

'I don't know. I've got a good sleeping-bag. Out in the open somewhere.'

'Sleeping rough? At your age?'

Gently mocking.

'Not so rough. It's warm. It's a class bag.'

They swayed on, then, in for a penny, he took the plunge.

'Have you . . . can you . . . suggest an alternative?'

'Maybe.'

Presently she withdrew her hands and reaching behind took his wrists and disengaged his. Without saying anything she took his hand and led him out of the square. And for the first time, as they passed close to the table where they had been sitting he saw two cowboy hats in the crowd beyond. But they weren't looking in their direction. He wondered if she had seen them and was moving off now because she did not want her travelling companions to see her with him.

They climbed the hill to the cathedral, passed through the square where the kiosk had been. Another band, another close throng of dancers, but she led him on round the edge, on to the narrow pavement, hugging the shop fronts and entries and out the other end. He felt dazed now, swimming in alcoholic, lustful euphoria, throbbing with anticipation of what might yet happen.

She pulled him into a doorway, pulled his face to hers with her left hand while her right hand wormed its way into the front of his chinos, getting hold of his now very tumescent prick. He did the same down the front of her skirt, got his middle finger into her very wet vulva when . . .

The big bang that created the universe was a non-starter compared with this. He took two double-fisted blows, one on his left ear, one on the right, then a pointed boot exactly between his anus and his coccyx. He screamed as he went down, but the same boot cut it off – his attacker stood on his face.

Yet he heard her.

'In his hip pocket. There should be about a thousand left. Don't take anything else.'

Then she stooped and he smelt the anise on her breath.

'This is for feeling up my bum in public.'

And she kicked him in the balls.

They left him in the road, close to the gutter. Much the same sort of situation as the one his dad had ended up in. He lay there waiting to be run over.

31

Coroner Criticises
of Car (*sic*)

FORMER BOGNOR SCHOOLMASTER'S TRAGIC DEATH

A YOUNG woman told the Coroner at Chichester on Wednesday how she stood in the roadway beside an unconscious man who had fallen off his moped, and waved both arms to stop an oncoming car from running into him. But the car came on.

'I had to move quickly to get out of its way. I did not see it hit the man, but I heard the noise of the car striking metal,' Miss Annabel H. F. Smith, domestic help, of Summertime Bungalows, Felpham, said.

The inquest was on 59-year-old Christopher Richard Tate Somers, retired schoolmaster, of Wroxham Way, Felpham, secretary of the Tithe Barn Club and staff manager for Mr Bob Murfett, turf accountant.

Asked by the Coroner (Mr M. P. A. Winslow) regarding trouble which Mr Somers apparently had with his moped in Upper Bognor Road, east of the junction with the High Street, Miss Smith said that the engine of the machine, which was travelling towards Felpham, stopped.

Deceased got it going again, but had trouble again about 15 yards further on. Then he started 'zigzagging all over the road' and fell off his machine on to his left side. She ran to him and was engaged in lifting the moped off his leg when she saw the car approaching. She stood up and waved to stop it.

CARRIED 39 FEET

Police-Sgt. Jenkins gave evidence of finding two pools of blood on the road, 39 ft. apart. Coroner: 'It looks as if the unfortunate man was carried 39 ft. by the car.' – Sgt. Jenkins: 'It would seem so.'

The Coroner told the jury that the accident occurred just after 10 p.m. on March 17th and deceased died the following afternoon in Bognor Regis War Memorial Hospital.

Dr W. F. Caine, pathologist, said that the left side of the deceased's skull was fractured, but it was not a serious fracture. This injury was quite consistent with deceased striking the roadway with the side of his head when he fell off the moped.

Deceased also had a fractured pelvis, which in itself was not a fatal injury, and also six ribs broken, three on each side, which would tend to increase shock to a substantial degree.

Asked by the Coroner whether, if deceased had only sustained the injuries through falling off his moped and 'nothing further had happened to him', he would have recovered, Dr Caine replied: 'I cannot say so.' He said it was very difficult to assess in connection with the head injuries.

Mr J. Pringle (For Mr Lewison, the driver of the motor car) asked how it could be certain that the fracture of the pelvis was caused by the motor car, Dr Caine replied that a fracture of the pelvis was almost always due to crushing. A pelvis could be crushed from a fall from a height. Coroner 'Is it consistent with deceased having been run over?' – 'Yes'.

BRAKES INEFFICIENT

PC Blake said that on testing Mr Lewison's car, a black saloon, the brake only acted efficiently on one wheel out of four. At ten miles-an-hour the car took three or four lengths to pull up.

The driver of the car, James Brian Lewison, chemist dispenser, of Rookery Cottage, Middleton, said his car was a 1939 model and he had driven for 37 years.

As he came eastwards along Upper Bognor Road, one of the vehicles coming up High Street went in front of him, causing him to slow down. His speed was 18 to 20 m.p.h., gradually increasing to 26 m.p.h.

By the light of his near-side headlamp he saw an object on the roadway when he was 10ft to 12ft away.

'I braked a little thinking to avoid what seemed like a sack.

'I never saw the girl waving. She was in a black spot on the road and I never saw her at all,' he said.

CAUGHT THE MOPED

Replying to Mr F. W. Alderson (for the relatives), he said: 'I did avoid the object (deceased) in the road. I turned right immediately but caught the moped and carried it along.'

Coroner: 'Do you not know that it is the duty of a motorist to so drive that he can stop within the limit of his vision?' – 'I didn't know that.' Coroner: 'A great many others drivers don't

(continued on Back Page)

either – so now you know.'

Miss Anne Frances Docherty, shop assistant, of 1, New Cottage, Middleton, told of travelling on her moped a little behind Mr Lewison's car. She saw something lying in the roadway, but she did not know what it was. A woman was standing in the road waving her arms. Coroner: 'Did you expect the car to stop?' – 'Yes, but it went straight on and hit the object.'

Tony Brown, student engineer, of 'Swallow', Middleton Road, Felpham, said he was a passenger on the top deck of the bus standing in the lay-by. On looking where a girl passenger was pointing he saw a person standing in the middle of the road waving her arms. As the car came up to her she jumped out of its way to the other side of the road.

'I didn't see the car hit anything. I just saw the car suddenly jump up in the air,' witness said.

Addressing the jury, the Coroner referred to the evidence regarding the inefficient condition of three of the four wheelbrakes.

'It is appalling,' he said, 'to find that a man of his age and responsibility should go out in a car such as has been described to you. If Dr Caine's evidence had been that the fracture of the skull had been so slight that deceased would have recovered and wouldn't have died if his later injuries had not happened, Mr Lewison would be in a different position.'

He told the jury that it was not for him but for the police to consider with what offence, if any, the driver of the car could be charged.

As directed by the Coroner, the jury returned a verdict of 'Death by Misadventure'.

32

With the side of his aching head resting against the bus's vibrating window, with the pain in his bum sharpened to flashes of agony every time they hit a bump or a pothole, Thomas was in no condition to take in the extraordinary beauty of the countryside around him. Steep meadows, once lush but now brown with the drought, dotted with small sugarloaf-shaped haystacks built round single tall poles, climbed to steeper slopes forested with beech and larch. Above it all the rounded eminences were covered with heather, purple still, and bracken prematurely yellowed by the lack of rain. On the increasingly frequent bends he could have seen, had he wanted to, the plain the bus was climbing from, back to Bayonne and the coast, hidden in violet haze thirty miles away.

Presently the Nive ran with the road, not yet the brown river that threaded Bayonne, but a cold grey stream, occasionally, where the valley narrowed, a torrent, pouring over and round grey rocks and breaking into white foam.

Confused images, recollections, anxieties stormed between his bruised ears: of the kind ordinary people, middle-aged, dressed unexotically, people *like himself*, who had not inter-vened while the hippies were beating him up and robbing him, there had not been time to, but who had helped him to his feet as soon as they had gone; who, in reply to his repeated plea of '*je veux une chambre*' had, against the odds in a town *en fête*, found him a room in a pension, only yards from where the beating had taken place; of the *patronne* who had been dubious at first but had accepted his Visa card as security and put him in a tiny room at the top of the tall narrow house, a room with a dormer window, a washbasin and a small towel – good people all, Good Samaritans. He'd have done the same had he been in their shoes.

Using the mirror set in the door of the small plywood wardrobe he had looked himself over: the blows and kicks that had so utterly destroyed him had left few marks. His left ear was swelling and the cheek hurt – there might be some bruising in the morning; there were superficial abrasions on his face and some dirt; the area round his anus and coccyx hurt more than it had but there was no sign of external bruising or bleeding. Later he had descended a half flight of narrow steep stairs and used the toilet. He bled quite a lot but not noticeably more than he had done over the previous five days: there was no reason to suppose that the kick had aggravated his condition. The pain in his testicles was fading quickly, as it does, though his penis felt sort of internally bruised and was swollen. He supposed that she must have held on to it when the first blows came.

The realization of this was almost the worst thing of all: the humiliation, the awareness of what a fool he had been, of how all along she must have secretly despised him, had gloried in the setting-up of the final scene even before it took place, all this filled him with chagrin, with bitter anger. He had to choke back tears or restrain himself from beating his fists on the back of the seat in front of him. And then, as if it were printed on the retina of his mind, or floated like photographic paper in the red light of a darkroom, her face came back, the spiky white-blond hair, the blue eyes, the tiny rings in her ears, the red bow of her mouth . . . the smile. How could he have been so stupid as to imagine a woman half his age could feel any sexual attraction to him? What had he been thinking of?

But really worst of all, and it was worse now, in the bus, and worse because he was not properly aware of what was happening to him, was the shock, the feeling of being 'all shook-up'. He felt hollow with it, emptied out, deeply bruised in some region where human tissue and the psyche are one, and this was the result not of what she had done to him but of the beating: his whole being's response to the enormity of being beaten up, something that had not happened to him since The Links.

It was this more than the actual injuries and humiliation that had led him to remain in bed for most of the following morning, only getting up when the landlady knocked on the door, threatening, as far as he understood her, to call a doctor. He drew more money from the hole in the wall, had a proper lunch of steak frites, and then, feeling some relief that he was doing so, caught the bus to St Jean Pied-de-Port, the last town below the Roncesvalles pass.

The bus swayed and climbed, dropped and climbed again through the broken foothills of the Pyrenees. The small homely farmsteads of the Basques, painted white for the most part with barns and outhouses attached, some with three storeys, the top one pierced to allow air-curing of hams, the drying of peppers, the maturation of cheeses and so on, passed the window. Each had a patch of maize a hectare or so big, still green but with ripe cobs and the tips of the spear-like leaves tinged with yellow, grown for fodder and to feed the hens that scratched and scavenged around their yards. In spite of the constantly un-dulating landscape, networked with valleys, it all seemed very tidy, well-husbanded, decent. In the state he was in Thomas found the concept of decency moving, and tears of a different sort pricked his eyes.

Presently the valley narrowed, twisted even more, the slopes on either side became steeper, in places fissured cliff faces broke through the trees and it seemed there was scarcely room enough for the road, the river and a single-track railway on the other side. Indeed the railway went through a couple of short tunnels and at one point the road was labelled 'sens unique'. He knew what it meant, one-way or single-line traffic, but the words became a toy in his head. Unique sense of what? Place, time? The mysterious sadness of humanity? The music of the uni-verse? The death of Dads?

Dad should have been happy in those last two years in Felpham. So should Mum. A house of their own. The furniture their own too apart from a few pieces Aunt Helen had let them keep because they actually liked them. But the Nefertiti head and the Venetian glass had gone – and Thomas still wished he'd been asked. Seventy-One had been his home as well as theirs. And all his books! The Edmund Crispins and Michael Inneses!

Even the *Children's Encyclopaedia* – never mind its racism, imperialism, volcanoes and skeletons, it also had good monochrome pictures of sculptures of nude women, the ones by Lord Leighton being particularly rewarding. He used to sit in his muck room for hours, modelling them crudely in plasticine, adding the genitals, exaggerating the nipples, and sometimes using his oil paints to paint them white.

They should have been happy. It was the 'You never had it so good' years. They had a telly, their first fridge, central heating that worked, a record player that played LPs. And that was another thing. Where had all the 78s gone? There was the 'Surprise' Symphony, the *Pastoral*. Music from *The Damnation of Faust* where you could actually hear Beecham drop the baton at the end of one piece, and say 'Thank you, gentlemen'. The Edith Sitwell-Constant Lambert version of *Façade* – that, on original shellac, must surely be worth a bob or two now. Tiana Lemnitz singing 'Dove Sono' and 'Porgi Amor'. The overtures to the *Marriage of Figaro* and *il Seraglio*, the former, according to Dad, exactly the right length to boil an egg to. But these were theirs. Also lost in the move were Thomas's own 78s. The 'March and Entry of the Guests' from *Tannhäuser*, the Prelude to *The Mastersingers*, the sort of stuff you throb to in late adolescence.

But it seemed they had not been as content as might have been expected, hardly content at all. Although they had a car, a Ford Prefect? Or Popular? Something of the sort, Mother hated being so far from Aldwick Bay, judged the new estate she was living on to be squalid. Dad, hurt by her rejection of the move he had organized, did not always rush home after closing Bob Murfett's office once the last dog race had been run, but instead went to a pub, usually the Orlando, and tanked up on Scotches before weaving his way home on his lethal moped.

Also, and surprisingly, he'd caught a nasty bout of religiosity, actually from Thomas himself. Thomas had had a brief phase of aesthetic Anglo-Catholicism – and Dad began going to church with him in the hols. The unfortunate thing about this was that the vicar banned Mum. She was divorced, had not even remarried. A scarlet woman. Meanwhile Father mopeded his hangovers to Felpham church without her. He rediscovered the poetry of Gerard Manley Hopkins and even bought an LP of an actress called Margaret Rawlins reading the better-known ones. Mother hated the sonorous sincerity of her performance and whenever he put the record on she went into the kitchen or the tiny new garden she was trying to make something of.

They'd had a row that day, she told Thomas later. Sensing her depression Dad had driven them out to the Devil's Dyke, north of Brighton, hoping that early spring weather, cowslips on the downs and daffodils in the Sussex villages, pussy willow in the hedges, would cheer her up. When it didn't, he'd said to her, 'Dess, the trouble with you is you are a perfectionist.' To which she had answered with genuine puzzlement, 'Isn't everyone?'

Already perhaps enough to make him stay out late that evening, but on top of that it was St Patrick's Day and the Orlando was Bognor's Irish pub. Dad, without joining in, enjoyed the atmosphere, the conviviality. And, at the bar, he fell in with just the sort of bloke he liked to meet, could get on well with – a minor belletrist, who often published mordant little pieces in the *New Statesman* or the *News Chronicle*, whose daughter was in rehearsal for the summer season at the new Chichester Festival Theatre. Thomas could imagine only too well how the presence of each had flattered the other – Dad very pleased to be chatting with a frequently published writer, who was probably even more delighted to find an educated gent in an Irish pub who had actually read his stuff. No wonder they stayed there through to ten o'clock, chucking-out time in those unconvivial days. The writer took the trouble to tell Mother all about it, a week or so later. He wanted to say what a nice person Pop was, and how he had enjoyed his company.

Two things not mentioned at the inquest. One: the moped being genuinely that, that is basically a bicycle with a small one-stroke engine mounted on the back wheel, and ordinary bicycle pedals. Dad's shoelace had come undone and snared in the pedal – hence the zigzagging before he fell over. Thomas in his bus climbing into the Pyrenees thirty-five years later had a sudden pang of sadness. He remembered his dad's shoes. They were always black, plain, slightly pointed, cheap, and often cracked. And often the shoelaces came undone.

Two. The sister, matron, whatever, in the hospital had told his mother, while she sat beside his bed, that they had never in her memory had a man in their care with so much alcohol in his blood. Mother had been disturbed by the fact that this nurse should feel it necessary to impart this information to a woman whose bloke was dying in front of her eyes. Now, in his bus, Thomas felt a sneaking, no, not sneaking at all, but open and ungrudging admiration for his dad. Considering how often drunks end up in hospital, that was quite a record. And, yes, he too could do with a drink right now.

They cremated Gerard Manley Hopkins with Dad, the book that is. The undertaker didn't think the crematorium people would take the LP. But before buying his own copy (the OUP Collected) Dad had marked up Thomas's copy with page numbers leading from one poem to the next, the sequence as read by Ms Rawlins. Thomas remembered how the sequence ended.

This Jack, joke, poor potsherd, patch, matchwood,
    immortal diamond,
        Is immortal diamond.

33

The road, skirted by a high dressed-stone wall on one side, with handsome stone-built villas above it, and a drop to the valley below on the other, wound into St Jean Pied-de-Port. Suddenly he felt it would not be a bad idea to stay where he was, just let the bus shuttle its way back to Bayonne with him still on board and then make his way to Hossegor. He felt an aching longing for them all – Katherine, Richard and Hannah-Rosa. Were they looking after her properly, were they keeping a watching eye on the edge of the surf, or were they all distracted by that damned *Championnat*? And it wasn't just the surf either, was it? The crowds along the beach would be thicker than before, how easy for some pervert to entice her into the Dune she still shuddered over because of the film . . .

The doors hissed open. He hesitated, then hauled himself upright, dragging his rucksack up from between his feet. He'd been through all this from dawn to late morning and he was not going to renege on the decision he had made then – he was not about to slink back to Hossegor like a whipped dog with a tale of being mugged and robbed of a hundred quid. Certainly he was not going to say anything about a freaky woman called Luke . . . But he'd phone some time soon, make sure.

The air outside the bus, which had been air-conditioned, was pleasantly warm and carried café au lait and chocolatines on its breath as well as Gauloises and garlic-flavoured petrol fumes. At four o'clock there was a pleasant air of busy-ness in the tiny square and Thomas suddenly felt altogether better. He wandered amongst the shops for a quarter of an hour or so, firming up his plans for the next stage of his odyssey. He bought a 1:100,000 map of the area and spent a few moments agonizing over boots. The walkers around were either students and totally unequipped for the mountains, relying on distressed sneakers, long hair and magic beads, or middle-aged to elderly and had the lot: rucksacks on frames, stout sticks bound with cord for handles below a grooved top where you put your thumb, water bottles. They wore knitted ski-hats, the sort of shirts Rugby footballers wear, but with designer labels, short shorts above thick stockings knitted from coarse Pyrenean wool the colour of porridge. But the *pièces de résistance* were the *grande randonnée* boots – stout leather, thick deeply treaded soles, padded ankles.

Thomas checked out prices in a shop window. You could pay a hundred and fifty quid for a pair of boots like that – and they didn't look that much different from his Wranglers.

The tourist office had *un bulletin météorologique* posted on the door. *Risque d'orages* in the mountains at night so he bought a plastic mac with a hood. Also *brouillards* in the *après-midis*. Get a compass? No, he'd stay on the road.

What else? Rations. He was really enjoying himself now, in the crowded sunny square beneath the deep eaves of the stuccoed houses, in front of the square-towered church with its round clock and a roof also deep eaved. Next to the book and gift shop where he had bought the map there was an *alimentation*. The usual small-town stuff – the fruit and vegetables tired, since the locals relied on the market for fresh produce, the tins and bottles dusty – but he got what he thought he needed. Two decades ago Moni had said you should always take *chocolat au lait*, *petits pains*, oranges or peaches, *saucisson sec* sliced thin, a litre of Evian. She disapproved of booze, saying alcohol and the mountains do not go together, but this was not advice Thomas felt able to follow. *Encore de Ricard?* No, the aniseed taste from the night before still floated round the back of his palate, but a half-litre of *eau de vie de marc* – cheap brandy – won't do us any harm. The label bore five stars circling a curlicued shield emblazoned with a floriated N. Just the thing to toast the defeat of the French on the hills above Sorauren.

A quarter to five. The last bus to Arnéguy and the border left at five. The temptation to settle in for the night was, Thomas decided, irresistible. He had already made a fool of himself, and fetching up on the crest of the Pyrenees at nightfall with nowhere to stay might seriously compound the folly of the night before. And too, the small spell of euphoria was wearing off, the aches and pains where he was bruised, the sense that he had been abused, seriously physically abused, was back.

He tried three pensions and of course they were all full. Panicking he returned to the tourist office where a kind lady rang round for him, using a list of out of town *chambres d'hôtes*. Still no luck. Eventually he had to settle for a room in a three-star hotel recommended by *Michelin* and costing six hundred francs for the night. When he got there the desk-clerk took one look at him, his bruised face, his one rucksack, his crumpled and grubby clothes and asked to be paid in advance. The hotel menu was similarly expensive and pretentious but he found a brasserie close to the railway station where he had a seafood pizza and a carafe of wine before returning to the room.

Now, he said to himself, looking round the standard fittings, I'm going to make the most of this. He had a long hot bath, and then, wrapped in towels, lay on the bed with the TV remote control, the brandy and the Evian water. No need to attack the mini-bar. He surfed the channels hoping for porn, but found nothing in that line other than a rock and pop channel whose videos were certainly fruitier than you get on British terrestrial but not enough to justify the music. Then he caught Alain Delon in *Le Samourai* and was asleep before it had finished.

He woke to the hissing blank screen at about two in the morning and found there was bright red blood on the towel beneath him. Drunk, frightened, he stumbled back to the bathroom and sat on the loo, wiping himself with toilet paper, then sponging himself with the already severely stained towel. Without a hand mirror he couldn't get a proper idea of what was going on. Certainly he was bruised and there was pain – but it came from the kicking he'd had, not, he felt sure, from whatever it was that was wrong above the sphincter. And he was not bleeding externally. Eventually he concluded that he had farted in his sleep, and probably woken himself up doing so.

And then he remembered he had gone to sleep without phoning home, well Hossegor anyway, and he felt a wave of longing that must have surpassed anything ET had suffered when he too could not make the right connections. In short, he knew what it is like to be alien.

He lay awake in the dark and remembered.

'He seemed to come to a little just once,' his mother had said. 'He moaned a little and tried to move, and he sort of breathed my name as if he knew I was there. Or wanted me to be there. Just "Dess", that's all. They didn't tell me he'd been run over, that his ribs and pelvis were crushed, not even that his skull was fractured. His face was terribly bruised, and his head had a huge bandage, but I thought he'd just fallen off his bike and hit it on the kerb. Which was why I wrote in the first telegram that I thought he was going to be all right. Then just about two o'clock in the afternoon he started breathing badly, sort of croaking, and I rang for the nurse, and she told me to wait in the corridor. Ten minutes later she came out and told me he had gone.'

That's all the second telegram had said.

Thomas, I'm so sorry but he's gone.

34

At five to eleven, and with a plastic bag to carry as well as the rucksack, he joined the short queue. It consisted, he guessed, of shift workers at the frontier *ventes* and cafés as well as walkers like himself.

This bus turned out to be very different from the one that had brought him from Bayonne. Its diesel fumes nearly made him sick as he waited for his turn to get on. It was old, the seats were hard, it shook and rattled. The driver/conductor was a large tank of a woman who wore a peaked cap too small for her mountain of permed ginger hair. When he tried to pay his fare he found her French impenetrable, apart from the odd *fou* and *salaud*, and he could not understand what she was on about.

'She requires you to tell her whether you would like a single ticket, a day return, or a period return.'

A tall man, in full *grande randonnée* gear, lean, bronzed, long fair hair tied back in a ponytail. Thomas put him down for one of those German bastards who speak English better than any of us can if you discount the plums in their mouths. And he could not for the life of him remember how to ask for a single fare, so the German had to do it for him. The woman cranked a handle and her machine spewed out a minuscule ticket.

Pushing down the aisle Thomas realized that if he took a window seat the German would probably take the one next to him and chat all the way, so he took a seat next to a beauty whom he took to be Spanish – olive skin, marvellous dark hair, thick eyebrows, haze of hair on her cheeks below and in front of her ears. She was about eighteen and wore an overall. As he squeezed in beside her she smiled shyly and budged up. When the bus started and began the short but steep climb out of St Jean Pied-de-Port it was inevitable that his thigh and his shoulder brushed against hers on the bends.

She kept her face turned three-quarters away as if she found the view fascinating and he could not help fantasizing about that haze of hair – how much of her body was hairy in the same way? It was so silly that women allowed themselves to be embarrassed by excess body hair. He loved it, if just once he could make love with such a woman... What with the warmth, this pleasant presence and the vibrations of the bus he began to feel he might be blessed with a stonker – an unwilled daytime erection. But no. Stonkers belong to your mid-teens, and he'd not copped one since he used to come back to Seventy-One on the last bus from Bognor after going to the Picturedrome or the Odeon on his own to escape the spiders on bridge nights. And on the way home his head might be filled with Vera-Ellen's legs, or that magic moment when in *Doctor at Sea* your first view of Brigitte Bardot was her back, her long, long back bare down to her bum...

The road levelled somewhat and there was a stretch of almost flat meadow, with a brown brook bubbling through it and big white cows with spreading horns and huge dewlaps, belled like ... cathedrals! Then more forest.

Thomas found he was looking at the back of the German's head in the window seat in front of him. He remembered the first time he'd met that particular model. It had been on his very first trip to Hossegor. Backing to do a turn he'd put the Bedford camper he was driving into the dune and up to its rear axle in sand. And this German had come by in a Merc cabriolet and towed them out. His final words had been, 'Trust the British to get stuck in the sand,' said in that immaculate accent.

'What about Rommel?' Thomas bellowed after him. 'Eh? What about the whole fucking Afrika Korps?' But too late, he had been well out of earshot going *brrrrm, brrrm* in his fancy car.

It was not a long ride, only five miles up to the frontier at Arnéguy. Thomas walked through the border, the first time, he realized, with childish pleasure, he had ever actually walked from one country to another. He changed three hundred francs for pesetas and went into the tacky *supermercado*. Since in spite of the EU a lot of things are still cheaper in Spain than France there are *supermercados* on the Spanish side of every border crossing. He wandered about for twenty minutes enjoying the Spanishness of it but in the end bought only a litre of Soberano, his favourite of the cheap Spanish brandies, to replace the marc and another bottle of Evian. He still had the food he'd bought the evening before.

When he got to the check-out he found that the dark furry beauty he had sat next to in the bus was at the till. She blushed slightly as she took his money and gave him change, and wouldn't look at him. He wondered what she had been doing in France. Had she just gone down for the morning to buy something? Did she live in St Jean, have a boyfriend there? He sensed the possibility of romance in her story, that perhaps she might not be Spanish at all but Greek or even Turkish – it was so easy nowadays to move about, live on one side of a frontier, work on the other, and all hundreds of miles from where you were born. But he had neither the nerve nor the language to ask her.

Once outside in the warm sun again he discovered his intention of walking the ten miles or so to the Roncesvalles pass had been based on a serious misreading of the map. He had assumed that the border post would be on or near the crest of the mountains, at the top of a pass, but the tumbled forested slopes still rose above him and a closer look at the map showed that the walk also involved a climb of at least two thousand feet. Was he up to it? Yes. Why not? He'd bloody better be. He might not be as fit as he should be, probably there was something seriously wrong with his lower bowel, but he wasn't decrepit. Yet.

The first four miles or so were no problem with only a couple of places where the road zigzagged steeply across the mountainside. There were plenty of trees, plenty of sun-dappled shade. Although the fumes from passing cars and lorries were a bother it was all very pleasant. A brook continued to prattle along over rocks and through pools (the map told him that it marked the border, that the other side was still France), there were patches of meadow, again with the cone-shaped haystacks, and still some flowers in the banks, mostly immortelles, scabious, valerian and teasels. Butterflies, fritillaries, for the most part, fluttered over them. A jay gave its rattling laugh and flew down into the valley, flashing blue, white and beige. The sky was almost clear, bright and pure apart from some puff-balls of cloud drifting up from behind the rounded mountains ahead. Presently he came to a village, Luzaide-Valcarlos. He stopped for an icy San Miguel beer, served on a narrow terrace above the road with a *tapa* of five tiny Manzanilla olives – although the other side of the valley was still France, this was Spain!

Leaving the village the road climbed almost continuously and for a time the valley was very narrow indeed, crags closed in, the rocks were hung with moss, there was little sunlight, and the traffic seemed to treat him as an expendable nuisance. His thighs began to ache, then his knees and ankles, the rucksack weighed heavier and heavier. And after an hour the outside of the big toe on his left foot began to get sore. Would boots costing five times more than the ones he was wearing have saved him? Probably not. He had inherited his mother's bunion and his father's varicose veins and fallen arches, which meant that for years his left foot had been half a size bigger than his right.

Two o'clock. He was very tired, thirsty, hungry, hot, miserable. The little river on his right bifurcated, one arm coming down a steep narrow valley on his left, the other continuing to follow the road. The map told him that the arm on his left still marked the border, and that the road was now leaving the frontier and climbing into Spain. It also told him that he was still only about halfway between Arnéguy and the watershed.

He pushed on for twenty minutes before coming to a point where the riverbed was only a few feet below the road. He climbed down over rocks and shingle and found a shady spot about a hundred yards away where a lichened boulder hung over a pool beneath a mountain ash, a rowan tree. The Rowans, Mottingham. This was a better place to bring up a tree than the bombed-out ambience of south-east London. The berries had formed but had not yet turned, were not the bright vermilion they would become. He delved into his plastic bag, set out on the rock beside him the plastic beaker, the Evian water, the Soberano, the packet of sliced *saucisson sec* still wrapped in heavy waxed paper, and two of the four *petits pains*. Then he savoured the moment.

The traffic noise and smell were no longer a pain. He was going to have a nice meal. There was no birdsong, the wrong time of day, but up over the mountains he could see two black spots slowly circling – could be golden eagles, since there were only two. The more common Griffon vultures usually hang about together in greater numbers – like the vultures in Disney's *Jungle Book*. He poured brandy and water, the water was warm, but what the hell, and drank. Magic. The river gurgled away and he could see brown fish in it, baby trout probably; the air was laden with a soft vanilla-ish coconut fragrance, and yes, there were flies, but butterflies too.

It didn't turn out quite as idyllically perfect as he had hoped. The bread was dry and the *saucisson* sweated grease with a sour tang to it. The peach was dry and pithy. He should have chucked the lot and bought fresh at the *supermercado* or the village where he'd had a beer. Even the chocolate was squishy, and stuck to his teeth and palate. He washed it all away with another beaker of brandy and water and began to pack up when suddenly he knew he was going to have to defecate. Do a busy. Shit!

He clambered about the rocks trying to find a hollow where he'd be invisible from the road, found one, a tiny patch of shingle between boulders, about three yards from the swirling stream. You shouldn't do this, you know, he said to himself, bad country practice to shit near running water, but, as Mother used to say, needs must when the devil drives.

The movement was easy, well shaped, not noxious to the nose. He used some of the wax paper, it wasn't a problem. When you squat it usually isn't. But there was blood, yes there was blood. Undiluted by toilet-bowl water he could get a better idea of how much. More than there had been on the towel the night before. Half a cupful? He gathered himself together again and then reached up to the boulder behind him. It was crowned with a low domed clump of flowering yellow broom, the source of the vanilla-ish fragrance. He put his hand into it to haul himself up, and out of it slithered a snake.

It was very quick, as frightened as he, fifteen inches long, hissing and jerking its head, black lightning flickering in front of its beady eyes, a body checked with triangles of black on silvery grey. The European asp whose venom kills by stopping the heart . . . or simply scaring the shit out of you.

Panting, heaving, he clambered back on to the road and then stood there for a minute or so cursing himself, his stupidity. He'd seen asps in the Pyrenees before. He knew they were there. Why had he forgotten? And why was he exposing himself to all this? Food-poisoning, hurtling vehicles, a serious bowel condition, freaky ladies who mugged you, drunkenness, heat-stroke, exhaustion, SNAKE BITE? 'What the fuck am I doing?' he cried – out loud. Onwards and upwards? Or back and down. Did it make a difference? Probably not. So. Onwards and upwards.

Hitching the rucksack into a more comfortable position, hoisting the plastic bag, now noticeably lighter, he set his face again to the climb ahead. A banner with the strange device – Excelsior. That's all he needed. That and the snow and ice to bear it through. At least there was much less traffic now – siesta time, both Spanish and French truckers observe it rigorously – the cars that swished by all had German, Dutch and occasionally British number plates. They were laden with roof-racked tenting, towed tiny trailers, the passenger seats were filled with small children car-sick because of the twisting road.

Onwards. Upwards. He grinned to himself. Back in the sixties he had taught in a north London secondary-modern, which had meant a railway journey every day to Camden Road and carriages shared with the nubile girls of Camden Girls School – all neat in their grammar-school jackets, badges emblazoned with the words 'Onwards and Upwards'. What a splendid motto for an all-girls' school . . . !

235

35

Midday on 25 July, 1813 a battle took place on the pass of Roncesvalles. For Thomas on the spur that ran north and downhill from the summit of Alto-Biscar, it was half-past two on 27 August, 1994.

He had made it to the watershed, labelled *Puerto de Ibañeta, 1057m* and then set off down a metalled but untarmaced track to the east. After a mile he turned north down the spur, leaving the height behind him. He was now stumbling through low heather whose tiny dried bells still held some colour, low yellowing coarse bracken, spiky grass. There were rocks and molehills, and lichen-covered whale-back boulders, and occasional declivities in the steeply sloping ground.

He stopped about half a mile down the ridge, set the plastic bag down carefully (but even so the Soberano bottle chinked hollowly), wriggled out of the rucksack, and sat down. The view in front was magnificent but hazed – mountains tumbled into hills which quickly lost any sharp definition. Or was it just that his head swam with exertion and brandy, his stomach heaved with the sour fatty meat, and he was very, very tired and very hot. Flies, on a scale with those in *Lord of the Flies*, soon swarmed around him – attracted perhaps by the smell of sweat and faeces that hung about him.

He hated that book. He had taught it to six different classes in the days of the old Certificate of Secondary Education. He had learnt to hate the cunning manipulation of emotion, the nihilism which the author himself could not face, but had to whiten, as one does a sepulchre, with the Christ-images and Simon drifting out to sea, luminous with starry plankton . . . what a cop-out!

He had once thought of rewriting it, recasting Jack as the hero he was in *Coral Island*, the lad whose practical inventiveness and sound leadership enabled the lads to survive in spite of Ralph's namby-pamby middle-class shittery, Piggy's four-eyed, four-square rationality and Simon's pseudo-mysticism. The unholy alliance of class, academia and religion holding back the inevitable victory of the common man, the proletariat. It had seemed a clever idea in the late sixties . . .

Why am I thinking about all that? The flies. He hauled out the Soberano. Had he really already drunk almost half a litre? Dear Lord, don't want to run dry before we reach the commissariat, do we? Meanwhile, another little drinkie won't do us any harm. He poured what he judged to be twenty centilitres into the plastic beaker, topped it up with the Evian which was not in quite such short supply, and saluted both parents from his eminence high in the Basses Pyrénées. Dead men, that's what they called empty bottles. 'Well, that one's dead,' Mother would say. 'Better open another.'

Dead men.

There must have been a few here.

The Griffon vultures, the black kites and the red kites dropped out of the sky where they had been waiting patiently all morning, riding effortlessly on thermals strengthened by the heat of battle. Rifleman Somers could see how the one closest to him was picking at a Frenchman he had himself killed, only sixty yards away, a brave man who had got nearer than most. The vulture (we are friends to the bitter end) now thrust its gouging beak into the man's backside and using the scaled claws of its shaggy foot for leverage hauled out flesh from which drooped the man's colon, dripping with blood and shit . . .

Funny, I've seen a lot of battlefields, and they always carry this aura, this chill presence, even in blazing hot weather. There's always a bleakness, a dull leadenness in the air – no, not the air, the air moves. There must be molecules in the earth, organic molecules, dead cells, with all the complexity that geneticists and micro-biologists and so on are only just beginning to unravel, that can hold in that complexity a memory of how the man they were part of died . . .

His head swam with the brandy, almost he thought he might faint, the blood thudded, a hundred and thirty to the minute, and in his ears . . . men died.

Here they come, tramping over the bodies of their mates, sending the vultures flapping and wheeling into the air. One dropped a liver, splat, on to the men below. The drums thudded, the tricolours drifted above the high black bonnets but only through the movement of the men. The bells beneath the eagles jingled. When five thousand men march together the earth shakes a little.

'Fire at will.'

Rifleman Somers pushed the black shako with its green feather to the back of his head, licked dry and cracked lips, rubbed his sweating palms down the sides of his blue canvas trousers and on the brass buttons, now patinated to green, no Brasso in those days, of his green jacket. Hang on. Maybe there was no Brasso, but there was plenty of horse urine and wood-ash about. That's what they used on brass in those days. Is that why Brasso smells the way it does? Perhaps. He lifted the Baker rifle, settled the oak stock in his shoulder, squinted down the highly polished brass sights. No need to crouch behind his rock; at two hundred yards they had nothing could hit him. Pick your man. This was the bit he didn't like. Playing God. He said to himself: if they get to us who is most likely to be the one to bayonet me, or slash his sabre through my collarbone and into my lungs. That one. With the big black beard.

Dropped him.

Reload. Takes time with a Baker. The Tower Musket can be fired four to the minute. The tighter fit and the rifling give the Baker its range and accuracy, but it's a fucking struggle to get the cartridge down the tight spout, even using the greased patches used for lubrication. Knew a girl like that. Once. Came wet in the end. Up to the shoulder again. Red-head this time. Never liked carrot-tops. Christ they're nearer – they'll be having a go at us before we know it. Got him.

Shouts from behind and a bugle call. Thank God, they're pulling us back.

*

Thomas stood, picked up the plastic bag and rucksack, walked backwards, his heel hit another boulder and he tumbled heavily so the back of his head landed in grass and rabbit droppings. Christ, I've been hit, it must have been one of those dratted *voltigeurs*. But the ball, almost spent, had only left him winded, his head singing, his poor old bum screaming, but more or less intact. And of course he had been falling uphill so the slope broke his fall. Nevertheless he felt the worst consequence might be another poo on the way.

One thing anyway, only Penis-ular War freaks like himself would be out here on this stretch of country, so no one would have seen him . . .

Except there's that fucking kraut from the bus looking at me through binoculars from the top of the Alto-Biscar. Him, or someone like him. Anyway, the light companies and the rifles are now filtering back through the thin red line, and I'd better catch up with them. And actually I think he's looking at the eagles, or vultures, not me.

'Well done, mate.'

'Welcome home.'

Rifleman Somers squeezed between the shoulders of two Wessex men, dark, their prematurely lined faces beneath the narrow peaks of their shakos the colour of medium-rare beef, and then between the two behind. A couple of steps up the slope and he could see between their headgear the continuing advance of the column below behind a screen of sharp-shooters.

'Don't fuck about, pick off the little runts in the front,' bellowed Sergeant Moore. As he reloaded he let his eye run down the line in front of him. Two hundred men, in black shakos over red jackets, formed up in two files of a hundred each, the colours in the centre. Here and there men dropped, or broke ranks howling with a femur or humerus shattered by a French ball. Calmly the men just moved inwards towards the colours.

Ratatatatatatat, at sixty yards the drums broke into double time, the front files of the column quickened their pace, but they were already puffed from the climb, the weight of their packs, and the heat built up inside their bonnets. Yet the sun glinted on their bayonets and Rifleman Somers had a sudden urge to be elsewhere.

'Present, Aim, Fire . . . at will.'

Two hundred muskets as one. A deafening crack above the already hellish row of battle, a swirl of powder smoke, two hundred tongues of red fire as burning cartridge papers followed the ball.

The thin red line is often romanticized as the epitome of gallantry in the face of appalling odds, the British David against the continental Goliath. No way. It was a deadly, machine-like weapon, trained to perform immaculately as on a drill ground, even under heavy fire, a robust killer.

The column reeled, eighty or ninety men dead or dying in the front three files. The muskets cracked again, and again, each achieving three or four rounds a minute, settling into a continuous roar. Then, when the carnage and chaos in the front files had brought the whole column of more than five thousand to a halt, the two hundred, down now to maybe one-seventy, fixed bayonets and charged. The front of the column broke as steel followed lead, bugles called, the beat of the drums changed rhythm and the French fell back, leaving four hundred dead and wounded behind them.

Between twelve and three this was repeated four times, and each time the thin red line became not thinner but shorter. At three the major-general who led the brigade ordered them back on to the even steeper slope of the Alto-Biscar where the tumbled rocks and boulders made their position virtually impregnable so long as their ammunition held out. However, Thomas, who now climbed up a further four hundred feet to the same position himself, could see that it was so, this new position did leave it open for the French to head east and turn the allied right.

And at four o'clock or thereabouts . . .

36

At half-past three European Summer Time Thomas sensed a general darkening of the valleys in front of him and a sudden drop in temperature. Seconds later wisps of cloud passed over him to the left and right, the Linduz disappeared behind a rolling cloud that changed from white to grey as the cloud behind him blotted out the sun, and then it was around him too. In seconds the slope that had spread below him was gone, the boulder which he had tripped over became a shadow of its former self, turned into a ghost, became mist.

I am, he said to himself, on the north face of a mountain. If I climb until I can climb no more because the slope is reversed I shall have crossed the mountain and be descending the southern side. I shall therefore, before long, meet the path or track I took away from the main road. When I reach it I shall follow it to my right and it will eventually take me back to the main road. Turning then to my left and going downhill, I shall make my descent further into Spain and hopefully out of this muck.

Pleased with this logical analysis of his predicament, achieved despite drunkenness, exhaustion, hunger, he set off – again onwards and upwards. The mist was so thick now that if he did not focus his eyes on the few grey objects he could see, the ground at his feet, the boulders as they loomed up like hunched old men, his retinae recorded to his brain the chains of plasma that swam across them. This sensation that he was seeing both blank mist outside and the interior but almost more physical world of the inside of his eye, filled him with vertigo.

Presently a sweet but pungent odour passed his nostrils. On a rock almost level with him, but seen through the corner of his left eye and at just that point where mist and rock dissolved into each other, a man sat with his back to him and pulled on a clay pipe in whose bowl he pressed a glowing wick. He pulled back the wick and half turned.

'Best to stay where you are, lad, until it clears. Else you might stumble into the boggers' lines and be took.'

The face of course was in an advanced state of decay. Fortunately Thomas recalled that in *An American Werewolf in London*, the werewolf's victim had just such a face when confronting the werewolf in a Piccadilly Circus cinema. The Living Dead. So he cheerfully told it to bugger off, knowing it to be a figment of his imag . . .

Put on a happy face, whistle a happy tune, tap your troubles away, this is the ghosts' high holiday, this is the ghosts' high noon. Ruddigore. His mother played the piano, a pretty Victorian upright. She said they sold it because her fingers were arthritic but Thomas suspected the real reason was that there was no room for it in the new bungalow. Why is a bungalow called a bungalow? If you're building a house and run out of bricks you bung a low roof on instead . . . Please yourselves.

Anyway the happy times included standing round the piano and working through stacks of Gilbert and Sullivan piano scores. Their favourites were the 'Policemen's Chorus' from the *Pirates* and the 'Entry of the Peers' from *Iolanthe*, as much for the words as the tunes. 'When the foeman bares his steel we uncomfortable feel . . . when threatened with *émeutes* and your heart is in your boots there is nothing brings it round like the trumpet's martial sound, like the trumpet's martial sound.'

What a card – to rhyme *émeutes* with boots!

Émeutes means riots. Not many people know that.

'Tanttanttara zing-boom,' bellowed Thomas stumbling through the mist. 'Bow, bow ye lower-middle classes, bow ye tradesmen, bow ye masses.' Was Gilbert a crypto-Marxist? Maybe. Am I going up or down, and is that a tree or what is it?

Yes, lots of trees. Scrub-oak, beech, some birch, none of them much above twenty feet and some hung with swathes of moss and all of them dripping with the mist. Where am I. Where the fuck am I? Spain? France? Outer space? Inner space?

Bells, no, jingling harness, clopping of hoofs, baaing of sheep and bleating of goats, must be a track ahead. And there through a screen of a holly-like plant, but the leaves smaller and not so sharp as the British variety, a small caravan goes by. A troop of light cavalry, horses snorting, harness jangling, the men cluttered with all their impedimenta of pelisses, dolmans, crimson and gold sashes, valises, sabres, sabretaches, pistols, carbines and what all, the mist dripping from their brown fur caps. Then a big barrel of a man on a big bay mare. He was wearing a cocked hat with a white plume, had blue facings to his red coat, gold lace and buttons, a crimson sash and his blue leggings had a crimson stripe. He reined in as another rider came through the screen of hussars and saluted the general by touching his crop to his hat.

'John? John Byng?' the big man called out. 'Is that you? Your lads did well up on that mountain.' Slight Irish burr in his voice.

'Thank you, sir. But I'm damned if I know what to do with them now. Damned if I can even find my way back to them.'

'Well, when you do, have them ready to move an hour before dawn. You'll get your route just as soon as this muck lifts enough for us to see where you are.'

'Sir Lowry, with respect, I understood My Lord had said we were to hold the pass for as long as we could. To the utmost. There's plenty of fight left in us yet.'

'Damn your eyes, John. Are you trying to tell me my duty?'

'Definitely not, sir.'

John Byng's black gelding began to piss the way only a horse can. He rose in the stirrups until it had finished. Then jogged off into the mist.

The convoy rumbled on. Behind Sir Lowry Cole came his big covered wagon and a small flock of sheep and goats. Then a couple more wagons.

'Cole,' Wellington said, 'gives the best dinners.'

There should have been a cow too, Thomas remembered. He's lost the cow he keeps for fresh milk . . .

Which way now? The most obvious answer was to follow Sir Lowry Cole and his caravan, but Thomas was not so far gone, yet, as not to be aware that he was willing hallucinations. He had done this before. The first occasion had been at the Easter High Communion in Chichester Cathedral at a time when the Dean had a high sense of drama and Thomas was suffering from Anglicanitis. Fasting, as he should be, he had cycled the seven miles and arrived early enough to get a canon's seat in the choir. Starvation induces hallucination anyway, add in incense, silver and white vestments, red-jacketed trumpeters in the clerestory gallery and it occurred to him there must be angels about. If there are angels about I should be able to see them. And of course there they were, swooping about the high, smoke-filled, sunbeamed spaces above, clad in shredded garments with a heraldic feel to them, metallic crimson, emerald and lapis lazuli, adding the unheard harmonies of the spheres to those of the earthly choir. Hail thee festival day, Day whereon Christ arose . . . But all through it, then as now, a corner of Thomas's mind, ever on the surface prone to romanticize though it was, retained the cool clarity of scepticism beneath. You can make yourself see anything if you want to enough, and Sir Lowry Cole with his wagons and sheep are small beer compared with the heavenly host.

It was now deathly quiet, chill and damp in the forest, and what had appeared to be track wide enough to take wagons soon became, or always had been, a path that eventually petered out in an undergrowth of saplings. The leaf-mould beneath his feet was soggy, spongy. Go back? But why? Head on down? But which was down? He felt panic now. Wait. Wait until the cloud lifts. But supposing it doesn't before nightfall?

Desperate now he pulled the map he had bought in St Jean Pied-de-Port from his rucksack, feeling that somehow it might help, though for the life of him he couldn't see why it should. He didn't even know which way was north, let alone whether he was in Spain or France. But, surprisingly, it did help for it showed rivers, streams, rising on both sides of the watershed. And on both sides these always eventually fed the main river of the main valley, the one that carried the road. He was standing, in a dry August, in a patch of something that was almost a bog – it had to be a spring, the rising point of one of these streams, or maybe an unmarked one, that eventually would feed into a marked one.

He scouted about the wet patch and sure enough found that one rim of it was wetter than the others and that there were bright patches of moss, some of it compacted of tiny star-shaped formations, brilliant green. And through them ran a tiny trickle of icy water.

37

If you were in the Allied army in Spain between 1808 and 1813 the one thing you did more than anything else was walk. Rifleman Somers walked from Lisbon into the middle of Spain and back three times. And by July 1813 he has walked from Ciudad Rodrigo on the Spanish-Portuguese border to the Pyrenees. And now he's walking back again. To Lisbon? Who knows?

Sometimes you walked in blazing heat, and sometimes in icy rain and snow. And sometimes, in the icy rain and snow, you had the parley-vous up your arse like at the back end of 1812, and if you loitered or went to the side for a shit, you could find your mates had gone and some Frenchie hussar was looking down at you from his horse, in the pouring rain, wondering what he should do with you.

On that occasion Rifleman Somers pulled up his pants, shrugged, grinned and walked off expecting to be shot in the back or sabred with every step he took, but when he turned after a hundred yards the hussar had gone.

This time it is hot but downhill.

'Hey, sarge, why the fuck are we running away? We licked the boggers yesterday, we can lick them today.'

Some of the rowdier element in the company sing as they lope round those spiralling bends, others break ranks for a moment to pick fat, juicy, ripe blackberries and then have to trot to catch up.

A mile or so behind and one hundred and eighty-odd years plus a month and a few hours later Thomas too loped down the same road, but metalled and tarred now and walled where there was a drop. His hunch about the bog he'd found himself in had turned out to be correct. It became a brook, and then something more substantial and, exactly as the map suggested, it ran past the tiny village of Orreaga – once known as Roncesvaux. He'd done well – found a tiny *fonda*, with a room which had a narrow bed and a damp sort of thin eiderdown for a cover, and a bar where he bought a plate of tiny fried cutlets and chips with a litre of fruity purplish red, before going to bed at the unheard-of early hour of nine o'clock. His bum hardly bled at all and he slept like a log.

For breakfast a toasted bun and a *cortado*. Cortado? An espresso (*café solo* in Spain) cut with a small amount of milk. And bliss. Always a surprise. How do they do it? You cross a border, twenty yards, and the café coffee is different. The Italian technology with the Latin American pure Arabicas – Costa Rican ... good, Colombian ... perfect. Just as our dead empire still gives us tolerable curries, and a French cous-cous is almost as good as a Moroccan, in Spain it's the coffee ...

Such were his thoughts as he stopped to pick a handful of blackberries before continuing in the footsteps, give or take an inch or two of tar, of the twelve thousand or so survivors of the previous day's fighting on the pass.

OK, he thought, so Wellington is the father I can respect and don't have to feel guilty about, but the interest in wars goes back beyond that. Why? Blame Hitler.

From age four to ten he had followed the maps, seen how his mother moved the tiny flags over them. He had seen propaganda features – *The Battle of the River Plate*, *Target for Tonight* and *Desert Victory*, as well as such fictions as *The Way Ahead*. And every time you went to the cinema (which of course was pretty often), there were the newsreels.

Deprived of the real thing, when it was all over he was still hooked – made tiny little men out of plasticine, armed with pins for muskets, and set them out in lines in the empty lot next to Seventy-One where he shot them to pieces with his BSA air rifle. The .177 calibre pellets were cannon balls to scale and did the same sort of damage to the plasticine men as round shot would have done. He used to wonder, as he did this, at his physical response – a warm sweat, a tightness in the throat, an erection.

Later, after Uncle Apples had given him the Arthur Bryant books about the Napoleonic wars, he went on to Oman's *A History of the Peninsular War*. And that more or less was why he was here now, hot, parched, hungry and dizzy, as after three miles the road swung west and began to climb ... again! This was less than fair – especially as the map marked the pass he was approaching as only three hundred feet lower than Roncesvalles.

'Look,' Rifleman Somers said to Rifleman Green from Nottingham. 'Just look at that.'

A cloud of dust a couple of miles away at the point where the road turns west and begins to climb again.

'Aye,' says his mate. 'The parley-vous. Anyroad the first of them.'

'No,' says Rifleman Somers a touch testily. 'That man coming up the road. Wearing dead funny clothes. Old man. Not too fit by the look of it.'

Podgy, balding, red in the face, with a haversack on his back and a bag made of some sort of shiny white stuff in his hand and wearing a pink but dirty shirt and trousers, but quite unlike any Rifleman Somers has ever seen before. And he's very puffed, stops, sways a little, and then sits down quite sharply on the bank just fifty yards from the top of the pass and the point where the last files of riflemen are rejoining the road.

'I think he needs help.'

'What the devil are ye talking aboot?'

'That old man sitting on the bank down there.'

'You're seeing things, Tom. There's no ol' bogger there.'

Rifleman Somers glances down at his feet and the loose earth and gravel, instinctively looking for a sound foothold before stepping across the ditch. And when he looks up again, the podgy man has gone.

Another six miles of winding climbing road take us to the top of yet another pass, and here the Fourth Division, with the Third in support, forms up again in much the same way as we did at Roncesvalles.

Again the riflemen are deployed ahead of the line but without the cover afforded by boulders. Thus exposed across the slope, and faced with an enemy even stronger in numbers than before, and with a good road to bring his columns up rather than the broken ground of Roncesvalles, we are soon driven in. Indeed I get a quite nasty knock from a spent ball full on the peak of my hat which, had it not been spent, would surely have dashed out my brains. As it is I am concussed and out of my mind for several seconds. I come to again and, for perhaps the space of a quarter of a minute, the figure I saw before is standing in front of me and panting fit to burst with his hand on his heart as if climbing the pass in that heat has been far too much for him. But then the vision fades and my friend Green helps me up and back through the thin red line.

Well, the French don't come on any more that evening. They want all up before they launch a serious attack. Meanwhile the generals share a sheep with their staff and dine off pot-roast mutton. During the meal they do some arithmetic, which show that we is up against close on twice the numbers.

So, yet again, a couple of hours before dawn our sergeant walks through the bivouacs (made from branches bent into hoops and covered with the blankets, one per man, that have made this campaign so much more comfortable than last year's, they and the metal cooking pots with a mule to carry them, one to every ten men, all ordered by Old Nosey himself, say what you like but he looks after us poor boggers like he was our daddy, walks through the bivouacs and kicks us awake.

Some men call these bivouacs *benders*.

38

The worst time poor Christopher Richard Somers had was also on a retreat. The retreat from Benghazi. Though it was years after the event before Thomas found out just how bad.

His mother had not kept any of the letters his dad sent her from the Middle East and Ceylon, and only one survived. However, he did have a score or more that Christopher had sent to his mother and sisters (Thomas's granny and aunts), and a diary he had kept on official Signal Office Diary paper from 22 December 1940 to 8 August 1941.

Pilot Officer, later Flying Officer and finally Flight Lieutenant Christopher Richard Somers had been adjutant of a mobile radar station, a unit with two officers and fifty men. As adjutant his particular duty was to look after the men's needs as best as he was able. And, from the letters, it was obvious that he was very able and his best was, as he would have said, a damn good one. Before the retreat from Benghazi there was the advance to it.

8/1/41

P/O C. R. Somers
216 MRU
C/O APO 590

Dear Ma & Family

At last a little time to write a proper letter. Within the limits of censorship regulations, I'll try to give you some idea of life out here.

First of all, for me, as far as the work and conditions are concerned, this is the happiest time of my life. The 'roughing it' is just enough to make you feel you're doing your share, and just enough to be called hardship. And the work is just what I love: I do all the 'administering' and organizing; getting rations, sanitation, camouflage, defence, welfare of men etc: [It was still sound orthographic practice in those days to mark an abbreviation with a colon.]

For about 3 weeks after landing we simply made preparations and sorted out equipment. Then a long journey with a convoy of vehicles: a few days round about Christmas at a desert station, and then several days' more journey, pitching camp each night at about 4 o'clock and getting off next morning by about 10. On 2 January we reached our site, and I only hope we stay here. We are quite on our own, living under canvas, and it's pleasantly warm in the day but very cold at night. At night I wear winter underclothes [that meant woollen vests to his knees and woollen long-johns – what you wore in winter in the north of England with no central heating], pyjamas [flannelette], a pullover, & sleep on a camp bed with four thicknesses of blanket & a greatcoat all tied up with the covering of my valise! In the day-time khaki shorts and a shirt.

Water is generally a bit short, and as a rule we can only allow one gallon per day per man for all purposes: but we manage quite well & I can arrange a 'laundry' day about once a fortnight. At present we are getting no bread or vegetables, but the cooks and I have invented a large variety of ways of dealing with bully beef and hard biscuits. Anyhow I'm trying to arrange a trip of fifty miles twice a week to a place [Sidi Barrani – seventy or so miles from the frontier between Libya and Egypt] where we hope to get 'soft' rations.

On our very first day here [the diary identifies the Halfaya Pass, twenty miles from the frontier] we had to put up a Group Captain and a Squadron Leader (= Colonel and Major in Army) for a couple of nights. The other officer & I slept in a dug-out & gave them our tent: they seemed to be quite pleased with everything, thanked us for the 'good food' they had had, and left us both a bottle of whisky!

The men are marvellous. Three of them are from Liverpool – one a reception clerk at the Adelphi. The way they settle down & start making the place habitable and comfortable, with a little encouragement, is lovely. Now that we have all our essentials well organized, they spend their spare time making little paths round the camp & sticking up notices. I only hope we don't get orders to move from here, as we're all beginning to look on this place as our 'home'.

There isn't really much more I can say. I was hit by a bullet 2 days ago! Some damn fool engineer started firing an Italian rifle, and as I leapt out of my tent to shout to them to stop, a bullet riccocheted (don't know how to spell it) off a rock and grazed my throat. It didn't hurt but I managed to swear at them for about ten minutes without repeating myself once. Our only other casualty was caused by one of our men picking up an Italian hand grenade in disobedience to orders. He blew his hand to bits, poor brute. I hate to see a man have his whole life ruined for one damn silly mistake: and it was the result of the one bad bit of discipline we've had the whole time.

I hope you're all right at home. I'll be glad when letters start arriving. Being cut off like this is the only snag in the life out here. In all other respects it's a damned good life. I hear it's pretty cold in England. Has Wilf: got his commission? Tell him that if not I'll expect him to pull out the hell of a salute when he meets me. [Wilf, his brother, was ten years younger.]

The Group Captain has just been along and told us where there is a canteen: so I'm going to lay in a stock of beer, chocolate, tooth-paste, soap etc: and start a canteen of our own in the camp. Profits will go to our 'Comfort Fund', and we're hoping to get a wireless set. At present we depend largely on rumours for any news.

                    Love to all,
                    Christopher

Life is likely to go on much as usual until we move from here, so I won't write often. There will be nothing to say.

The diary entry for the same day reads:

Better rations this morning: potatoes, onions & tinned sausages.

Sent Martinson to 2/7th Australian Field Ambulance

with *otitis media*. [Inflammation of the middle ear, something Pop knew about all too well.] Strength now 43 O.Rs. [Other ranks.]

Found Naafi & opened credit a/c.

Some bombing during the night, but nothing very serious.

The radar station travelled in lorries and cars from Mersa Matruh via Tobruk to Benghazi in the successful campaign against the Italians and then back again rather more quickly, with Rommel and the Afrika Korps up their arses. Through it all Pilot Officer Christopher Richard Somers made sure the rations and water got through, that the accounts were kept, that petrol and paraffin were available, that the men's health was looked after properly, even that they washed their clothes (dhobi duty) when water was available, everything you could think of. He organized entertainments, quizzes, whistdrives, censored their letters, sorted out their emotional problems... And this through sandstorms, periods from Benghazi onwards when they were bombed and machine-gunned from the air, while all the time the lorries and cars broke down or got 'bogged' in the sand, and during which he had four teeth out without anaesthetic, got a boil on his bottom which had to be lanced, fell head-first into a six foot slit trench, had an abscess in one ear and a perforated eardrum in the other... Thomas thought, Welly would have been proud of him.

He was a father to those men and he loved it when they accepted him in turn, even though he was a toff, and even though the other officers rather disapproved or envied his easy bonhomie. Much as, two decades later, Thomas was proud of the rapport he had with deprived inner-city kids, a rapport that proved elusive to his more experienced colleagues. It was, he later realized, a belief not universally held, though every Somers he had ever known held it, that all youmans are worthy of precisely the same, that is total, respect.

Finally, through a decision and an act which left him more or less a broken man for the rest of his life he probably saved the lives of almost his entire unit, just the one man dead and a few others scratched . . .

So much a father to his men, they stopped calling him Topher and called him Pop instead.

He could, thought Thomas as he reached the top of yet another fucking pass, with his blood pounding in his ear, and sweat pouring off him, a sudden pain in his chest so he put his hand on his heart, he could have been a bit more of a dad to me.

39

Today's walk is only a short one and all downhill or level through meadows with a river on our left, the Arga. The meadows are rank and grown over with sorrel and bramble, and many of the churches roofless, since the heathen French who have been here these five years have slaughtered the cattle and burnt the convents and knocked down the churches apart from the towers, which they keep for observation points.

By eight o'clock in the morning we have covered close on three leagues and can see ahead the city of Pampeluna. A giant tricolour still floats above the fortifications and when our van gets within a mile, puffs of smoke pop up, then come the distant bangs and right behind them roundshot and canister land only a hundred yards short of us.

After a time of scouting about they move us up on to the crest of a long, steep hill some five miles north of the town which has a deep declivity in front of it which then rises to a second hill. The two hills are joined near their east end by a saddle somewhat lower than the crests of the hills.

At the mouth of the valley that separates the hills there lies a small village called Sorauren which sits above the road that leads north to the rest of the allied army, and a bridge across another river, the Ulzana. A chalky track climbs from this bridge up on to the southern hill and is marked near the top by a small hermitage or chapel.

By half-ten our army is spread along this southern ridge or hill, but when Byng's Brigade, to which our company of Rifles is attached, held in reserve behind the main line, because in the preceding days we bore the brunt of the fighting.

And as we take up our positions so, to the north, the ridge opposing us fills up with corps upon corps of the French, nearly double our numbers in total, commanded by the wiliest of

French commanders, Marshal Soult, whose presence is now clearly to be seen, surrounded by his staff with all their plumes and fol-de-rols.

'Are we caught?' I ask Rifleman Green, standing at ease to my left.

'Aye, maybe. But not with our pants down. We'll give them a good taste of lead and cold steel before they get us off this hill. Hey-up. Where's yer spy-glass?'

I'm wise to this. If Rifleman Green wants to borrow the spy-glass I picked up on the field of Vitoria back in June, then there's something worth looking at, and I'm not so foolish as to let him have it until I've had a good look myself.

I rummage in my haversack to find it. It was clapped not to, but in the eye of a gunnery lieutenant in charge of a French battery and I had to clean some eyeball and bone and stuff off it, but it's a handy instrument, quality lens ground in Geneva, nice furniture – gun-metal bound in kid.

'Where, what's there to see?'

'Come on, gi-us it.'

'Fuck off. Where's the action then?'

'No, you idjit, let me.'

'Gerrorff.'

'Further left, the bridge.'

I swing the glass left and down a bit, and can see two men at the far end of the bridge, one on a dark bay, almost black, he's a young man, an ADC, the other on a frisky chestnut I know I've seen before.

'Shit,' I say, 'that's Copenhagen!'

'You daft prick. It's Nosey.'

'Jesus, you're right.'

There's a troop of the French hussars coming into the north end of the village.

'Those fuckers'll get him.'

'If they do, we're fucked.'

In spite of the closeness of the French, the two men have dismounted. Nosey's scribbling a note using the parapet of the bridge for a desk. Shit, man, get a move on.

At the bridge near Sorauren, 27 July, 1813, 11 a.m.

Our troops are formed on the heights on this side of
Pamplona, the enemy in front. The enemy's right is close
to the road to Ostiz, near this village. The road therefore
by Ostiz can no longer be used.

As soon as the 6th division have cooked, they, and all
the artillery at Olague, are to march to Lizaso. Hill should
march this night, if possible to Lanz, leaving a post at the
head of the Pass, which he should withdraw in the morning.

The 7th division should also march towards Lizaso.

Wellington.

The young man grabs the paper and gallops up the western
bank of the river, the opposite side from the French. Nosey
remounts Copenhagen, pulls his small black plumeless cocked
hat lower over his eyes, straightens his short grey coat, and
gallops across the bridge. Glancing over his shoulder he gives
Copenhagen a smack and he's off like Pegasus, flying up the
chalky path towards us.

It was rather alarming, certainly, and it was a close run
thing.

As he comes nearer he almost fills the circle of my spy-glass. I
can see the great Roman nose, the high-arched brows, and
nearer still the strong hands on the rein, the firm set of the
mouth that does not smile much, but smiled a little then, as
reaching the crest, five yards from us, he reins up in an easy
little pirouette and briefly doffs his hat – as much at the French
across the way as at us.

'*Douro, Douro, Douro,*' The Portuguese cry, using the title their
Regency has bestowed upon him.

'*Viva el Velintón y viva la Nación,*' cheer the Spanish.

And a file or two away from me, I hear an Irishman exclaim:
'By Jasus – it's Atty, old Nosey himself, the long-nosed bogger
that licks the French.'

I look down at my feet where I mark mauve-tinted scabious, sage, and yellow trefoil, and a cinnamon-coloured butterfly with small black spots hovering and flitting above the flowers . . .

'That's all right then,' says Rifleman Green. 'We'll win.'

'Thirty-five thousand against eighteen?'

'His Lordship's worth ten. And twenty-eight of this army can beat thirty-five from anywhere else in the world.'

Daddy . . .

40

Unit 216, mobile radar unit, based at the top of the Halfaya Pass near the Egyptian/Libyan border remained relatively inactive for the first three weeks of 1941 while the army under Auchinleck pushed the Italians back to Tobruk and then further west towards Benghazi.

23/1/41   2 teeth out at Bandia and had boil on my bottom
          lanced. Returning found that immediate move
          to T. likely. Got ahead with arrangements for
          move.
24/1/41   Indications now are that move to Tobruk will be
          delayed.
              P.M. Took party for bathe and got 96 bottles of
          beer.
25/1/41   Received orders to move up to Tobruk tomorrow.
          Men worked well and preparations well forward by
          evening.
26/1/41   From Halfaya Pass to 80 km E. of Tobruk.
              Convoy moved off at 1100 hours. Considerable
          delay at FSD [Forward Supply Depot] as rations,
          ordered yesterday, not ready. Further delay at
          Capuzzo where we got more water.
              P.M. Splendid progress: better roads than further
          East: went straight on until 16.15. Total mileage
          about 45.
              Leaves broken in Stamp's lorry & defect in brake
          drum of water trailer.
28/1/41   Fort Acroma
              E and I again went ahead in clear weather &
          found the site without difficulty. We decided to
          use Fort Acroma as billets although it is 1¼ miles

from the site. The billets are filthy but can be made satisfactory.

Cooks in a bad flap. Otherwise things going well.

29/1/41 Billets now v:g: Spent A.M. making clearly marked 'road' between billets and site. Two men in small tank turned up. They had spent 8 days on 2 days' rations, but were cheerful and optimistic.

P.M. Went to Tobruk (25 miles) in Humber with Cpl Waite & Humphries. Nothing yet organized, but managed to scrounge some rations – including lemons and Vichy water . . .

The first two weeks at this new site went well enough, but then things began to go wrong. There were serious difficulties over fresh supplies and there were frequent sandstorms . . .

7/2/41 Men cleaned billets etc: of sand. Wind still high but no sand blowing.

Food situation now really bad. No bread, no potatoes, no oatmeal, no jam & only one tin of cheese, no bacon, sausages or beans. Sugar getting very low. But we have stacks of tea & the water supply has been good.

8/2/41 Returned from technical job & found Edgley had run over an Italian land mine 7 miles away. He was stone deaf, badly shaken & exhausted. Took him to hospital in Tobruk.

Rain fell heavily P.M.

The next week was grim. Lorries broke down, telephone communication broke down, the technical side failed to work, possibly as a result of storm damage and possibly because the absent Edgley was the officer in charge of it. But meanwhile Benghazi fell – the final achievement of what had been a startlingly successful campaign, overshadowed by the terrible retreat and then by the even more successful campaign that started at El Alamein.

15/2/41   I was just setting out with the ration party at 0730
           when a signal arrived ordering immediate move to
           Benghazi . . .

In spite of the usual mechanical failures with the lorries, and having to be re-routed when it was discovered a bridge had been blown up, it took them only three days to get the three hundred miles from Tobruk to their next site near Benghazi. And they found time to have a bathe at Derma – a place and experience so beautiful Pop talked about it many times in the years after. They were now well into Cyrenaica, the ex-Roman province expropriated by Mussolini and colonized by the Italians during the previous decade or so. Orchards flourished, the roads were good, there were new comfortable buildings . . .

19/2/41   Perfect site from domestic point of view. Large,
           clean ex-Road House with beautiful gardens and
           useful outbuildings. Said to have been favourite
           haunt of Graziani [who was, I believe, the marshal
           or whatever leading the Italian army they had just
           defeated – or maybe the one who 'conquered' Libya
           in the first place].
21/2/41   Most successful day – except that Carter had to be
           taken to hospital – probably appendicitis.
               Found ration depot. Australian unit for drilling
           picket holes [I think there's a joke here – against the
           Australians – but blest if I know how it works] – &
           remarkable opportunities for scrounging.
               P.M. Drew rations including bread and vegetables
           and 'won' about 100 bottles of chianti, 2 cases of
           milk and one of fruit: also quantities of jam &
           marmalade.
               Meanwhile men blacked out airmen's mess &
           cleaned place up.
               Good progress technically.

11/3/41   Fairly heavy raids in evening & night. Unit con-
           gratulated on work.

This was the beginning of Rommel's offensive, which drove
the Allies back into Egypt, though clearly Dad had no idea of
what was about to happen. The euphoria was sustained right up
to the nineteenth when he wrote this letter to his sister Olive –
the one married to the Liverpool haemorrhoid specialist.

19.3.41   P/O C. R. Somers
                                            216 MRU
                                            APO 590
Dear Olive
        Many thanks for parcel posted Dec: 8th. You asked
what we needed most. It is:– News from home, Reading
matter, Chocolate, Darts. Old Penguins would be much appre-
ciated by the men.
        I've been writing letters to 'Family' so I hope you've had a
few of them. In case not, I'll say that for several weeks we were
in the desert, living in tents, generally miles from anywhere:
toughish sort of conditions, but not too hard except during
sandstorms, and for one short period when the only water
obtainable had been salted by the Italians. Now we are in
fertile country again & billeted in a large building: however I've
got used to being out of doors & don't like sleeping in a house,
so I've fitted up a box lorry with a good bed ('won' from an
empty hotel), table & chair & telephone & use it as a bed-
sitting-orderly Room. Very pleasant. It's lovely to have a real
bed after months of a 'camp' species.
        Also it's marvellous to see trees & even a little grass after
nothing but sand and stone. Trees here are chiefly palms,
oranges, & lemons. The orange trees are in blossom & the
lemons are ripe. There is also lots of cactus and mimosa & that
beautiful purple stuff that you've probably seen in the S. of
France. [Bougainvillaea? Jacaranda?]
        The natives remind you of pictures of Biblical times & have
probably remained at about the same stage of development.

We buy eggs off them and I can count up to 20 in Arabic now which makes it easier than it used to be at first. I run a canteen for the men, selling everything at 10% profit: then spend the profit on buying extras like eggs to add to the normal rations.

Rations, by the way, are quite good here. For weeks & weeks we had no bread, no potatoes or vegetables, no fresh meat & no fruit either fresh or tinned. Now we get *all* these things. The men were amazingly good during our harder times, held sing-songs in the Mess Tent etc: & were always quite cheerful. They're a good crowd. By the way we have a piano and an excellent wireless set. The piano was rather funny. When we first arrived here things weren't 'organized' & the ration arrived back with all sorts of things they had scrounged. I went out to them and said jokingly, 'What! No piano!' And they said, 'Yes sir, we can get one if you'll sign a chit for it, & we thought, sir, if you'll let us take one of the big lorries, we'd get it straight away.'

A few nights ago we had a Unit Concert & asked officers and men from other units. It was really very good & included Exhibition Waltz by Sgt Stephenson & A. C. Ross (!) [The exclamation mark because the name and rank are the same as the ones adopted by Lawrence of Arabia when he joined the RFC after WWI], tap-dancing by a youth from Croxteth Road, the usual songs and dirty jokes etc: – and free beer (from last month's Canteen profits) . . .

On the hill above Sorauren Thomas remembered snatches of them that he had heard his father sing: 'Oh what a pity, she's only one titty to feed the baby on, Poor little bugger he'll never play rugger, he's not sufficiently strong, dadadadaaah, dadadadaah, He's the Queen of the Fairies,' and a routine that began, 'And you, Corporal Smith, will carry the drum. Not me, Sir, I'm in the family way. You're in everyone's way, you, Smith, will carry the drum' . . . and so on.

. . . I've been quite fit out here, except that my teeth started to 'go' on the hard biscuits and I've had 3 out – and a boil on my bottom. We've had bombs near us on a few occasions: I don't mind them as much as I thought I would, but have a couple of seconds of intense fear when I hear the whistle of them coming down. However that hasn't happened often.

I like the life here. I think it's what I always wanted to do, but we feel very cut off from home & and all hope it won't last *too* long. I think that if the war's over in about a year I shall be damn glad I did this: but if it's much longer than that I get very home-sick and Decima-sick. If only Dess could come & live Cairo or Alex: & I could get a week's leave occasionally it would be grand! Certainly as far as work's concerned, I like this better than any job I've had except perhaps for my 2 years as headmaster in Liverpool.

Love to all of you

Christopher

Please send this on to Ma.

41

The gap between the ridges was very deep and very steep, grown over with brambles and littered with quartzy boulders that look like melting blocks of ice. Just below the saddle the slope was at its steepest, at times almost a climb. Near the top it levelled a little and there were signs of terracing, also of the flattened ramparts of an iron-age fort. On the top there was turf and a low cover of sage, thorns, some clover and vetch, and curry plant. There was a hot wind everywhere except in the valley, which at midday and in the afternoon became an oven. A lot of men died on the slopes, and the wind in the brambles still seemed to Thomas to have something to say about it.

> In the short time after they had taken up their ground, the enemy attacked the hill on the right of the 4th division. Our troops defended their ground, and drove the enemy from it with the bayonet . . .
>   Nearly at the same time that the enemy attacked this height on the 27, they took possession of the village of Sorauren on the road to Ostiz . . . and they kept up a fire of musketry along the line until it was dark.

That night there was the usual horrendous thunderstorm that preluded so many of Wellington's victories. There are, of course, thunderstorms in any of the mountains of Spain two or three times a week in July and August. This one passed before midnight when the men on the hill looked back to see Pamplona illuminated by the garrison in celebration of the relief they were sure would come next day.

Both Thomases were terrified: the rifleman no less than the podgy son of Pilot Officer Christopher Richard Somers. At times it seemed as if bolts were raining around them and the thunder came in sulphuric cracks that deafened even more than cannon fire or the explosion of an Italian land mine. The rifleman cowered beneath his blanket and endeavoured to keep his bandolier of sixty cartridges dry beneath him, the twentieth-century educationist in search of himself did likewise, wearing his plastic mac inside the sleeping-bag Elvira had lent him.

Both adopted foetal positions with their left thumbs in their mouths and their right hands inside their trousers clutching their genitals. Both felt the steady seep of water into the gaps and the increasing discomfort of the rocks and thorns beneath them – but they dared not shift for fear of letting in more water. And both speculated as to their chances of being struck and what it would feel like if they were.

Once the storm was passed both admired the illuminations. Those in 1813 were produced by several hundred candles and lanterns hung along the fortifications and on the cathedral, those in 1994 by conventional floodlighting. Thomas, not the rifleman, was by then hungry, wet and cold. He considered going down the hill and walking into the town to look for lodgings, but at past midnight what chance would there be of finding any? And at that moment the floodlighting was turned off and by the light of a moon still a quarter off full he found his way back into the sleeping-bag. Towards dawn he slept, and was blessed with erotic dreams: a cheerful, fat woman knelt in front of him and let him mount her from behind, while he, in the sort of anatomical improbabilities that dreams confer on us, contrived to kiss and lick large breasts that hung above him. No doubt the rifleman's dreams were similar.

Towards their respective dawns both woke with erections and a masterful desire to pee. Both did, the difference was that the rifleman was in the company of about eighteen thousand men doing the same. The more recent Thomas then got back into his sleeping-bag and waited for the sun to come up. He knew it would be instant warmth when it did, and he was prepared to wait.

The 6th division had scarcely taken their position when they were attacked by a very large force of the enemy which had been assembled in the village of Sorauren . . .

Which was where Thomas had a coffee and an omelette *boccadillo* before buying more sandwiches, coffee, mineral water and a litre carton of Navarra wine. He wondered at the looks he was getting until he went to the *caballeros* and saw himself in a mirror. The bruising had all but gone, but he was a mess – face streaked with muddy rain, hair spiky, a three-day beard, and his clothes unkempt and filthy. He cleaned himself up as well as he could and spent the rest of the morning and the early afternoon climbing the ridges, tumbling down them, dragging himself through brambles, getting stung by a wasp. Early on he felt the possibility of sunstroke, took off his shirt and draped it over his head and got burnt shoulders instead.

Their front was however so well defended by the fire of their own light troops from the heights on their left, and by the fire from the heights occupied by the 4th division that the enemy were soon driven back with immense loss from a fire on their front, both flanks, and rear.

The battle now became general along the whole front of the heights . . .

His Lordship does not see fit to employ us until well after midday, and indeed, because we are behind the ridge we have little knowledge of how the matter is being settled, though repeated 'huzzas' drowning out the rattle of the Frenchmen's drums give news that though they are coming at us with an advantage of two to one, our lads are holding back the tide.

Then, with the sun just past its greatest height, up trots an ADC and begs to inform Mr Byng that His Lordship would be obliged if he would bring his brigade over the crest and fill a gap between the brigades of Major Generals Ross and Anson. We come over the crest above the very steepest part of the slope, steep enough for a man to need hands as well as feet if he is to make a comfortable ascent. Not easy when you're holding a musket and the likes of us are popping away at you.

There's a lot of red coats stretched along the ground at the top, and many hundreds of blue and white on the slopes beneath, some spread out with their heads way below their ankles, others rolled up like rag-dolls, and a few at the very bottom caught in a thicket of brambles whose stems are an inch in diameter and whose thorns, spikes I'd call them, are up to two inches long. Some of these still howl, and curse as they bleed to death cocooned in thorns. It occurs to me you could make a fine and efficacious defence for infantry if you could somehow make giant watch-springs out of iron or steel and fix sharps to them and thus emulate these thorns.

And there's the smell too, the smell of battlefields that brings the vultures in from leagues around. Already the air above, high, high above has filled with these slowly wheeling sailing ships in space. The smell is of blood and powder mainly, but burnt flesh and shit as well, for while a few men shit themselves with fear almost all let go when they die.

And then I see him yet again, about a third of the way down the slope, behind a quartzy boulder where the quartz looks like grease or molten wax, and he has his trousers down, those strange trousers which go right down to cuffs at his ankles, but right now the whole article is round them and he's doing his business. And he wipes himself with paper, which is a novelty in itself, and then examines it as if to seek out omens but what he sees is blood, bright red; even at this distance I am not mistaken.

I think again to search out my spy-glass and take a closer look, but now the drums are beating again and the frenchies are formed up in their columns and are coming down the slopes and across the saddle, and it's time to check my piece, find a rock that may protect me, and when I look up again, he's gone.

So here they come, and, welladay, they're a scrawny gaggle of youngsters is all, and look terrified, none more than eighteen at the most . . . they say there are no grown men left in France, only old men and boys . . .

I never saw such fighting as we have had here. The battle of the 28th was fair bludgeon work and the loss of the enemy was immense. Our loss has likewise been very severe, but not of a nature to cripple us. I escaped as usual unhurt, and I begin to feel the finger of God is upon me . . .

Wellington used the phrase once more – after Waterloo.

At three in the afternoon, seeking some shade, twentieth-century Thomas put his back to the north wall of the hermitage, set his copy of *Wellington's War* on one side, and ate what was left of his sandwiches. He asked himself just what the hell he thought he was doing. A penance, he supposed, was the answer, but for what? He still had four days (or was it three?) to go before he would have lived longer than Dad had, so he need not feel bad about that until he'd done it. He drank half a litre of the rich fruity wine, and closed his eyes.

21–23/3/41	Conflicting orders over possible move to Escarpment. Eventually move postponed, but all domestic equipment packed and ready.
1/4/41	A few bombs. S/L Barclay asked if everything ready for immediate move. General flap increasing.
2/4/41	Hostile plane intercepted and almost certainly shot down. Unit congratulated.
3 & 4/4/41	0830. Received orders to move at once. Good progress with packing & all ready by 1230.

Made towards Benghazi aiming to strike main
B – Barce road, but within a few minutes of our
start dumps of It ammo began to be blown up by
the road. Flames and shrapnel across road, terrific
explosions. Commer (15cwt van) hit twice.
Managed to turn vehicles round & then made for
escarpment via Benina. – Further destruction
there, but no danger to us – [the pencil P/O
Somers normally wrote in is crossed out here.
Above the deletion he wrote in the fountain-pen
ink used in some later entries.] Although we had
been warned not to take this road as it had been
mined. [The entry continues in pencil.] Expected
to find considerable defences on top of
escarpment, but found place deserted. Reached
Barce 18.30 & told by G/C Brown push on.
Refuelled beyond Barce and had late meal.
I suggested driving on till moonset & parking
at cross-roads [underlined words bracketed in
ink], but E decided to go on through the night.
All well for 100 miles, then the Commer ditched

and turned over. While we were waiting on pass
down to Derma, lorry of another unit let 2 wheels
over dip opposite one of our vehicles. Bowman's
lorry sent down hill to turn: when opposite ditched
vehicle had head-on collision with yet another vehicle
coming down with no lights & apparently out of
control. B's lorry now U/S. Consequently left [written
over in ink with: 'had to leave'] much camp
equipment behind . . .

And so it went on as they got themselves back through,
behind and occasionally in front of a retreating army, right back
to Halfaya Pass where it seemed they might stop and begin to
operate again as a radar station from the same spot they had left
six weeks earlier. On the way tow-bars broke, were repaired,
broke again. The men got dysentery. All Edgley (E) could
think of was saving the radar masts. The men were Pop's
responsibility.

8/4/41   Situation now as follows:– Men have little but what
          they stand up in: Commer and one Crossley (de-
          stroyed) in enemy hands: one mast trailer cannot
          be moved: Ford U/S.

By the thirteenth they were right back in Mersa Matruh well
inside Egypt, and there at last the retreat halted – mainly
because Rommel had extended his supply lines far too far and
had to wait for supplies and support to catch up. On the way
they lost more vehicles and equipment, but not men. And at one
time they had to drive through detonating petrol dumps. It was
either during this last phase, or the earlier one outside Benghazi
when the ammunition dumps were being blown up, that it
happened. Probably it was outside Benghazi – however, the
diary was rewritten for the later part: the pencil entries are very
scant but are supplemented by ink entries obviously filled in
after the event. This possibly suggests the horror occurred in the
last stages.

*

During the two years after his father was killed Thomas's mother sold the Wroxham Way bungalow and bought one very similar close to the Bay Estate. It was there, in October 1962, that Thomas had his first opportunity to spend a few days with her on their own. He had been teaching English in Ankara University, Turkey.

They spent the evenings in what she called the front room, and what the estate agents called a lounge-diner, drinking G and Ts after a supper of poached egg on toast.

Most of the furniture was not what had been bought for Wroxham Way – she had thrown all that out apart from one armchair and one small sofa. The rest was all from Seventy-One including a grandmother clock made in 'Scarboro' by an Italian called Vasalli, a walnut veneer wall-table which could be pulled apart and the top folded out to make a square, green-baized card-table, a gate-leg table and an elegant rocking chair.

The card-table was what she called a boon. The Widows who came to play bridge with her were all enormously more wealthy than she was, but none had a card-table to match it. Nor did they have Real Old Willow Pattern, in that inimitable blue with the gold-leaf rim, a set still complete enough to lay on a bridge tea for four without showing a chip. Several of Aunt Helen's ornaments had resurfaced too. Thomas wondered about this. Mum had resented not being able to furnish Seventy-One with stuff of her own, but now seemed content to use some of the left-overs, though really she didn't have to. Was it because she now had title to them? Or that they were of a quality that would impress the Widows? Or had they, after all, over the years, become not only familiar but actually liked?

There was a small coal-fire set in grey glazed tiles. Another decade had to pass before fitted carpets and smart, modern gas-fires came in.

Thomas sat in the rocking chair and occasionally rocked. His mother sat opposite him, with the low gate-leg table between them, and to the side of them, the anthracite glowed hot in the small grate. On the table there was an ashtray, small, silver, inscribed:

To
C. R. Somers
Master at
Sutton Court School
1947–1954
From all the Boys

which she had to empty into the solid basket-work waste-paper basket at her elbow about once every half-hour. Instead of Weights she now smoked tipped Senior Service through a short silver and amber holder he had bought for her in Turkey. He smoked Camel – the only cigarettes readily available in England at the time which had some Turkish tobacco in them. She used a tiny chrome lighter, he a Zippo. They drank very strong G and Ts without lemon or ice out of cut-crystal whisky glasses which she must have bought herself. And why not?

'No point,' she said, reaching for the Gordon's, 'if you can't taste the gin.'

Her hair was stylishly permed with a hint of blue rinse. As ever she smelt of Coty's *L'Aimant*. She was wearing a mottled green and brown pleated Crimplene dress, and a necklace of silver and silver-gilt filigree flowers. Delicate, perfectly proportioned so as to be noticeable, not showy, it was lovely. Pop had bought it in Jerusalem, the major city of what had been a Turkish colony called Palestine, inhabited by Arabs, and was then a British protectorate.

And, Thomas remembers, as he briefly opens his eyes to look across the narrow steep valley, twenty years later, just before Alzheimer's got a serious hold on her, she freely and unprompted gave the necklace to Katherine. It was a gesture of sublime magnanimity, incredible. It was without doubt her most treasured single possession. It was perhaps a gift to her son who, obviously, would never wear it himself, but when Katherine wore it he would look at it. It also demonstrated faith: Thomas had cocked-up before. With Katherine Decima realized, he quite probably would not cock-up again and the necklace would remain in the family. There was another dimension too. Through the twenty-three years or so Thomas and Katherine had lived together he had tried again and again to give her gifts as precious, as good (forget commodity exchange – this necklace we're talking about has no serious monetary worth at all), but had never found anything as lovely. So there you go. The best token of love your partner has was given by your father to your mother who gave it to your partner. Something to be celebrated.

Thomas rolled over, took a swig from his wine and lived and dreamed on. The wasp sting was no longer a bother and the sun was still warm.

'There are things I should tell you about your poor dad . . . '

'Oh? Yes?' Wary now of possible embarrassment, he lit another Camel. Really his mum was, he thought, in pretty good nick. Probably more in charge of her own destiny than she had ever been. Sixty-four years old, left tolerably well off with half the income from Dad's share of Grandad's estate (the other half going to the execrable April), she still worked for twenty hours a week in Bob Murfett's Pagham branch office and she was having a whale of a time planning a decent bit of garden the way she wanted it. A Romneya, and a purple, small-flowering, hardy hibiscus, a hedge of mallow and a bay tree in the front, some good shrubs and trees including a eucalyptus at the back, a hedge of roses, and a vegetable patch behind it. All of course immature then, but ready to flourish in their own good time. Some years yet for her to enjoy it before the Alzheimer's set in.

'Like what?'

'He was sexually very repressed.'

And you weren't? Already his toes were curling, his scrotum contracting, but if this was something she wanted to talk about, so be it.

'When we first began to sleep together he was terribly nervous. He came out in a sort of nervous eczema. Like measles.'

Psoriasis, I bet, murmured Thomas to himself, on the hill above Sorauren, thirty-plus years later.

'But he got over it. Often it was very, very good for him. He said so.'

She smiled, a touch grimly, not at Thomas, but at the cigarette holder as she used her thumbnail to lever the Senior Service filter out of it and insert another. He wanted to ask her: And how was it for you?

He should have asked her. He'd never know now. At the time the implication he had received was that she had done her duty and made her bloke a happy man, all that people of her sex, class and age were meant to do, but perhaps that was quite wrong. Maybe she'd had a ball. But he couldn't, couldn't ask her. In 1962 you'd only just begun to talk openly about sex, and then not with much knowledge and certainly with no wisdom, to one's partner. But not with one's parents. And certainly not about *their* sex lives.

She looked up, eyes expressionless behind her new bifocals.

'Earth moved and all that, you know?'

For Whom the Bell Tolls had meant as much to her generation as *Lady Chatterley's Lover* had to his.

He recalled his father at prize-giving during those two years he had been headmaster of his own school and the photograph there was of him doing it. Lean, yes, but robust in a way he never had been later, and confident too, even saturnine. The point was that at thirty-eight he had been his own boss, had sired a son on a woman reputed to be sterile and the earth moved . . . quite often.

'But he'd lost it when he came back.'

'Oh?!'

'He was a mess.'

'Really?'

'I don't mean just in bed.'

Thomas then, back in 1962, recalled the rows heard through thin walls during the hols, the despair. How, almost as soon as they were in Seventy-One his parents had slept in separate bedrooms. Why? Daddy snores was the answer given.

'Three times he threatened to shoot himself. Once he threatened to shoot me. He got very drunk, you see. And then, far later than I should have done, I got him to tell me all about it. You see ... I thought he'd had an affair with someone, I don't know, a tea-planter's sister or wife in Ceylon. A nurse in the hospital he spent three months in in Gaza.' She giggled a little. 'You know, he wrote to his family that he was eyeless somewhere and at the mill with slaves. The censorship wouldn't let him say the real name. They were worried out of their minds, thought he had been blinded and was in some frightful concentration camp. Of course I could tell them he meant Gaza. Milton.'

She smiled with satisfaction at the memory. They'd always looked down on her – but she knew her Eng. Lit. better than they did.

'Anyway, that's what I thought was the trouble. He had a mistress somewhere he wanted to go off with or back to, and she was in bed with us every time he tried to ... Another little drop, eh? Dead Man. There's another in the cupboard.'

Thomas did the honours.

'Where was I? Yes. So eventually, not till after we had been at Seventy-One a year, I got it out of him. What the matter was.'

'And?'

She shifted a little, spread her knees, angled herself towards the fire, and talked to it rather than to him.

'The retreat from Benghazi. He never expected to be in that sort of business. He was forty when he joined up. Yes, he'd volunteered for overseas – we needed the money and you got extra. But he thought that even abroad he'd only have a desk to fly. Anyway he was adjutant to this radar convoy, looking after the men, and they had to get out quick. Convoy of lorries and he was in the one in front. And they started blowing up all the ammunition dumps and the petrol dumps just as they were going past them, and they were being bombed at the same time. The lorry he was in was hit twice with shrapnel, and the second time ... he was sitting beside the driver, you see?'

'Yes ...'

'And either from a bomb or the explosions all around them the driver got hit. In the head. Badly. Fell forward over the wheel, couldn't steer ... or drive at all. And all these explosions going on all round them ... '

She looked up at him, now almost over her shoulder, she was so hunched forward, took a drag on her amber holder. Then she turned back to the fire, looked into the glowing coals.

'He, the driver, was bleeding terribly, the side of his face and head caved in. Imagine. Poor Pop. He didn't know what to do. The men at the back were shouting, screaming at him to get a move on. Several bombs fell straddling the road in front. Blocking it. The next ones ... He leant across the driver, opened the door and pushed him out. Then he took his place and turned the lorry round, in a tight circle, and the ones behind followed him. They said later he'd run over the driver ... '

'Later?'

'There was an inquiry. Most of the men believed he'd saved their lives, but two or three of them were friends of the driver and said he probably wasn't dead. They said Pop could have pulled him into the passenger seat then gone round and got into the driver's seat from the outside. They said Pop was frightened and had done it all to save himself. The inquiry found for him, said he'd done the right thing. The important thing after they had been hit twice was to get out as quickly as possible. And that's what he did. He saved the rest of the unit, and the driver would have died soon if he wasn't already dead. But Pop *was* frightened, terrified. Even so, he did actually try to pull the man along the bench seat, but he was all tangled up with the steering wheel and the gears and his feet with the pedals, so he gave up and leant over and got the door open and pushed. But he could never be sure that the decision was not made to save his own life as well as, or even rather than, those of the men he was meant to look after. That's what ruined him. That doubt.'

She reached over, picked up a small poker and gave the coals a rattle they did not need. Sparks flew upwards.

'All that time he couldn't tell me about it, just the horrible nightmares he had, waking up in a sweat and drinking, and wanting to kill himself. He should never have been there. It ... stained the rest of his life.'

Blame Hitler.

Blame fucking ... no, he didn't do a lot of that from all accounts, just Hitler. Blame Hitler.

'I say, old chap, Are you all right?'

I, however, determined to attack their position and ordered Dalhousie to possess himself of the top of the mountain in his front, by which the enemy's right would be turned: and Picton to cross the heights on which the enemy's left had stood, and to turn their left by the road to Roncesvalles. All the arrangements were made to attack the front of the enemy's position, as soon as the effect of these movements on their flanks should begin to appear. Packenham turned the village of Sorauren as soon as Dalhousie had driven the enemy from the mountain by which that flank was defended; and the 6th division and Byng's brigade instantly attacked and carried that village.

'I say, old chap. Are you all right?'

Byng's Brigade? That's our lot. Come on, chaps, down the slope again, past the hermitage, watch out for those brambles, there's the village, Oooops, poor old Rifleman Green, got his head knocked off by a four-pound shot. If I'd been in front instead of him, it would have been ... SHIT!!!

'I say, old chap. Are you all right?'

43

It was, of course, the German. He had been hiking along the northern ridge, the one the French were driven from on the morning of 30 July, 1813. Looking south and west his attention had been caught by a figure galumphing down the steep path towards the village. As he watched, the man, whom he did not yet recognize as the plump, almost elderly, Englishman who had boarded the bus in St Jean Pied-de-Port four days earlier, left the path and hurtled straight down the slope rather than obliquely across it. Inevitably he took a tumble, tripped by a greasy-looking boulder that projected through the turf, and flew arse over tip into a briar patch.

Thomas was stunned. Although he had actually made a complete turn in the air so it was his back and backside that hit the ground first, the slope was so steep that he had gone on into a second roll, not airborne, which had ended up with a crack on his head only partially broken by the brambles. Those brambles. Even the vultures could not penetrate to get at the blackened, swelling bodies killed there two days before. The German could not see or smell them, the way Thomas could, though perhaps he sensed the melancholy of that hot still place without knowing its cause.

'Nothing broken, I hope.'

'I don't think so.'

'Your head took a bit of a knock. You could have received a concussion. Look at the sun, please. That's fine, your irises respond. Move your head from side to side. No loss of movement? Chin on your chest. No sudden pain? Splendid! Let's see if we can get you to your feet. These thorns are a blessed nuisance, are they not?'

His face was very close to Thomas's now. Pale blue eyes, very serious, strong cheekbones, long straw-blond hair tied back in a ponytail. Strong brown hands holding Thomas's elbows.

'Up we come. Oops. Steady now.'

'You're very kind.'

'Not at all. There. Nothing broken.'

'No. But I do feel . . . shaken.'

'Of course you do. Why not sit down again? Here. On this rock. Let me . . . '

Thomas sat, shook his head. It hurt. Worse still his backside hurt, felt jarred, much the way it had the last time Katherine and he had taken the children ice-skating and he took a tumble. And then as now, a side effect was a desire to empty his bowels.

'I think I'm all right, but I'm bloody thirsty.'

The German handed him a flattened water bottle clad in webbing. Thomas pushed back the wired cap, wiped the top with his sleeve, the way kids do, and drank it all. About half a litre.

'Yes. You are all right. But you should not be left here on your own, I think. Where are you headed?'

'I don't know. Pamplona I suppose.' He looked at his watch. Twenty-past nine. And then, without really thinking why, pressed the button that changed the digital part of the display to the day and date.

'Oh shit! Is that right? Wednesday the thirty-first?'

'That is correct. Is something the matter?'

'I'm meant to meet my wife and children in Jaca at half-past one.'

'Hmmm! Problem, I think.' The German pulled a map from the side pocket of his rucksack, unfolded it. 'Sixty-eight and forty-three, that's one hundred and eleven kilometres.'

Miles, man. What's that in miles? eighty's fifty . . . oh come on, it's the autoroute speed limit, seventy miles, give or take.

'Railway?'

'None shown on the map. A bus may be possible . . . but first we must get you into the town. It's about eight kilometres to the centre . . . can you manage that?'

'I'll try. I bloody have to.'

Ten minutes later and the road only a hundred yards or so away . . .

'I'm sorry. I have to take a shit. I'll . . . I'll go behind that wall.'

Low, drystone, stubble on one side, a patch of ochre and yellow maize on the other.

Hunkered down yet again, pulling the seat of his trousers well forward between his ankles, he pushed and considered. Getting on for ten o'clock and this was the day. At last. Four hours and a bit to a quarter past two. But would he make it? More important now though, even than living or not living as long as his dad had, was whether or not he could get the seventy miles to Jaca in three and a half hours. She'll murder me if I don't. Anyway if I'm seriously late by, say, an hour or two. Yes . . . well.

It'll have to be a taxi. Nothing else for it.

He looked round and down.

Blood.

Hans, yes, his name was Hans, was a brick; what was more he spoke excellent Spanish as well as class English. While Thomas was occupying his space behind the wall Hans decided that a five mile walk was out of the question and took him instead into the village, crossing the very bridge on which Lord Wellington had scribbled the note that won the Battle of the Pyrenees. There Thomas drank more water, mineral water, in a tiny bar, while they waited ten minutes for the small local shuttle bus which took them to Pamplona bus station just below the ramparts of the citadel. Hans found out that there was a long-distance bus to Jaca, that it left at eleven-thirty and took two hours.

They had forty minutes to wait. They went to the *caballeros*. As they zipped up and Hans washed his hands, Thomas said, 'You've been very good to me, very kind.'

'Not a thing! How's the head?'

Thomas shook it.

'Bangs a bit. But not too bad.'

'And the rest?'

'Sore. But bearable. I'm still so bloody thirsty though.'

Hans turned, eyed him, head on one side, then grimaced.

'Dehydration. I hope you do not mind my saying this, but, if your children are young they will take fright at the sight of you.'

Thomas looked in the mirror. His forearms were scabbed and

his face scratched. There was a tear in his shirt which was blotched with grass stains and sweat. His off-white chinos were crumpled and smudged. His boots were badly scuffed.

'Not a lot I can do about it.'

'Have a good wash then you can buy a T-shirt and a pair of jeans. You have enough money?'

'I've got plastic.'

He bought both garments in a Simago which they found nearby and then they went to a café. The T-shirt was a leftover from San Fermín – a raging bull with *banderillas* fluttering behind its horns charged like death out of a splash of red above *Los Fermínes 1994* written in floriated capitals. Thomas changed in another *caballeros* while Hans ordered *café con leche* and *churros*, strips of fried choux pastry with sugar shaken on them. Brilliant. And more mineral water.

In the loo Thomas carefully rolled up his old shirt and trousers and opened his rucksack. In it he found the answer, in part at any rate, to the question that had been nagging ever since Hans had found him and he had checked the date. What had happened to the missing day, the missing night?

The clue was an almost empty litre bottle of pacharrán, the red liqueur of Navarra, a non-sweet form of *anis*, wrapped up in the sleeping-bag. Katherine and he had been to San Fermín many years earlier. They had met a Norwegian writer who had insisted they drink the local cocktail: pacharrán and brandy, half and half. It had nearly killed him then.

And he now suspected that a) this one bottle was only half the story, and that somewhere up on the hill there was the empty brandy bottle that constituted the other half, and that b) the combination had probably nearly killed him again. The thing was he had actually lost a whole day, sure, not a lost weekend, but a day and a night. At some point he had bought this bottle, and possibly a Soberano to go with it, and he could not remember where or when. He remembered lying against the wall of the hermitage, with *Wellington's War* on the dry grass beside him, he remembered the red wine from a carton ... and after that dreams and visions. I have had a most rare vision. I have had a dream. I shall write a ballad of this dream. It shall be called 'Bottom's Dream'. Yes, well.

So why didn't he have a hangover? But he did. What he had attributed to the consequences of his mad tumble was at least half hangover. And the dehydration was part of it.

Outside on the pavement but protected from the already hot sunlight by the café awning they drank coffee and dunked the *churros*. Not many Spaniards about, but plenty of tourists. And then a youth went by on a Vespa with a gorgeous miniskirted girl riding pillion side-saddle behind him. She had one arm round his waist and held a cigarette in her free hand. Neither wore a helmet. Now that is an image of the real Spain, Thomas thought to himself. Then he remembered what could happen if you didn't wear a helmet, and he wanted to rush after them and tell them.

He glanced at his watch. Five to. They'd have to go back to the bus station. Suddenly emotional he covered the back of Hans's hand with both his own.

'Probably,' he murmured, and his voice snagged as he said it, 'you saved my life.'

'Oh, come on. I do not think so.'

'A couple of hours unconscious in this heat would have fried my brains.'

'But you were not unconscious.'

'Damn nearly. Could easily have just stayed where I was and gone to sleep. Anyway. Thanks.'

At the bus station, waiting in line to get on the big modern bus, Thomas shook his hand.

'You British. Always ready to shake the hands.' For a moment Hans seemed shy, awkward.

'I hope the bus doesn't break down or something,' said Thomas.

'It won't.' The long perfect vowel on 'woooon't', not a hint of a diphthong. 'It's a Mercedes.'

Thomas got on the bus, sat by a window near the back, looked out, thinking to wave. But the German had already gone.

Look – no Hans!

44

'Cool T-shirt, Dad.'

'Thanks, Richard.'

'You made it to Pamplona then.'

'Daddy, why is your face scratched?'

'Took a tumble on a hillside. Nothing serious.'

'You don't look as bad as I thought you might.'

'Good.'

'Pity you didn't shave.'

Oh well. Perhaps that was why their kiss had not been as prolonged as he had hoped. But she never had been a dedicated kisser. All the rest, sure, yes. But not a kisser.

La Fragúa, it means the forge, was where they had left it thirteen years before, in one of several alleys that linked the two main streets. Inevitably it had changed – but not a lot. There were now individual tables for four with proper chairs instead of long wooden tables with benches. The bar was no longer a bar where locals or passers-by could come in for a drink and a *tapa*, or a coffee, but just a short serving area where the waitresses picked up the drinks orders. But there was a big black and white framed photograph showing it as it had been, with others that showed it as an actual delapidated forge with anvils and extinct furnaces. The important thing though was the cooking area, laid out behind cabinets of cold stuffs, salads, chorizos and cheeses. This, the centre and heart of the place, remained unchanged – a big open charcoal fire beneath a semicircular stone chimney piece. Best of all was the fact that *el Proprietario* was still the same lean, intellectual, bespectacled Merlin of the *parrilla* they had known – a touch greyer, wiser perhaps, but a true wizard to find at the end of the rainbow, at the end of the yellow brick road, no charlatan he.

'What's *pollo*, Mummy?'

'French *poulet*, Hannah-Rosa.'

'And *parrilla*?'

'Grill, grid-iron for grilling, griddle.'

'So *pollo alla parrilla* is grilled chicken. I'll have that.'

Thomas ordered grilled cutlets, Katherine *gambas alla plancha*. Richard insisted on having an omelette, even though the grills were the speciality. Thomas hit a problem when it came to wine. Either you ordered a posh bottle or you accepted a litre of house red – Cariñema, purplish, blackcurranty, the wine of Aragon, heaven – and no halves.

'Go on,' said Katherine. 'I'm driving anyway.'

Along with the children she ordered diet cola.

Thomas watched his watch. The wine arrived at two-thirteen. He poured a glass and waited. The LCD digits shifted. Two-fifteen. He raised the glass, eyes filling, and drank.

'You did it then?'

'I did it.'

'Well done!' She covered his hand and squeezed. But she remembered the still unaltered clock in the car which, she knew, would be indicating one-fifteen. Or sixteen. She bit her lip and looked up at him. Their eyes met and they smiled at each other, openly and happily. He put his glass down, leant back in his chair. He looked better, indeed well, in spite of the mess he was. She forbore to point out that Spanish time is European time and an hour ahead of British. Back home it was still only one-fifteen.

'And happy birthday too, Dad. Well. In twelve days' time. It would have been his ninety-fourth birthday.'

They drank their cola again, wondering at the strange high, lit mood he was in. Katherine thought of doing the sums – had he really got it right? Then a thought crossed her mind. Leap years! Had he taken them into account? Her mouth set into a line as she decided – best to keep shtum about that one.

'So! What have you lot been up to?' he asked.

'Sunday evening we drove up to Pau and stayed in Monique's flat. It was very hot and Richard and I were poorly . . . '

'Oh, I am sorry.'

'Not all the time . . . '

'And I wasn't ill at all,' Hannah-Rosa said proudly. 'But we went to Lourdes and they seemed to get better . . . '

'Not really,' said Richard. 'It was after Lourdes that I got that really bad stomach.'

'It only lasted a few hours and your *chaud-froid* got better.'

They prattled on. Crushed in the crowds at the grotto (pretty grotty, said Richard; not pretty at all, said Hannah-Rosa) they had been shushed first by the pilgrims close to them and then over the PA system.

They'd been to the Cirque de Gavarnie but had walked rather than taking the pony or donkey ride, and seen La Brêche de Roland, the gap in the sheerest knife ridge at the top of the granite Pyrenees which Roland had hacked out with his sword.

'Ah,' said Thomas, 'but I went through Roncesvalles . . . '

'What's that?' cried Hannah-Rosa – it was all getting to her now, she loved restaurants, she loved having her dad back.

'It was where Roland was killed. He blew on his horn so the Emperor Charlemagne might come and help him, but Charlemagne let him down.'

'Bastard,' said Richard.

Roland, Orlando, thought Thomas. Orlando, the pub sign in Bognor was a horn, the horn that Orlando blew in vain. He raised his glass again – to a ghost he hoped would be, not laid, that he did not want, but more benign.

And so it went on. Sunday poorly, Monday Lourdes and Gavarnie.

'And yesterday we didn't do much because silly Richard wanted to buy his silly gunpowder . . . '

'Gunpowder?'

But now he remembered. Richard wanted to buy bangers the way you can buy them in France and Spain, and smuggle them back to Britain.

'Well we couldn't find a firework shop, we walked miles, and then Moni's boyfriend . . . '

'What's he like?'

'Weird, Weeee-erd.'

'No he's not.'

'He only said you'd get better if you wore a black beret all the time.'

'Anyway . . . ' Katherine took up the tale again, 'he said why not make gunpowder, why not buy sulphur, and saltpetre, they use it for curing sausages, and there's no problem getting charcoal—'

'But that's just what I said. Before we left.'

'Really? But could we persuade anyone to sell us sulphur or saltpetre? Apparently there's some sort of licensing system. After the third shop, this was in that agricultural area near the market, you remember?'

Thomas remembered. Big shops selling small tractors and chemicals by the hundredweight – or whatever.

'I called a halt. I felt sure they thought we were shopping for the IRA . . . '

'But in the evening we went up into the mountains and saw hang-gliding and para-gliding, and Richard bought a handmade knife.'

Richard passed it across the table – a simple clasp-knife but with a crudely carved handle in the shape of a bird of prey with wings folded.

'I like it,' he said, 'because it's not mass-produced. It's the only one just like that in the whole world.'

Christ, thought Thomas. I was going to give him the one I bought in Bayonne. But it's gone. Lost. And, in the event, just as well. Oh damn, and that silly book too, *Wellington's War*. Oh well. There's only so much baggage you can carry around with you, good to shed some every now and then.

'There was this artisan shop up in the mountains. Quite nice really. Anyway, we reckon Richard will be able to buy the bangers he wants here in Jaca – when the shops reopen after lunch.'

Plates full of small bones were whisked away.

'Dessert?'

'I should say so.'

The children and Katherine had exotic ice-creams, Thomas a large slice of Manchega cheese to accompany the last third of his wine.

At last, and it was nearly four o'clock, it was over. The restaurant, which had been full and noisy, was beginning to empty. Thomas paid the bill with the pesetas he had got from a hole in the wall in Pamplona, and then, just as they were leaving, he turned and went to the grill at the back.

'Excuse me,' he said to *el Proprietario*, 'Do you speak English?'

The man turned from the last grid-iron of cutlets he would cook that lunchtime.

'Yes, I do.'

'I thought so. I mean I remember that you do.'

The eyes behind the glasses twinkled a little.

'We've been here before, but not since 1981. The first time we came here was in 1975.'

'Ah. That was three years after we opened.'

The accent was perfect – not Hans's perfection, but completely natural.

'Anyway, I just wanted to say it was lovely for us to come back and bring the children and find it all . . . just as good as we always remembered it was.'

'Thank you. I'm glad you remembered.' Earnest now but kind. 'I'm glad you came back. You will understand and forgive me but of course – I do not remember you. But if you come back soon, I shall.'

They were waiting for him outside in the hot sunlight.

Richard murmured to him: 'Why are you crying?'

'I don't know,' Thomas said. 'But I don't think it's Hitler's fault.'

He took Katherine's hand.

'Now let's see if we can't buy some fireworks.'